Date Knight

Bridget Essex

Other Books by Bridget Essex

Wolf Heart
Wolf Queen
Falling for Summer
The Guardian Angel
The Vampire Next Door
A Wolf for Valentine's Day
A Wolf for the Holidays
Don't Say Goodbye
Forever and a Knight
A Knight to Remember
Wolf Town
Dark Angel
Big, Bad Wolf
Meeting Eternity: The Sullivan Vampires, Vol. 1

About the Author

My name is Bridget Essex, and I've been writing about vampires for almost two decades. I'm influenced most by classic vampires– the vision of CARMILLA (it's one of the oldest lesbian novels!) and DRACULA. My vampires have always been kind of traditional (powerful), but with the added self-torture of regret and the human touch of guilt.

I have a vast collection of knitting needles and teacups, and like to listen to classical music when I write. My first date with my wife was strolling in a garden, so it's safe to say I'm a bit old fashioned. I have a black cat I love very much, and a brown dog who actually convinces me to go outside. When I'm actually outside, I begin to realize that writing isn't all there is to life. Just most of it! I'm married to the love of my life, author Natalie Vivien.

The love story of the beautiful but tragic vampire Kane Sullivan and her sweetheart Rose Clyde is my magnum opus, and I'm thrilled to share it with you in ***The Sullivan Vampires*** series, published by **Rose and Star Press**! Find out more at **www.LesbianRomance.org** and **http://BridgetEssex.Wordpress.com**

Date Knight

Published by Rose and Star Press
First edition, November 2015

ISBN: 1519101732

ISBN-13: 978-1519101730

Date Knight

DEDICATION

Always and forever to my own lady knight in shining armor. I love you, baby.

And this book is especially dedicated to Sir Terry Pratchett. You will never know what you meant to the twelve-year-old girl who needed your magic so very much. Beyond the grave, I salute you and I thank you with deepest love. This story – and I – would not exist without you.

Chapter 1: The One-Week Anniversary

I jump up and down and cheer at the top of my lungs as I wave my little blue-and-black pennant like a madwoman over my head. Down in the Knights of Valor "jousting arena"—which is just an area of the dog park that's been cordoned off with fraying rope on haphazardly placed plastic stakes—the knight in shining armor lifts her lance to me in triumph as she wheels her horse around with a practiced hand, trotting that enormous black beast along the fence line and posting in the saddle with a gorgeous behind that I'm totally not staring at.

(I lied. I am.)

Though there's currently a big medieval-style helmet covering the knight's beautiful face, hiding her smoldering blue eyes and that certain expression she gives me when she's just won a joust...I know it's all there, anyway, even though I can't see it.

Because that knight in shining armor just happens to be my new girlfriend, Virago.

Who, I'd like to point out, just happens to be a knight from another world.

A few weeks ago, I did not have said girlfriend. A few weeks ago, I was living a vastly different life...

So I think it's safe it's safe to say that it's been

one hell of a month.

"Dude, did you *see* how she just walloped that other knight off his horse?" asks Carly, as she jumps up and down, too, waving her blue-and-black flag just as hard as I'm waving mine. My best friend's bright red curls are flying all over the place, and her enthusiasm is pretty much off the charts. "That was *awesome!*" she hoots, pumping her fist in the air. "Take *that,* red-and-black knight who we're supposed to boo for, for absolutely no reason!" she hollers down onto the field.

The red-and-black knight, currently huddled in a small ball in the middle of the arena, winces a little, swiveling his helmet around to see who shouted at him. I feel, in that moment, a little sorry for the knight...who's probably going to be nursing some pretty nasty bruises on his bottom since Virago hit him with the butt of her lance...

I've got to remind her—for probably the millionth time—that she's not *really* jousting for anyone's hand or honor right now. She's supposed to be jousting *theatrically.*

Old habits die hard, I guess.

I'm still waving my flag like crazy when Virago wheels her horse back around toward us, pacing her mount beautifully along the fence. She's riding a gorgeous, big-boned black horse that's probably either a full-blooded Percheron (think large, black relations of the Budweiser Clydesdales) or related to one. Either way, because of how tall that horse is, Virago is currently sitting about eight feet off the ground, which is pretty damn high, but she's perched up there like she's perfectly comfortable, like she does this every day, and doesn't even have to think about it. It's pure effortlessness, the way she works her legs smoothly against the horse's sides, the way she sits back in the saddle, handling the reins like the trained professional that she is.

But she's reaching up now and taking off her helmet, holding her reins and the lance in her other leather-gloved hand as she slows her horse to a standstill. The gelding comes a stop, pawing at the ground and snorting.

Suddenly, the world starts to move in slow motion (or, at least, it *seems* to), a distant, hard rock ballad blasting out of someone's faraway car in the parking lot. The ballad playing is about sexy ladies, appropriately enough, as Virago takes her helmet off, shaking out her long, black hair and tossing it over her armored shoulder. Virago rakes a gloved hand through her hair, the strands now falling in perfect black waves over her metal-clad arms, down her back, the tips curling and shining against the spirals carved into her armored back-piece. And now she stops, rising up in her saddle. Virago searches through the crowd with her piercing blue eyes as she stands in the stirrups, her gaze trailing over the assembled people gathered along the fence line, her brow furrowed, just a little, as she searches...

And then her gaze finds me.

And when her eyes light on mine, the entire "arena" of the Knights of Valor Festival starts to glow as brightly as the surface of the sun. Because those bright blue eyes fix me in their sights, sparkling with energy, with delight, and her full lips turn up at the corners revealing dazzling, white teeth, and...my God...the smile that unfurls... It's utterly enchanting.

I can feel my knees weaken immediately, my heart rate accelerating like I just ran a mile in a second, as I hold her gaze, and I smile, too.

Because Virago is looking at me right now with a mixture of triumph—Carly's right; she really *did* wallop that other knight, poor guy—but also this kind of pure, radiating joy at seeing me in the audience, watching her do one of the things she's best at: being a knight. Her bright blue eyes dazzle, and the planes and curves of her face, naked of makeup, radiate with a flush of exertion and exhilaration. But there's more to her expression than that.

Because there's this specific look that Virago has that she saves, only for me.

It's love. Love, pure and simple, perfect and absolute. When Virago gazes at me, it's like nothing in the world exists except the two of us. Like everything else around us and outside of us—the people, the houses, the city of Boston, the world—fades away until there is only us and the connection that's between us, so bright and vibrant, pulsing like a newly born star. I can practically feel it, like a shining thread that binds my heart to hers.

I think it's safe to say that, in all of the relationships I've had, I have *never* been looked at in the way that Virago looks at me. Honestly, I didn't think that people *ever* looked at each other like that.

Admittedly, I'm an incurable romantic, and I've read about a billion lesbian romance novels—give or take a few. Hey, I'm a librarian. It's practically my *job* to read. But I thought all those furtive glances were hyped up for effect. That "meaningful look across the room," that "stolen moment where we glance at one another." I mean, it was romantic and heart-fluttery to read about smoldering gazes, but I'd often wondered how based in reality that sexy, happily-ever-after stuff could possibly be. It *couldn't* be real, I'd thought...and I'd believed it. Life had beaten me down, and I didn't believe in the possibility of true love, or soul mates, or even people who just really, unconditionally loved each other.

Until I met Virago.

Until I fell in *love.*

And I'm pretty sure I look at her in that exact same way that she looks at me.

"Hey, earth to Holly! Come, in Holly," says Carly, good-naturedly elbowing my ribs with a laugh, her smile wide as she shoves some of her curls out of her face; it's a little windy today. "Cartoon hearts are bouncing around above your head," she chuckles at me, with a little eyeroll, a manicured brow raised impishly. "And *now* said hearts are popping like tiny balloons and showering me with love-colored confetti." She pantomimes brushing something invisible off of her shoulders.

"Cartoon hearts. Sure. I'd believe it," I sigh happily, then grin at Carly. "Okay, so what's 'love-colored' look like, exactly?"

"Pink and red with a few white ones," Carly replies automatically, still grinning as Virago turns her horse around and begins to trot him back toward the makeshift tent-turned-stable where the horses for the Knights of Valor Festival are kept while the festival is in progress. She posts in the saddle easily, rising and falling in the perfect rhythm of the horse's hooves, and I'm having a *very* difficult time not looking at her leather-covered behind again. I can already feel my cheeks blushing as I look back at my best friend, my best friend who is absolutely *not* hiding the fact that she's making fun of me.

"Hey, you know, I realize how sappy we're both being," I admit gently as I tuck my blue-and-black flag into my oversized purse, pushing my purse's strap back up onto my shoulder. "And I'm really sorry that we're infecting you with love cooties," I tell her, with a wink.

"Oh, you had to deal with me when I first got together with David," says Carly with a shrug, "and I'm highly aware that I shed *a lot* of love cooties in those first few years. And, you know, even now," she tells me, with a chuckle and a shake of her head. She pauses for a moment, holding my gaze; then she takes a deep breath. "I don't mind all the cartoon hearts, Holly," she says, her voice dropping to a conspiratorial whisper as she snakes an arm around my waist and draws me into a surprise hug. "It's *really* wonderful. You have no idea *how* wonderful it is—to see you so damn happy. You're, like, radiating. Like Godzilla, when he got radiation pumped into him in that one movie. But in a *good* way," she tells me sincerely.

I'm laughing. "Hey, coming from you, that's the ultimate compliment," I tell her, squeezing my geeky friend tightly before letting her go.

"I mean, do you realize how lucky you are, Holly?" asks Carly, holding me out at arm's length and searching my face. "I just want to make sure, 'cause I seem to remember, like...oh, a month or so ago, a rather *different* visit to the Knights of Valor festival. Remember? One where you were pretty damn *depressed* because that ridiculous woman you called your *girlfriend* was being a total *asshat?* Just wondering if the *asshat* reference jogs your memory at all," she says wryly, sticking her tongue out at me.

I open my mouth, ready to defend my ex—and then I remember that Nicole *was* cheating on me for a year. I snap my mouth shut, shaking my head with a small sigh.

"*Holly*," Carly tells me, her face shining as she beams at me. "That woman right now, in the armor?" She points across the field at Virago. "The woman you're madly in love with? She came for you across *worlds*. I just...I just hope you know how lucky you are to have found each other."

I glance across the lawn, at Virago astride that big, black horse, talking to one of the knights down on ground level, a big grin stretching across her face. I can't hear what they're saying, but Virago tilts back her head at that moment and lets out such a joyous peal of laughter that, even over the noise of the rest of the Knights of Valor Festival, I can hear it, can hear how bright and happy her laugh is, like ringing bells.

The sound of her laughter makes my heart skip a beat.

"Yeah," I tell Carly, and I realize that there are probably even *more* cartoon hearts rising out of my head now and popping like tiny balloons, showering my friend with "love-colored" confetti. "I do know how lucky I am." I smile contentedly.

That's the deepest truth I know.

I'm the luckiest woman in this world. And, you know, pretty much any other world.

"Good," Carly says with a satisfied nod, hooking her arm tightly through mine. "So, don't you think that we should go congratulate your lovely knight on yet another fine performance?"

"Sure."

"By the way," Carly tells me, a brow up as we begin to step over the knee-high rope fencing. "I think it's pretty awesome that the festival lets Virago participate in the jousts and everything"—Carly gestures forward, her tone a little incredulous—"without a *single* page of paperwork documenting her previous work experience. Which happened to all take place on another world," says Carly with a laugh, as we thread our way through the exiting crowd, aiming for the back tent. "I mean, how did you convince the festival guys? Virago doesn't even have a driver's license! No passport! No nothing!"

"Well..." I shrug. "Virago just tried out for the joust like everybody else and really impressed them with how she handled the lance work and the horse. And, you know, considering that she jousted for my hand a few weeks ago at the festival, before the whole Beast thing happened... I mean, it *was* a few weeks ago, but obviously some gorgeous lady knight asking eloquently for the right to prove herself behind a lance for her lady's hand... That's pretty much something that nobody's going to forget."

"True, that," says Carly, shoving her hands into her jeans pockets. "But, still, I think it's pretty awesome that they're letting her do this without references or...well, anything," she says, glancing sidelong at me.

"Are you suggesting that Virago used some sort of magic to convince them to let her joust?" I ask, innocently batting my eyelashes. "Why, madame—the nerve!" I tell her, as her eyes grow wider, her mouth open in a little, round "o."

"You know what? I'm sorry I asked," she quips, eyes still wide, hands up in an "I surrender; please stop talking about it" sort of gesture.

"Okay, okay. It was just a *little* magic," I tell her, holding my thumb and forefinger a hair's breadth apart as she shakes her head, rolling her eyes and trying not to smile.

Yeah, I've got to admit, it's kind of questionable that we decided to use magic for that. But it's the only time we've ever used magic on *anyone*, and it was for a *super* good cause. Virago loves being able to joust at the festival (and it was only a "these are not the droids you're looking for" moment. I promise).

Carly and I move through the crowd, and then the people part...

And there she is.

As we approach Virago, my heart starts to flutter against my rib cage, my mouth turning up at the corners as I look at the gorgeous woman perched atop that massive horse. Virago gazes down at me for a moment, looking as pleased as a cat who just ate an entire pet shop's worth of canaries. She swings a leg over the rump of her big horse and hops down onto the ground effortlessly, her armor clanking as she settles. Virago lifts her chin then and gazes at me with those perfect bright blue eyes.

"Hello, my love," she growls happily. And then Virago leans forward, the leather thongs along her sides creaking as she wraps her strong arms around my middle, drawing me close, my costume dress pressing against the front of her armor with its glorious, scroll-worked breastplate, covered in tiny spirals. And then she's kissing me. Fiercely. Her mouth is hot and soft and fiery against mine.

Virago tastes of white-hot mint, and her lips are full and warm against me, electric. She kisses me, tasting me, holding me tightly. I wrap my arms around her neck and draw her down, happiness filling every atom of my body.

We stand, of course, next to a massive horse along the edge of the arena. And the massive horse chooses this moment to stomp one of his massive hooves, flicking his tail at flies, glancing over his shoulder with a very long-suffering sigh. Since Virago started jousting here just a few days ago, it's our kissing that delays the horse from his oats each evening. I'm starting to get a complex that the creature kind of hates me because of it.

Carly coughs politely and clears her throat. "Not that I don't enjoy watching a nice makeout session between a woman I kind of consider a sister—so, you know, therefore, *cooties*—and a knight from another world," she tells us mildly, "but..."

I'm laughing as I back away a little from Virago, shaking my head as my blush deepens. "Sorry, Carly," I tell her, but she's chuckling, too.

"Hey, I don't want to interrupt something as hot as all that," she tells us with a wicked grin, "but I've got to get going. I promised David I'd be home to cook him my specialty!"

"Takeout pizza?" I ask her, returning the grin.

She spreads her hands and smiles as beatifically as the pope. Or Oprah. "*You* get a takeout pizza! *You* get a takeout pizza!" she says, in perfect pantomime of Oprah's Favorite Things, as she points at random people in the crowd. They look a little surprised but shrug and keep going about their business, because—frankly—this is a Renaissance festival, and there are much weirder things going on around here.

"But no, seriously," Carly grins at me, "I'm probably just going to get a frozen pizza," she says with a little shrug. "And what are *your* plans for this evening?" she asks us, then covers her eyes, holding up a hand, "and try to be G-rated, please."

I'm laughing, and Virago is, too, because I explained the rating system for movies just last night when I showed her *Jaws* and she wanted to understand what the gigantic "R" on the screen had to do with a really big shark. (I'm ashamed to admit that, at first, I joked that it stood for "Really big shark.")

"Well, you know," I say then, lifting my chin as my smile deepens, "today just *happens* to be our one-week anniversary!"

Carly's already groaning (in anticipation of our "love cooties," I'm sure) as Virago's smile deepens, too, and she leans close, bending down her head slowly, gently, to brush her warm mouth against the curve of my neck and shoulder, bared by the ridiculously low-cut costume gown.

"And it will be a night to remember," she murmurs, gazing at me with eyes that suddenly seem to spark. A tremor of desire moves through me as she looks at me with total and unabashed lust, her bright blue eyes visibly darkening with desire in an instant. Good Lord—I'm fairly certain that, right this moment, she's undressing me with her eyes...

"Before you guys start exuding cartoon hearts again," Carly interjects wryly, stepping forward and shaking her head, "I wanted to tell you good job, Virago," she says with a wide smile. She gently punches Virago's upper arm like I've seen guys in locker rooms or on sports fields do. "I'm really glad you're enjoying the joust so much. It's obvious that you're passionate about your work," she says, shoving her hands into her jeans pockets then and rocking back on her heels as she considers the two of us.

"It has been very easy for me, this 'theatrical'

jousting," says Virago, "for I have a good mount." She reaches back and affectionately pats the large horse's shoulder. "It is true," she says, her voice dropping to a conspiratorial whisper as she shakes her head a little, "Brute is not as good as my beloved mare back on Agrotera, but he is willing to learn and is quite responsive. And I think I can teach him," she says, beaming. "It should only take a moon, possibly two, before he listens as well as Aphelion. Aphelion," she explains easily to Carly, "is my battle mare."

Carly shoots me a questioning look just then, her brows very, very high. I can read Carly like a book, and while Carly *could* be thinking in my general direction, *a* battle *mare?*, I know that, in fact, Carly is currently telepathically asking me, "You didn't tell Virago that the Knights of Valor Festival is closing in a *week*?" I shake my head just a little, biting my lip as I squeeze Virago's hand tighter. I take a deep breath at that moment and very adamantly avoid meeting Carly's eyes.

"Soooooo," says Carly then, dragging out the word as she rocks back onto her heels, trying to quell the momentary awkwardness. Momentary awkwardness, I might add, that Virago does not seem to notice. "It's your one-week anniversary," Carly says with a wink. "Knowing you guys, you probably have elaborate, romantic plans, yeah?"

"Quite," says Virago, taking a big breath and standing triumphantly as she raises my hand into the air. "We are going," she says, with a flourish, and a small bow aimed in my direction, her body curving forward gracefully, "on a *date night.* I just learned of this thing," she says, rising easily and gazing earnestly at Carly. "It is, apparently, a ritual where a couple leaves the house and goes to do something romantic together, such as visiting a fine restaurant, or embarking on an epic quest to slay a—"

"—or going to a movie," I insert hastily, then smile.

"I mean, I can think of a few Republican presidential candidates I'd like you to slay," says Carly, her grin conveying a hint of menace before she chuckles. "But we kid, we kid," she tells us with a wink. "That's awesome, you guys... So which of those things are you going to do?" she asks, folding her arms and cocking her head.

"A fancy dinner," I tell Carly, with a warm smile. "And then possibly a movie. Or mini golf!"

Carly blinks at me. Then she takes in Virago, standing next to me with her sword strapped to her back, her lance on the ground beside her horse.

"Sure," says Carly, rolling her shoulders back. "Mini golf. That...sounds like something a knight would be interested in. Why not?" She's chuckling a little as she shakes her head. "Hey, it sounds like it'll be a fun night for the two of you, sincerely." And I know she's being sincere. She glances down at her watch just then. "Have a fantastic time, okay? I've got to go do the grueling work of preheating that oven. And, seriously, Virago, great joust. You're a natural," she says, lifting a brow.

"Thank you, lady Carly. It is an honor that you say so," says Virago, smiling companionably.

"Call me later," Carly mouths to me, lifting her thumb and pinkie to her ear and mouth, one brow raised as she shakes her head a little. Knowing Carly like I do, she's either going to call to ask if the frozen pizza box is accurate in its assumption that you don't *really* need a pan and can just put it directly on the rack...or ask me why the hell I haven't told Virago that the festival is ending very, very soon.

That pizza question I can answer. The other is going to be a little more complicated...

"Bye, lovebirds. And happy anniversary," Carly tells us with a wink before she turns, her hands shoved into her pockets as she makes her way into the crowd, disappearing into the Knights of Valor festival.

"I must cool Brute down," says Virago, squeezing my hand before letting me go again. She takes a step back, gathers up her mount's reins, and untethers him from the makeshift hitching post. "It won't take me very long," she tells me, curving her gloved fingers into a slim space between her breastplate and her leather shirt on the right side of her chest. My eyes grow a little wide (and my hearts skips about *ten* beats in a row) until I realize that she's pulling out a leather thong that she then uses to gather up her hair, tying the leather around a makeshift ponytail. She chuckles at my expression when she catches it (she wasn't *trying* to be sexy, but that's the thing about Virago: she *is* sexy, effortlessly), and then she smiles slowly, seductively at me before leaning in, wrapping an arm around my waist and pulling me close again.

"My love," she tells me in a low whisper, her brow up as she gazes down at me, her lips wet, her bright blue eyes smoldering. "When do we have to be at the restaurant?" she purrs into my ear as she leans down, pressing a very (*very*) indelicate, hot, rather intense kiss at the nape of my neck again.

"Um...whenever you want. It's not a place that...um...takes reservations or anything," I tell her breathlessly, my knees going weak again, my legs struggling to hold me up as her hand slides down my waist and rests almost innocently against the curve of my rear.

But it's so *not* innocent as Virago gently, delicately, squeezes my butt.

Her eyes are dancing now as she chuckles a little, and I'm laughing, too, even though it was pretty sexy and I shouldn't be laughing—but we both are. Virago curls her hand around the curve of my waist alone, and I press the palm of my hand against the plate of armor that's covering her stomach, feel the scrolled metal beneath my skin, feel the warmth of that metal because Virago's body heat has made the metal hot. The levity leaves me, and desire takes over, pulsing through me like my blood, making me feel ridiculously heady. I shiver.

"Oh, good," Virago tells me then, stepping back again, lifting up her chin, her eyes flashing with an intense brightness. "I had a few things I wanted to...take care of first. Before dinner," she murmurs, nodding to me with a knowing, secret smile.

I'm laughing breathlessly as I nod, trying to still my erratic heartbeat.

Yeah, Carly was right about those cartoon hearts. I can practically see them dancing above my head as a blush reddens my cheeks, making my whole body feel flushed.

"Um..." I take a deep breath and wrap my arms around Virago's neck again as I lean forward, my breasts squishing against her metal breastplate. Don't ask me why that's super sexy, but for some reason, it *is*. "We don't...we don't *have* to go to dinner for our one-week anniversary," I'm telling her, my voice low and purring in what I hope to be a sexy timbre.

Virago is shaking her head wildly then, placing both hands on my hips firmly and holding my gaze.

"Lady Holly," she says, in her no-nonsense-this-is-serious-business voice, "you have told me that a 'date night' is a sacred and time-honored tradition of your world—"

"I mean, sort of," I tell her hastily.

"And this will be our first one!" she says, searching my gaze. "Our very first date night," she reiterates, enunciating each word like it's an incantation to a sensual spell. "That it *is* our first means that it is special and sacred, and deserves to be treated with respect. So dinner and mini golf must happen in order for the tradition to remain unsullied and pure, and to commemorate our one week together."

I never thought the words "mini golf" could be uttered in a sultry tone, but then I hadn't met Virago until about a month ago, so... She could sing the Presidents song we were all taught in school, and it would be a feast for the senses. And I *may* have taught her that song a few nights ago, just to prove to myself that she could sing it sexily. *And, wow, she did.* "Monroe, Adams..." I mean, I get shivers right now just thinking about Taft, and that's a little weird.

"All right, all right," I tell her, squeezing her in an embrace and pecking a final kiss on her cheek before letting her go and taking a step back. "We'll do dinner. It's not that I don't *want* to do dinner..." I tell her, one brow up, head tilted to the side.

"We have time enough for *all* things," says Virago, her voice low and husky as she smiles at me. And now her eyes are flashing even brighter, and her blue gaze travels the length of my body appreciatively before moving back up to my eyes again.

That single glance just told me that we're going to have a *lot* of fun before dinner.

"Meet you at the car," I tell her, still breathless, and she nods confidently before walking away with Brute to cool him down. The horse lets out another long-suffering sigh—which I translate as *finally*—and as he walks past, the horse swishes his tail and nearly thwacks me in the face. Yeah, I'm definitely not his favorite person...

I turn on my heel and make my way through the Knights of Valor Festival. And on my way back to the car, I pass people telling Shakespearean jokes, people selling hush puppies and turkey legs, Coca-Cola and mead, crystals and hand-rolled incense. I pass women in elaborate dresses and armor, and men in armor and breeches and, yeah, a few men in dresses. It's a pretty friendly festival, and Boston is a pretty friendly city, in general. I pass an alpaca and a small petting zoo that consists entirely of a rotund, annoyed-looking donkey and his turkey friend. That the petting zoo pen is positioned right next to the booth selling turkey legs is in bad taste, I think.

But I don't really *see* any of that stuff. Because my heart is beating irregularly (it's *probably* not cause for a visit to the cardiologist, since this is what Virago does to me every damn day, making my heart skip beats), and my face is likely flushed to the color of a ruby.

If I were in a movie, right about now is when I'd start in on my first major musical number, singing about the most wonderful woman in the world and how madly in love with her I am. There would be a flame thrower or three in said musical number, and it'd end with confetti guns spewing a metric ton of golden glitter into the air.

God, I have it bad.

The thing about falling in love—in real, mad, true love—is that pretty much everything else in your life feels like a musical number, anyway. Or maybe that's just me. I really don't have any basis for comparison, because I've never felt this before, and God knows I'm not much of a dancer...or singer, for that matter. I'd be the first one to admit that my strengths and superpowers are all librarian-based. But I'm so in love with Virago that I can't *help* but think in lyrics from cheesy musical numbers, where someone declares devotion and everlasting love.

There's a large part of me that can't quite believe this is happening to me. *Me,* the woman who, historically, *always* goes after the wrong woman. I've acquired a long list of terrible dating experiences throughout my life, ranging from the hilarious (like that one time that I dated my literary criticism professor, and she failed me for a test because the date we'd been on the night before "missed the mark entirely." True story.) to the tragic (like the time that the woman I'd been dating for *four* years, the woman who I thought I would *marry,* had secretly been cheating on me for an entire *year* behind my back with her assistant). But, for some wonderful and miraculous reason, my bad luck in the romance department has dried up and has been replaced by a vision in shining armor.

Virago is literally a dream come true. *My* dream come true.

So, yeah, I'm seriously considering that musical number as I walk through the Knights of Valor Festival, as I weave through the laughing, happy crowd milling around in the sunshine, the minstrel singing a ballad across the little path from a jester juggling a dozen brightly colored balls. The jester's face is a slightly creepy mask, but his juggling is pretty topnotch. He's doing a ridiculous bit where he's *acting* as if he can't keep up with the balls swirling through the air, and he's staggering all over the place as if he's about to drop them. But he always catches them at the last possible second. Like most of the people who have been walking past him, I stop to watch his act for a moment...

And, for that single moment, it's still all song-and-dance numbers inside of me, with the jester staggering around, singing a song to himself, the kids in front of the crowd surrounding him laughing. Everything is nice and wonderful and picture-perfect...

But then a cloud scuttles across the sun, obscuring the brightness of the sunbeams. The cloud is very black, and the scene transforms from brightly lit, a gorgeous summer's day...to darkness. Darkness descends all around us like we've just stepped into a gray-scale photograph. The jester drops one of his balls, and then another; soon enough, they all fall to the ground.

Everyone looks to the sky, murmuring quietly.

Hmm.

This isn't ominous at all. Nope...

In denial, I glance up at the sky, too, shielding my eyes as I shiver. I'm remembering what was, a mere moment ago, a perfectly cloudless day, the kind of day that artists paint pictures of, or seventies-style rockers write songs about...

But I can see, above the treeline surrounding the dog park, and all along the horizon, that there are storm clouds forming, big, pillowy mounds of dark gray clouds that are starting to pile on top of each other, billowing taller, bigger, closer.

And there, across the sun, is a single small, dark cloud. And even though it's much smaller than the bank of clouds growing along the horizon, for some reason, this one looks just a little bit more menacing.

I wrap my arms around myself and stare up at that little cloud. Odd... It was *supposed* to be a gorgeous afternoon and evening. But now, even as I glance at the far bank of clouds building up over the city, I can see the unmistakable crackle of distant lightning, thread-like but white-hot. There's a soft rumble from the sky. Thunder.

Even though there shouldn't be—not a single meteorologist predicted it—there's going to be a storm tonight.

Well, it's not as if the weather guys and gals are always right, and after last winter, I should know better than to trust them. Plus, considering that I'm acquainted with some of the weather forecasters at Carly's public access television station, it's surprising that I *ever* trusted them in the first place... But I checked multiple weather sites online, and even called Carly at the station earlier, because I wanted to make absolutely, positively certain that it was going to be a perfect night for mini golf. (I know, I know—*mini golf.* Kind of a guilty pleasure of mine. But it's no fun playing play put-put in the pouring rain.)

As if in answer to my inner musings, there's another flicker of lightning along the dark gray bellies of the clouds and—far distant—a small, grumpy, and yet surprisingly ominous growl of thunder.

My skin breaks out into goosebumps as I stare up at the sky.

I'm sure it's nothing, no big deal, I tell myself, which

is denial again, because that's not what I'm thinking at *all.* I have a lot of really terrible memories about storms...

Like the one about a month ago, when a tremendous storm brought Virago to me...but it brought with her a monstrous beast. Virago has told me now that it's because of the violent power of the storm that the portal between our worlds was able to be opened. That the storm made the link work, the door between Agrotera and Earth swinging wide. At least...she *thinks* that's how it worked. But, either way, the storm delivered something wonderful...and something horrible at the same time.

Something horrible that almost took that something wonderful away from me forever.

It's not as if I have a fear of thunderstorms now; there have been several that happened since Virago came through the portal to Earth. It's been a pretty stormy summer, after all.

But—and I couldn't tell you exactly *why*—there's just something sinister about this one. Maybe it's how quickly the clouds appeared, billowing and rising like a distant, nefarious castle. Maybe it's how the lightning flickers, crackling along the underside of the clouds as if it's some sort of strange, electrical monster, searching for something...

Okay, Holly, whoa. That's letting your magnificent imagination get a little *bit carried away there. It's* just *a storm,* I remind myself, turning away from the jester who's attempting to pick up all of his balls (there's a joke in there somewhere...). I aim for my car.

But as I walk through the rest of the festival, past the ticket turret entrance and into the greater parking lot, to wait for Virago, I feel that ominous dread inside of me grow. I snatch glimpses of the darkening sky from moment to moment, watching those clouds grow bigger, darker, stronger. I bite my lip, unlock the car door and sit in the driver's seat, unrolling the window to gaze out at the nightmarish clouds.

I think the real problem here is that this just doesn't *feel* like a natural storm. I know that sounds silly, but it's true. And if I'd been paying closer attention the night that the portal opened, the night that Virago and the Boston Beast appeared in my backyard, locked in an epic, otherworldly battle, I would have noticed a *lot* quicker that there was something unnatural about the storm that night, too.

Here and now, along the edge of the horizon, a single bolt of lightning flickers, dazzlingly bright. I glance over my shoulder, toward the festival's opening gates, and I'm relieved to see a familiar silhouette making her way toward me through the darkening afternoon. As Virago opens the car door a few moments later, another ragged bolt of lightning rips open the sky, and I'm trembling as I put my key into the ignition. For some reason, right now...I really, really want to get home.

"Hello," Virago says companionably as she leans down and glances at me through the passenger-side opening with a soft smile. She watches me through her long, black lashes, her blue eyes sparkling just as much as the lightning. Then she turns and opens up the back door to deposit her jousting armor, her leather clothes and her sword and scabbard.

"Virago," I begin, glancing nervously up at the sky as she folds her long, lean length into the passenger seat. "Do you think... Um, I know this is weird," I say, worrying at my lip. "But don't you think that storm came up awfully quickly?"

Virago lifts her chin and glances up at the clouds, regarding the lightning with a careful, calculating expression, her blue eyes narrowed.

"I'm not certain," she tells me then, her voice a low growl. "Why has it unsettled you, my love?" She casts me a sidelong glance, concern making her full mouth downturn as she reaches across the space between us and settles her long, bare fingers, on top of my thigh.

"I don't know," I tell her, suddenly distracted by the fact that she's gently stroking my thigh through my skirt, her thumb smoothing back and forth, back and forth. It's very distracting, but it's also somehow calming. "When you came through that first night," I tell her, "that storm was exactly like this one. I don't know. It just seems...odd," I finish weakly, with a little shrug.

"Do not worry yourself," Virago tells me, her chin lifting up and her frown turning into a smile almost instantly. "For there is nothing to fear. The beast is held safely. There is no way that she can escape from her prison. All is well," she tells me, still stroking my thigh. Her fingers against the fabric of my skirt are warm and strong and soft, all at once. I concentrate on her touch, concentrate on the good, slow, soft sound of her breathing. I concentrate on the fact that she's right here, right here beside me.

It's silly to be unsettled by a thunderstorm. I know better. I wrap my fingers around the steering wheel, give Virago a sidelong smile, and then I'm pulling off the lawn/parking lot surrounding the Knights of Valor Festival, and I turn onto the highway.

Along the cloud bank, the lightning is getting thicker, larger, more jagged as it dances along the curves of the clouds. There hasn't been any lightning striking ground as far as I can see, no spears of electricity arcing down from the sky...but that doesn't mean it won't happen.

When we get home, the clouds along the edge of the horizon have, well, migrated. Because now the entire sky, that just a half hour before was blue and cloudless, is almost as dark as night. It's nearly August, and the sun doesn't set until nine o'clock. But here it is, six o'clock in the evening, and the sky outside is ominously black. Lightning makes the clouds flicker constantly now, but I can't see any more bolts, just flashes of light.

The strange thing is, that with all of the clouds overhead, with the constant roar of thunder and flickers of lightning...there still hasn't been a drop of rain.

It's as if the clouds are hovering overhead, waiting for something.

I pull into my driveway and turn off the ignition, tossing the set of keys in my purse as I turn to look at Virago. Along with the dark pair of fitted jeans that she's magnificently filling out, she's currently wearing the *hell* out of a black, button-down shirt, her equally black, satiny mane pulled back with that leather thong into a messy ponytail. There are loose wisps of blue-black hair framing her face, with its high cheekbones and those large, bright blue eyes. She's wearing no makeup, but her long lashes blink slowly at me, her gaze piercing me through, her full lips wet because she just licked them—slowly, sensuously, her tongue dragging across them as her mouth turned up into a slow, seductive smile.

Everything is still and quiet in the car. The windows are rolled up, and the car's off, but it's been a cool enough day (surprisingly, for a summer in Boston) that the car is simply comfortable to sit in. In the stillness, all I can hear is the distant rumble of thunder, the somewhat closer sound of Bill, the guy who lives next door, mowing his backyard...and the sound of our mingled breathing, slow and steady.

But as I glance sidelong at Virago, as I watch her lick her lips again, as I watch her lean a little closer to me, hearing the rustle of the fabric of her shirt, hearing the soft shush of her jeans moving against the seat beneath her, hearing the whisper of her hair falling over her shoulder...my breathing starts to come just a little faster.

Virago holds my gaze for a very long moment as my heart rate skyrockets. And then she murmurs three words in a gentle, growling voice; they invade my senses, making me tremble.

"I want you," Virago whispers across the space between us, as—overhead—a rumble of thunder makes the car shake.

But I don't pay attention to the thunder, and I'm certainly not paying attention to the ominous sky anymore as Virago reaches for me with maddening ease, and slowly, with a great deal of self-control, traces a single finger across my right breast, down my side, and along the inner curve of my thigh. She accomplishes all of this over the fabric of my clothes, but her touch, in that moment, is searing. I gasp out loud.

Virago is the mistress of the slow seduction, something I've never been good at, as much as I keep trying to beat her at her own game. Ha. It's pretty pathetic when I try to hold out, try to be all slow and sensual when I'm arching over her in the middle of the night—and I suddenly have *zero* self-control, and Virago is chuckling under me as I lean down and kiss her or do any of the million-and-one acts I was just teasing her would be excruciatingly slow in coming...and then totally *isn't*.

But there's something about the energy of the air tonight—it's too alive. Too electric. It's as if there's no time for lingering, sultry endeavors.

There's only this moment, right now. And there's a deep, abiding urgency...

Virago leans forward as another rumble of thunder echoes overhead. She wraps an arm around my shoulders, drawing me close smoothly, quickly, threading her fingers through my hair, cupping my cheek with her palm as her breath intensifies, hot against me. She captures my mouth, in that instant, with another kiss.

But this is not the languid kiss that we shared post-joust, as she smiled against me, as the horse stomped impatiently next to us and Carly teased us. No, this is the kind of kiss that makes my toes curl, that makes me gasp. It's a full-of-passion kind of kiss, full of blatant, obvious need and desire, a need and desire that I return instantaneously as my knight draws me close, wrapping me tightly in her arms, pressing my chest against hers, her breath hot and quick, her fingers curling tighter in my hair as her mouth finds mine.

Okay, so this is kind of embarrassing, but I haven't made out in a car since...well, I don't think I even made out in a car, not even in high school. In my defense, I came out pretty early in my teens, and there weren't any lesbians or bi-ladies besides me who were out at my high school at the time, so my dating life back then was pretty sad.

But my driveway is hidden pretty well from both sets of neighbors by some robust, I-have-to-constantly-trim-them hedges, and, anyway...what the hell. I honestly don't even care if someone sees us. If Mrs. Whitter saw us, it might even do away with her "When are you going to start dating a man, dear?" comments, once and for all.

And as I taste Virago, as my hands find the top few buttons of her blouse, fire races through me. I trace my fingertips under the edge of the neckline, feeling the searing heat of her skin against my own—and then the sky erupts.

A torrential downpour deluges my car. It sounds like a million metal trash cans being knocked over. As the rain roars against the roof, it covers the windshield in water, making it impossible to see out. I stare in surprise as I realize that I can't even see my house, which is a mere few feet away—and has bright purple shutters, so it's usually visible from space.

All I can see is the rain. And Virago, who is watching me with luminous blue eyes, her cheeks reddened, her lips open, wet, panting...

Again, Virago draws my attention away from the storm.

My earlier worries about the storm being somehow magical or malevolent evaporate as I consider instead that making love in the middle of a violent rainstorm...yeah, that sounds pretty damn sexy to me.

"Come on," I whisper to her, my voice almost squeaking, I'm so excited, as I open my car door.

And, yes, it *is* a deluge out (thoughts of childhood Sunday school classes and cartoon Noahs on boats with giraffes peeking out of the windows pop up into my head unbidden). The roar of the water drowns out everything else as we empty out of the car and run, together, up the walkway and the few steps onto the front porch.

Maybe it's the energy of the storm; maybe it's the closeness of this incredible woman, this woman that I'm so deeply attracted to—body, soul and spirit... Maybe it's the dazzling blue of her eyes as she looks at me, every atom of her being desiring me. Maybe it's a combination of all of these things, but every inch of me feels alive, more alive than I've ever felt before, as I fumble with the keys at the door, shoving my soaked red curls out of my face as I finally shove the damn thing open.

We're through the doorway in a heartbeat, and Shelley, my crazy, wonderful dog, is jumping up on us excitedly, *ecstatic* that we're finally home. She keeps pushing her big white paws on my stomach, practically using it as a springboard, and I'm laughing, trying to push her down, back onto four paws, as Virago gathers me up in her arms again, as she holds me tightly to her, the both of us drenched from the rainstorm. And she kisses me.

The door is still wide open behind us, but Shelley is *super*-aware of the fact that she is *not* allowed out the front door without a leash, and for some reason, this is the one law in the universe that she obeys. So, instead of bolting outside, she sits beside us, staring adoringly at the both of us, blinking her long, brown lashes and sighing contentedly.

Outside, the thunder resounds so loudly that it rattles the windows in their casements. I'm breathless as we kiss each other, highly aware of Virago's curves pressing against me, of the muscles of her stomach (Her *stomach* has *muscles.* I mean, seriously.) against my fingers as I drift my hands over her torso and then wrap my fingers around her hips, digging into them with my fingernails. I gasp against her. Because Virago has wasted no time; she is lifting her long fingers to the piece of string that I use to keep my costume bodice cinched up.

I think it says a lot about me that I've fantasized about a moment like this, where Virago is about to unlace my not-historically-accurate-but-it's-all-I-could-afford costume bodice. I know that the image of unlacing bodices is traditionally synonymous with straight romance novel covers (that is, again, quite a bit less than historically accurate), but who cares? Because this moment? This moment is as *not* straight as you can get, considering that an incredible female knight is pressing her breasts against mine, grinning slyly and tucking her long fingers into the lacing, raising a single brow suggestively.

I feel, for half a heartbeat, that I've died and gone to some incredible version of nirvana, that I've seemingly done everything right in life and been given everything I ever desired, all wrapped up in the body and mind and heart of this woman... But as I kick the front door closed behind us, intent on pretty much doing it right here and right now, Shelley starts to jump around us again, determined to interrupt us in a way that can't be ignored. Because this time, she's leaping quite a bit more emphatically, propelling her front paws off of my stomach as if I'm a walking trampoline.

"Urgh... I'm really sorry," I manage to croak to Virago as I take a step back, holding an arm over my stomach so Shelley will stop bouncing off of it. "But, um...Shelley really has to go outside," I tell her with a sigh. And Virago, who—amazing woman that she is—understands about animal needs, takes a step back, raking a hand through her messy ponytail as she holds me in her bright blue gaze.

"Of course, of course," she murmurs, taking a step back from me, her mouth still parted, still drawing my gaze like a gravity. "This," she tells me, raising one brow and chuckling a little, "can wait a moment. Small beasts in our care must come first," she tells Shelley indulgently, who is practically in raptures at her feet, her white-gold tail blurring as she wags it violently, staring up at Virago with her adoring brown eyes.

"She's going to get so soaked," I moan, walking past Shelley, who turns and pounces across the floor after me. "But there's no help for it," I mutter, glancing up at the dark sky through the sliding glass door in my living room. The curtains and blinds are open, and outside, after another bit of jagged lightning rakes across the sky, I can hardly see the yard for all the torrential rain, coming down in waterfalls against the glass.

"Sorry about this, girl," I mutter to Shelley, and open the door for her. But my crazy dog doesn't care about the rain as she rips right out of the house and scampers across the back porch, leaping down the few steps and onto the lawn, euphoric to pee on every inch of my yard to inform the other neighborhood dogs that this is *her* turf.

I turn to glance back at Virago, who has padded stealthily up behind me. She wraps her arms around my middle, pressing her front against my back and her chin onto my shoulder. I reach up, wrapping an arms around hers. We stay like this, tightly embracing, our bodies interwoven, as we gaze out into the backyard. The backyard where everything happened, where my entire life changed forever, just a little less than a month ago.

As we wait for Shelley to finish her business—she's currently racing across the backyard, her nose down to the ground, while she follows the trail of an animal who probably scampered over the grass hours ago—I can feel Virago against me, can feel the heat of her breath on my neck. The rain is turning cold outside, and as I turn my head slightly, as I lean forward just a little, the heat of her breath passes over the bare skin of my neck, and I can see her exhale standing in the air, like smoke. It's cold enough to see breath. I shiver.

Virago's arms slowly loosen around me. Her movements are purposeful, sensuous, as she reaches up with her long fingers, her front pressing against my back. And her fingers wrap loosely around the laces of my bodice.

She pulls.

The bow comes undone, and the tightness of the bodice, squishing my boobs up in customary Ye Olde Renaissance Fashion, causes the laces to unravel pretty quickly. Virago tugs at the lacing, pulling it out of the grommets along the bodice until the entire front comes loose.

This is one of my favorite, most comfortable outfits that I have to wear to Renaissance festivals, and it's pretty common. The bodice and overskirt, both in a bright, happy red that go well with my natural red hair, are layered over a baggy white chemise with bell sleeves, then tied tightly to accentuate all the curves. So when Virago undoes my corset, there isn't immediate skin accessible to her—as much as I wish there was. The bodice is just now undone, and that means the skirt and chemise are still on, still between me and her.

But Virago is well versed in the workings of Renaissance-type clothing (even the kind that comes from the Halloween store and is very, very cheap, apparently), because she trails her fingers up my arms to the elastic top of the chemise.

She tugs it down, over my shoulders. I shiver against her as she places one hot kiss on my right shoulder, trailing her tongue over my skin, over my neck, as I tilt my head to the side, gasping as she kisses me there, there, there, a lot of wet, hot kisses, until she shimmies the chemise lower, the elastic giving easily.

There are hedges along my fence, and—honestly—it's too stormy for me to worry much about any of my neighbors watching my girlfriend strip me of my bodice and chemise...

I turn to her now. I can't take it anymore. She's being too slow, too tantalizing, and since I watched her jousting this afternoon, I've been wanting her. Well, since I woke up this morning, I've been wanting her. She is everything I want, everything I'm attracted to, everything I love, and *I want her.* I can't take this teasing. I need her now.

Virago was just about to pull the chemise below my breasts, but when I reach up, the chemise pulls up again, because I'm wrapping my arms around Virago's neck, drawing her in for a kiss.

Shelley is still tearing around in the backyard, so we leave the back door open for her, the rain slanting in the direction opposite of the open door, and Virago pulls me toward the couch. The couch is where Virago usually sets her sword, Wolfslayer, so—out of force of habit—I glance behind me before I sit on the couch, pulling Virago after me.

She must have left the sword in the car, because it's not on the couch. I immediately lie down on my side, pulling Virago after me, hooking my fingers in her leather belt as she rises over me, an indulgent smile tugging at her lips.

"You're loving this, aren't you, milady?" she asks me, her voice a low, sexual growl as she dips her head down, brushing her lips along the elastic hem of my chemise.

"Yes," I tell her, panting, tugging at her belt. "You have *no idea* how badly I've wanted to make love to you while wearing this damn thing," I tell her, gesturing down at myself with a free hand.

"Wouldn't you rather," she whispers, kissing the hollow of my neck, "that I was wearing," she growls, kissing my bare shoulder, "my armor?" She trails her tongue down, down, pushing the chemise lower, my breasts straining against the elastic now.

"Oh, you know, this is just fine," I manage, wrapping my fingers in her hair as she draws my chemise over my breasts now, freeing them.

"Because I could always stop," says Virago, her bright blue eyes flickering in the dimly lit room as she glances down at me, as her mouth turns up at the corners and she grins at me almost wickedly, "and put on my armor." She tilts her head to the side, raising one brow as her smile deepens, her lips glistening in the shadows.

"You're so mean," I tell her breathlessly, and then I'm laughing, shaking my head as I stare at her, propping myself up on my elbows. I pull her down to me, and I'm kissing her hard, fiercely. "You're a knight even without the armor, baby," I tell her, with a little laugh, as she breaks our kiss off, trailing kisses down my neck again, aiming—God, I *hope* she's aiming—for my breasts.

But as her head hovers above my breasts, as she reaches down, about to gather their curves in her hands, about to kiss them, taste them...

The lights in the living room that I just turned on flicker.

I glance over my shoulder at the small, dimly lit lamp on the table beside the couch. It's one of my favorite unicorn lamps (Don't ask how many unicorn lamps I have. The number is staggering. But, hey, everyone needs ample lighting in their home, right?), a ceramic one from the eighties, with a rainbow-haired unicorn rearing below the bright pink lampshade. The unicorn lights up; there's a small light bulb in his stomach, as well as the light bulb in the actual lamp, and as I watch, both the unicorn and the main bulb flicker as if they're trying to sync up with a Christmas song.

They flicker. And then they go out altogether.

The room is plunged into darkness.

On top of me, straddling me, Virago sighs. I can't see her in the dark, but I can feel her as she sits up, as she reaches across me and pulls me up, too, her arm around my right shoulder.

I turn to look back at the backyard, and I can see the houses that are visible over the fence. All of their lights are out, too.

I can't help it. As I sit there on the couch, my heart rises in my throat, and I grip Virago's arms tightly as she draws me to her, holding me against her chest.

I flashback to a month ago. I remember

crossing my living room to that exact same sliding glass door. I remember staring out into the torrential downpour at something that couldn't possibly have existed...but did. I stared out that night at a massive, towering monster who had just obliterated my shed with its enormous body. And, that night, I also stared out at a woman wearing armor, who was wielding a sword and challenging that massive beast to fight.

But as my heart rate skyrockets, as my breathing comes fast, I tug my chemise back up, back over my shoulders. And I rise up from the couch, padding silently to the open sliding glass door as I draw my bodice closed. And I stare out at my backyard.

Behind me, silently, Virago stands up and follows, crossing my living room to come stand behind me again, wrapping her arms tightly around my waist and drawing my back to her front. I can feel the steadiness of her heartbeat as I stare out into the blackness of the night. I can feel the steadiness of Virago herself.

And, out in the backyard, I am very gratified to see...well, nothing. There's nothing out there. There's no beast. And the knight that came through that evening a month ago, my knight, is standing here with me, holding me close.

It's ridiculous that I'm afraid of thunderstorms. It's ridiculous that another power outage would unsettle me so much. I'm just being silly, I tell myself, as I take a deep, calming breath. Power outages happen. Storms happen. It doesn't mean anything at all.

But as the rain intensifies, as even more buckets of water slosh out of the clouds, Shelley, currently obscured out in that downpour (how she can still be running around, sniffing things and peeing on them, I'll never know—she must be utterly soaked!), lets out a strange, high-pitched bark.

I peer out, and so does Virago, her body stiffening behind me, her arms tensing, her breathing slowing even more.

Lightning arches overhead, and my backyard, for just a heartbeat, is illuminated.

And I see...people.

Chapter 2: Three Knights and a Queen

There are four people standing in my backyard.

And they're all women.

Oh, my God.

I stare out into the backyard, trying to peer through the rain and make out shapes in the intermittent flashes of lightning.

And there's another flash of lightning now, so bright and dazzling that it lights up the entire sky.

And that's when I realize that it's really true, what I thought I saw.

Because all four women in the backyard?

They're wearing armor. They're carrying swords.

They're *knights.*

Virago realizes this at the exact same moment that I do, and then she's racing past me, through the open door and into the torrential downpour with a wordless exclamation of joy. She leaps off the porch, over the three steps, and then she's running across the backyard, whooping now with a kind of happiness that's completely catching. My fear and (ridiculous) worry about the monster coming back was unfounded. There are knights in my backyard. *Knights.*

Of course it's all right. These are Virago's

knights, knights she knows. There isn't any *monster*. But still, I can't help but glance around, just to be sure, gazing over the tops of the houses, up at the sky, even peering around the corner, out to the front yard, to make certain there's nothing prowling the Boston streets. But, no, there are only the four knights.

There's no beast. I take a deep breath, turn my attentions back to the women slogging through the pouring rain and Virago eager to meet them.

There's no beast, I think to myself, trying to calm my roaring heartbeat.

But, for some reason, it won't be calmed.

Virago is shouting something excitedly, and the knights are shouting back excitedly, but it's just one big, loud sound that's merging with the near-constant thunder, and I can't hear specific words. When I look hard, though, I can see the many embraces, the happy expressions, the joy at reunion. I make sure that my chemise is up and over my shoulders, and then I slog out of my living room happily, over the porch and into my backyard, determined to herd all of the knights somewhere drier.

And, as the lightning crackles overhead, spearing down out of the sky and striking a nearby house, I make an amendment: somewhere drier and *safer*.

"Alinor!" I hear Virago cry jubilantly, drawing a shorter woman to her and squeezing her tightly. The woman, I can vaguely make out through the downpour, seems to have very short hair. "And *Kell*!" Virago yells, flinging her arms now around a woman with long, dripping hair. Everyone's wearing armor, but in the darkness and the intermittent lightning bursts, I can see that some of them are wearing an armor that's similar to Virago's, but some are wearing a different kind...

"It's *you!*" this last woman, Kell, is shouting, practically jumping in place. "I wasn't sure if we could even *find* you, Virago, but then we started to open the portal, and we used your battle mare as an anchor for the spell, and—"

"Aphelion *hates* having spells anchored to her," says Virago, shaking her head, but she hasn't stopped smiling, so this comes out as ecstatic, too. Anchors? Spells? Battle mares? I don't pretend to understand what they're talking about as I step across the last few feet to reach her. Virago's hair is glued to her back now with water, her pants, shirt, and, I'm assuming, shoes are utterly saturated, but she doesn't care; she just keeps grabbing different women and hugging them tightly in turn, before grabbing another one to embrace enthusiastically.

"Virago, the storm—you guys are getting soaked!" I tell her, reaching out and touching her shoulder. Virago wheels around, and then the smile that blossoms on her face is as bright as a thousand suns as another bolt of lightning arches overhead, temporarily illuminating the entire world.

"My fellow knights!" Virago yells triumphantly, folding forward into an effortless, graceful bend, and she's now kneeling in front of me on one knee...in my flooded backyard. The mud *squelches* around her knee. Virago spreads her arms to encompass me, and I think she's about to start a Shakespearean soliloquy, but she doesn't. Instead, she inhales deeply and announces, with a huge, happy smile: "This is the love of my life!" she shouts. "It is my deepest pleasure to introduce to you the lady Holly, my lover!"

"Lady Holly!" all of the knights chorus

instantly, cheering and raising their fists to me in knightly salutation. I'm immediately blushing, even though it's freezing, and my chemise is paper thin. Virago reaches out, takes my hand and presses the back of it to her warm mouth. All of the knights are still cheering as they watch, and then Kell makes a sound that I can only interpret as another world's version of the classic "bow-chicka-wow-wow." And my blushing intensifies.

"Virago, we are overjoyed to meet your lover," says one of the knights, her voice low and warm, her eyes sparking with kindness, even in the dark. She has long black hair, high cheekbones and a very aristocratic nose. I recognize her a little, and I wrack my brains for a moment until I realize that this is the knight that we handed Virago through the portal to, the one standing in the meadow when we opened the portal to save Virago. This is Magel, I realize, then. Virago said that she was the head of the Royal Knights of Arktos City.

I guess this means that Magel is Virago's boss?

But as I offer an arm down to help Virago up from her position, kneeling in the muddy quicksand that my backyard is turning into, Magel steps forward easily and holds out her hand to me, smiling warmly. I take it, and she shakes it emphatically, pumping my arm up and down like she's trying to get water up from the bottom of a very deep well.

"It is an honor to meet you, Lady Holly," she says, her voice low and warm as she nods to me. "That you have tamed our wildest knight, oh, that is a pleasure long in coming," she says with a chuckle.

Wildest...knight? What in the world does that mean? I'm blinking back the rain, trying to see through it and gauge her face when another knight steps forward, wiping the water out of her eyes.

"Let's get inside, yeah?" asks the shorter woman—Virago called her Alinor, I think. She hooks her thumbs in the leather loops around the waist of her armor as she waggles her eyebrows at me. "Then we can all look at your lovely lady, Virago! It'll be a right treat!"

One of the other knights whoops tiredly, and that's when I realize that, despite the enthusiastic greeting they gave Virago, they all must be exhausted. It's no easy trick to create a portal and move through it, and they must have done both of those things to be standing right now in my backyard. I'm still very unclear as to how all of this portal business works, but Virago told me that the effort to come back through a week ago, in order to find me again, exhausted her utterly. She had to tune the portal to a specific person. Me. So it must have been very hard, I'm assuming, for the knights to find Virago here.

My heart flutters inside of me as the women begin to slog through the backyard toward the sliding glass door. Shelley is bounding around triumphantly, barking her head off with joy as she leaps around the knights, but for a moment...I don't share her excitement.

Because, yes, it's obvious that those knights are very close to Virago, are her closest friends, in fact, and—for all intents and purposes—they are also her family.

But they wouldn't have come through the portal just to meet her new girlfriend.

There must be a very important reason that they sought out Virago. They must need her for something.

There must be something wrong.

Something's wrong back on Agrotera, and Virago's presence is required.

And that scares me to death.

I don't know *why* my brain immediately feeds me the idea that they must have built the portal and come through it for a *bad* reason, but then, I'm also highly, *highly* aware of all of the stories that Virago told me about the campaigns she and her fellow knights have participated in. I mean, the only reason that Virago even came through the portal to Earth in the first place is because her company of knights was sent by Queen Calla, the queen of Arktos City, to rid the northern mountains of a *massive, man-killing beast.* And, yes, the queen had every reason to believe that the knights would be able to vanquish the creature, but they almost *didn't.* They almost didn't come out of that campaign alive.

And Virago has been on *many* other campaigns, ones even *more* dangerous than her recent run-in with the beast, starting with the very first campaign she ever went on—which was to kill a pack of savage, cannibal werewolves.

A *pack* of *cannibal werewolves.*

When Virago tells me the stories of the beasts she's vanquished, or the terrible people she's brought to justice, and how she always, always helps keep Arktos City safe...I'd be lying if I didn't tell you that a *large* part of myself is very, very grateful that she isn't currently doing any of these things.

Yes, Virago has bested massive monsters and evil enchanters and natural disasters. She has come out of all of these *incredibly* dangerous situations victoriously. But that was *before* she was my girlfriend.

I...don't really know if her being in that much

danger all the time is something I could handle.

I finally know what the romantic partners of cops feel like. But I've never heard of a cop dealing with a pack of cannibal werewolves.

When we trudge through the backyard and make our way up the steps onto the back porch, the lights inside flicker, on and off and on and off, stuttering light onto the porch, and then in one blaze of brightness, all of the electricity is switched on again. All of us, dripping and creating puddles beneath us, shuffle into the living room. I draw the door shut behind us.

Okay, I have to admit: it's...pretty *surreal* to see four female knights—and my girlfriend, who is also a knight—standing, larger than life, dripping water on my living room floor. Even though they're soaking wet, they still stand regally, at ease, and that's impressive, considering how much like a drowned rat *I* currently feel. I push my sodden red curls out of my eyes, and then Virago is moving quickly into the kitchen, opening the cupboard beneath the sink. She emerges with stacks of hand towels and begins to pass them out, and then I find myself racing upstairs to grab a bunch of thicker towels from the linen closet in the hallway.

"Oh, thank you," says Kell happily, when I come back down the stairs and hand her a big, fluffy pink towel. She leans forward at the waist and shakes out her hair to dangle in front of her. And what a massive amount of blonde curls she has, seriously—they're waist-long and so thick. She wraps her hair in the towel and begins to rub it vigorously, sniffling.

Alinor is definitely shorter than Virago, but you'd never know she's shorter, standing next to her. Alinor's got a big personality, something that's evident when she darts forward, wraps her arms around me and squeezes me like she's using my body to make a fresh cup of orange juice.

"Lovely to meet ya, Holly, my girl!" she booms in my ear, squeezing me even *harder*. Her arm muscles are like rocks, and I can actually hear my ribs popping as I gasp for breath and give Alinor a watery smile.

"Nice to meet you...too..." I manage, before Virago is clearing her throat.

"Alinor, please don't kill my lover," she chuckles, and then Alinor lets me go, taking a step back and giving me a flourishing bow. She's already used a kitchen towel to dry her hair, and the short, blonde ends of it are sticking up in all sorts of directions.

Alinor's armor and Kell's armor are very similar, I realize, glancing around at the knights in my living room. But the rest of the knights wear armor more like Virago's, the more traditional type of armor that you'd see at a Renaissance festival or in a book about medieval knights. It's full-body armor, with chest plates and back plates, and though Virago doesn't have a helmet (she borrows one from the faire whenever she jousts), almost every inch of her leather-clad body is covered by metal plating, each large, hammered piece attaching to the next with leather thongs.

But all Alinor and Kell are wearing is leather pants topped with leather skirts, and a leather bra. These things are covered in metal bits, including metal spirals over their breasts, but their arms and stomachs are noticeably bare—and their stomachs, I note, are just as muscled as Virago's. What kind of training program do they have for these knights? And why hasn't Jillian Michaels gotten in on this yet? Kell and Alinor have some leather thongs tied around their arms, but other than those few leather straps...that's it.

It's not just the armor that's giving them this certain look, but their faces and their expressions—honestly, both Alinor and Kell look much wilder than the other knights. The kind of warrior women who aren't afraid in the slightest, who rush into battle without any anxiety or even the slightest wavering of their bravery, swinging their swords (or axes, or other ridiculously terrifying, sharp, pointy fantasy-type weapons). And it seems that I'm right about this, because Alinor beams at me just then, her bright brown eyes warm and...a little intense. Wild. She has a scar that traces over her face and her right cheek, and she wears it quite proudly as she lifts her chin, holding me in her confidant gaze.

"All right—it is time for introductions," says Virago then, straightening and rolling her shoulders back, her voice taking on that storyteller cadence that she uses when she's about to tell me a particularly good tale. She wraps her arm around my shoulders. "These," she says, gesturing forward, "are *my* knights," she tells me proudly. "This here is Alinor," Virago tells me, turning and gesturing to the shorter knight with the close-cropped sandy blonde hair. Alinor bows low at the waist, lifting her chin and giving me a bright smile when she rises.

"This is Kell," says Virago with a wide smile. Kell stops toweling off her hair and flings it down her back again as she stands up straight. Even though her hair was just completely drenched, the toweling actually dried it pretty well, because it's starting to curl in massive waves. She has a *lot* of hair, a gorgeous blonde color that tumbles over her shoulders. And, yes, she—like Alinor—looks a little wild, and a little, well, crazy. In a nice, I'm-going-to-fling-myself-into-battle-come-what-may kind of way. She has bright blue eyes, and those eyes rove over me in our moment of introduction, training very, very slowly over my breasts.

I'm wearing that paper-thin white chemise—which is now utterly soaked, and my bodice is completely open. I sigh, blushing, as I fold my arms in front of myself and give Kell a weak smile. She chuckles a little, her head tilted the side as she glances at Virago.

"She's lovely, Virago," says Kell, then nods to me, bowing low at the waist. "Pleasure, milady," she says, her voice dropping about an octave to become this growly, sensual thing. I blink, then nod, trying to remember my manners as I realize that Kell was possibly just hitting on me.

"Ignore her," says Virago, smiling and leaning close. "She would try to seduce a goddess statue if she thought she could get away with it."

"I would!" says Kell blithely. The remaining knights chuckle and make "oh, you," sounds while they shake their heads. They must be very used to this.

"This is Magel," says Virago, continuing, gesturing to the woman who stands even *taller* than Virago...which is a little shocking. Virago is about six feet tall, and this woman stands about an inch above that. What do they *feed* the knights on Agrotera?

Magel has warm brown skin, the kind of gorgeous, dark eyes that people write sonnets about, high cheekbones, and a beautiful, long nose. Her straight black hair is pulled back with a ponytail, and she inclines her head to me gracefully as she steps forward, sinking to one knee before me.

"Milady Holly," says Magel, bringing the back of my hand to her lips. She's not doing it in a flirtatious way, though. She gazes up at me through her long black lashes as she kisses the tops of my knuckles, and then she's standing straight again beside us, smiling down at me warmly. "It is so good to meet the woman who Virago loves so very, very much," she says, reaching out and curling her fingers over my shoulder. She squeezes her fingers gently against me before letting me go. "You have made my friend very happy, Holly," she says, her voice low as she gazes at me earnestly. "That is a debt I can never repay you."

"It's...it's my honor," I stammer, my cheeks reddening even more as I flush under that high praise. Magel smiles and nods at me, turning to glance at the last of the four knights.

"And this..." says Virago, regarding the last knight, too. She takes a step forward, her brows raised. "This is..." She pauses, glancing to Magel and Kell and Alinor. "Surely, I am not seeing what I think I see," says Virago then, her voice soft and hushed, gazing incredulously at the fourth woman.

This fourth knight is wearing the same type of armor that Magel and Virago wear, armored plates over leather clothes, her entire body covered in armor. But she's also wearing a thick black cape, with a hood pulled down low over her face. She now lifts up her leather-gloved hands and slowly, gently, pushes back the hood.

The woman staring out at us from beneath that black brim of hood is wide-eyed and pale. She has bright green eyes that almost glow, they're so incandescent, and though she's just as tall as Virago, she looks slighter when standing next to these muscular, battle-trained women. The armor that's tied to her body seems to hang in some places, as if weren't made for her at all but for someone bigger. She looks a little younger than me, maybe in her late twenties, and when I gaze at her, she reminds me of...well, of me. The "me" of a little over a week ago, the me who didn't know if Virago was alive or dead, who wondered if I'd ever see her again. The me who had almost completely given up hope on everything.

This woman is beautiful in the way that paintings or a sumptuous piece of art is beautiful. She moves with elegance and grace, her face refined, with a classic, Golden Hollywood vibe. Her long, auburn hair falls in graceful waves over her shoulders, under the hood.

She's stunning.

But she also looks utterly heartbroken.

"My...my queen," says Virago, her voice catching as she sinks down to one knee in front of her. "Please forgive me," she whispers, her voice hoarse. "I did not... I did not expect you."

As I gaze at this fourth woman in shock, I realize my mouth is hanging open. I shut it. But...this is the queen? Queen Calla? I stare at this woman, this woman with the face of a ghost, and feel my heart ache for her.

What must have happened to her to make her look so sad?

"Please, Virago," Queen Calla murmurs, her voice soft as she holds out a gloved hand. "Please rise."

Virago takes the queen's hand and brings the back of it to her lips, pressing a kiss to it before letting it go and rising smoothly. She's glancing sidelong at her fellow knights, one brow raised.

I'm guessing it's probably abnormal for the queen of Arktos to go gallivanting off to another world.

"Why have you come?" asks Virago then, her voice heavy, the earlier mirth gone as Virago takes in Alinor, Magel, Kell and Calla, who stand in a semicircle about us, faces grim.

For a long moment, the knights and the queen are silent. Each of the knights holds Virago's gaze in turn; Calla is looking out the back sliding glass door, her wide eyes trained on the lightning outside. But I somehow think she's not seeing it at all.

Her heart is somewhere else.

"We came," says Magel with a long sigh, then, glancing at the queen, "because there was an attempt on Her Majesty's life."

Virago pales as she sinks down, back onto the couch that, only a few moments ago, we were about to get frisky on. Instead, her fellow knights are now standing in my living room, about to regale her with some very bad news.

And everything, I realize, has changed.

"What do you mean?" asks Virago, raking her fingers back through her hair, gazing worriedly at Queen Calla. "Are you hurt, milady?" she asks breathlessly. "What *happened*?"

"Don't worry so," says Kell, flopping herself down into one of my two overstuffed blue armchairs. She puts her muddy, booted feet up on my coffee table, and Virago glances at her mildly, one brow still raised. And, to my absolute shock, Kell takes her feet off of the coffee table almost instantly, instead crossing her legs in front of her and steepling her fingers over her stomach. "*Any*way," she says, huffing out a breath a bit like a disgruntled teenager might, "the queen is *obviously* safe. That's all that matters."

"I need details," says Virago, glancing at Magel,

who nods and sits down beside Virago on the couch, her wet leather clothes creaking dully beneath the plated armor.

"It was yesterday," says Magel, shaking her head. "You must know, Virago, that the Hero's Tournament is soon?"

I can see Virago actually perk up, her shoulders smoothing back, her chin lifting, her back straightening, her eyes flashing. "Yes," she says, her voice calm and steady, but there's a tremor of excitement beneath it. "I remembered," she tells Magel.

"As you also well know, Arktos City was chosen to be the host for the tournament this year," says Kell lazily, tapping her foot in the air. "And that means that there's a huge influx of people coming into the city from all parts, different countries. The taverns and inns are bursting. We've upped the guards, everyone's on high alert, whatever, but the queen was still making her bread run to Ratter Prison, despite the influx of strangers."

Virago's eyes flicker over to me. I don't know much about Arktos City, Virago's beloved home city, but I do remember that Ratter Prison is where Virago told me she grew up. I also know it's the poorest part of the city: the slums.

"The very first time that I met you was on a bread run," murmurs Calla then, looking back from the sliding glass door to gaze at Virago instead, as she smiles softly.

I glance from Calla to Virago with surprise. There's still so much I don't know about Virago that I wish I did. Is this how Virago was picked to start training for the Royal Knights of Arktos City? Because Calla found her while, I'm assuming, she was handing out bread to the poor?

"So Her Majesty was on her way to Ratter Prison, but we were passing through the market," says Kell with a sigh, "and an archer tried to pick her off from a third floor window," she growls, her eyes flashing with a very dangerous light. "He used an arrow wiped with a natural poison from a fenris mushroom, so that it could get through the magical defenses and shields and have a chance of striking the queen."

Virago stares in alarm at Calla. "Were you pierced? Did the arrow touch you?" she asks, about to spring up from the couch, but Magel reaches out a calming hand to rest on Virago's shoulder, shaking her head.

"What do you think?" Kell practically chirps, lifting her chin triumphantly. "I caught the arrow's shaft with my bare hand. Of *course*," she sniffs, as if she's annoyed that Virago would ask such questions. "But that's not even the worse part," she says, her head tilted to the side. She's sober for a long moment before she says, "It's the colors that archer was wearing—"

"He was dressed in the robes of a priest of the Goddess Cower," says Alinor bluntly, her arms folded in front of her. "And he wore an armband with the colors of Furo."

"Furo," Virago breathes, her eyes wide. "*Cower?*" Now she looks utterly alarmed.

I feel worried and lost as I sit down beside Virago. She blinks, shaking her head, like she's just woken up from a very bad dream. "I am sorry, my love," she tells me then, her voice thick with emotion. "You...you, of course, know the Goddess Cower. It was you who vanquished her," she says, holding my eyes with her bright blue gaze as she reaches across the space between us and takes my hands in her own, squeezing them tightly. "You know that Cower is currently imprisoned. There is no way that she can rise again. But there are people, still, who worship her and her message of the end of the world."

I nod, squeezing her hand back.

"Well, these people, these followers of the Goddess Cower—they are currently looking for her," says Kell, shaking her head. "They plan to release the goddess from prison, get her back to her old self with—I don't know—blood sacrifices or something. And then they want to loose her on all of Agrotera again, even more powerful than before."

"Furo is a country to the north of Arktos," says Magel to me. "It is a country that we have had a longstanding conflict with, but we have been peaceful together, Furo and Arktos, for many years now."

"But a king came to power there—a new king—about two moons ago," says Kell, a brow raised. "And he's a warmonger. He's utterly reckless."

"Are you saying," says Virago, glancing from Kell to Magel, "that you think the king of Furo may be a worshiper of Cower?"

"We don't know. The priest may have been wearing the Furo armband because he's from Furo, or for any number of reasons. For all we know, he was trying to confuse us," says Kell, her piercing blue gaze trained on Virago now. "But we'll never know for sure, because he jumped to his death after trying to shoot the queen, and there have been no accomplices found. And the diplomat sent to the king of Furo returned with nothing but nice things to say. We think he paid her off," mutters Kell disgustedly.

Virago steeples her hands and presses her index fingers against her mouth, lost in thought, her brow deeply furrowed. "This is very bad, my friends," she murmurs. "So very, very bad..." And then she lifts her gaze to Calla. Calla who has stood there, leaning against my living room wall, during this entire discussion, with a faraway look in her sad eyes. Calla who has not spoken a single word since she mentioned first meeting Virago on a bread run.

"Your Majesty," says Virago then, rising, taking a step closer to the queen. As if waking from a trance, Calla shakes her head, turning her gaze back into the room.

"I am sorry," she says, her voice shaking a little as she lifts her chin and meets Virago's gaze. "I must admit, I was not listening. What is it?"

Virago exchanges a knowing glance with Magel, and then she takes a step forward, curling her long fingers around Calla's elbow gently. "Your Majesty," Virago says, her voice soft, "I am so sorry about the assassination attempt. I am so sorry that I was not there to protect you, but I am so very glad that the others were. Are you...are you all right?"

Calla flicks her gaze, in that moment, to me.

"Do not apologize, dear knight," she whispers then, her voice quavering, but she clears her throat and continues. "Your place is here now," she says, and she inclines her head to me. "With your lover, Holly."

Virago opens and shuts her mouth as she glances at me, concern etching her brow with several deep lines. She's about to say something else, but then Kell shakes her head, gets up from the chair she was sprawling in.

"Calla...tell Virago what you told us?" she asks

then. Her voice is uncharacteristically soft, kind, as she speaks to the queen. I glance at Kell, and I'm surprised to see her eyes soften when she looks at her queen. "Please?" she whispers.

For a long moment, nothing happens. But then Calla nods, and she gazes up at Virago for a heartbeat of silence before she leans forward. And when she leans forward, shaking her head just a little, she whispers something into Virago's ear.

The whisper doesn't take very long, and within a few seconds, Calla is silent again. But when Calla is done speaking, Virago takes a single step back, searching Calla's face. Virago visibly pales in that moment, her eyes sparking with concern.

And then Virago turns to me.

"Beloved," she says, the word clipped, her tone sharp. I blink, surprised. "Please take the queen to our bedroom? She is quite tired from her journey, and I need to...have a counsel with my knights. Just for a few minutes? Let Her Majesty lie down, get her bearings?" she asks me.

Virago is looking at me with wide blue eyes. And I can tell, in that moment, that she's trying to communicate something. Something that she doesn't want the rest to know.

But I'm not that psychic! That's my brother; he's *totally* psychic. I bite the inside of my lip, but then I'm nodding, coming forward to stand awkwardly beside the tall queen.

"Um...this way...Your Majesty," I murmur. I have no idea how you're supposed to address royalty if they aren't *your* ruler. Virago reaches out across the space between us, and then she's curling her fingers around my elbow.

She leans down as if to brush a kiss on my cheek, but instead, she whispers, "She needs your kindness."

Of course I'm going to be kind to her, but as Queen Calla follows me up the stairs toward our bedroom, I'm worried that, since I didn't quite understand what Virago was trying to telepathically tell me with her eyes, I've missed something crucial.

But I figure it out in a moment, anyway.

"Poor Virago," sighs Calla, climbing the last few steps to the top of the landing wearily. "I must have frightened her badly if she wants to speak to her knights alone."

When I glance back at Calla's face, I pause for a long moment. There is so much pain in her expression—so much sadness.

"Pardon me for...um...wondering," I say then, biting at my lip again. "But...are you upset about the assassination attempt? I mean, I'd feel pretty rotten if someone wanted me dead. I can't even imagine it. But you look...just...heartbroken. I mean...I'm just sorry is all," I murmur, stammering. *Real smooth, Holly*, I think, despairing as I watch several emotions flit across Calla's face, too fast for me to pick up on what she could possibly be thinking.

Calla, of course, doesn't respond to that jumble of words with anything more than a quiet shake of her head (so she's *not* sad about the assassination attempt, I guess), and we walk silently down the rest of the hallway until we reach what was, up until a week ago, solely my bedroom. I flick on the light, wincing as we step inside. I glance around like Calla, seeing my bedroom for what it probably is: really weird. There are many unicorn figurines positioned around the room, and my few groaning bookshelves are sagging to the side because they're *literally* stuffed with books. Once I stopped caring and realized that I would *never* have enough bookshelves for the amount of books I wanted to read in this lifetime, I just started stacking the books along my wall. If you squint, the differently sized stacks of books look just like the Boston city skyline. At least, I think they do.

And then there's my *other* unicorn lamp on my bedside table. This one is of a mother unicorn and her baby unicorn. The baby unicorn has an extra light bulb in his behind, a little bit like a firefly. In my defense, they made really weird lamps in the eighties.

Calla, the queen, is taking in all of this. I feel more than a little self-conscious. I'm escorting royalty into my unicorn-infested bedroom.

There's silence between us for a long moment as Calla crosses the threshold into the room. But then she turns back to me. Her eyes are very soft—very kind. I can see a hint of the ruler she must have been once, before whatever happened broke her heart. She must have been compassionate and wise, a good person to serve as queen.

"You are very kind to me, Holly," says Calla quietly, lifting her chin. "So I will abate your curiosity."

"I'm not... No, I'm not curious," I tell her holding up my hands quickly. "I'm sorry. It's your business. You shouldn't have to tell me anything. I'm just sorry you're sad," I murmur to her then. "I remember... I remember what that was like. I didn't know if Virago was alive or dead," I tell her, waving my hand in the air, gulping down air as I remember the intensity of that pain, the pain I felt for almost an entire *month* before Virago came back. "I thought she was dead," I whisper, "but I didn't know, and I hadn't been quick enough to follow her through the portal...so I felt like I'd left her alone. It was rough. I don't know what you've been through," I tell her, shaking my head, "but I'm sorry you're hurting."

An emotion flickers over Calla's face, and, in that moment, her eyes fill with tears.

She's standing there, and I can tell that she's trying to be strong. Her hands are curled into fists, her shoulders are tense, her breathing is coming fast, but she's not bending to the many tears that fill her eyes.

I can't imagine having to be so strong all the time—the ruler of a country, a ruler that everyone depends on. I can't imagine what it must be like, to have people coming after you who want you dead.

I don't know what happened to Calla, but it must have been truly terrible. And I'm not sure if she has a safe space where she feels free to let those tears out.

So...I do the only thing I can imagine doing. It doesn't matter that this person is a queen. It doesn't matter that I've known her for exactly five minutes.

I open my arms, tilt my head to the side. "Um," I say, my voice soft, "do you want...a hug? Maybe?"

For half a heartbeat, she looks at me, her eyes wide, the tears filling her eyes ready to spill down her cheeks but not yet doing so.

And then she steps forward quickly, stepping into my arms, putting her face down onto my shoulder...

And Queen Calla starts to sob.

Her sobs are muted, the kind of sobs that someone makes when they're trying to be quiet and let no one else hear them. Sadly, I learned how to make those same types of sobs when I was in high school. Between periods, I holed up in the girls' restrooms, crying because I was known as "Holly the homo" to every single one of my classmates. To them, I wasn't, you know, an actual person. My high school years were hell, but at least I had the *tiny* satisfaction of knowing that someday, I would graduate, and I would be able to leave those terrible hallways forever.

I don't know why Calla's sad right now, but it's heartbreaking to witness, so I just hold her, letting her cry on my already soaked shoulder. Her own shoulders shake quietly, and she smells like flowers, a very nice scent, but I'm too distracted by how upset she is, and by the fact that I have no idea what else to do to comfort her or help her in any way. So I hold her while she cries, and I worry.

"Do you... Um, do you want to talk about it?" I ask Calla then. I'm a little shocked when I realize that that's something my mother always asked me. And I sounded a lot like her when I said it. My mom would always catch me when I came home, would gather me into her arms and want to know what was the matter. And I told her; I didn't keep any secrets from my mother. My mother and brother and Carly were the most supportive people in the universe. Does Calla have that kind of support? I mean, she's the queen; she must.

Right?

"I am... I am so sorry," Calla sniffs, taking a step back, shaking her head, trying to dry her eyes on the hem of her sodden woolen cloak. I take a tissue out of my unicorn tissue box (They made everything with unicorns on it in the eighties! Really!) and hand her one. She takes it from me, gazing down at the tissue and blinking.

"It's a tissue," I tell her, trying to figure out a word she might know. "A handkerchief?" I try.

"Thank you," she says, her nose a little stuffed up. But then she blows it on the tissue. I have never, in all my days, heard anyone blow their nose so daintily.

And then Calla sits down on the edge of my bed and looks up at me, her face exhausted, her eyes dull.

"Please forgive me, Lady Holly," she says then, quietly, tiredly. "I did not mean to weep on your chemise," she says, gesturing to my clothes.

"It's all right," I tell her earnestly, sitting down next to her. I don't know why: maybe it's the exact same reason that I chauffeur injured birds to the wildlife rehabilitation center, or the fact that I'm a sucker for any sad puppy or kitten story. But I feel terribly, *terribly* sorry for Calla and wish that I could help, in any way, with her pain. And, probably because of that, I really feel a connection with her, have felt one since I first saw her. And I know it's only been a week since I felt that much pain myself, wondering if Virago was alive or dead, wondering if I'd ever see her again, and it's only been a few years since my mother passed away, only a few years to deal with all of the pain I felt when I lost her.

But if there's anything I've learned because of that pain, it's this: no one can help you with your pain or your grief. They can help distract you; they can give you comfort and love and companionship. But they can't take that grief away from you.

The grief remains. Grief is the price of love. And, for my mother, I paid it willingly.

And I would have paid it for Virago, too.

I'm just so, so, so deeply grateful that I didn't have to.

Calla searches my eyes then, carefully folding the used tissue in her lap. "I must admit, Lady Holly—I am mortified that I wept on you like that," she says, her voice quiet. "It has been...a trying few days," she says. The way she's looking at me, desperately hoping I'll forget the whole thing...I know what I have to do then.

I take another tissue out of the unicorn tissue box. On second thought, I shake my head, handing the entire box to the queen.

"It's obvious that you're soaked to the bone, and the rain outside was freezing," I tell her in a soothing tone. "So we really should get you out of those wet clothes. What do you like to wear?"

"Gowns," says the queen immediately, her head to the side as she watches me with perceptive eyes. The corners of her mouth are turning up now, too. She looks utterly relieved that I've changed the subject. "Dresses," she says then, as if she's worried I'm not going to know what a gown is.

"I have a lot of dresses, but you're much taller than me," I say, wrinkling my nose thoughtfully and crossing the room to my closet. I open the doors, peer inside.

Just then, there's a knock on the open door to the bedroom, and I look back, startled, to see Virago standing in the doorway. She's leaning against it gracefully, watching the two of us with hooded eyes, a tense smile on her lips.

"Your Majesty," says Virago, straightening off the door frame, clearing her throat. But she turns to me. "Beloved, can I speak with you for a moment?" she asks, her head to the side.

"Here," I tell Calla, gesturing to the closet. "Anything you want to wear is yours. And, um, don't look in that box over there..." I say, wincing and pointing to a large, bright pink box in the corner that has some of our sexual unmentionables in it.

"Surely," says the queen, standing and examining the unicorn tissue box. "That is interesting. They have unicorns on this world, too?" she asks me quietly, before handing the tissue box back to me.

"Wait—what now?" I squeak, clutching the box, but Virago pulls me smoothly out of the bedroom and shuts the door behind her.

We're standing in the hallway, our bedroom door closed as Virago leans down and presses her forehead to my shoulder, right where Calla wept only a few minutes ago.

"This is very bad, my love," Virago whispers, groaning a little. "So very, very bad."

"What's happening?" I whisper to her, my eyes wide as Virago straightens a little, gazing at me with her bright blue eyes narrowed in concern. "Calla just cried on my shoulder... Something terrible must have happened to her, aside from the arrow," I tell her, all in a hushed breath.

Virago's face is grim. Honestly, she's the most optimistic person I know, and I've never seen her look so unhappy. Or so serious.

"According to my fellow knights," she murmurs to me, her full mouth downturning at the corners, "Calla has made talk of abdicating her throne. And she just told me as much downstairs."

I stare at her. "She doesn't want to be queen

anymore?"

Virago shrugs, shaking her head, her frown deepening. "Though she said as much...I don't know, not for certain. She is very...very troubled. By what happened..." Virago waves her hand and then closes it in a fist. "It is not my place to say," she breathes to me, lowering her voice, "but Calla's grief is destroying her. And it could destroy Arktos, too."

I stare at Virago.

"If Calla abdicates," says Virago, her face pained, her brow furrowed with worry, "it will send the country into a turmoil it has not seen in five hundred years. Furo wants to take over Arktos, and if there was no ruler, they could do it easily, plunging the country into darkness." Virago searches my face now. "There is so much that could go wrong with this, but the worst part... The *worst* part," Virago whispers, as she holds my gaze, "is that the castle has been infiltrated in Arktos City. I think someone put Calla up to this thinking, telling her that she should abdicate. Someone who wants to rule in her stead."

"Who in the world would do that?" I ask Virago. She works her jaw now, clenching it.

"There is only one woman I can think of who would even dream of such a thing," she tells me in the lowest growl.

I watch her carefully as she takes a deep breath. And then, she murmurs a single word softly.

"Charaxus."

A little shiver runs through me. "Charaxus... Well, that...that sounds like a nice name for a...oh, no, not so nice?" I ask her, when she starts to shake her head slowly and determinedly.

"Charaxus," Virago whispers, spitting out the

word again almost like it's a curse—which surprises me. Virago never speaks ill of *anyone.* Not even the mail guy who was ripping up my packages because he found out I was a Red Sox fan (he's a Yankee guy—how he survives on his Boston route, I will *never* know). "Charaxus is the vice queen to Queen Calla," says Virago. "The second in command. If anything were to happen to Calla, she would take over ruling Arktos. But this also means that if Calla abdicated the throne, with no current heir...the throne would then go to Charaxus. Usually, the vice queen is a good choice to rule after the queen. But...but I *know* Charaxus. We went to the Knight Academy together," she says, her eyes flashing a dangerous color now. "We were not friends."

"Okay," I say, drawing out the word. "So what are we going to do?"

"Calla can*not* abdicate the throne," says Virago determinedly, shaking her head for emphasis, "and we *must* keep her safe from assassins, of which there will probably be more, considering the Hero's Tournament is coming up, and there is a plot for her life. Calla *must* be kept safe," she says, searching my eyes. "Holly..."

I watch her carefully, uncertain about what she's going to say next, worrying that she's about to tell me that she has to go back home, back to Agrotera. I understand that she has to; Calla has to be kept safe. But I don't want her to go.

Still, I never could have predicted what she tells me next:

"The knights have asked me to come back with them to Agrotera," Virago whispers, "just for the Hero's Tournament. Just to make absolutely certain that Calla is kept safe. I was one of the main knights set to guard Calla, so I'm the best woman for the job," she tells me, still searching my eyes. "I was hoping..." she murmurs, licking her lips, "that you would...well, that you would come with us? For the tournament?"

I stare at Virago for a long moment, unresponsive—because I'm so damn excited. And then...I actually start to jump up and down. I leap up, wrapping my arms around my girlfriend's neck.

I was the kid who tried to go through all the backs of the wardrobes in the furniture stores, trying to find Narnia. I was the girl who read *The Knight of the Rose* over and over again until my book became threadbare.

It has been my lifelong dream that there were other worlds, magical worlds.

And now my knight girlfriend is asking me to come visit hers.

"Are you serious?" I ask her, squeezing her tightly. "Oh, my *God,* Virago!"

"Holly," Virago tells me softly, her eyes shining, "it would be the greatest honor I can imagine to show you my beloved Arktos City."

She smiles against me then, and slowly, carefully, she places her hands on the walls behind my head as she leans her head down, bending to me. I lift my chin and capture her mouth with a kiss, threading my fingers through her satiny hair, pulling her down to meet me as I draw her into a deep, ecstatic embrace.

At that moment, Calla opens the bedroom door...and there we are, making out in the hallway. Virago straightens immediately, and I glance at Calla, feeling a little self-conscious (I mean, she was just crying on my shoulder, and now I'm having happy makeout times right outside the door? Real nice,

Holly)...but she stands a little straighter, lifting her chin regally.

Calla has changed into one of my dresses, a purple satin gown that I got for the fancy work holiday party that we have every year at the country club (no, I promise your tax dollars aren't going to fund lavish librarian holiday parties; one of our fellow librarians belongs to the country club and gets us the place for cheap because she's *awesome*). No one has noticed yet that this is the dress I wear *every* year, but it's a timeless kind of dress, and that helps me pull off wearing it over and over. It has a plunging front neckline and is very long on me (I trip on the hem), so it's about tea-length on Calla. She's raked a brush through her hair and has pinned the strands up in looping spirals with bobby pins, and she looks... Well, she looks very regal—and utterly gorgeous, not like she was just crying on my shoulder a few moments ago.

"Have the knights plied you with their question, Virago?" asks Calla formally, glancing at Virago with a soft smile. "Will you stay upon this world, or will you return home one last time for the Hero's Tournament?"

I blink. Wait a second... One last time? Has Virago talked to her knights and her queen about this before?

When Virago came to me, across the worlds...did she do it intending to stay...well...forever?

I file that thought away for a think later, because Virago is nodding to Calla, wrapping an arm around my shoulders and drawing me to her.

"I will come," she tells the queen solemnly. "And I am bringing my lover with me."

Calla nods genteelly, but she looks at me with soft, thankful eyes as her smile deepens. "That will be lovely," she says, and though her words are low and her voice is hoarse, she still looks like she means them.

"The portal will not open again until the morning," says Virago, glancing at me now as I hold her arm and try not to vibrate in place from excitement. I don't think it's working—I'm pretty sure I *am* vibrating. "So...we have one night left on Earth," she says, her head to the side. "And I was thinking... Well, the knights are *very* curious about this world."

"As am I," says the queen, drawing herself up to her full height, her green eyes finally taking on life as they flash. My dress hugs her curves beautifully. She places a hand on her hip and tilts her head. "I would like to explore it, as well," she says in a tone that brooks no argument.

"Wait, wait. Explore it? Earth?" I ask, biting my lip. I glance at Calla with worry, but then there's a loud *crash* from downstairs. That crash had the particular cadence of one of my dinner plates breaking into tiny, unrecognizable shards on the floor.

"*That* one is Alinor's fault!" Kell pipes up happily from down in the living room.

Virago glances at me, a smile tugging at the corner of her mouth, one brow raised.

Four knights and a queen from *another world* go out on the town in Boston on a Friday night...

This seems like it'll make for a pretty bad idea...but, also, a *really* memorable evening.

"Um..." I swallow, wondering if bribing them with pizza and Showtime would keep them in the house, but it probably wouldn't. "Sure, yeah, yeah, we can go out," I squeak. "But they need clothes," I tell Virago urgently, shaking my head with wide eyes that I'm hoping convey, *Armored ladies in downtown Boston: not a good idea.*

"But of course," Virago says indulgently, squeezing me and pecking my cheek before letting me go. Then she turns in the hallway and lets out a short, piercing whistle over her shoulder. Almost immediately all of the knights are up the stairs and crowded together in the hallway, standing or draping on the banister languidly, as if they've always been here.

Kell winks at me.

In this moment, I worry that this isn't only a bad idea...but a *spectacularly* bad idea.

"A change of clothing, m'ladies," says Virago with a smile. "And then, we ride! To our date night!"

The cheers in my hallway are deafening.

Well. It's not the date night I expected...but it's still going to be fun. I think. As I glance around at the happy faces (Calla's face carefully neutral), I feel my spirits lift.

This could prove to be a wonderful night.

But still, there's a slight uneasiness as I head back into our bedroom, as I open my closet door and start to choose a dress.

Four knights and a queen on the town...what could possibly go wrong?

Chapter 3: Knights on the Town

I feel like I'm in the locker room getting ready for some super-famous sports magazine to photograph a winning lady's soccer team in street clothes.

Admittedly, I don't think they'd pick short, non-muscular women (you know, like *me*) for the Royal Knights. Royal Knights, I have learned today, are different from the regular knights of Arktos City, because the Royal Knights are, technically, Calla's right-hand ladies. Their main concern, different from the other knights' concerns (like saving the country and protecting cities) is keeping the *queen* and the queen alone safe (or doing the queen big favors like going into the northern mountains to chase after a beast). So, because they're mostly with the queen all the time, with her for all of her dignitary meetings and throne room hours, it means that they have to be impressive-looking. If a foreign dignitary from a far-off country comes calling, these knights are some of the first sights they see upon entering the palace, and apparently their presence sends a message, loud and clear.

These knights belong to Arktos. So don't mess with Arktos.

Here and now, these women may not be wearing armor...but it doesn't *matter* if they're wearing armor or not, because they have the bearing of knights, anyway, in or out of metal plating. They're tall, muscled, curvy, gorgeous...and they're dressed in the street clothes that I've gotten for Virago since she started living with me. Which means they're all wearing variations of button-down shirts, blazers, jackets and jeans.

It really does look like a sports photo shoot is about to break out at any second in my living room.

"You know, we might get stopped, anyway," I mutter, glancing sidelong at Virago with a smile. "People are going to think they're famous for something relating to... I don't know." My mind stretches as hard as it can to find a sports-related metaphor. "Nets or hockey pucks or something," I finish.

Virago smiles at me and squeezes my shoulder.

I have never been happier that she was from another world and could not possibly understand how terrible that joke was.

So, obviously, I would be lying if I didn't acknowledge that all of these women are gorgeous, graceful and sexy. They're all *lady knights*, which has kind of been my happy mental default when I think sexy thoughts since I hit *puberty.* But I'm being perfectly honest right now when I say that I don't even really see them. Don't get me wrong: they're *beautiful* to look at, like a piece of art is lovely to look at, or some pride of lionesses out on the Serengeti would be a breathtaking sight to witness.

But when I look at Virago... It's not that she's more beautiful than any of the other women here. Or more graceful, or sexier, or more confidant. She and her fellow knights are really evenly matched, and that's impressive. You can tell that they trained together, that they have fought together, and I'm not doubting in the slightest that any of these knights here would take a bullet (or a sword blade, as the case may be) for each other. They are a tightly knit group of women who are tremendously loyal to one another.

But *when I look at Virago*, my heart lifts up inside of me, growing, pressing against my ribs and knocking loudly against my bones, because there's a bright connection between us, pulsing just like my heartbeat, alive and well.

Virago is the love of my life. I'm surrounded by gorgeous lady knights, and the only sight I have eyes for is my beautiful girlfriend, who—when she gazes at me—sees to the deepest parts of me, with her bright blue eyes, her mouth turning up at the corners into that secret smile that's all for me.

I'm in a kind of love that takes my breath away.

Because *she* takes my breath away.

Virago's all dressed to go out now, with her hair in a high ponytail, and it's falling over her shoulders like an inky black waterfall. She's wearing a suit that we bought in the men's department, but then we took the suit to a tailor who made it fit her curves perfectly. Hell, she's even wearing a black silk tie to complete the ensemble, the tie dangling loose around her neck, because the top three buttons of that button-down shirt, beneath the jacket, are teasingly undone...and that small bit of creamy skin that I can see is driving me crazy in the best possible way.

And she *knows* it, too, because when I glance at her, she holds my gaze, smoothing the lapels of her jacket with her thumbs, looking at me through hooded eyes with her sexiest smirk.

"So..." I stammer, clearing my throat. "I figured that we could introduce you ladies to Boston by way of something that would be...um..." I turn my hand in the air, trying to find the right words. "Less of a culture shock," I tell them with a smile.

According to Virago, there are a *lot* of taverns on Agrotera, and a *lot* of taverns in Arktos City, and, also according to her, drinking is one of a knight's favorite pastimes. So I figured we'd take them to Queenie's, a lesbian bar in the South End. We can all get there on the T, and Queenie's has burgers and fries (and one of the best veggie burgers in the city, believe it or not), so the knights and queen can get dinner, entertainment, possible lady-action... It's all there. And, in one place, I can keep tabs on all of the knights and make sure they don't get into trouble.

I mean...I know they're grown women and can obviously take care of themselves. But in the time that they've been in my house, they've already broken three plates, broken my dishwasher (What in the world were they *doing* to it?) and recorded eight hours of TLC because they were playing with the remote.

In a highly populated city on a world they've never visited? For some reason, I have a feeling they could get into a *lot* of trouble if they're not kept under constant watch.

Virago doesn't share my concerns (I don't think she's even had the thought), because she's ecstatic that her best friends are here and that she can show them the world she found.

"Just know that, when we leave this house, my friends, we mustn't get separated," Virago tells the knights solemnly, but her eyes are shining as she holds the gaze of each one, then Calla, and then me. When she looks at me, she begins to smile, and she's smiling that special smile, the one that's so sexy it drives me crazy, and so love-filled that I reach across the space between us to take her hand, pulled to her like gravity.

"We're going to have a *wonderful* time tonight, my friends," Virago tells everyone, practically glowing as she steps forward, as she wraps her fingers around my waist and hips...and then she's actually *lifting* me to spin me around in a circle as I laugh, her hands wrapped tightly, but gently, around me, lifting me like I weigh nothing at all. And, I assure you, I do weigh a lot of somethings.

Virago is so, so happy, I realize, as she sets me down, and as she gathers me close in her arms. Her happiness is infectious; I tilt back my head, reach up and kiss her, and she kisses me, kisses me *fiercely*.

All of the knights surrounding us whoop and begin to clap, laughing good-naturedly, but Kell clears her throat, her eyes flashing as she puts her hands on her jeans-clad hips.

"I'm happy for you, my friend, truly," Kell says to Virago, her head to the side as she grins, "but I'm ready to find my *own* woman to kiss."

I'm chuckling, my cheeks flushing from one-part embarrassment (I mean, they were just clapping while we were kissing), and three-parts attraction to the woman I was just passionately kissing. "All right," I tell them, standing straighter and pointing to the front door. "To the bar it is!"

When we step out, I watch the knights and queen closely. Like Virago, they are suitably impressed by this other world but not overwhelmed by it. We set off down the sidewalk, aiming in the direction of the nearest T stop, and the knights gaze wonderingly at cars, large trucks, the crane and construction site at the corner and the flashing lights and crazy neon colors of all the signs and billboards surrounding them. The advertising on the blocks near my house runs the gamut from the different plays that are currently in town, different alcoholic beverages and—somewhat out of place, but completely welcome among all the buy-me-now advertising—a billboard urging us to take care of our national forests.

"Do you not have horses here?" asks Magel then, her hands buried deep in the pockets of the dress pants she's borrowed from Virago. Her hair is plaited down her back in one long, thick braid, and she looks so striking in the black button-down shirt she's wearing. She gazes at me with those deep, dark eyes, and she looks like she's taken in everything and processed it in about a second.

FYI, it's not Magel I'm currently worried about taking to the bar.

Before I can answer, Calla is speaking. "I'm not certain if they have horses, but they certainly have unicorns," she says pleasantly, gazing at me then. "Holly has several statues of them in her bedroom."

And before I can correct the assumption that we have unicorns on this world (as much as Carly and her Cryptozoology Club would argue about that), Kell answers back with a smirk. "Ah, she has many unicorn statues," she chuckles. "It figures."

I blink, then turn to Kell.

"Wait a second. 'It figures'? What's that supposed to mean?" I ask her, raising a brow.

Virago snorts, then glances at Kell, eyes wide, shaking her head as she tries to cover a smile with her hand. "Kell, must we start the—" she begins, but Kell is grinning like a very happy cat right now, and she talks right over her friend.

"'It figures,' because you must consider the horn on a unicorn, milady," she says mildly, leaning close and raising one brow.

"Yeah, I've considered it. I know it's a phallic symbol," I tell her with an exacting shrug as I return her grin. I realize I just sounded like a twelve-year-old who has no knowledge of below-the-belt stuff, but dammit, two can play at this game—and I wasn't born yesterday. I got my lesbian card pretty damn early, so...

My internal monologue is cut very, very short when Kell leans closer to me, her eyes flashing with obvious delight.

"Well, on Agrotera," she murmurs to me, her grin deepening to a very, very wicked one, "when you're a woman who loves women, we use naturally fallen unicorn horns, sand the edge down so it's not sharp, and we—"

"And that's a *plane*," says Virago loudly, pointing above us as a plane circles overhead, aiming for Logan airport. "*Planes* are used to transport people in the air. Much like our winged horses," she adds very quickly.

Calla, walking beside me, gazes at me with bemusement, shaking her head. I guess I look shocked.

"Well, here on Earth," I soldier on, determined not to be out-knowledged (is that even a word?) by a knight who looks so damn smug, "we make our dildos out of *plastic*," I tell her. "And...and lots of other stuff."

Kell's actively laughing now. "What is this word?" she asks, her head to the side in an exaggerated motion. "Dildo?" she says, sounding it out loud. We get a couple stares on the sidewalk, and Virago is currently covering her entire face, trying not to show me her laughter. "What does it mean?" asks Kell obnoxiously.

Virago glances at me then, clearly unable to hide her mirth as she shakes her head, looking just as bemused as Calla. "This discussion need not continue, my love," she says, a brow up, but I continue on, anyway—because I'm stubborn.

Sometimes, being stubborn is not such a great trait.

"It's. Um. It's a thing. That you use. Well, you don't *have* to use it. But some people use it to make love. It's great for penetration," I tell Kell, trying to put on my best librarian game face, the same librarian game face I use when teenage boys are being stupid to us librarians and asking where the porn section is.

Kell's laughing so hard there are almost tears streaming down her face, Alinor joining in now while Magcl is trying very, *very* hard not to smile. "We have that word on Agrotera, milady Holly. I just wanted to hear you explain it," says Kell with a wink.

I say the only thing I can think of to say, but I realize I'm chuckling, too. "You're such a jerk," I mutter.

"I have been called many things," she says, sweeping a low bow to me, "and that is one of the nicest yet!"

Virago chuckles, putting an arm around my waist and drawing me close to her as we walk along the sidewalk. "They but tease you," she tells me softly, one brow up.

"I know," I tell her, putting an arm around her waist, too, as I smile up at her. "Just a thought, but are they *always* this sex-obsessed?"

Virago's laughing. "Just Kell," she mutters, glancing over her shoulder and shaking her head at the knights behind us.

"I heard that," says Kell happily.

We reach the T stop and board the bus with a *surprising* amount of civility and understanding from everyone involved. I mean, I'm starting to expect it from Magel and Calla. But Alinor and Kell are beginning to strike me as Navy ladies who have just been given shore leave after about ten years on the high seas without another woman in *sight*.

For example, the very first thing that Kell does, after climbing up and onto the bus, is sit down in one of the seats, cross her legs elegantly, and tilt her chin up, her eyes flashing, as she winks at a woman two seats back. This woman appears to be out for a night of partying, too, because she's in a club dress, her long, blonde hair in elaborate waves, her makeup spot on. But when she glances at Kell, she sighs, rolling her eyes, diving back into her phone—probably to unhappily tweet that a woman just hit on her.

"I'm sorry, Kell, but not everyone here is like, well, us," I tell Kell, with a shake of my head, biting my lip as I try to figure out how to explain this to her.

"Us?" she asks, raising one brow, completely not understanding.

"On our world," I say, clearing my throat, "it's called 'being a lesbian.'" I draw my fingers in a circle to encompass all of the knights, the queen and me. "It means that you love women," I tell her, defining the word in the simplest way possible.

"The thing about Kell," says Alinor, leaning forward onto the back of her seat with a wide grin, "is that she *never* met a woman who wouldn't love her."

"What?" I ask, bewildered.

"She's just that good," says Alinor, spreading

her hands with a shrug.

"But...but not everyone is attracted to the same thing," I'm beginning, but Kell shakes out her hair, works her shoulders back, lowers her chin and makes her eyes utterly dazzling (I'm not sure exactly how she's doing it, but it seems that the temperature *actually goes up around her* when she does this). Kell then stands and prowls her way across the crowded bus to stand next to the woman who had—a moment earlier—looked like Kell's wink may have made her throw up a little in her mouth.

"On our world," says Calla quietly, glancing sidelong at me as she tries to hide a smile again, "we have a belief that the Goddess made women with the ability to love everyone. So, if you have not yet loved a woman before, there is some place inside of you where you hold the possibility of that love."

I blink. "I mean..." I trail off, considering things. "There have been studies on our world saying that all women are bi..." I start, but I realize I'd have to explain a lot about that sentence, so I clear my throat. "Huh," is what I follow that up with. "But...that woman looked pretty unhappy that Kell was giving her attention."

"See for yourself," says Alinor, inclining her head toward the back of the bus.

Kell and the woman who rolled her eyes so hard that they were in danger of falling out of her head...

Are currently making out.

"She talked to her for, like, a minute," I whisper, awed. The woman that Kell is kissing pretty passionately is *initiating* it, is—in fact—looking like this is the best moment of her entire life.

I'd expect someone on the T to say something about a making-out session that is so, well, *robust*, but surprisingly no one makes a single remark. Maybe it's the presence of all the women toward the front of the bus that Kell came in with—strong, muscular women who could probably take down anyone they wanted to.

But, for a moment, I realize what it must be like to live on Agrotera, or—more specifically—to live in Arktos, a country ruled by a woman who loves women, in a city of women who love women. Where this is completely the norm.

I mean...isn't that every lesbian's secret fantasy? To be in a place where she's not just "tolerated" or, on the negative side, in danger at any given time. To not be considered the minority or an abnormality or different...

But to be *normal.* And to be surrounded by women who are *just like you.*

I tuck a red curl behind my ear and smile up at Virago as I cross my arms over my chest. Virago grins down at me, wrapping me in her arms and holding me close as Kell and that lady go to town on each other.

All things considered, this is starting to shape up to being a *very* strange night.

I don't know how much stranger it could get.

Yet.

The bus grinds to a brake-screeching halt near Queenie's, and when we get off the bus, we're no longer the group of six women who climbed up onto the bus. We seem to have gained an additional member.

"My name's Jeana," says Jeana, the woman who Kell was making out with, who Kell now has an arm around, a satisfied smirk making her wet mouth round up at the corners. "I'm from Georgia," says Jeana, her smirk deepening. She fishes around in her purse and takes out a pack of cigarettes and a lighter. "Nice to meet y'all."

She already sounds pretty drunk. Jeana taps the bottom of the cigarette pack, taking a cigarette out, and—holding it between two bright red nails—she offers this cigarette to Kell.

Kell's about to take it, gazing at it with curiosity, but I move too fast for her.

"She doesn't smoke!" I pipe up, getting between Kell and Jeana in that instant (no small feat since I don't think *atoms* are currently capable of squeaking between their bodies, they're pressed so tightly to one another). "She...she quit. It'd be bad for her to have another cigarette," I'm stammering, holding up my hands like I'm in some desperately under-budget after-school program to teach kids not to smoke. All I need is to get Kell hooked on Earth's nicotine...

"Suit yourself," Jeana mutters, rolling out from under Kell's arm. "I've got places to go," she says, waving over her shoulder.

Kell looks slightly annoyed as she glances at me then, but she shakes her head, obviously undaunted by the woman's departure.

"Where we're going, there are many women?" she asks me, raising a brow.

"Loads," I tell her, putting my hands at the small of her back and propelling her gently down the swarming sidewalk towards Queenie's.

The door to Queenie's is opening and shutting as women make their way in and out of the bar, and the loud music is pouring out of the door every time it's opened, washing the sidewalk in poignant, wailing hard rock. I actually think it's a live band tonight, which will be much more interesting for the knights than the usual, overly loud DJ with all of the premixed club songs. I guess it means that I'm well and truly in my thirties that the prospect of listening to loud, mixed club music isn't making me excited. But to see a live band? Especially if it's one of the hard rock, woman-fronted ones that Queenie's often has? Yeah, that makes me feel pretty stoked.

And as we make our way into the dimly lit bar, I can see the stage at the back of the large room, and I'm happy to see a band I recognize, Batty Sisters, a local hard rock act that's comprised of four women—all lesbians. It seems like a very nice omen for the night, like the knights are going to have a good time because there's a leather-wearing, sexy musician on stage, swaggering around and crooning into the microphone like she owns the universe.

When Kell, Alinor, and Magel's eyes adjust to the darkness, they look around the place, taking in the sight of all of the ladies. An immediate swarm of women descends on them, and by the time I turn around from the bar, two overly full glasses of beer in my hands, one for me and one for Virago, the knights have completely disappeared into the sea of women. Calla, too.

Virago laughs as she takes the beer from me, holding it up in a small salute. "That was quick," she says mildly, sipping the foam off the top of the beer. "Thank you for the drink, my love."

"This really worries me, baby..." I tell her, glancing around the bar as I try to spot the knights, but all I see are women writhing together on the dance floor, and women chatting each other up at the bar. "What if something happens?" I ask Virago, biting my lip. I trail off as I realize that Virago's arm is around my waist and that she's pulling me toward her.

"Do not worry so," she growls into my ear, making me shiver as the band's energy increases, the guitar vamping up to a loud, almost primal *thrumming* that makes my bones feel like they're vibrating, my breath coming faster. "They are knights," Virago murmurs into my ear, her mouth against my skin. "They can take care of themselves, and they know to stay close to us. Now," she says, taking a step back from me. The rush of cold air between our bodies drives me crazy...just like she thought it would, because she gives me a slow, sensual smile before turning to her glass and drinking down the rest of her beer in a few swallows. She upends the glass onto the bar's counter so hard I'm surprised the glass didn't break—and then she turns to me. "Will you dance with me, beloved?" she asks me, her eyes sparking with a very welcome fire.

I try to drink my beer down, too, but I'm a total lightweight these days (Ha! Who am I fooling? I've always been a lightweight), and when I upend my glass on the bar's counter, too, I feel the effects of the alcohol almost immediately.

I'm already tipsy? From one beer? My college self is laughing...in that my college self would be tipsy from one beer, too.

I lean on Virago a little as she pulls me onto the dance floor of the bar. Out here, among all the women dancing with (and—let's be honest—grinding on) each other, I can feel the energy of the room, the energy of the music, of all the people surrounding us. Maybe it's just because I'm tipsy (okay, *probably* because I'm tipsy), but that energy fills me as I gaze up into Virago's bright blue eyes. She's smiling down at me, her mouth rounded at the corners into a soft, sexy grin, and when her hands grip my hips, when I meet her stare, I can feel her want and need. I have just as much want and need, so I wrap my arms around her neck, pulling her head down, pulling her mouth to mine for a kiss.

She's electric, her kiss potent and powerful as the *thrum* of love and lust (never quite knowing where one stops and the other starts or where they both merge) jolts straight through me.

The tempo of the song changes, becomes more energetic now, hard and pulsing like the blood pounding quickly through my veins. The woman on stage locks the microphone into the mic stand, and she leans the mic forward, gazing out at the crowded bar with hair that sweeps in front of her eyes. She lowers her tone, her shoulders curving, her breath coming fast, impassioned, as her eyes narrow, as the power of the song compels her.

"I feel you, under my skin," the woman growls into the microphone, raking her eyes over the women dancing in front of her. "I feel you..."

I turn on the dance floor, and Virago turns with me as we press tightly together, her fingers in my hair now, pulling me closer as I dig my own fingers into her hips, gripping her, breathless.

In the back of my head, I realize that this is the last night I have here on Earth—literally. And Agrotera isn't the safest place. There is a chance that something *bad* could happen to me while I'm there. Monsters roam Agrotera: cannibal werewolves, massive beasts. And I'm aware—highly aware, in this moment—that this could be my last—truly *last*—day here.

But you know what? If this *was* my last day, it would be *such* a good day that I don't think I would regret a damn thing. My mother always talked like that, reminding me over and over again that the days that make up our lives are important, that to make a conscious effort to be happy every single day means you're living happily ever after. And, dammit, right now I am so happy I could burst, really and truly happy, as I dance with my knight on the dance floor, as the performer sings her heart out on stage, as the other knights whirl around us with women in their arms.

It seems like they're pretty happy in this moment, too. I've caught glimpses of Magel, Kell and Alinor, and while Magel and Alinor have been dancing with the same two women (and they look pleased to be doing so), Kell...has not been dancing with only one woman.

This is the fourth woman I've seen her dancing with since we've arrived at the bar. And Kell is dancing closely with this new lady, a smaller, lovely woman with long brunette hair that's as straight as a pin, and—like us—Kell and she are making out unabashedly in public.

A little bit of my happiness leaves me, then, because I realize that I haven't seen Calla dancing with *anyone* at all.

Actually, since we arrived at the bar and Calla first disappeared...I haven't seen her once.

I'm fairly certain that an assassin following the knights and queen from Agrotera to Earth is an impossibility. But just because there aren't assassins on this world who would seek to kill the queen of Arktos, that doesn't mean that a bar in Boston is a completely *safe* space. It worries me that I haven't glimpsed her, and now I can't rest until I find her—just to make sure she's okay.

"I'll be back in just a second," I tell Virago,

reaching up and brushing my mouth against hers, exchanging one hot, short kiss, before extricating myself from her embrace as the song the band was playing comes to a final, long-held note. The song ends, and the crowd cheers the band on voraciously. "I'll be right back," I repeat, shouting to Virago over all the yelling, and she nods. "Keep dancing!" I mouth to her with a smile; then I'm moving through the crowd, trying to find the queen.

I trust that Calla can handle herself, just like her knights can handle themselves. But she was just...so *sad* earlier. I want to make certain she's all right. Hell, I'd be thrilled if I found her slow-dancing with a woman, or making out with one... But when I finally spot her across the crowded bar, that's not, unfortunately, the case.

Calla is sitting at the bar, her back to it, nursing a glass of what *appears* to be only water, her expression distant. She's staring out at the crowd of happy, intoxicated women, and she looks like she's not really seeing them at all. Her eyes are unfocused, as if she's a million miles away. She stirs the little plastic straw in her glass before taking a small sip with a downturned mouth.

I reach her, then clear my throat, hoping not to startle her—but she must have seen me coming. She turns to me expectantly with a small sigh, like she's about to take an audience with a dignitary.

"Hey," I murmur to her, leaning against the bar beside her. "Are you...all right?"

"Don't even try with her," says a woman on my left, a woman who's pretty inebriated, judging by how hard she's leaning on me, her hooded eyes blinking slowly. "I just tried to get her to dance, and she was all like, 'No, thank you,' like she was declining an award or somethin'." The woman hiccups in my face.

I ignore her as she makes a show of shrugging and pushing off the bar. Calla gazes unhappily at the floor now, twirling her straw in her hand. I bite my lip and clear my throat again, having to shout over the band as they start a new song, "Hey," I repeat, "are you all right?"

Calla glances sidelong at me, and a single tear leaks out of her right eye, tracing its way down her pale cheek.

So, no, then. Not all right.

"They have all been very kind here," she says, indicating the bar at large. "I have had many offers," she says, smiling sadly. "It is enough to make a woman blush," she says, tucking a strand of blonde hair behind her ear as she lowers her lashes. "But I can not be with anyone."

My brow furrows as I try to understand what she's talking about. After a moment, things start to click into place in my head, and as I watch Calla gazing wistfully out at the room full of women, I wonder...is she so heartbroken *because* of a woman?

"What are you drinking? Can I buy you another one?" I ask Calla, and she shakes her head at me, lifting up the glass.

"Do not bother, dear Holly. I am only drinking water," she says simply, her shoulders rolling in an elegant shrug. She uncrosses her long legs and crosses them the other way, raising a brow as she glances at me. "I wanted to keep my wits about me on a new world."

"More ale!" Alinor bellows next to us, appearing out of thin air to slap her open palm on the bar, her other arm around a slip of a woman who's clinging to her happily. Alinor looks...pretty drunk already, actually. We haven't even *been* here that long!

Calla smiles a little indulgently as she shakes her head. "Obviously, my knights do not share my philosophy," she says, glancing at Alinor with affectionate eyes.

Alinor takes the "ale" that the bartender just gave her (it looks like he just poured her a beer) and stumbles off to drink it down and dance with the woman she's with. Calla's gaze follows her, and it's equal parts affectionate and pensive.

"Um...it must be pretty wonderful—to have *knights*," I tell her, inwardly cursing myself for such a ridiculous conversation opener.

Calla glances at me quickly and then looks away. She doesn't say anything for a long moment as she bites at her full bottom lip, rotating the glass in her hands. She gazes down at the water, her mind turned inward.

As the music starts to wind down, I realize that the band is preparing to play a slow song...

And it's at this moment when everything begins to fall apart.

Here's a pro tip: if you have knights visiting you from another world, *never take them to a bar.* This is something that I have to apparently learn the hard way.

A tall woman wearing a backwards baseball cap and a t-shirt emblazoned with the Boston Red Sox logo is currently stomping her way across the dance floor, shoving women aside and generally being rude as she makes a beeline toward...

Oh, crap.

Kell.

Currently, Kell is slow dancing with yet another woman. Well, they're not so much dancing as grinding on each other, Kell's front against the woman's back, the woman's arms reaching over her own shoulders and cradling Kell's head. Kell is kissing the woman's neck, her hands sliding beneath the woman's blouse...

And this Red Sox-shirted woman is stomping toward Kell and her dance partner with a determined scowl. She's just as tall as Kell, and she looks like she works out, muscular arms evident beneath her t-shirt. But more importantly than anything else? She looks *pissed.*

And now that the music is quieting, it's the perfect lull for voices to be easily carried throughout the bar.

Yeah, I didn't want the knights to draw any attention, but it's apparently a bit too late for that.

The angry woman finally makes her way through the mass of bodies gyrating on the dance floor, and she taps Kell pretty hard on the shoulder with a jabby finger. Her face is glowering so much that I'm surprised a storm cloud hasn't rolled into the bar, aiming miniature-sized lightning bolts at Kell.

It's obviously aggressive, how this woman gets Kell's attention, but Kell does what I'm assuming any trained knight would do. She turns around slowly, pivoting on the back of her heel. Her guard is up, and she's staring at her challenger intensely, as if her ice blue eyes could turn someone to stone.

"Hey, you're dancing with my girlfriend, *asshole,*" says this new woman to Kell. She shouts it at her, actually, her hands curling into fists at her sides, and because the music is so quiet, the sound of her voice *does* carry throughout the bar, and the entire crowd falls silent in that moment, people flicking their eyes to what is clearly about to become a scene.

Kell glances, her brow raised in question, to the woman she was kissing half a heartbeat ago. This woman, with disheveled hair, her shirt untucked (and unbuttoned at the bottom), simply shrugs. Then Kell turns back to the woman who just interrupted them.

"That's not what she said a minute ago," Kell informs her, almost sweetly.

And then she ducks a punch.

That punch came from nowhere, and with the strength that the woman threw it, it could have knocked Kell out cold if it had actually hit home. But it didn't. Kell was standing one second, and then she just...wasn't. She moved so fluidly and quickly, I never actually saw her do it; she just bowed like a dancer, avoiding the punch.

The woman lets out a groan of annoyance, and she gets ready to throw another punch, but then Virago arrives at Kell's side, appearing there in a heartbeat's time. She stands as a barrier between Kell and her opponent, her hands up, her expression conciliatory, friendly.

"I am so sorry, friend," she tells the woman, her tone mollifying. "It was but a mistake, truly. Kell is not from this country, and she is unfamiliar with the customs. She only arrived here today. Please forgive her. Let me buy you a drink, show you there is no need for animosity," says Virago, offering her hand to the woman and smiling.

But Virago's soothing words don't fix things. Not even a little.

"That *jerk* had her hands all over my girlfriend's ass!" shouts the angry woman, taking a step forward and shoving Virago's shoulders.

"Well, it's a *nice* rear," says Kell, shrugging, as if

she doesn't understand what the fuss is about.

The seething woman takes in what Kell just said, as if she's drunk and has to process the words (or maybe it just takes her a minute to realize all that was implied by Kell's statement). But when she understands it, it's like a *hurricane* has settled in the bar.

"That *does* it!" the woman shouts, and then she steps forward so quickly that her body is a blur as she aims a very aggressive, savage punch, not at Kell...but at Virago, who still happens to be standing between them. Virago is a barrier to Kell, and it's obvious that this woman is going to do *everything she can* to get through that barrier and unleash her fury on Kell.

But the punch that she threw at Virago doesn't touch her. Instead, Virago catches the woman's first in midair, her palm and fingers curling over the other woman's wrist in a calm but no-nonsense grip. "Friend," sighs Virago, shaking her head, "Kell was wrong to dance with your girlfriend. It was just a misunderstanding. Please, I urge you again—let me buy you a drink."

But the angry woman doesn't seem to hear a word Virago is saying. Her rage only grows more potent: she snarls, and then she tries to punch Virago with her *other* hand.

Yes, obviously, Kell should *not* have been dancing with the girlfriend of another woman. But no matter what, this woman shouldn't have tried to punch Virago, someone who was playing peacemaker and trying to make sure a fight didn't start.

I've never seen Virago in a combat situation outside of jousting, and it's all fake jousting at that. So the speed with which Virago moves right now...well, it's kind of breathtaking. Because, one moment, Virago is standing calmly between Kell and the angry woman. And the next moment, somehow, the woman has been flipped through the air and is lying on her back on the ground.

Virago executed the flip elegantly, just by grabbing the woman's hand and using her body weight to help her complete the arc through the air.

Though I watched it happen with my own two eyes, the ease of the action is almost unbelievable to me. The woman turns over, and she's now lying in a fetal position on the club floor, coughing. I think she got the breath knocked out of her. Virago bends down and offers a hand to the woman again. For a single heartbeat, I think the woman is going to take it and finally accept Virago's offer of a drink.

But nothing's ever that easy. And though the woman just had her breath knocked out of her lungs, she pushes Virago's hand aside, rolls over, gets on all fours, and then slowly, slowly, rises to her feet again.

I'm not prepared for what happens next. The angry woman delivers a vicious short kick with her leg, aiming for Virago's middle.

But Virago sidesteps the kick easily, as if she did expect it, and then she's crouching low, like a lioness about to leap on an unsuspecting gazelle. There is raw power moving through every inch of her muscled body as she leaps gracefully through the air and does a quick spinning kick with her right foot.

In mere seconds, the angry woman is on her back again on the floor.

Virago crouches over her for the second time, a small line furrowing her brow. "Friend, please let me buy you that drink," she tells the coughing woman companionably. The woman on the ground has broken out in a sweat and is breathing hard, her chest rising and falling as she stares up at Virago with what really looks to be pure loathing. Virago, on the other hand, appears exactly as she did a moment ago, every hair in place, a bright smile on her face.

This time the woman *does* take her hand as she struggles to stand. Virago pulls her upright easily and then guides her to the bar, where she raises a finger to the bartender, who races over, eyes wide, with two new beers.

The woman Kell was dancing with has left Kell, following the woman and Virago to the bar unhappily. This means that Kell is now alone, and that's something that Kell is not going to stand for. Almost immediately—after a sigh and frown in the direction of the retreating woman—Kell is circling the dance floor of women again, her head to the side, swaggering with her hands deep in her pockets, a thoughtful expression on her face.

The heads of nearly every woman on that dance floor turn and watch her, and I'm fairly certain they're not interested in her because she was just part of a fight a moment ago. No, Kell is prowling like a tigress as she circles that floor, a noble, gorgeous predator, ready to find her next willing prey.

It's a very short hunt before she has another woman in her arms.

"You did well," says Calla, as Virago approaches us, walking along the bar with her head held high, her eyes flashing with a potent fire. Virago tugs down the sleeves of her suit jacket with a small shrug, but you can tell that she's pleased by the queen's praise, her lips turning up at the corners in a small smile that she tries to stifle.

"Milady, it was nothing," she says then, and her smile for the queen grows. But then she glances from me to Calla and realizes the same thing that I did: Calla is sitting here, nursing a glass of water, alone.

"Are you not enjoying yourself, milady?" asks Virago, her voice dropping low as she leans toward the queen. "There are many women—" she begins, but then she seems to think better of her sentence, and she pales a little, straightening. "Forgive me, Your Majesty," she says, her voice suddenly solemn.

"There is nothing to forgive," Calla murmurs to Virago, though the slim smile is gone from her face. For a long moment, she says nothing more, and Virago and I turn, looking out at the dance floor. Virago's jaw is working, and I can tell she's holding something back, holding words in, but there's no time for her to utter them.

Calla rises easily, pushing off from the bar stool and straightening the bottom half of her dress with long fingers before she sighs and lifts her chin. "Is there a washroom?" she asks me then, and I nod.

I start to tell her how to get to it, but the problem is that Queenie's restroom is located near the kitchen, and there are a lot of different turns to get there. She'll probably end up *in* the kitchen, because I'm terrible at giving directions. "I can...I can just show you," I tell her with a little shrug, and I glance at Virago, who apparently had something to say to the queen...but no longer does. She nods, taking a step back.

"I'll be here," she murmurs to me, and then the crowd swallows her up.

As Calla and I make our way along the hallway, the din of the music, the laughter, and the shouting from back at the bar starts to fade. It's replaced, instead, with muted conversations and the din of pots and pans banging in the kitchen ahead. Halfway down the hallway, we join a line, because of course there's a line stretching around the corner for access to the toilets. But I've seen the line longer than this; it should move fairly quickly.

We stand in silence together. Two ladies in front of us are making bets that their friend will break up with someone named Ashley. A few people behind us, a woman is arguing loudly with someone on her cellphone about lawn maintenance. I lean against the wall and stand up on my toes to take the pressures off the balls of my feet. I'm too old to wear heels to bars.

I'm not expecting what Calla tells me then.

"You move beautifully together, you know," says Calla solemnly, glancing at me as she leans on the wall, her arms folded in front of her, her shoulders curving forward. "You and Virago," she supplies, her head to the side.

I blush a little, tucking another curl behind my ear as I bite my lip. I can't keep from smiling.

"Virago is a prize," says Calla, and she sounds like she means it as she gazes forward, lifting her chin. "She is loyal and good and kind," Calla tells me, "though she can be stubborn. And, perhaps, too protective," she says, her mouth rounding up at the corners into a soft smile. "But she is a good match for you, Holly. I am glad that you found one another."

"Thank you, Your Ma—um, Calla. Thank you," I tell her.

There are several people making out in the line, including the people directly ahead of us, and I'm suddenly self-conscious as I think about my theory that

Calla's sadness is caused by a woman.

"They look happy," says Calla wistfully, gazing at the nearest couple. I'm fairly certain that these two aren't headed to the bathroom because they need a potty break.

Calla's eyes fill with tears as she watches them making out. She's biting her lip when she finally turns away, tears streaking down her cheeks in silent succession.

I have a pack of tissues in my purse, and I offer these to her automatically.

"Oh, Holly, you are quite good," she tells me with a sniff, immediately trying to put on a brave face and completely denying that she was crying at all with her actions. "You're always at the ready with a...what did you call these?" she asks, unfolding the packet and taking a tissue to her eyes, dabbing along the edges and shaking her head. She's obviously trying to keep from crying further, and I bite my lip. It seems that Calla isn't fond of being overly emotional in public. I want to respect that, so I try to distract her.

But, God, she's in so much pain. It's hard to watch, to witness someone's heart aching like this.

"They're tissues," I tell her quietly, clearing my throat. "So, *tissue* is a fun word, huh? Tissue. Tis-sue," I repeat, realizing that I'm getting funny looks from the women on the other side of us. "Anyway, unicorns, really?" I say, raising my brows. Whatever. I've heard weirder conversations in the bathroom line.

"Yes, there are unicorns on Agrotera," says Calla, smiling a watery smile. "I think you'll like seeing them."

Blessedly, it's our turn in line then, and the both of us use the extremely *filthy* restroom (*Welcome to Earth,*

Queen Calla! I think to myself miserably as I toilet-paper my seat. *You're never going to want to come back again!*), but Calla is apparently a true class act, because she doesn't seem to notice or pass judgment on the state of the facilities...or the fact that two women are clearly bow-chicka-wow-wow-ing in the handicap stall, as evidenced by their spectacularly overexaggerated moans.

I know that, in a lot of bars, having sex in the restrooms is not encouraged, but...they're pretty flexible about that sort of thing here. After all, Queenie's has been around for a very long time, and they turn a blind eye to hanky-panky—which is probably why even more lesbians frequent this bar than any other in the city.

As I'm washing my hands, waiting for Calla to exit her stall, a cheer goes up from the waiting women in line when the door to the handicap stall opens.

I turn around as I grab a paper towel from the dispenser, and then I'm staring with my mouth open.

Striding out of that handicap stall comes Kell with yet *another* woman. This is not the woman she was making out with right *before* we entered the restroom, but, in fact, a *different* one. I mean, seriously, how does she do it? And how in the world did she get a woman in that stall so quickly? Or, you know, go through the line to the restroom that quickly? Kell swaggers out of the stall, grinning widely at the cheers, and holds up the woman's hand as if they've both just won an Olympic gold medal or something. And then she smirks as she walks past me, tossing her hair over her shoulder and pinning me to the spot with a satisfied blue gaze.

I shrug and give her a thumbs-up sign, which I realize Kell probably has no context for. Calla comes out of her stall in enough time to see Kell and the other woman exit the restroom, Kell's arm draped around the woman's shoulders loosely, their head angled close.

Calla chuckles as she washes her hands. "That's our Kell," she says, taking the paper towel I hand to her.

"Is she always like this?" I ask, with a bewildered smile. "Because...wow. I mean, she certainly has a lot of, um..." I turn my hand in the air with a grin. "*Stamina.*"

Calla smirks, shaking her head. "Kell has not yet found the right woman to settle down with. I used to think that she wouldn't find the one, that this is the way she wants to live her life," says Calla, gesturing at the line of women angling back toward the bar. I'm fairly certain that she's gesturing to the many, many couples making out. "But then Kell told me something a few moons back, and now I think...Kell is ready. Ready for someone new, someone she can give her heart to." Calla sighs a little, her head to the side. "Do you think me a romantic?"

"Hey, I'm one, too," I tell her with a soft smile. We're entering the bar proper, and the music and voices are deafening.

For a moment, back in the quieter hallway and in the restroom, Calla seemed calmer, happier, more talkative. But when we step down onto the dance floor, her queenly mask slides right back into place, and she's suddenly aloof, her chin tilted upward, her regal bearing evident.

"Calla," I call to her, reaching out to touch her arm. I shout, over the din, "Do you want to go?" I ask her. "Is this place making you unhappy?" I gesture around at the bar.

Calla looks at me in surprise. "Why would you think it makes me unhappy?" she asks then, the words coming out a little stiff as she tries to look nonchalant, but something flitted across her face, an expression of sadness so deep, so painful, that it twisted my stomach and my heart.

Calla clears her throat, shakes her head a little, taking a deep breath and settling her shoulders back, like a diplomat about to attack a problem. "It is...it is *good* to see women in love. Good to see that love still exists..." But then her face flickers again, and she says softly, sadly, "It exists for other women." She trails off, and then Calla folds her arms around her middle carefully, like she's cold. "But it will never exist for me," she whispers.

I had to strain to hear her final words over the din, and now I'm opening my mouth, about to ask her what she means, when Virago spots us from across the room. She's leaning against the wall beside Alinor, the both of them nursing beers, but when she sees me, she pushes off from the wall and strides purposefully through the crowd. Surprisingly, the dancers clear a path for her with no comment, moving around her as if she has a presence that fills up a room.

And she does. Virago's bright blue gaze pins me to the spot when she catches my eye, and together, Calla and I wait for her to reach us.

When Virago is close enough, she puts a hand on the curve of my waist, drawing me closer to her so that she can murmur in my ear. "I think that maybe we should go," she says, her mouth to the side as she leans close to me. "The knights are always...quite a handful whenever we have leave, but you're right, my love. If they are mischievous on this world, it makes things even more...complicated," she says tactfully.

She has to shout these last few words to be

heard over Kell's whoops as she crawls up onto the bar right in front of us, very, *very* drunk. She rotates her hand in the air as she wiggles her hips, and then she's dragging another woman up beside her onto the bar. The woman is probably even more drunk than Kell, and they're both standing on the bar, dancing together. As Kell draws the woman toward her, they begin to make out rather enthusiastically, the heel of Kell's boot shattering a shot glass that someone left on the bar top.

This woman, I would like to point out, is *not* the woman Kell was with in the restroom.

"Alinor already did *that*," says Virago, inclining her head toward Kell's antics, "while you and Calla were in the restroom," she tells me, folding her arms in front of her with her head tilted to the side. The long-suffering expression she's wearing tells me that both Alinor and Kell have performed such antics many, *many* times...just on another world..

"Uh, yeah, we can totally get going," I murmur quickly. "I'll go find Magel. Um, honey," I tell Virago, flashing her a grin, "why don't *you* coax Kell down from there?"

"Sure," says Virago with a sigh and a smile.

"And I spot Alinor—" I cut myself off, and then I'm angling across the dance floor, keeping Alinor firmly in my sights to avoid losing her in the crowd.

It doesn't look like Alinor is going anywhere soon, though, because she's gyrating against a woman who looks even drunker than she is. It's not even that late! How are there so many drunk people already in this club? Alinor's eyes are half-closed, and she has her arms around the woman's neck, drawing the two of them tightly together. Alinor has been dancing with this woman all night, and I'm a little sad that I have to separate them. I mean, what if Alinor was really hitting it off with her?

But we *have* to go.

I'm busy trying to make my way through the inebriated dancers, aiming for Alinor...

But then the dancing just *stops* around me. Because the music, the constant, pulsing, pounding music...stops, too.

The band was right in the middle of a fast-paced cover of "Come to My Window," the lead singer leaning into the microphone stand as if it were a lover, growling the words in her super-sexy voice. The cover had the whole bar roaring with applause, and everyone was dancing close and tight. I mean, isn't that song *everyone's* romantic anthem? But the band is now still, silence descending over the bar like a deafening bomb. I glance up to the stage in shock.

The lead singer is standing up there now, gripping the mic stand as she stares over the crowd...and toward the entrance of the club. Her eyes are wide, her mouth open—like she just saw a ghost.

I turn, along with everyone else around me.

There's a woman standing at the top of the stairs, poised at the entrance, and every single person in the club is staring at *her*.

"Oh, shit," I mutter, my heart beating a million miles a minute, my mouth suddenly dry, a lump in my throat.

Standing on those steps, impossibly, is another knight.

But saying that she's "another knight" makes it seem as if she's like the knights I've already met, and I've got to confess, yeah, that's not the case *at all*.

True, the woman at the top of the stairs is

wearing armor, like the other knights were when they first came over from Agrotera. But this knight's armor?

It's jet black.

And it has *spikes* on it.

She honestly looks as if she just arrived from the site of a brutal medieval battle, because her sword is out and held at attention, gripped in a black-leather gloved hand. Every knight's sword is different, I know, and is an expression of that knight's personality—or so Virago has told me. This woman's sword is massive, long and wicked-looking, with a serrated edge and a brightly gleaming blade. The pommel is covered in black gems that flash in the low light of the club, and the pommel itself is huge, heavy-looking. You could probably kill someone if you hit them with it.

So the armor and the sword set her apart from her fellow knights. But there's more to it than that.

She's tall, taller than Virago (again, I'm assuming they just grow giant women in Agrotera), but her presence is bigger than her physical height. She seems to fill the whole room, just by stepping into it. She has long black hair that falls in luscious waves down her back, spilling over her shoulders and down her front. Her high cheekbones and long, aristocratic nose give her an air of nobility.

But her eyes... I can't tell what color they are from across the room—but I don't need to. They're *electric*, and they're dancing with an ill-boding light.

Energy seems to pulse around her as she descends the steps with the grace of a jaguar. I've seen big cats move in zoos, stalking the perimeters of their enclosures as if they're constantly looking for a means of escape, but I've never seen a human being move like them...until now. She moves into the bar, one step at a time, the world seeming to shimmer and shift around her, as if she's a spark prepared to set off a tremendous blaze.

This new woman, this new *knight*, descends into the startlingly silent room. The air seems to waver around her; I feel like I'm staring at her through the glass of a fish bowl, and things are starting to look a little out of proportion. I'm reminded of the House of Mirrors I walked through at a carnival when I was a kid. I rub at my eyes, and then Virago is there beside me, and she's gripping my arm with strong fingers, her jaw clenched as she watches the knight approach.

The woman in black armor prowls into the very center of the room, dancers falling all over themselves in order to get away from her. The entire dance floor seems to be empty now, and the knight stands in the very center of it.

She stands, and she stares at Virago.

Actually, "staring" isn't the right word for what she's doing.

Because if this woman's eyes were actual weapons, Virago would be dead right now.

"What have you done?" the woman murmurs. It's so quiet in the club that you could hear a pin drop, but even if it weren't so quiet, even if the music were playing and everyone was dancing and laughing and yelling, you would have been able to make out this woman's words. They carry across the space with the cutting edge of an ax: sharp, shining...and deadly.

I shiver, standing next to Virago, and I'm ashamed to say that, in that moment, I want to step behind her so that this woman is not directly in front of me. But I don't. I find some scraps of courage from somewhere deep inside myself, and I hold my ground.

But just barely.

Beside me, I can feel the heat of anger rising off of my knight. Virago's leaning forward, her entire body tense, her bright blue eyes flashing with their own icy fire.

And in that space, Virago whispers one word, like a warning. Like a curse.

"Charaxus," she hisses.

I stare at the woman with her terrifying sword, with her spiky, black armor that would probably wound anyone who dared to bump to against it. I stare at her as I finally understand who she is. *Charaxus*—the vice queen. Queen Calla's vice queen, and—apparently—second in line to the throne of Arktos.

This new knight, Charaxus, holds the sword above the ground like it weighs nothing, even though, from the length of the blade and heft of the pommel, I know that's absolutely not the case. Charaxus' nostrils flare as she lifts her chin, as she pins Virago with her gaze.

This close to her, I can tell that Charaxus' eyes are just as bright and blue as Virago's. But there is so much to Virago's eyes besides the color, because her gaze is always full of kindness, even when she's angry, even when she's about to take on a monster. There is strength and courage to her eyes, but you can tell that she has such a big heart, just from her gaze, just from the softness at the edges of her eyes whenever she looks at me, love evident in a simple glance.

In this moment, I can't tell if Charaxus has a big heart, or if she's ever had a kind thought in her life.

Because, in *this* moment, all I see is the pure fury burning through her, sparking in her gaze, a rampant fire of ice (a maelstrom of dueling, potent energies) that could consume the world and destroy all of it.

Charaxus lifts her sword easily from where the tip was resting on the floor. She lifts it without even flexing her arm, and then she raises it level with her heart. And she points the enormous, wickedly flashing blade at Virago.

"*Where*," Charaxus growls the word, and the very floor beneath us seems to quake from the strength of that single syllable, "is Queen Calla?" she snarls. The lights overhead flash off of the sword blade, making it appear even deadlier, and my heart is pounding in my throat as I stare at that sword, at this cold, rage-filled woman who crossed over from another world to be here, now, her black armor glittering in a silenced bar, a deadly weapon aimed at my girlfriend's throat.

If Charaxus is an icy inferno, Calla is the calm at the center of the storm. Queen Calla regally glides over to come stand beside us, and all eyes move from Charaxus and focus on the queen, her noble bearing obvious, awe-inspiring. She steps with grace and dignity, and her chin is raised high, her eyes flashing brightly. And dangerously.

Since I've met Calla, I've come to sympathize with her. I *really* like her, and I think we would make good friends, if I get to have that chance. Never, in the moments since our meeting, have I seen her act with anything but gentility, calmness and kindness.

But, in this moment, there is a rampant, blazing strength that billows around her like a shimmering cloud of lightning, dazzling and bright...and just as deadly as Charaxus.

The queen doesn't look at us as she draws herself up to her full height. She's gazing at Charaxus with a frown that makes the corners of her mouth downturn severely.

She leans forward, her arms loose and dangling at her sides as the storm of energy seems to swirl around her. She bends toward Charaxus.

"Charaxus, stop," she commands, and—like Charaxus' voice—Calla's makes the ground beneath us seem to shift and rumble, just a little, the floor quaking with the raw power of her words. I wonder if she and Charaxus are using magic to do this, and I'm worried that, if they'd use magic so casually, what *else* might they use it for in this tense situation?

When Charaxus' eyes alight on Calla, a great deal of the fire in them fades—all at once. The sword's point lowers as if it's been forcibly pushed down, and then Charaxus' head is bowing forward, her hair falling on either side of her face as she lowers her entire body. "Your Majesty," she murmurs, and she's kneeling deeply, dropping to one knee in a fluid, graceful movement that makes her cape—I didn't realize she was wearing a black cape over her armor until this moment—flare out around her; she sinks to the ground. "Your Majesty," she repeats from where she kneels, her eyes flashing again, her jaw clenched as she places a gloved hand over her heart. "Have you been kidnapped?" Charaxus asks, her eyes roving over the queen as if to search for any sign of damage or hurt.

Calla's gaze tires as she looks at Charaxus, regarding her wearily. "No," she says simply, shaking her head as she spreads her hands. "I came here of my own free will. Rise, please, Charaxus."

Charaxus' eyes flash again, her fist, made over her heart and kept there in honor of the queen, tightens as Charaxus turns her gaze from Calla to Virago...as if it was Virago that put her up to this, I realize. She rises instantly, flowing upward, her eyes narrowing further.

"*Magel* thought it best, since the attack happened so recently," says Calla firmly, and Charaxus looks back at the queen, thunderstruck. She obviously thought this was all Virago's fault.

Why would she think that?

I remember Virago telling me that she and Charaxus were schoolmates as they trained to become knights, and that they "didn't get along," whatever that means. But this is much more than not getting along.

This is two very powerful knights at odds.

And it can't possibly be good.

"We came in *search* of Virago," Calla says formally, inclining her head in Virago's direction while still holding Charaxus' gaze, "and we have found her. And she will kindly return with us to keep me safe during the Hero's Tournament."

Charaxus' eyes narrow at that, and her hands fall to her sides. The sword is lying on its side on the ground where she set it when she knelt in genuflection to the queen, but she keeps it there for a long moment as Virago and Charaxus stare at each other with sharp eyes.

While said knightly staring contest takes place, I am highly aware that one of the bartenders has brought the cordless bar phone to her ear and is calling the cops, whispering into the phone as quietly as she can. I can't blame her: an extra-tall, super-imposing lady just walked into her establishment wearing spiky black armor and carrying a pointy sword. I would be calling the cops, too, if I didn't know we weren't in danger.

I mean, I don't *think* we're in danger. I *hope* we're not in danger. But, at that moment, Charaxus turns to Virago again. She bows down, picks up the sword in a gloved hand, and she raises the sword level with her heart.

She's pointing the tip of the blade at Virago, the sharp thing flashing from the lights overhead.

"Your Majesty knows that you are not in the best state of mind to make emotional decisions," says Charaxus, her voice low. "That you would risk your life to pass through the portal, to come all this way to another world to find a knight *hardly* worth finding...this leads me to believe that you are not thinking clearly."

Virago snarls at that, her jaw clenched, her teeth bared, her hands curled into tight fists at her sides. I can feel her entire body tensing beside me, but Virago surprisingly says nothing.

Instead, Calla draws herself up to her full height again, her shoulders back, her chin up, her hands in fists at her sides, too. And though she's wearing my formal gown—and a purple one, no less, complete with frills and lace—in that moment, I've never seen her look more queenly. She lifts her chin, eyes flashing with a raw, green fire that's as potent as any blaze.

There is pure power in her bearing as she stares at Charaxus.

"You will address me more formally, Charaxus, and you will not question my judgment," she says, voice steady, the floorboards beneath our feet shaking just a little, as if a tremor is passing through the earth. Her words are so soft, I almost can't hear them, but the gravity of them is a strength I can feel in my bones. "You *will* have respect for the decisions I make," Queen Calla growls.

For a long moment, Charaxus' blade does not waver; she holds it, strong and still, aimed at Virago's heart. But then the point of the blade falls, resting against the floor as Charaxus takes a deep breath, as her noble face pales, her lips downturning into a pained frown.

And then, surprisingly, Charaxus kneels again, folding elegantly forward and pressing one knee to the floor as she places her hand, curled into a fist again, over her heart. She sets the sword on the ground beside her.

“Please forgive me, Your Majesty. I was concerned for your safety,” she murmurs. This time, the floor doesn't quake beneath us as she speaks the words. There is pain in her tone, but she keeps her voice ceremonial as she gazes up at the queen.

There's something in that gaze, something I can't quite place, as Charaxus stares at Queen Calla—but then, whatever it is vanishes as the rest of the bar seems to wake up from its trance, women coughing and murmuring amongst themselves as the singer glances at the bartender and shrugs, tapping the mic.

“Hey, guys,” she says into the microphone, squinting against the lights trained on her. “Um...everyone remain calm, okay?”

Kell hops down off the bar in a surprisingly fluid motion for someone so very, very drunk. She turns and grabs the woman she was dancing with around the waist gently and helps the woman down off the bar, too, lifting her easily and setting her on the floor as if she's a large doll. The woman smiles up at Kell, but Kell isn't even looking at her. Instead, Kell is staring and glaring at Charaxus, anger quite evident on her features as her mouth downturns into a particularly snarly frown.

“Party's over,” Kell mutters to the woman she

was dancing with, and then she turns away from her, striding over to us, her hands on her hips as she sneers at Charaxus, who remains down on one knee in front of Queen Calla.

"Well, look who decided to grace us with her presence. The queen's *pet*," Kell mutters to Charaxus, obviously to Charaxus, and Charaxus' eyes glitter dangerously as the two women stare at one another. But then Kell lifts her chin and moves in front of us almost casually. I think she's aiming to go stand beside Alinor, but she kicks Charaxus' sword, lying on the floor beside her, away from the knight.

It was just a little kick with the toe of Kell's boot, a kick that made the blade spin around. It was made to look accidental, but I'm pretty sure I know enough about Kell at this point to realize that this was one-hundred percent intentional.

And Charaxus seems to know this, too, because she is on her feet in a heartbeat, sword somehow already in her hand, pointing the blade at Kell's heart as her eyes flash with a cool fire.

Charaxus is crouched in a fighting stance, and Kell is almost too drunk to stand, but she somehow manages to turn on her heel. Kell's obviously laughing at Charaxus as she shakes her head, daring Charaxus with her mocking gaze to try something. But then Kell is reaching over her back for her own sword...

But Kell is wearing clothes she borrowed from Virago. The sword that she came through the portal with is back at home, neatly stacked on my couch alongside Magel, Alinor and, yes, even Virago's swords.

So Kell is weaponless.

The woman at the bar hangs up the phone and holds onto the receiver nervously. If she really was calling the cops, then they are on their way here *right this minute.*

And it's going to be awfully difficult to explain to the police who exactly these women are, why they have no ID or passports, or, really, anything that marks them as citizens of Earth...

Because they aren't.

In that moment, my already overactive imagination takes over, and I'm starting to imagine all of the ways that this could go horribly, *horribly* wrong. Like, for instance, the knights and queen (and, hey, maybe me) being detained in jail or sent to the FBI for questioning. Or what if they press charges and something terrible happens and Virago ends up in *prison* on our world because she was in the wrong place at the wrong time without any ID?

I have a *very* overactive imagination, but the terrible thing is that *any* of those scenarios are possible in this dangerous situation we're all participating in.

"Oh, my God, we need to *go*," I whisper to Virago, gripping her arm as I turn to look up at her. "Right *now*, baby," I mutter, gripping her even tighter, trying to put a tremendous urgency in my touch. Virago glances down at me in surprise, and I whisper into her ear, "I think the woman at the bar called the cops. We need to get the hell out of Dodge."

Virago nods and doesn't waste another moment. "Your Majesty," says Virago immediately, smoothly, stepping forward. Her voice lowers as she inclines her head toward the queen. "We need to go."

Calla, too, seems to understand the urgency of the situation, because she casts a single glance around the room, at all the women staring at us, at the band no longer playing, and realizes the danger this has put us in.

"Kell. Charaxus," she says immediately, pointing out a single finger. "End this immediately. We are done here."

The blade of Charaxus' sword drops, but she and Kell are still glaring daggers at one another as Virago crosses the room quickly, tapping Magel on the shoulder and helping Alinor—who's currently having a little bit of difficulty standing upright—back to the group.

"There's a back door," I tell Virago, inclining my head toward the hallway that leads to the kitchen, the restrooms...and eventually a way out to the alleyway between Queenie's and another bar, Murphy's. The alleyway perpetually smells like pee and rotten lobster, but it'll probably be the easiest way for everyone to leave this bar quickly.

"This way," says Virago, then, her voice quiet enough for all the knights to hear her, but low enough that the rest of the women in the bar do not. Blessedly, the bartender is signaling to the lead singer of the band to start up again, and she does, crooning into the microphone as the rest of her band members fall into sync haphazardly behind her, the drummer last as she drops her drumsticks and picks them up again, fishing for a new, unbroken one under her seat.

The knights and the queen fall into single file behind me and move swiftly through the bar as the music starts to fill the space. Soon we're in the bar's hallway, and I'm leading the way, my heart pounding loudly in my throat, shoving blood through my veins in a much-too-quick manner that's making me feel a little lightheaded.

We all tumble out into the alleyway as Charaxus

sheaths her sword over her head, staring with a displeased grimace at Virago. I inhale a breath of fresh air (that smells a little like pee and rotten lobsters, but then beggars can't be choosers).

"We both know that the queen would never have risked coming to another world if it was not for you," murmurs Charaxus, and she comes close enough to Virago that they're facing off, the air crackling.

"I said, *enough*," says Calla, and then she's stepping between them, a hand at both of their chests, pushing them away from one another with surprisingly strong arms. The knights oblige their queen, but it's obvious, *painfully* obvious, that there is no love lost between Virago and Charaxus.

"If you say again that I came for any other reason than my own free will, there will be consequences, Charaxus," says Calla, lifting a finger as if daring Charaxus to argue with her. The knight's lips close into a thin, tight line, and again, she surprisingly listens to the smaller, daintier woman, bowing to her wishes as Calla turns, then, bright green eyes just as sharp as she looks at Virago.

"Your rivalry is starting to impede upon your work, Virago," she says, her voice low. "Do not allow it to continue."

I blink, but—like Charaxus—Virago acquiesces to the queen's wishes and softens her gaze.

"We must leave here right now, yes, Holly?" asks Calla, turning to me with wide eyes.

I can already hear police sirens, faint but getting closer out on the street, and I stiffen, watching the red lights reflect off of the brick walls that tower overhead. We're going to be found soon—very soon.

"Um...that's not good," I mutter, glancing

behind me at the equally solid brick wall. The alleyway is a dead end full of Dumpsters, no way out other than the mouth of the alleyway and entering the club we just exited—the club that will, at any moment now, be swarming with cops.

We're trapped.

Charaxus opens a small leather pouch that's tied to her thick black belt. She reaches in with gloved fingers, and then she's holding a tiny shard of glass. She sighs and lifts her hand. "Milady," she says quietly to Queen Calla.

Calla gasps, crossing the space between them to stand close to Charaxus, looking down at the wickedly glinting, sharp bit of glass in the knight's hand. "Where did you get this?" she whispers, gazing at the black-armored knight with wide eyes. "*How* did you get this?" she asks, lowering her voice.

Charaxus shrugs smoothly, but for half a heartbeat, a small smile flits across her naturally downturned mouth. "I have no time to explain," she tells the queen softly, her tone kind, but then she glances at the rest of the knights around her, and her expression hardens. "Be ready," she murmurs to them.

"Wait, wait... Be ready for what?" I ask, stepping forward.

Charaxus gazes down at me bemusedly, as if I'm beneath her notice, but then she holds up the little shard of glass. "We will use this to open a portal between worlds and enter Agrotera once more," she says simply.

Virago glances at me with alarm. "Wait, we can't do that!" I tell Charaxus, my mouth suddenly dry. Charaxus now stares at me as if I'm a cockroach that has invaded her space.

"And, pray tell, why not?" she asks calmly. "Are we not being pursued?" She gestures to the red lights. "Is it not best that we retreat, with haste?"

"Yes, and yes. But we can't go to Agrotera right *now*. The knights... They don't have their swords," I tell her quickly.

And, more importantly, I don't have my *dog*.

I have had no chance to ask Carly or Aidan to watch Shelley for me, and I don't know how long I'm going to be gone in Agrotera. I can't leave my beloved pet in my house without food or water.

I might have to fight to the death for this, though, because Charaxus is about to open her mouth, her frown turning into an impatient smile. She's about to tell me tough luck about those swords—but Calla reaches up and gently touches Charaxus' arm.

"Charaxus," she murmurs softly. "Can you focus the portal to also be anyplace in this world?"

Charaxus sighs, lowering her gaze, but she nods. "Yes, milady," she says, almost tiredly.

"If you have the shard, it costs you nothing to return to Lady Holly's home and let her...gather what she needs to gather."

When Calla glances over Charaxus' shoulder at me, I can see the small smile flit over her face.

Does she know that I want to bring Shelley? Does she know the panic that was about to fill my heart when I realized we might be leaving Shelley alone? Something passed between us when she spoke to Charaxus.

I think Calla and I are going to be good friends.

"Yes, milady," says Charaxus, and then she glances at me with narrowed eyes. "If you would but take my hand," she whispers, proffering her gloved hand to me.

Okay, a little over a month ago, if a super-sexy lady knight had asked to hold my hand, I'm not going to lie: I would have been *all over that.* But there's something about Charaxus, something that rubs me the wrong way...

I don't know; maybe it has something to do with the *death glare* she's currently aiming at my girlfriend.

But, "Sure," I mutter, and I take Charaxus' hand.

Her grip is strong, but it's not painful (for some reason, I thought she was going to break my fingers or something), and then Charaxus is turning the shard of glass so that it catches the red, spinning lights from the police cars.

A guy on a megaphone—I'm assuming he's a policeman—is yelling back into the alleyway, "Put your weapons on the ground!"

"Oh, crap," I mutter, swallowing.

Absolutely *nothing* seems to happen for a long, terrifying moment—the kind of moment that takes an *eternity* to pass (and ages you about a hundred years in the process)—as Charaxus holds up that shard of glass and narrows her eyes, concentrating on turning the shard *just so.* It reflects a bit of light from the police cars onto the brick wall opposite us, a bit of light in the same shape as the shard...

"Cooperate," says the guy, shouting over the megaphone.

My heart is in my throat as I stare at the light on wall. I hope, hope, hope that Charaxus knows what she's doing...

One second, the tiny shard of light is just a

reflection. And the next instant, it's a a dazzling portal the size of two wide doors. It's a bright, pulsing light, just like the portal that my brother opened for Virago.

It's a *portal.*

"We go," says Charaxus, her voice low, and—still holding my hand—she prowls through the portal. I walk alongside her, every hair on my body at attention. There's an electric feeling, like there's about to be a major lightning storm, or I'm about to put my hand on a live wire. And then there's a bright flash of light, so bright and intense that, after looking at the portal itself, I'm practically blinded...

And the next instant, somehow, *impossibly*, I'm standing in my living room, and Shelley is jumping up on me, wagging her tail and peppering my face with slobbery, dog kisses. I've never smelled anything more comforting than the scent of the lavender potpourri that I keep on the coffee table, and I don't think I've ever seen anything as comforting as my beautiful dog's face. I smoosh her with my hands, crouching down and hugging her tightly.

"That actually worked?" asks Calla then, her hand to her stomach as she sags against the far wall.

Charaxus shrugs, pocketing the shard and folding her arms in front of her. "There is a first time," she says, lifting her chin, eyes flashing, "for everything."

"We almost just died," Kell tells me helpfully, with a much-too-large smile.

I hug my dog a little tighter, feeling my legs turn to Jell-o beneath me.

Chapter 4: Unexpected Guest

I'm going...

I stare down at the text I've begun to type on my phone, then erase all of the letters. I blink down at the blank screen now, and I take a deep breath.

I'm going to Agrotera.

I slowly delete all of *those* letters and roll my eyes at myself as I tap my phone against my bed's coverlet in frustration. I'm doing my best to try and think of a succinct, tactful way to say my goodbyes to my best friend and brother.

Somehow, I don't think a text message is going to cut it, but Charaxus said we have to leave *right now*—about five minutes ago.

If I survive Agrotera and get back to Earth safe and sound, Carly's *going to kill me* for this.

I start typing gingerly, wincing. *I'm going to Agrotera. Everything's fine.* I stare at the blinking cursor after the word *fine,* and I know that's not *exactly* true... I mean, Virago has been asked to return to Agrotera to protect the queen from assassins, so everything isn't *fine.* But I don't want to worry Aidan or Carly more than is necessary. I type a little more and stare at my phone. *I'm sorry I have to go so quickly. I should be back...*

And that's when I stop typing and realize I have no idea when I'm going to be back.

And a teeny, tiny best-left-unnoticed part of me

wonders if I'm *ever* going to be back, considering the fact that this new world is apparently full of monsters, cannibal werewolves and, you know, *Charaxus.* I shudder a little and sigh.

I opt not to type out any details and stick with *I should be back soon. I love you!*

I send the text immediately to Carly and my brother, Aidan, and I stand up, dragging my much-heavier-than-an-airline-would-allow suitcase off the bed. Thank God I'm not traveling on an airline, I guess.

I'm about to set my phone in the center of the bed, leaving it here in the house—I doubt I'll get good reception in another world, and there's certain to be no plug where I can recharge, so why bother taking it?—when it *dings* with a received text.

I scoop it up off the coverlet, just as Virago trots up the stairs and strides down the hallway toward our bedroom. She's already fully dressed in her leather underclothes and her armor, with her sword's scabbard strapped to her back. Her hair is done up in its tall ponytail, the wolf's tail tied to it with a leather thong and draping gracefully over her right shoulder. Her knight's moon necklace glitters at her throat.

"We must leave, my love," she says, standing in the doorway and leaning against the frame. "Are you ready?" Her eyes rove over all of the open dresser drawers, all of the dresses and skirts and blouses, and—let's be serious—every piece of clothing I own spilling out of my closet as if a very irate Tasmanian Devil whirlwinded his way through the place.

Looking at the mess, I'm worried for the umpteenth time that I didn't pack everything I needed...but that's the age-old worry for any trip, right?

It's just a little more worrisome when you're visiting another world...

"Yeah, I'm ready," I murmur to Virago, and she crosses the room to take my suitcase and carry it downstairs for me.

With trepidation, I slide the unlock screen on my phone, and I open the text I just got from Carly.

It reads:

*WAIT WHAT YOU'RE GOING TO AGROTERA? WTH? **WHEN?***

Yeah, that's pretty much what I expected.

I type back quickly:

We have to leave right now. I'm so sorry, Carly—we have to go. I love you!

Instantly she texts back with:

OMG, BUT...BUT...

And then, a second later.

I love you, too. Please be safe.

And it's *that* that causes the tears to stream down my face as I hold my phone to my chest and wonder if I'll ever see my best friend again.

I wish she'd texted back with a joke. Like, "Bring me back a baby dragon egg!" (I have no idea if Agrotera has dragons) or, "You're going to be the first human to have sex on *another planet.* Do you realize you're making history?"

Or she could have texted back with something angry. I could totally deal with anger. But what if this is the last communication we ever have? It seems so small, just a few words on a screen. I wish I could give her a hug; I wish she could tell me something funny and I could tell her something funny back, and then we could cry on each other and tell each other best friend mushy stuff, like, "Take care of yourself," and, "I love you."

I just saw her today, but already it seems like a lifetime ago. And now I don't know when I'm going to see her next.

And Aidan. He hasn't texted back yet. I talked to him about a week ago, and the last thing he told me? "Holly, if you love me, then please never, ever, *ever* bring your cupcakes to meditation *again*." I mean, he was joking when he said it (it's not like I baked those cupcakes; I bought them at the grocery store. But I guess that's what made it extra funny. Buying them at the grocery store *is* my version of "baking cupcakes"), but still... That will be the last thing he said to me before I vanish into another world. His last words were about bad grocery store cupcakes...

Virago pauses in the doorway, glancing over her shoulder, but then she really stops, turning to come back into the room, her brows furrowed in concern as she holds my gaze.

"My love," she murmurs, cupping my cheek with her hand and searching my eyes. "Are you all right?"

"Oh, you know...I'm just peachy," I tell her with a shake of my head, as I wipe a tear from the corner of my eye, refusing to let it fall. I try to smile at her. "I'm excited, baby. I mean, I'm *really* excited about going to Agrotera," I tell her, sniffling a little and wiping my nose on the bell sleeve of the *other* Renaissance-era costume dress I own. (I figured, what the hell. Maybe I won't stand out like a sore thumb if this is what I'm wearing on Agrotera). "It's just...Aidan...Carly..." I drift off, not really sure what to say.

Virago searches my face then, her blue gaze glittering with warmth. "Holly," she says, her voice soft and soothing as she wraps her hand at my waist, her fingers curling over my curves with a comforting strength. "You're coming back to Earth," she tells me, murmuring the words like absolute truth as she holds my gaze. "We *both* are," she tells me then meaningfully, one brow raised.

I blink, my brow furrowing as I reach up, run a nervous hand through her ponytail; her hair is satin and slides over my fingers like water. "How...how did you know that's what I was worried about?" I ask her then. She says nothing for a long moment, and I reach up and place my hand over hers, which is still cupping my cheek gently.

My eyes close, and I lean against her, breathing in the good, sweet scent of mint and the deep, dark sexy aroma of leather and metal and something a little like sandalwood, the scent of all that is Virago. She is so warm, so soft and gentle as she curves her hand on my face, her thumb gently caressing the side of my mouth. I lean into her hand, breathing out, feeling her love wash over me; I can feel that love pulsing through me like my own heartbeat. Like hers.

"I knew," says Virago, her voice dropping huskily as she leans forward, as she bends her beautiful head to meet mine, our foreheads touching, "because I know *you*. I will never, *ever* let anything happen to you on Agrotera," she tells me fiercely. "We will be gone just as long as the Hero's Tournament takes, which is seven days. In a mere seven days' time, I swear to you, by my blood and bone, you will be back safely. I *promise* you," she says, staring into my eyes, her blue gaze flashing with a fire that she saves only for me.

As I lean against her, as I take in the scent of her, reaching out and curling my fingers around her hips, too, feeling her strength and solidity...I trust her. I know she would never let anything happen to me there, or anywhere. I mean, she's my knight in shining armor, after all, and I know she's going to keep me safe.

But as much as I love and appreciate that Virago will always be there for me, protecting me when I need it...I really want to be able to fight my own fights, too.

I wielded a sword once, to keep my beloved safe, and I was completely inexperienced; I had no idea what I was doing. It could have ended very, *very* badly, but I still did it.

An idea has been circling in my head lately, and I voice it now. If we're going to be on Agrotera, it makes sense to me.

"Actually, Virago," I tell her, smiling softly as I lean against her, placing a soft kiss upon her cheek. She raises a brow and smiles down at me now, realizing that I'm about to ask for something she might not necessarily be up for. "I've been thinking," I tell her, "and I really, really want to learn how to use a sword, okay? I figure, Hero's Tournament, there's probably a lot of swords involved... I'd like you to give me a lesson or two," I say, a small grin turning up the corners of my mouth as I look up at her. "I want to be able to take care of myself," I finish.

She gazes down at me in surprise for a heartbeat; then a happy smile spreads across her face. "It would be my greatest honor to teach you the way of the blade, my love," she says, her head to the side as she gazes at me with warm eyes, full of pride. "But you know that you have already bested a beast with a sword, so you are well on your way to knighthood!"

I shiver as I think about the Boston Beast, how

I pierced it through with Virago's sword, the blade sinking into...*ugh.* Even thinking about the sensation of the blade sliding into the beast is enough to make me feel nauseated. I shake myself a little and sigh.

"Let's not start the training on big old monsters yet, okay?"

She nods at me, still smiling as she picks up my suitcase again. I look at my phone one more time; no text message or call back from my brother, which worries me. But I'm coming back home, I remind myself. I *know* I am. I'll speak to my brother again, before I know it.

So I set the phone on the center of the bed, gazing at it with nervousness before steeling my resolve, straightening and glancing around my room one last time, trying to shove down that annoying feeling that I *must* have forgotten to pack something crucial, or forgotten to do something Very Important.

I already put in a call to my boss at the library. I have about a thousand years of paid time off saved up (give or take—I never really took vacations), so she was surprised by the late hour of the phone call but was totally up for my having the week off. I'm taking Shelley with me (which is going to provide its own set of problems, but at least I won't have to worry about her tearing up the house, or herself, while I'm gone). I've brought pain medication and tampons (I'm *prepared,* dammit!), my favorite book, candy, tea, including lots and lots of chamomile, which just happens to be my favorite, and my favorite mug, the one with my brother's Pagan shop logo on it.

Um...I mean, I *think* that's everything that I need.

You know that game you play when you're kids,

the one where you wonder what you'd bring with you to a deserted island? Yeah, I kind of feel like I'm playing it for real right now. But the upside is that I know that Agrotera isn't some destitute place. I know they have tea houses and taverns, palaces and queens, and I know they have a lot of magic. Whatever I need, if I've forgotten it, they'll probably have it there.

I scoop up a piece of rose quartz that I usually keep on my bedside table. My brother gave it to me when he first opened his shop, quite a few years ago now. It's just a large tumbled stone—it fits in the palm of my hand—but its warm, pink-hued, and it feels smooth and comforting in my hand. Aidan told me, when he gave it to me, that rose quartz is specifically for love, for drawing love to you, for loving yourself... He said a lot of other stuff, but I was already fantasizing about the mystical powers of the rose quartz getting me laid that night in the bar (it did *not*), so I didn't really absorb the rest of the stone's properties.

Since then, I've joked with him about it, how it keeps me safe in car accidents (it was with me when I totaled my Buick, and the car may have been in tiny smithereens, but I walked right out of the wreck and into a Starbucks) and helps get me the job (I brought it with me on my job interview at the library), but that it has never, *ever* helped me get a girl.

But I *did* find Virago... Maybe it really does work.

I don't know; I'm certainly no magic expert. Mostly, now, I keep the stone on my bedside table, but tonight I just want to take it with me. It's something small and comforting to remind me of home in this magical new world. So I slip it into the convenient pocket of my costume dress.

"I'm ready!" I tell Virago, swallowing a little as I turn and give her a huge smile. I realize that that smile is partially ecstatic about venturing into a completely different world, and also partially terrified. I feel a little like Neil Armstrong might have felt on the rocket ride up to the moon, if said moon were populated by aliens.

"One small step for woman," I murmur, taking Virago's free hand and threading my fingers through hers. "One giant *leap* for librarian kind."

Virago raises a brow, but she's already shaking her head and chuckling as we both make our way downstairs. To her credit, she doesn't tease me about what I said at all. Which proves, for the umpteenth millionth time, that she's a keeper.

When we reach the living room, I gaze around at the assembled knights, and my heart rises in me. They're all wearing their armor and their swords, their hair tied in leather thongs (or, in the case of Kell, spilling over her shoulders, because I'm beginning to realize that Kell doesn't give a damn about *anything*. And she still manages to do awesome stuff, so, really, more power to her), their scabbards strapped tightly to their backs. The knights are lounging on the couch and against the living room wall, but it's a very controlled-looking lounging. They're ready to go, awaiting Virago and me.

I'm suddenly self-conscious at having held up the party. "Sorry that took so long," I say quickly, but Charaxus raises a leather-gloved hand, curling her fingers into a very tight fist.

"You *are* ready, yes?" she asks, her eyes sparking, her mouth set in a semi-permanent frown.

"Um, yes," I manage, swallowing again. My mouth is suddenly dry. Going through the portal from the bar wasn't that difficult, but Kell *did* say that we could have died. I didn't get any further clarification on that statement, but then again, I probably don't want any. And as Charaxus takes the little mirror shard out of her small leather pouch again, I have to wonder. Virago told me that going through portals is very difficult, and I'm going to believe her over anyone else. So what is it about this shard of glass or mirror that makes it so easy to open one?

And does opening a portal so easily come at a price?

"I would much rather we not use the relic," says Calla softly then, reaching up and staying Charaxus' hand, curling her fingers over the knight's fist. Charaxus was just beginning to use the shard of glass to reflect the light shining down from my overhead fan onto the far living room wall. But she stops now. She tenses when Calla touches her, but then Charaxus covers the shard with the palm of her other hand, hiding it from the light in one fluid motion.

"Milady," Charaxus says, searching Calla's eyes. "It costs nothing to use the relic." Her voice may be low and gravelly, but it's soft as velvet when she speaks to Calla. Calla straightens a little, lifting her head high, regal as she draws her cape a little closer about her shoulders.

"We don't know that," says Calla, lowering her voice and raising a brow. "Please. Put it away, Charaxus. We do not need the relic to return to Agrotera. It will be taxing," she says, lifting a hand as Charaxus is about to say something else, "but it would be better to use our own magics than to borrow from something we know so little about." These last words are spoken adamantly, her eyes wide as she holds

Charaxus' gaze.

Charaxus' mouth shifts into a thin, hard line, and she sighs but acquiesces to the queen, inclining her head gracefully as she pockets the shard.

"As you will, milady," she says softly.

"Come then, my fine knights," says Calla tiredly, with a small smile, as she steps forward. "We must all hold hands," she says, then, and she takes Charaxus' gloved hand in one of her own and reaches out for mine with the other. "And we will have to summon up the energy to open the portal ourselves."

Charaxus tightens her jaw again, but she takes her queen's hand, and when Charaxus glances at the queen in that moment—it's so strange. I've known Charaxus for a handful of moments, but I never would have imagined that Charaxus has the capability to be anything but hard. Still, she softens in this heartbeat, softens completely. Her ice blue eyes train over the queen and change, transforming from the purest ice to something just a little bit melted. I realize she's looking at the queen with affection. Not only respect but genuine affection.

Huh.

We're all assembled in the circle now, and the last two women to link up are Virago and me.

But as I reach across the space to take Virago's hand, that's when the doorbell rings, the *ding-dong* echoing strangely from the front hallway into the living room.

For a moment, I stand there, stricken. For all I know, it's a bunch of religious people on the porch with pamphlets, and if it *is* religious people, I can only imagine their terrified faces when I inform them that I'm a lesbian. They'd leap off the porch as if the house were on fire. This has actually happened. *Or* it could be some poor guy misdelivering a pizza. I pause in my thoughts as I realize that taking a pizza to a new world would make me a *hero.*

I should probably get the door, then.

All joking aside, I have no real idea why I'm so drawn to the door at this moment, but I really am. I need to open it. "I just... I'm just going to get that, okay? It'll take two seconds," I tell the knights, holding up a finger and turning to hurry toward the door. Admittedly, I know it's probably not the pizza delivery guy; it's probably not anyone important at all, or even anyone I know. But I just really feel that I have to answer that door.

And I know *exactly* why once I open said door.

It's my brother, Aidan. He's standing on my front doorstep, and he's smiling at me with his good-natured smile, holding out a dozen cupcakes on a pretty silver tray. The cupcakes are pink and white, and I can tell he made them himself, because they're liberally sprinkled with edible confetti in the shape of witch hats.

"Hey, sis, I thought I'd bring these over, and we could have a fun night in," he tells me with a wide grin. "I mean, I didn't know what your plans were, but I woke up this morning, and I was all like, *I need to make cupcakes and go visit my sister and her girlfriend,* so here I am! With cupcakes!" he tells me, beaming and holding the tray of cupcakes aloft.

Aidan is a witch, and—as such—he prides himself on his strong powers of intuition. Granted, these are the same powers of intuition that told him Britney Spears would become as classic as Madonna... But, often enough, my brother gets it very, very right. Like knowing that, tonight of all nights, he had to come see me.

I swallow, emotion filling me as I stare at my brother with wide eyes. "I...I can't believe you're here," I manage. "We're...about to leave. For...um...Agrotera."

My brother stares at me, and I stare at him, and then he's stepping forward, depositing the plate of cupcakes on the table beside the door. Then he hugs me very tightly. He smells of cotton candy (because my brother has a sweet tooth) and sandalwood incense from his shop, and it's one of the most comforting things in the world right now, my brother's scent and his warm hug...

I didn't expect to get choked up right now, but I am as I return my brother's hug.

"Oh, my God—are you coming back?" he asks me then, holding me out at arm's length to watch my face carefully.

I shake my head, drawing him in for another tight hug, setting my chin on his shoulder and squeezing. "Of *course* I'm coming back, silly," I tell him lightly—even though my voice comes out as choked—as I step back. "I mean, I can't imagine living without your cupcakes, so..." I grin as I take up the plate and make a big show of hiding it behind my back, like I'm about to steal it from him. I hope the gesture conceals the fact that my eyes are full of tears.

Virago peers around the corner of the hallway just then, her brows rising when she spots my brother. "Sir Aidan!" she calls out, striding down the hall to embrace him tightly, smacking him on the back with probably a bit more gusto than would be comfortable. My brother winces a little, but he still smiles at Virago, until he clears his throat, looking from me to her.

"Virago, what's going on?" he asks then, searching her face.

"My friend, I go to protect the queen of Arktos during one of our tournaments," says Virago, gripping his arm tightly in a knight's handshake. "I swear to you, I will bring your sister back unscathed after the tournament has run its course."

"Well...I mean, *unscathed* sounds good," says Aidan, turning to me then, his worried expression dissolving. "That doesn't sound so bad! Do you want me to watch Shelley while you guys are gone?" he asks me then, as if Virago just told him we were about to embark on a road trip to Provincetown, and not—you know—slide through a portal to another world.

"Thanks, but don't worry about it, Aidan. I'm going to be taking Shel with us," I tell him, grabbing her leash from the little hook on the wall. "I, uh, admittedly don't know if a new world is *ready* for Shelley," I quip, "but we're going to make the best of it. And that way you don't have to watch her, and Hex doesn't have to be a gigantic ball of hissing fluff for seven days," I add apologetically. Hex is Aidan's cat, and the moment that Shelley and Hex met, it was hate at first sight. I would never ask my brother to watch Shelley when there would be such a blood feud going on in the sacred space of his apartment.

"That's nice of you," chuckles Aidan; then he turns to look at Virago again as he chews on his lower lip. He sighs. "This is, sadly, where I have to be super macho and tell you that you have to bring my sister back safe and sound, okay?" he tells her, folding his arms in front of him and lifting a brow.

She nods seriously. "Of course. It will be my honor, sir," she says, then curls her hand into a fist and taps it gently over her heart three times. "I have sworn it to you," she says, lifting her chin. "By my blood and bone, it will be done."

"Well, blood and bone—that's all right, then!" says my brother, winking at Virago and me. "Take the cupcakes," he says, indicating the tray with a small, mischievous smile, "and you will be a hero among the knights!"

"So humble," I smile, and then I feel a great wave of emotion move through me again, and I feel tears fill my eyes—but I don't let them even think about falling. I smile at my brother before he can notice a slip of my expression... But he's too perceptive.

"Hey, be good, okay? Don't do anything crazy or super valiant or whatever," he says, stepping forward and wrapping his arms around me to give me another squeeze. His voice is thick with emotion, and I'm about to burst into tears if we don't blow this popsicle stand in the next minute.

Virago seems to sense that, too, because she inclines her head to my brother again and murmurs, "Aidan, if you could but help us... We are trying to open a portal, and who is better at opening portals but you?" She smiles widely at my brother, who rubs the back of his neck and actually *blushes.*

"You're going to make my head grow too big to fit through the door," he grins at her, "but, sure, it'd be a privilege."

"Um...there are a lot of other knights here," I mutter to him, as we all turn and go back down the hallway, toward the living room.

"What now?" he asks, but he follows us, mystified, and stops in his tracks when he reaches the entrance to the living room.

"Wow," he murmurs. "You weren't kidding."

Charaxus is standing in the center of the circle, and she is glowering as she stares at me in all of her black-armored glory. From Aidan's eyes, seeing her for the first time...I mean, she looks positively scary, frowning like that.

"If the lady is done delaying the *queen*, we might get started," Charaxus says, folding her arms in front of her as her tone conveys the sharpness of a horde of angry bees.

"I'm sorry, Your Majesty," I tell Calla at the exact same moment that the queen waves her hand at me, shaking her head.

"Don't trouble yourself, dear Holly," Calla says with a small smile. "But who is this?" she asks, gazing curiously around my shoulder at Aidan. Aidan, who is just as dwarfed as I am by these knights.

"This is my brother Aidan," I tell Calla, putting an arm around him. "And he's a witch and can help us with the portal."

"Thank the Goddess," mutters Kell, rolling her eyes. "If we had to wait for Charaxus to summon it, we'd be here until the next full moon," she murmurs, raising a brow and glaring daggers at Charaxus. Oh, great. Their feud is apparently still ongoing.

But Charaxus doesn't even bother to glance in Kell's direction. "And if the knights who were put in place to protect the queen didn't *kidnap* her and take her to another *world*, thereby placing her in *grave* danger," she says, with poison in her tone, "this portal would not even be necessary."

"For the last time..." Kell snarls, and her gloved hands are suddenly in fists, her mouth set in a savage frown. She's about to lunge at Charaxus, starting a fight, but Magel steps politely in her way and locks her arm across Kell's shoulders, barring her from leaping forward.

Being restrained doesn't appear to matter to Kell, though. She keeps talking, anyway. "We did *not* kidnap the queen, and we *have* kept her safe," she says, her lips drawn over her teeth. She reminds me of a wolf.

But Charaxus is no prey, and she actually laughs in face of Kell's anger. "Hotheaded as a pot of boiling water," she observes, her eyes glittering like daggers. "Do you really believe that your temper aids your queen in any way? Or do you, perhaps, realize that your temper might get our beloved queen killed? Like someone else we once knew."

"You go too far," whispers Kell, in the suddenly still room. Her eyes are wide, and she stares at Charaxus as if the black-armored knight just tore out her heart. Kell pales as she stares at Charaxus, but Charaxus does not back down.

"Please," says Calla then, and the word is thick with exhaustion. "Let us just return home."

Kell is staring at Charaxus as if fire is about to come out of her eyes. Charaxus is ignoring her, already done with her... But after Calla speaks, Kell's intensity dies down a bit, and she actually takes a step back, Magel's arm going slack over her shoulders. Kell turns away from Charaxus and returns to her place in the circle, and though she won't lift her eyes, and though she grits her teeth, the fight appears to have been suspended. For now.

Virago said that she and Charaxus didn't get along in knight school. And I can tell, obviously, that Charaxus isn't the easiest person in the world to get along with, even if you're as easygoing as Virago. But what in the world could have happened for there to be such a gap between these knights and Charaxus? It can't possibly be that Charaxus is Vice Queen, and therefore more powerful than them. I don't think they care about power that way, because they defer to Queen Calla with love and admiration immediately. No, it has to be something else, something I haven't been made aware of yet.

I grasp my brother's hand and Virago's now, as Aidan steps into the circle.

"Hello, ladies," he says reverently, inclining his head to the women assembled here, in my living room. "It's wonderful to meet you," he says warmly, and it's obvious that he means it. He licks his lips and smiles with chagrin then. "I, uh...I'm by no means an expert at creating portals. But I can certainly try."

"We appreciate your help, Sir Aidan," says Calla, smiling and inclining her head to him, too. "My knights and I are strong, but our strength lies in things other than magic. Your aid is appreciated."

Aidan closes his eyes then, grasping my hand and Calla's hand as he takes a deep breath. He practically inflates himself, as he's suddenly standing perfectly straight, his chest out, his shoulders back, and his chin lifted. When he speaks again, his voice is richer, deeper, stronger, and he begins to intone: "By the powers of air and fire, by the powers of earth and water, I call upon the elements to aid us this night."

Whenever Aidan gets into his witchy mode, he becomes someone else entirely. Gone is the brother who ate booger candies in the eighties; instead, he's replaced by this strong, powerful guy who I couldn't be prouder of. He has a particular cadence when he speaks the words, and I shiver a little as I feel the energy in the room shift.

"Now, please concentrate on the center of the floor in the circle," says Aidan, his voice dropping to a low whisper. "Concentrate on the center, and imagine that it is glowing with a bright...white...light..."

I take a deep breath, and I concentrate with all my heart.

And in the center of the floor, after a long, tense moment, something begins to glow.

It's odd: at first, I think my eyes are playing tricks on me. It's night, but the overhead light from the fan is very bright in the living room. My eyes *shouldn't* be playing tricks on me...but then there it is again, what I thought I saw a moment ago. A spark, floating in midair, a little like a firefly...

But then that spark starts to glow brighter, and I realize that it's really there, really glowing, about a foot off the ground, not imagined at all but *real.* It's small, this spark, about the size of a piece of hard candy, but then it grows bigger and bigger, taller than the knights now, as it grows and lengthens, growing brighter, too, as we stare at it, as we concentrate on it.

"Okay," says my brother, and though he's still intoning the words as majestically as before, I know him, and I can hear his breathless excitement. To him, this is pretty much the coolest thing in the world. Modern Pagans don't ride on broomsticks, and the magick spells they cast don't usually have such, well, theatrical results.

The glowing oval is hovering about a foot off the ground right in front of us, taller than the knights themselves in height.

"This is it!" says my brother, whispering the

words almost reverently. "I did everything just like before, so...I'm pretty sure this is a portal to Agrotera, you guys."

And, indeed, as the oval spins slowly in front of us, I start to see something through the glowing white. Something that looks a lot like trees and a meadow in daylight. And something rising over the trees...

Is that...a castle?

"Knights, assemble," says Calla, and one by one, the knights let go of each other's hands and form a line, lining right up to the portal. Charaxus is at the front of the line, which I find interesting. She must know the inherent danger of going through an untested portal, but she's the first one willing to go through. That marks her as having just as much fight as Kell, and just as much courage as Virago.

Again...interesting.

Charaxus lifts her chin, straightens her shoulders. And then she steps through the portal.

One by one, the knights step through, too, as the oval spins in front of them. One by one, they enter, until the only people remaining in my living room are me, Virago, Aidan, and Queen Calla.

I take up Shelley's leash from the coffee table and clip it to her collar. "Be good when we go through this, okay, baby girl?" I beg her nervously, and Shelley just thumps her tail against the floor, grinning up at me with her wide, collie grin as if to say, "I'm always good!" which is, in fact, a total lie. But I grasp the leash tightly and turn back to Virago.

"I will hold your hand," she tells me quietly, reaching across the space between us and taking my free hand in her gloved one. "Stay right beside me," she tells me, her eyes bright, "and it will be over in a flash."

"Take care," says my brother, then, and the words come out choked up; I think a see a tear in his eye, but I dart forward before he can say another word and embrace him tightly. One last time.

"Goodbye," I tell him, and then I turn and take Virago's hand again.

And grasping Shelley's leash, holding tightly to Virago...we step through the portal together.

Chapter 5: A Whole New World

You know that scene in *The Wizard of Oz*, when Dorothy leaves her old house—that has been plucked up by a tornado and whisked away to Oz—and she steps through the door from a grayscale world into one of amazing color? I remember watching that movie for the first time when I was very, very little, and I still remember gasping with delight when the television's screen switched from dull monochrome to vibrant, jaw-dropping color.

I realize, as I step through the portal, as I take my very first step into a whole new world, onto Agrotera...that that's exactly what's happening now.

Not that Earth was monochrome, obviously. There's color everywhere—in bright billboards and flowers and people's clothing and the ocean and sky and grass and buildings. There's color everywhere on Earth.

I guess it's just a different kind of color.

Because when I step through that portal, gripping tightly to the leash and Virago both...I actually gasp out loud.

I glimpsed Agrotera for a moment through a portal once. That's the first time that I saw Magel and the other knights, as I stared down at a meadow. It had looked just like any other normal meadow.

But nothing looks normal now that I'm actually

here.

Right now, we are standing with the rest of the knights in the middle of a meadow, just like the meadow I saw that day. The grass is a *dazzling* green and tall, up to my hips. Luscious. I reach out my hand, still gripping Shelley's leash, and, spellbound, brush my palm over the tip of one of the pieces of hay. It's soft to the touch, grazing my fingertips like a feather. There are flowers sprinkled throughout the meadow, and their color has been "turned up" so much that they're almost blindingly bright. I've never seen any of these flowers before, but there are ones that look a little similar to daisies that are bright purple, with pink centers, and ones that look a little like roses, though their stems aren't woody or thorned, their petals such an astonishing, burnished gold that I stare at them, mesmerized.

All around the meadow itself, lanky pine-like trees arch overhead, as tall as skyscrapers. What's odd is that these trees aren't as bright as the meadow. They're much taller than any trees I've ever seen, but aside from that, they look familiar, a deep, vibrant green that's beautiful, but, yeah, normal.

"What is this place?" I whisper, taking a step forward. I turn, searching for the portal, but it's not there; it's vanished.

We're in Agrotera for keeps.

For now.

Virago watches me happily, folding her arms in front of her as she glances about the meadow, taking in the flowers and grasses. The sunshine spilling down from the cloudless sky makes every golden rose glow.

"This is the Meadow of Memory," she says, inhaling deeply as she lifts her chin up. She gazes at the meadow with soft fondness as she tilts her head a little. "This is where all knights are buried," she tells me in a hushed voice.

I blink, then glance down at my feet and around the rest of the scene. There are no burial stones that I can see, no grave markers. Just astonishingly beautiful flowers everywhere. But then, it's such a serene place, the definition of hallowed ground, I think.

Calla glances around, too, her lips softly curved. "Good, good," she says, when she sees that all the knights are accounted for. "Now, let us go," she says, turning to wave her hand in a direction opposite the sun.

Over the tops of the trees, I can see a tower peeking out among the sharp pines. My heart rises in my throat, and my blood starts to rush through me in excitement as I realize what I'm looking at. The tower is built of white stone that seems to shimmer in the sunshine, and the golden roof of the tower is fluted and lovingly shaped. The architecture is exact, precise, and just gorgeous. Flapping from the post above the tower is a pennant that is a bright cobalt blue, covered in stars.

"Let us return to Arktos City," says Calla companionably to her knights.

The excitement inside of me is building to dangerously high levels as my heart rises...but then something happens that I must have imagined. I realize I'm on a magical, different world, but I couldn't possibly have just seen what I thought I saw.

Because flying right by that merrily flapping pennant on the top of the tower...

I stand there, staring, blinking, disbelieving, as I watch the flying horse zip right past the tower, pumping his wings mightily and lifting his head to neigh. His legs are arched beneath him like he's a carousel horse, and he's bright white, with a bright white mane and a long, flowing tail as soft-looking as clouds.

The horse with wings, um... It looks like Pegasus.

“Am I really seeing that?” I breathe to Virago, clinging to her arm so I don't keel over from shock.

“You *must* have those in your world, beloved,” says Virago, shaking her head and chuckling at me. “You have a picture of one hanging in your bedroom!”

“I... Yeah, we don't have those,” I tell her, finally realizing that I'm not hallucinating. There is an honest-to-goodness flying horse making circles overhead.

“Just...don't stand beneath it,” says Virago, glancing up and frowning a little. “They are quite messy.”

“Right,” I manage, and then we're moving across the meadow as the flying horse comes to land in the center of it, staring at us with suspicion before snatching up one of the golden roses and crunching happily on it.

Toto, we're not in Kansas anymore.

“It's a very short walk to the city itself,” says Calla, falling back to walk beside Virago and myself. “But I can call for the royal carriage if you're not well, dear Holly. You're looking quite flushed,” she tells me kindly.

“Oh... Oh, I'm well,” I tell her, gulping air. “I just saw a flying horse, so that was kind of weird and awesome, but I'm totally fine.” A smile breaks out over my face as I peer over my shoulder and watch that flying horse eat another golden rose, snorting and arching his wings overhead, as if he's stretching them in the late afternoon sunshine. Just like a bird would do.

"They're quite a nuisance, I'm afraid," says Calla with a small smile. "We have managed to tame a small percentage of them, but they have bird brains. They are not nearly as smart as horses or alicorns, and as such, it is difficult to train them. Ah, well, they are quite pretty to look at, no?" she says.

I nod, still speechless. What's next, *dragons?*

No, don't think about that, Holly; you'll have a heart attack.

And then Calla is moving a little quicker to walk alongside Charaxus, who is at the head of our little group, as we enter the forest beneath the cool pines, stepping onto the needles that hush our footfalls.

"Welcome to my world, my love," says Virago, putting an arm around me and squeezing tightly. The romance of the moment is truncated when Shelley sniffs at a tree and then pees against it.

I laugh a little and tug her leash after she's done, though she circles the tree again and sniffs with her fuzzy snout. "I can't believe I'm here..." I tell Virago, and then I feel a little choked up as I try to figure out how to tell her exactly what this means to me, the kid who searched her entire childhood for a portal to another world and never found one, and the adult who eventually stopped believing in magic because she lost her mother... And here it is, right in front of me, everything that I always wished for with my entire heart. A world full of magic.

Another world.

"My love," says Virago then, stepping forward and tracing the thumb of her leather glove beneath my eye to catch my tears. "I am very glad," she tells me gruffly, her voice thick with emotion, "that it means so much to you. It means so much to *me* that you are here, beside me. I love you," she tells me then, holding my gaze. "You are my beloved, and you are here, in my homeland. My heart," she whispers then, her blue gaze glittering, "is full."

My heart is full, too, as I stare up at my girlfriend, and I stand on my tiptoes, wrapping my arms around her neck. I'm about to kiss her—fiercely—when we're interrupted.

"Hey, lovers!" Kell shouts back, chuckling as she shakes her head. "We'd like to arrive in the city before next winter!"

"We're coming," Virago chuckles after clearing her throat, and I chuckle, too, kissing her lightly on the mouth before letting her go. I take her hand again, and then we walk through the quiet woods together quickly, catching up with the rest of the knights and the queen.

I'm surprised that there isn't much to the woods, and we're soon through them, stepping out from the rich loam and earth of the forest floor, onto bright white cobblestones.

I stare up at the city before me, utterly breathless.

The broad, white cobbled road that we're now standing on leads to a massive, sprawling city right out of a fantasy novel cover...but prettier, if you'd believe that. Yeah, actually, it's gorgeous beyond measure. There is a super-tall wall around the perimeter of the city that appears to be built on a hill. The wall itself, while imposing, is also decorated by carved scrollwork, an ornamentation of vines and leaves that spiral into each other all the way down the wall, drawing the eye.

There is a wrought-iron gate at the entrance of the city, where the cobbled road leads, and those gates are currently flung wide—opening up into the city itself.

At the very top of the city is what I'm assuming is the palace, with many white towers; pointed golden roofs and brightly colored pennants flap merrily in the breeze.

It's breathtaking. And we're going there *right now.*

As we walk across the cobblestones, I honestly feel like a kid again, waking up Christmas morning, ecstatic to see exactly what Santa Claus has brought me. Virago squeezes my hand, and as I look up at my knight, I catch her smiling warmly as she watches me take everything in. I'm in awe, in absolute wonder, as I stare up at the wall that we're about to pass through, at the wrought-iron gates that are as tall as some churches back home. I've never seen anything more amazing.

Well...aside from the woman who brought me here.

I glance sidelong at her, and she reaches out, wrapping her arm around my waist as she holds me close, pressing her mouth down onto the top of my head and placing a warm kiss there.

Shelley, by the way, is amazed by all of this, too—which, granted, is her usual state of being, even back on Earth. But here on Agrotera, there are even *more* interesting things to smell and try to roll in, like that bit of horse refuse lying in the street. She's trying with *all of her might* to drag me toward it so that she can sniff it. But I'm not letting her, so, instead, I pull my almost-horizontal dog (she's tugging *that* hard!) along behind me until she finds something new to smell and forgets about the horse poop.

There are some women riding horses alongside us on the cobblestone road leading up to Arktos City, and of course Shelley wants to go visit the horses and make friends. She's floundering like a fish on the end of a line, trying to get at these animals.

That's an interesting thing, actually: there are no men that I can see. Everyone else on the road with us is a woman.

"Hey," I murmur to Virago, and she glances sidelong at me, a brow up. "Are men allowed in Arktos City?"

Virago laughs then, a rich rumble. "But of course, my love," she says, shaking her head. "Arktos City is open to everyone. And you will see many men within the city when we enter it, because of the Hero's Tournament coming up," she tells me, her head to the side, "but there are not many men who *wish* to live in Arktos City. There are not many women who would couple with them there, you see." She shrugs. "People go where they are most comfortable, where they feel like they belong," she tells me now, speaking the words tenderly as she holds me a little closer. "Arktos City is my home, has always been my home, because who I am is what everyone else is there."

I nod. It makes sense. We want to go where we feel like we belong. But as Virago was talking, my stomach turned inside of me. I mean, she has every *right* to love her home city. But the way she spoke of it, the obvious love she has for this place...

How can I possibly take her away from this?

Okay, Holly, focus; now is no time to get sad about things. I can think about all of that later. I take a deep breath, and then we're stepping through the wrought-iron gates.

On either side of the gate, there are female knights wearing armor very similar to Virago's. But whereas Virago's armor is silver, these ladies are wearing armor that looks gold in tone.

The knights grin when they see Virago and the others, but the one on the right, the one closest to us, with long red hair that she has drawn up in a high ponytail, stops smiling immediately when she sees Calla. Calla has her hood up and pulled over her face, but she can't disguise her royal bearing, and some of her blonde hair is spilling out over her shoulder. The knight holds herself at attention immediately, drawing her sword and holding it at the level of her stomach so that the blade is pointed toward the sky.

Calla steps close to the knight, lowering her voice and leaning close, a gentle hand on the woman's armored forearm.

"No need to salute me, Galatea," says Calla. "I am in disguise at present."

Galatea's full mouth turns up at the corners, and then slowly, gently, she reaches up and tucks the errant piece of blonde hair that was curving over Calla's shoulder back under the hood of her cape.

It was an intimate gesture, yes, but I'm beginning to realize that most of the people in Arktos City (or, at the very least, the knights) are pretty touchy-feely with each other, and this doesn't necessarily mean anything. I'm fairly certain that's just how they are.

But still... Since I'm standing near Charaxus at this moment, I notice her reaction to the knight's gesture. And it's a very subtle reaction, but it's there all the same. Charaxus' jaw clenches when she sees this knight, Galatea, reach out with her gloved hand to tuck back the queen's hair. And Charaxus' hand, open by her side, curls into an instantaneous fist.

"Be careful, Your Majesty," says Galatea then, relaxing her posture. "There are many newcomers here for the Hero's Tournament. Should I call more knights to escort you back to the palace?"

Virago actually laughs at that, a brow raised as her mouth curls into a smile. "Galatea, you insult me," she says, but she's serious when she leans forward, her eyes glittering. "We will get the queen back safely."

Galatea winks at Virago, then nods to all of us, and we are ushered into Arktos City.

There's a lot of chaos. Maybe it's because the Hero's Tournament is in town (or maybe Arktos City is really just this populated), but there are so many people and so many animals, all trying to go in different directions on the streets. Brushing past us is a group of women in floor-length dresses that drape over their beautiful brown bodies like water running down a hillside. A little bit ahead on the road is a woman dressed in breeches and a big red coat with a cascade of lace at her throat, her hair formed into long, black dreads down her back. There are women on horses, urging the animals to trot slowly through the press of people, and women on donkeys, and...oh, my God...

"Is that..." I whisper, gripping Virago's arm. She looks in the direction of my gaze, and then she chuckles.

"Yes, beloved," she whispers to me. "That is an alicorn." She winks at me then. "But I have heard you call them *unicorns*."

And it *is* a unicorn. There's a woman riding an honest-to-goodness unicorn down the city street. As someone who grew up in the eighties, I can't even tell you what this moment feels like to me, but I'll try, because suddenly I'm full, full to the brim; an explosion of happiness just occurred in my chest.

The unicorn is about as tall as the closest horse (which is a big, heavy horse, like the Clydesdales on our world), but the unicorn is not as heavy-boned as that horse. Its bones are actually very thin, and its body is narrow and lanky. It has a long neck and a little beard spilling from its lower jaw, and hair around its cloven hooves. It looks more deer-like than horse-like, and the woman seated atop the unicorn is just as slim and fragile-looking as the unicorn itself. But I have a feeling that she's not fragile at all. She's wearing armor that looks crystalline, faceted and shining in the light, and she's wearing a crystalline helmet, too, with a long, purple plume that rests on her back. She has bronze-colored skin, and when she glances to the side, I see that her eyes are a warm, rich amber. Honestly, this whole moment is probably one of the most beautiful of my life. The unicorn proceeds in a stately fashion through the street, the woman sitting as regal as a queen upon its back.

"That's one of the challengers for the Hero's Tournament," says Magel, then, leaning forward and murmuring into Virago's ear. "She is known as Citra, and she hails from Lumina, to the east."

"Lumina," Virago breathes, her eyes wide. "I have heard stories but have never seen one of their warriors in person. Do you think she is as skilled as the tales say?"

Magel's brows are raised as she shrugs elegantly. "Who knows? But I think it is telling that they have sent a warrior for *this* Hero's Tournament, if you get my meaning."

Calla stares back, her face pale. "You...you

speak of the King of Furo coming for the tournament? That this is the reason Lumina would wish to send someone?"

Magel's mouth moves into a thin, hard line. "I am, milady. I think that people besides ourselves are unhappy with his coming to power. I think that others are also worried that he seeks to expand his lands by force. That he wants war, by any means necessary, with anyone he deems a threat. And he deems everyone a threat, I believe," she murmurs, her eyes flashing dangerously.

"War," Calla breathes, looking after the woman on the horned creature's back with unseeing eyes. "There has not been a war here in Arktos for so many cycles of seasons. It would be the first war in generations." She grows smaller, like she's deflating. "We cannot have a war," she says, shaking her head resolutely. "We must do everything we can to prevent it. Charaxus," says Calla, lifting her head to her vice queen. "When does the King of Furo arrive in Arktos City?"

Charaxus tilts her head, gazing up at the sun. "He was supposed to arrive this day," she says, her voice low. "At any time, milady."

Calla rolls her shoulders back, taking a deep breath. "Then we simply must impress him with our knights, show him that he does not, indeed, wish to go to war with such a powerful country."

Virago and Magel exchange a glance, but Charaxus is nodding, not looking back at the other knights.

"Then we must get to the palace, and quickly, so that you are ready to receive him," says Charaxus, whispering.

"Let us go," says Calla, moving forward at a faster pace now.

But before we walk a handful of steps, we're stopped—because standing in the middle of the busy street is a very angry woman.

And she's staring right at Kell.

This is starting to be a regular occurrence.

The woman standing in front of us right now looks a little different from the one at the bar, however. For one, this woman is dressed in breeches and a very sumptuous-looking brocade coat, with a big hat and feather plume on her head. Her outfit reminds me of something a French nobleman would have worn during Marie Antoinette's era. She looks, in other words, very *fancy*, with elaborately long, curled hair spilling over her shoulders, lace at her throat and wrists, and wide-buckled shoes on her feet.

She's also holding a huge sword at the level of her heart, and she's pointing it at Kell.

"Stand and face me, daughter of pigs!" the woman bellows.

"Damn," mutters Kell, then lifts her chin and steps forward, her hands open in a conciliatory gesture.

"Do I...um...know you?" Kell asks the woman brightly.

The woman, who—up until now—has sported a pretty regular, tanned skin tone, turns as red as a strawberry, her eyes going wide, her mouth falling open.

"No, you do not know *me,* you swine! You *slept* with my *wife*!" says the woman; then she waves toward a woman standing off to the side wearing an elaborate red dress with a bell skirt, the neckline so low that I can almost see the entirety of her breasts.

She's smiling warmly at Kell and wiggling her

fingers. And then, she actually winks.

"*Oh*," says Kell, and she takes a step forward, bowing low to the woman in the dress. "*Now* I remember." Head tilted to the side, Kell offers up a rogueish smile.

"*Ahem*," says her challenger, raising the sword, lifting up her other hand as she sinks into a theatrical fighting stance. "I demand retribution!" she says loudly. "I must duel you for my wife's honor!"

Kell shrugs lazily, unsheathing her sword with a *shing* of metal that echoes off of the surrounding buildings.

"You can't fight her, Kell," says Virago firmly, placing an arm in front of Kell's chest and shaking her head. Her voice drops. "She knows not what she does."

I glance at the woman in the fighting stance, and I realize she looks a little like a *painting* of someone about to fight. And, hell, I'm certainly no fighter, but I've never seen the knights look so...well, *posed.* Her feet are positioned wide apart, she's holding up her other arm like she expects a high five at any moment, and her head is thrown back so that the little bit of wind that we're getting here, between the buildings, is sweeping her curls back elegantly.

Kell glances sidelong at the woman in the dress, the woman who—if we were on our planet—would probably be mouthing, "Call me." As it is, she's leaning forward a little, one brow raised, so that Kell can have full view of her chest.

"This is preposterous!" yells the swordswoman, sinking even lower into the fighting stance. Right now, she looks as if she's squatting at the gym. "You slept with my wife! Honor has been breeched! I demand retribution!"

"Those *breeches* are about to be breeched," Kell mutters, indicating the tightness of the woman's trousers as she sinks lower into her bend. Kell sighs then, with a great amount of boredom.

"Kell," says Magel, folding her arms before her, "did you know this woman was married when you slept with her?"

Kell shrugs. "Of *course* not. I have more honor than that," she mutters, gritting her teeth as the woman with the sword starts to waggle her weapon in the air inexpertly.

"Stand and face me, knave!" the woman is shouting—and then Calla steps forward.

The queen removes the hood from her head. I didn't realize it until this moment, but Calla is wearing a slim, silver circlet over her blonde hair and brow. The effect is subtle, but as she rises up to her full height, her shoulders back, her chin lifted, it's fairly obvious to anyone watching that the queen herself is here.

The crowd around us hushes as more and more people realize Queen Calla stands among them.

"Fine citizen," says Calla then, her words smooth and just loud enough for everyone within the vicinity to hear as she steps forward. "I am so sorry that there has been a misunderstanding."

The woman actually *drops* her sword, and it clangs on the white cobblestones like a cheap prop. "Uh...ah, Your *Majesty*," she says, and she takes off her enormous hat and holds it in front of her as she performs a very sweeping, melodramatic bow. I'm not quite sure why I think it's melodramatic. Maybe because it takes about a minute to execute, and she makes little flourishes with her hands as she floats down, pointing her toe forward as if she's about to ask Calla to dance. "I am Lady Von Epsendice, your majesty. Maybe you remember me from court? I have been invited to many of your fine dinners and dances," she says, smiling hugely.

"Of course," says Calla, her smile soft. "Now, let me apologize for my knight, Kell. She assures me that she knew nothing of your wife's prior commitment to yourself when she had her dalliance, I assure you."

Kell sighs for a long moment, but then sheathes her sword and steps forward, her hands up again in a gesture of surrender.

"I apologize, Lady Von Epsendice," says Kell, gritting her teeth. "I did not meant to cause any harm. I thought your wife was unattached."

The woman in the dress, the wife in question, is about to say something, her brow furrowed, but the Lady Von Epsendice steps in front of her.

"Yes, yes, all is forgiven!" says the lady then, folding forward into another ridiculously elaborate bow. "Will we be invited to the formal banquet this night, Your Majesty?"

The words are calculated, as if she was hoping for this outcome. Well. That's pretty jerky. But Queen Calla, surrounded by all of these people, and forced to diffuse the situation, seemingly has no choice. If she wants to look good in front of her citizens, she'll have to agree to the lady's demand to come to a royal dinner party...

But Calla surprises me:

"*All* are invited to the banquet this night," says Calla, smiling as she lifts her voice and gazes around at her people, now a large crowd, surrounding us on the street. "Please, tell your friends and loved ones. This night, in Arktos City, will be a night to remember," she says, raising her arms.

There's a loud cheer all around us—even as Charaxus stares at her queen while biting her lip...and holding her tongue.

The cheering becomes a little deafening; women throw open the shutters of the windows in the nearby buildings and stare down at the proceedings, taking up the cheer, too. The roar of approval seems to spread like wildfire, and I can hear it coming from multiple streets; we're standing at a crossroads in the city right now.

Wow.

Word spreads *fast* around here.

Lady Von Epsendice is currently bright purple. I'm sure that she couldn't have predicted this outcome. And though I've known the lady for all of a handful of moments, she strikes me as the kind of person who doesn't want to associate with "lesser folks."

"It...it will be a pleasure to attend the banquet," mutters the lady then, doing a fumbling bow that is less elegant and theatrical than her previous attempt, and then she's grabbing her wife's hand and tugging the woman after her, effectively disappearing into the crowd.

"We had best make our way to the palace, milady," says Magel, a smile making her lips turn upwards at the corners as she steps forward and curls her gloved hand around the queen's elbow, shaking her head with a low chuckle. "A big evening is now ahead of us."

Calla turns back, and the smile that lights up her face just then makes me feel like I'm looking at the queen who once was...and the queen who could be again. The light that emanates from her eyes is bright enough to light up a city. "If the King of Furo thinks that war is a good idea, I can show him the women who would be fighting against him. And that, I think, will give him pause," she says, her smile faintly mischievous.

"I've got a bad feeling about this," sighs Kell, but she turns back with a grin for the queen. "Thank you for saving my rear, milady," she tells Calla, and then Kell executes a showy bow to the queen, as the other knights chuckle.

"My pleasure. But please, make certain you know who you sleep with next time, yes?" Calla tilts her head to the side as she smiles affectionately at Kell.

And, to my complete surprise, Kell actually *blushes.*

Chapter 6: Stars and Stars Forever

We arrive at the palace after a quicker walk through Arktos City than I would have liked, but—as Virago tells me—I have an entire week to explore the city, and time is of the essence right now.

So, Arktos City is *big*. It's certainly not New York City-big, but there are so many buildings and temples and shops, and the palace itself, sitting at the top of the city like a crown jewel, is enormous, with about twelve towers (that I could count, with a limited view of the skyline). All that being said...Calla just invited *every single person* in the city, from the people who live there on a daily basis to the people who have journeyed here for the Hero's Tournament, to *dinner*.

How in the world is she going to prepare for that many people on such short notice? How is she going to *feed* so many mouths? But every single time that I glance over at Calla, chatting with Charaxus or Magel, as the two knights escort Calla through the city, making a clear path for her through the crowded streets, I'm surprised to see that the queen looks calm, dignified...

If I were tasked with feeding hundreds, possibly *thousands* of people, I would probably look a little more frazzled than she does right now.

When we finally pass through the palace gates, Calla removes her cape and hood and gives them to an awaiting attendant, a woman in a long dress covered in a white apron, errant hairs flying out of her black braid. Calla runs a gloved hand through her own hair and sighs as she glances around.

We're standing in the very entrance of the palace, having just walked up the white stone steps and through the massive wooden door. The door was painted in vibrant purple, blue and silver, with five-pointed golden stars covering all of the cobalt blue areas. Past the door is a very long hallway, with a cobalt blue rug beneath our feet that stretches to the *next* set of doors. The ceiling is far above us, covered with paintings of women sitting on clouds. There are white columns all along the hall, and Gothic arched windows along the hallway letting in a decent amount of late-afternoon sunshine.

"We need to prepare for this evening immediately," says Calla, lifting her chin, her eyes flashing as if she's just been given a particularly exciting challenge, and she can't wait to confront it. "I will, of course, need a meeting with Asha. Can you arrange that, Charaxus?" she asks her vice queen.

Charaxus nods, her mouth thin, hard. "Your head cook will not be pleased with you, milady," she says wryly.

"Asha can just drag out the Cauldron of Plenty," says Calla, waving her hand dismissively. "We've used it before. I know she'll be frustrated that there's no time to present her usual gourmet cuisine, but beggars cannot be choosers. Now," says Calla, turning on her heel. She glances at Virago and me and smiles. "Normally," she tells me, taking a step forward, her much-too-big armor clanking as the maid steps forward again and begins to undo the straps at her shoulders, "Virago would stay with her fellow knights in the barracks. But this is a special occasion. And a *guest* cannot stay in the barracks. It's not seemly," she tells me, gesturing to me with a smile. "So you and Virago will stay in the far north tower guest room, Holly. My treat."

"Milady," says Virago, paling. "We deserve no special treatment."

Kell snorts. "No, no—she's giving *us* the special treatment, Virago. I don't want to lie awake at night and hear the two of you worshiping the Goddess of Love in the bunk next to mine."

This earns hearty laughter from Alinor, and Magel chuckles before hiding her mouth behind her hand as Virago sighs, a single brow arching.

"That you would think that I should ever be so crass," she begins to tell Kell, but then Kell is shaking her head, chuckling.

"It is good that you have found your lady," says Kell, glancing sidelong at me with a smirk. "And we are glad of it. But take the queen's offer. It is given in kindness so poor Holly doesn't have to sleep on a bed of straw. And it is a kindness to us, yes, but it is a kindness to you, too, so your *virtue* may remain unchallenged, and you need not revere the Goddess of Love in our presence." Kell sticks out her tongue at Virago, and Virago laughs.

Calla is chuckling, too. "That may have been *one* of my considerations, yes," she says, and when she glances at me now, she looks almost wistful, as if she's remembering something she once had... But the expression fades in a moment, when she turns back to Charaxus. "I must meet with my head cook, Asha, now," she calls to us over her shoulder. "Virago, I know you know where the room is. Please go to it, with my compliments. And visit the court seamstresses, will you?" With that, Calla's all the way down the long hallway and gone around a corner.

Magel rocks back on her heels, a brow raised. "The banquet will be soon. We must get into our best armor."

Virago glances down at herself and shrugs. "I must go in this, I'm afraid. My best armor is in the barracks, and I haven't time to change."

"You don't need to win a pretty girl, anyway," says Kell with a chuckle. "You already have one!"

"Go show your pretty girl to your rooms," says Alinor, thumping Virago on the back as the three knights turn, ready to leave us. "We will meet you at the banquet?"

"I look forward to it," says Virago, touching her forehead with her two first fingers and tipping her hand forward in a small salute. The knights leave, and then Virago is weaving her arm through mine as I try to convince Shelley that she doesn't want to go after the maid who just took off down the hallway.

"Let us go," says Virago companionably, and we begin to walk through the palace of Arktos City.

The maid may have already scampered off down the hallway, but coming back down towards us as quickly as her feet can move her is another woman. Her black hair is done up in a set of elaborate braids that spiral and build themselves into a rather impressive bouffant on her head. She is wearing a waistcoat, vest, white shirt with lace at the throat and wrists, and breeches that end in leggings and buckle shoes. She bows, and when she stands back up, her smile is dazzling.

"Milady Holly?" she asks, holding out her brown hand to me. I take it, and then she's shaking it vigorously as her smile deepens. "I am Joy, head tailor and seamstress to Queen Calla, and she told me to see you right away to procure an outfit for the banquet this evening."

I'm a little dismayed as I look down at myself and realize that my Super! Clever! Plan! to wear a cheap Renaissance costume dress didn't go over so well, but Joy is watching me, taking a step back as if to get a better look.

"No, you look fine, lovely," she tells me, her voice warm and soothing, as if she could read my thoughts, "but the banquet will be a fancy affair. Right, Virago?" Joy asks, winking. Virago takes a step back, holding up her hands.

"Right," says my knight with a chuckle. "Joy used to be a knight, Holly," she says then, grinning at the woman who has taken a little cloth measuring tape out of her sleeve now and is kneeling in front of me, measuring and making strange faces as she mumbles numbers. "But the call of the cloth was much more interesting to her than sword fighting," says Virago with a shrug. "So, after ten years of carrying the sword...she put it down in exchange for a needle."

"Wow, that's pretty cool," I tell Joy as she asks me to lift my arms from my sides. Shelley chooses this exact moment to pepper the woman's face with kisses, which Joy takes in stride, petting Shelley's head absentmindedly as she rises and finishes my arm measurements.

"It's never too late," says Joy, her eyes twinkling, "to be what you might have been. Now, stand up straight, please."

I feel a little self-conscious, letting this woman measure me in what is, effectively, the palace's foyer, but I acquiesce, and the measuring is over in another minute. Joy tilts her head to the side as she counts something on her fingers now, her eyes taking on that distinctive far-off look as she drapes her measuring tape over her shoulders and straightens, tugging on the arms of her coat with a flourish.

"Your room is in the north-most tower?" she asks for clarification, and I nod with a small shrug.

"I...think so?" I mutter, and glance at Virago, who nods.

Joy holds out her hand to me and smiles widely. "All right, then! Hold on tightly, and close your eyes."

Virago steps forward at that moment and takes my hand, which also grips Shelley's leash, and I awkwardly take Joy's hand, too.

And everything around us...changes.

Honestly, it's as if the hallway we were just standing in had been painted on a theater's backdrop, and the backdrop fell away to reveal an entirely new room. Because one moment, we are standing in the front hallway of the palace, and the next, we're standing someplace else entirely.

"Wow," I breathe, spellbound.

We're in a tower room; I can tell because the ceiling slants upward, and in the very center, it rises into an inverse point. To our right is a cozy bed with a bright blue canopy, and a cobalt-blue duvet covered with embroidered golden stars. Across from the bed, there's a fireplace made out of the same white stone as the cobblestones on the streets of the city, and in the fireplace, a fire roars merrily away. Around the edges of this circular room, there are bookshelves built to hug the curved wall, crammed with many old, bound books.

"All right, let me see," says Joy, stepping quickly across the sumptuous, cobalt-blue rugs to stand in front of the wardrobe that's situated next to the fireplace. The wardrobe is tall and ornamented, with carved vines and stars trailing down the warm, honey-colored sides. She throws open the doors to reveal a completely empty wardrobe.

Joy glances at me over her shoulder and looks me up and down. "I must ask this, though I think I already have a sense of your style," she says, her mouth turning upwards at the corners. "But do you dress like a knight, a lady, a lady knight, or somewhere in between all of those?"

"Um..." Perplexed, I glance down at myself. "I like dresses, mostly," I tell her.

"Lady it is," Joy tells me, and she closes the wardrobe. She's holding tightly to the door handle, and she bows her head. For a moment, I think something's wrong, but then Joy snaps her head back up, and she opens the wardrobe doors, dramatically flinging them wide.

The wardrobe is no longer empty but *filled* with dresses.

Joy turns back to me. "I would recommend a dress that compliments your hair," she tells me, tapping the side of her nose, "but then, anything in there should do nicely. My work here is done," she says, with another bow. "I will see you at the banquet?"

"But...but...how did you..." I step forward, reaching out toward the dresses in the wardrobe. My fingers pass over a silky skirt, and the fabric—color-shifting from red to orange, and back to red in the firelight—is so soft and smooth that it makes me shiver to imagine wearing something so beautiful.

Joy leans forward and smiles at me as she shrugs. "*Magic*," she whispers. Then she nods to Virago and me, and—in an instant—she disappears.

I let out a very long breath, and I glance around, just to make sure Joy is really gone and that I didn't just imagine it.

"Well, that was...weird. And very, *very* cool," I tell Virago, who smiles at me as she kneels down, unclipping Shelley's leash from her collar. Shelley bounds around Virago and then makes a beeline for the bed, leaping up onto it, twirling around three times like the wonderful, neurotic dog that she is, and then curling up into a tight ball at the foot.

"Try on one of those dresses," says Virago, then, indicating the wardrobe. She sighs tiredly, and she reaches up to her chest to unbuckle the sword belt that hangs from her back. "Any of those will look lovely on you," says Virago, her smile small and earnest as she gazes at me with soft eyes. "Joy does impeccable work."

"Did she use magic to get us from the front hallway to here? And to just make these dresses appear out of thin air?" I ask her, mystified, as I set Shelley's leash down on a small, ornate table by the side of the bed and cross the room to the open wardrobe. "Because, if she did, that's pretty kick-ass and amazing, and I think I may need a lie-down to process all of this soon." I reach out again and finger the material of another dress, this one bright, emerald green. It's as sumptuous and soft as velvet, but it isn't *quite* velvet, so it's not heavy in my hand. I let the skirt fall from my fingers, putting my hands on my hips to stare at the contents of the wardrobe with wide eyes.

"Of course she used magic," says Virago, letting her sword sheath fall onto the bed. She takes off her leather gloves and sets them down beside the sword; then she reaches up and begins to undo the leather thongs that connect the armored pieces over her shoulders. "Magic is... Well, it is everywhere here. It is used for many things. Small transportation spells, like you just experienced, and then transformation spells, which Joy performed upon the wardrobe." Her chest piece falls off in her hands, and she lets the back piece fall back onto the bed, setting the chest piece gently beside it. She removes her metal shoulder pads, and the metal bits around her upper arms, and then she's taking off her leather boots and letting the metal fall from her thighs as she undoes her armor's ties.

I turn back to Virago, suddenly inspired. "You told me once," I say, with a small smile, "that your magic on earth was much less powerful because you were on a different planet. If Joy just did all that... Well, what can *you* do here?"

Virago's brows go up, and she glances at me in surprise. She's now standing before me in just her leather pants and her leather shirt, and as I look at her, a little thrill of heat runs through me.

God, she's beautiful.

Virago thinks for a long moment, her hands on her hips, and then she smiles a slow, seductive smile.

"I can do things like this," she murmurs, her voice low, and then she's taking a step forward and wrapping her fingers around my waist, drawing me to her. All around us, something seems to shift and change, because...

Well, I know it's impossible, but we're suddenly surrounded by stars.

I remember going to the Hayden Planetarium when I was a kid. They had this show where you sat in a circle and looked up at the ceiling, and the stars and galaxies were projected on it a little like it would appear if you were out in space, gazing at all of the wonders around you. I'll never forget that moment; I was breathless, staring up at the badly focused projection, dreaming of the other worlds out there. It was one of the most magical moments of my life. Because, yes, I couldn't find the door to Narnia, no matter how hard I tried looking for it, and I couldn't get to Middle-earth, but staring up at those stars, projected flatly on the ceiling above my head, I wondered if there *were* other worlds with other people out in that great, big universe. Maybe even worlds with magic. It sustained my faith in something bigger than me.

Here and now, there are no stars badly projected on a ceiling; there are stars *swirling* around us, right alongside us, dazzling and white-hot, amorphous, taking my breath away. There are shooting stars orbiting us slowly; wide, bright galaxies with whorls of color pouring out of the hearts of stars; all miniature, all moving around us as if they're real. I actually reach out to touch a shooting star that soars past us, but my fingers drift right through it.

"It's just an illusion," Virago whispers into my ear, her breath hot against my skin. "I am not good at magic. I can only do small spells, but this is one I thought might please you."

"Please me?" I repeat, turning back to her, tears standing in my eyes. "It's so *beautiful*," I breathe, and then I wrap my arms around her neck and pull her down toward me. "*You* are so beautiful," I tell her.

She smiles a little, and then I capture that warm

mouth with my own as galaxies spin around us, as molten white stars explode into being, infinitesimally smaller than they are in real life, but here and now, they are tiny and perfect, an illusion created entirely for me.

Heat rises in my body, and I'm suddenly feeling everything: the fact that we're on Virago's world, the fact that Virago is here, with me, in a magical tower in a magical palace in a magical city...

Who knew that all of this would turn a fantasy nerd on *so much*? But, yeah, it does. And I'm pressing tighter against her, then, letting my fingers stray under the collar of her leather shirt. I can feel Virago moving against me, too, know that the heat of desire is rising inside of her, fueling her to grip my hips with tight fingers, to growl a little against me as her kisses travel down to my chin and my neck, her mouth molten against mine, igniting a white-hot need until I feel like a star myself...

But that's where she stops.

"No...no...don't stop," I mutter, arching up against her, but Virago is leaning away from me, her cheeks flushed, her mouth wet, her lips swollen from her hard kisses, her eyes dark with longing.

"We... We can't. The banquet is happening so soon," she murmurs regretfully, and she's right. From somewhere outside of the open windows, I can hear shouting and cheering coming from far below, in the city streets. The sun is sinking toward the horizon lower and lower, almost touching the edge of the world now, and if I remember correctly, the banquet was supposed to start at sundown.

I moan a little in frustration, and then I shake my head slowly, licking my lips. "Okay, fine. But seriously," I murmur, breathless, adjusting the collar of my bad costume dress as Virago takes a step back, raking her hand through her hair and trying—and failing—not to look at me with her wanting eyes. I swallow a little and feel the electricity crackling between us as the galaxies begin to wink out of existence. "We need to get down to business after the banquet," I murmur to her. "Because, new world, new bed...I mean..." I drift off with my brows raised, and then Virago glances at my face and laughs as she adjusts her ponytail.

"Do not worry," she tells me, her voice low enough to cause me to shiver. "I will have you," she growls then, laughter halting as she steps forward, as she stands so close to me but doesn't, *maddeningly,* touch me, "very, very soon," she breathes, her eyes glittering.

For a long moment, we stare at one another, close enough to touch, but not touching at all, and power—scintillating, raw power—radiates, pulsing, between us.

"I'll have you, too," I whisper, laughing a little more high-pitched than I intended, but that impish smile on her face sends heat through me almost more than anything else she does. There's a promise in that smile. It ignites something inside of me, like a spark.

"You should change," says Virago, lifting her chin as her eyes still glitter. She arches a brow, too. Then she turns around and walks back to the bed, sitting on the edge of it, leaning back on her hands as she crosses her legs. "And I," she rumbles, her eyes burning into me, "shall watch."

My breathing is coming a little fast as I look at the wardrobe, and then back at my gorgeous girlfriend, sitting on the edge of the bed, leaning back like she's in the most comfortable position in the universe, like she could sit there all day, waiting for me to disrobe.

Well, she's not going to have to wait that long.

I really have no self-control when it comes to Virago. Virago has gobs and *gobs* of self-control about everything...but it's like she has *extra* self-control when it comes to me. Being a knight probably helps with that. I mean, I'm the kind of woman who, if I even *think* about a drink from Starbucks, it's in my hands before the end of the day. If I want pizza, I get pizza. I'm not really into denying myself anything.

But Virago is different. She told me a few days ago that the longer you wait for something, the more delicious it is when you attain it. It helps me understand her better, that she can wait, patient, controlled, until the perfect moment.

Also, I've learned that waiting and teasing has a pretty profound effect on sex, by the way.

Like right now. This cheap costume dress is actually a little itchy (it was just meant to be worn for a Halloween evening), so I reach up and undo the polyester corset while keeping my eyes trained on Virago.

I'm not the world's most sexually confident person; I'm actually pretty awkward about things if I'm not already on the bed or in a darkened room. I tend to get a little self-conscious, too. But Virago has brought out something in me that I never really thought I'd have before. It's as if I can finally see myself clearly through the lens of her loving eyes. Maybe I *was* sexy all these years, but my girlfriends didn't bother to ever mention it. Or maybe I wasn't sexy to them, but I am to Virago.

Either way, I can feel it in myself now, this newly awakening confidence that gives me the courage to do stuff that, a few months ago, I would have thought was utterly crazy.

Like what I'm about to do right now.

I turn around, my heart racing, to look over the dresses in the open wardrobe that Joy magicked into being. Okay—after that amazing show of stars and galaxies in the room, and realizing that the flag of Arktos is cobalt blue with golden stars on it...that dress on the end, of cobalt blue velvet with embroidered gold stars, *that's* the one that I'll be wearing to the banquet.

Taking a deep breath, I turn back to Virago. And with my undone bodice, I slip the over-layer of my dress off of my shoulders and let it pool on the floor at my feet.

I am now only wearing a chemise, a plain, white dress that's see-through, and because a bodice is always tight and designed to support your breasts, I'm not wearing a bra.

I know I'm blushing as I reach up and undo the tie that keeps the chemise's neckline gathered. Virago is watching the motions of my hands with glittering, hooded eyes, and as I pull gently on the cord that's tied in a bow, she licks her lips.

She may be lounging back, like she hasn't a care in the world, but I know her well enough to spot her "tells." Like when she's trying to appear nonchalant about something, her thighs and calves tense, as if she's about to rise up in an instant. Her arm muscles flex, too, and it's subtle, spotting these muscles tensing beneath her leather clothing, but I can see it all the same.

She's watching me very closely right now. *Very* closely. So I might as well make this good.

I hook my fingers around the neckline of the chemise, and I tug it down gently, smoothly. The gather of the neckline begins to loosen as the cord gives way, and the neckline—which can be tied to be super revealing, scooped around your shoulders, or not revealing at all, tied tightly around your neck—grows wider. The fabric slides over my shoulders, and I can't help it—I shiver *again* as I glance up at Virago, at her darkening eyes and the way she's watching me, so closely, her breath coming fast.

The fabric falls down to my chest, and then I pull it all the way off. And the chemise flutters to the floor, pooling around my feet in a circle.

I'm wearing my Supergirl underwear, with the big “S” logo front and center, which makes this moment a little less dramatic, but Virago always likes these panties, and her mouth curling up at the corners as she watches me place my hands on my hips, tilting my head to the side, is utterly priceless.

The moment lingers, and I'm highly aware of the little things right now. Like the fact that my chest is rising and falling quickly—and drawing Virago's gaze. That her smile gets more sultry as she tips her head back, as she grins at me. Electricity crackles between us as I turn away from her slightly, taking the gown out of the wardrobe.

I'm not really sure how to get into it, but I hold it over my head and go up through the skirt, like most dresses that don't have a zipper or fastener (that I can see). But when it pools down over my arms and settles over my chest and waist, I realize that there's corseting in the back...and that Virago needs to do it up, since I certainly can't reach around behind me.

I bite my lip a little and smile at my girlfriend, who has just realized my predicament.

“Could you do me up?” I ask her, my head to

the side as she rises smoothly, prowling across the space between us.

"My pleasure," she whispers, placing her hands at my hips and turning me purposefully. I move as she directs me, and then I'm standing there, my back to her; she gathers the corset laces in her hands.

This dress is beautiful, majestic. There is an ornate mirror hanging on the doors of the wardrobe, so I can see how the dress was magically made to fit my shape. The gown has a scooped neckline and lies off the shoulder, with the arms beginning over the edge of my biceps with puffed organza sleeves. The corset part of the dress is heavily embroidered with golden stars, but the voluminous skirt, a different material from the velvety upper part, is made of gauze-like fabric, peppered with tiny, golden stars that have been sewn into the mesh material. Some people call these types of dresses "cake toppers," because you essentially look like an enormous bridal cake decoration, but you know what? This dress is *awesome.* I have never had an occasion in my life to wear one like it, and I'm enjoying the hell out of this.

I'm also enjoying the look that Virago is giving me in the mirror.

She's staring down at me, which makes her eyes appear even more hooded than before. Her mouth is parted, just a little, and I can see her shoulders rising and falling gently but quickly; she's breathing hard as she holds the corset laces in her hands, as she stares down at my bare neck and shoulders.

I tilt my head to the side, let my red hair fall over the other shoulder, so that the curve of my neck is perfectly available to her, my mouth turning up at the corners as my own breathing increases, as Virago bends forward...

And she places one soft, hot kiss at the curve of my neck.

And then she begins to tighten the corset.

I've worn corsets to most Renaissance festivals, and, yeah, they're not that comfortable, but people nowadays would *never* tighten the corset as much as people in historical periods did (I mean, *some* people do, but that's their prerogative). I don't like tight corsets, because I enjoy doing things like breathing and having normal-shaped organs inside of me. Virago knows this, so she does the laces up carefully, and just tight enough where my breasts are cradled by the bodice of the dress and my waist is accentuated, but I'll still be able to sit down and eat. When she's done, she completes the final knot and tucks it into the top of the corset, so that the bow of the laces isn't visible.

Outside, trumpeting is beginning to sound. I glance out the window, and the gorgeous, golden sun is just beginning to dip below the horizon.

It's time.

In the bottom of the wardrobe, there is a handful of ribbons in colors that complement or outright match the dresses above them, so I scoop up a cobalt blue one, weave a quick, thick braid of my hair and tie the ribbon high within the braid. Then I turn to look at Virago.

"Ready?" I ask her breathlessly.

Virago nods, and then she takes a step back.

She was just wearing her leather clothes before, the undergarments that are necessary beneath the armor so that she's fully protected. But now, growing over her leather shirt and pants is something else entirely.

At first, I think my eyes are playing tricks on

me. The stars and galaxies have slowly dissolved away to nothingness in the room, but when I glance at Virago, I wonder if they're back. But no—there's light coming over her form, but this isn't the illusion of stars spiraling out over her torso. This is living armor, growing and morphing and changing, made of molten metal that elongates and actually *grows* over her, like silver vines and leaves rising up out of the earth to scale her.

When the process is done, Virago lifts her chin, takes up her scabbard from the bed and places it on her back, doing up the buckle over her chest with nimble fingers before turning back to look at me with a smile, opening her arms.

"What do you think?" she asks.

I step forward and touch the spiraling armor that now covers her. It moves seamlessly with her, and unlike the stars and galaxies before, I can actually touch this armor. It's *real.* And it's beautiful. It looks completely organic, and like it would protect her better than her normal, knight armor would. "That's amazing," I tell her simply.

"I was just going to wear my old armor," she explains, gesturing to the armor lying on the bed, "but I decided to use a bit of magic for this," she says, shrugging her shoulders a little. "It's important," she tells me, her eyes far off as she gazes out the window now, "that the knights leave a good impression on everyone who will be at the dinner." Her jaw is tight now, and she's no longer smiling as she gazes down at the crowds of people below, visible through the open window.

I reach out and touch her arm, and warmth flickers back into her eyes as she smiles at me. "Well," she says, clearing her throat, "let's go." Virago pets Shelley behind her ears. My dog is sprawled out on the bed, and she gives a halfhearted wag of her tail before going back to sleep, closing her eyes and beginning to snore contentedly, her tail occasionally flopping as she dreams.

Virago takes my hand, twining her gloved fingers through mine, and we leave the room, ready or not for this party on another world.

Chapter 7: Not Your Average Dinner Party

We go down and down and down about a hundred flights of stairs, each set of steps growing progressively wider than the last. We pass by floors filled with large, ornate doors, and then floors with even taller hallways, until finally I *assume* we're on the floor that houses the banquet hall, because the ceiling is so far above me... But, nope, there's still one more floor to go, and, seriously, I think the *Titanic* could have fit into this hallway quite nicely.

When we start to go down the final staircase, spiraling down, down, I'm staring at the people below in shock.

That's...a *lot* of people.

Think Times Square in New York City on New Year's Eve. The place is *that* packed, but everyone's milling about orderly, and pretty much everyone has a goblet of some kind in hand, filled with different-colored liquids.

Speaking of different colors, there are so many bright things to draw the eye, from the hats and coats to the enormous dresses, to the glinting armor in every type of metal I can imagine—and then, *wow,* some I totally never could have. The woman from before, the one riding the unicorn in the crystalline armor, is probably down there, or at least someone who looks like her, with her crystal armor capturing the light from the chandeliers covered in candles, throwing the fractured prisms of light up to the ceiling.

The large hallway below branches out to different hallways, and as we reach the floor level, I can see this hallway opening up to the massive banquet hall.

Far, far ahead of us is the banquet hall itself. On a dais, overlooking the crowd, is a single, long table positioned lengthwise to the wall behind it, with Queen Calla sitting at the very center. I know it's Queen Calla because she's wearing a large crown that I can make out from this far back, and her blonde hair is loose, falling over her shoulders and the front of her dress.

I also know it's Calla, because, beside Calla, standing on her right, is Charaxus, conspicuous because of her height and her black armor. I don't have the best view (seriously, you could fit a football stadium in here without any problem), but Charaxus appears to be bending to the queen and whispering something into her ear.

"Come," says Virago, placing a protective arm around my waist. "The knights have a table near the queen."

I see that there are many long tables as we move through the press of people. It seems that almost everyone is already drunk with whatever they have in those little goblets in their hands.

"That's Magin," says Virago, indicating the goblet of the woman nearest to us. The woman herself is wearing an overly large, awesome hat with about a billion different-colored feathers sticking out of it. She's saying something unintelligible to her companions, slurring the words.

Virago smiles at me. "Magin is our drink of choice at gatherings, because it intoxicates quickly, but it also filters out of your body quickly, leaving no side effects," she chuckles. Virago picks up a goblet from the tray of a woman walking by, and she hands the glass to me. "Would you care to try it?"

What the hell. This is research, right? I'm the first person from Earth to visit another world. If I don't partake of the local cuisine...

Oh, who am I kidding? I'm just really, really curious about what a magical beverage tastes like.

I sniff the contents of the goblet as we keep walking through the crowd, and I'm captivated. There are so many notes to the scent of this liquor: the first is something citrusy. I can't quite place which citrus fruit, but I realize they probably wouldn't have the same fruits here on Agrotera that they have on Earth. Then, spiraling over that citrus note is the rich, decadent darkness of chocolate, followed by a bright inhale of vanilla.

Virago smiles at me as I close my eyes, as I tip the goblet back and take the first sip.

The scent of the drink was very strong, but in my mouth, it's an explosion of flavor. I swallow it down, relishing the citrus that merges so beautifully with that chocolate—the best chocolate-tasting thing I've ever had in my life, by the way, and I've always considered myself a chocolate connoisseur. The mellow blossom of vanilla finishes out the array of tastes with a flourish. I gasp as I swallow it, and then I open my eyes, staring up at Virago.

"I've never tasted anything like that," I breathe to her, and Virago smiles at me, taking the goblet from my hand and setting it on another tray that whirls by and is whisked away.

"A warning: the effects should take hold in a moment or two," she tells me as we continue across the floor. "But you didn't drink that much, so you should be fine."

I nod and thread my arm through hers, glancing up at the chandeliers above us. They're enormous, each one with dozens of fluted, metal arms supporting candles that illuminate the hall with a warm, golden light. There are also orbs of light around the edges of the wall, about knight-height (definitely above my head) that seem to just hover there. There is nothing that connects them to the wall; the golden orbs simply hang, suspended from nothing, making the perimeter glow.

Because the room is so well lit, I can easily take in the splendor. There are about twenty long tables (one woman sitting at the end of one table is *screaming* at someone at the *other* end of the table, and said person keeps yelling back "What? Huh? I can't hear you!"), all with cobalt blue table runners shot through with embroidered golden stars, adorned with blue flowers in tall silver vases. Many people are moving to sit down at these tables now, but there are still plenty of bystanders milling about, waiting—I suppose—to see what's going to happen.

Queen Calla stands up at this moment in a smooth unfolding of her body, and the entire room, surprisingly, falls into silence, as if everyone is holding their breath. You could hear a pin drop in the sudden hush.

"Welcome, one and all!" Calla calls, lifting up her arms and smiling at the assembled mass, her voice carrying throughout the room. "Please enjoy our banquet. You are very welcome here," she says, and then she sits back down amidst thunderous applause as, somewhat behind her and to the right, two massive double doors open wide, and people come out bearing silver trays of food, carried high over their heads triumphantly.

I wouldn't be startled right now if inanimate objects started to sing about "being our guest," because the servers move through the doors as if they're dancing, and music starts up—though I don't know where it's coming from. I can't see a string quartet anywhere in the crowd, but the music sounds live. The servers, all women, colorfully dressed in costumes with flowing cobalt veils attached to their shoulders, bring these plates of food to the tables and dance away.

More and more women bearing more and more food enter the hall. It's a never-ending line of strange-looking dishes, some of which I might actually be brave enough to try. I *did* just down another world's booze, after all. Some of the concotions look like rice, and some look a little like pasta, and there are vegetables for *days*, and fruit (I think it's fruit?) cracked open and formed into the shapes of different animals, all brightly colored and delicious-looking. There are pies and cakes and puddings and tarts, and as a server walks by with something that looks like a pot of tea, I cave and wave her down, asking for a cup.

"Here you are, milady!" she says, pouring the tea out with a theatrical flourish and handing me the cup with a wide smile. "Enjoy!"

I peer down into the cobalt blue china cup and stare at the tea: it's actually *glittering*. And it smells glorious, like blueberry green tea.

"Ah, you'll like that," says Virago with a smile, before her brow furrows a bit with worry. "Are you feeling the effects of the Magin yet, my love?"

"No, I feel *great*," I tell her, sipping at the tea and sighing happily. "Oh, my God, that is so good."

"I'm glad..." Virago begins, but then she trails off, lifting her face, eyes wide. I've never seen her look like that before. I set the cup back down on the table, my mouth suddenly dry.

There's a grimness that comes over her face, a frown so deep and dark that it gives me a chill.

And again, suddenly, the room is silenced. It's shocking, as if an entire movie theater's worth of sound is immediately cut out. I follow the direction of Virago's gaze, searching throughout the room, trying to figure out what could possibly have happened to make everyone stop talking, stop laughing, stop partying...

All heads, including Virago's, are turned in only one direction, and it takes mere seconds for me to see what caused the hush.

At the entrance to the dining hall stands a man. But this isn't just any random man off the streets. This guy is wearing a massive, thick fur coat, stands just as tall as the knights (which, you know, is a feat in and of itself), and on top of his head, he wears a crown. It's scary-looking, that crown, because it appears to be made of several hundred nails that were slightly melted, oozing together and then forced into a crown-like shape. He has long, black, wavy hair, and his expression...

God, he's terrifying. He has bright blue eyes, a long, wolfish nose and a scowl that seems to be the result of him trying to suppress an outright snarl (it's not working).

As he lifts his chin, as he strides into the room with several black armored men (their armor looks a whole hell of a lot like Charaxus' black armor) falling into line behind him, I can see Calla at the front of the room standing genteelly, folding her hands in front of her but lifting her chin, eyes flashing.

Calla is no pushover.

I realize, at this moment, that this is probably that king that everyone's worried about, and I find out I'm right when Virago leans close to me, her lips brushing against my ear as she whispers, "This is the king of Furo, Charix," she tells me, her voice hard and flat; I've never heard her sound so unhappy.

I look up at her, eyes wide, and I whisper the very first thing that comes into my head. "That's weird. That's such a similar name to..." I drift off when Virago shakes her head gently.

She raises a single brow and murmurs to me, "King Charix is Charaxus' brother."

My mouth gapes as I glance at Charaxus then, standing uneasily on the dais, her chin raised uncomfortably high, her face pointed in a completely different direction from her brother, the king. Charix, on the other hand, is staring *holes* into his sister's head, his eyes full of a raging fire that I feel uncomfortable to witness. His expression is predatory, and I shiver, glancing away.

"Oh, my God," I mutter, shaken. "So...so this means that Charaxus is from his country? She's from *Furo*? The country that has everyone worried?" I ask Virago, and she nods to me, her mouth set in a thin, hard line as she watches the king advancing toward the queen's table, prowling between the tables like a ravenous lion.

"It is one of many reasons that Charaxus and I have never seen eye to eye," Virago murmurs, her jaw clenched with tension. "It is not good that Furo was invited to take part in the Hero's Tournament. All countries are typically invited, but Furo is simply too unstable now, with Charix as its new ruler. And there is too much at stake. Allowing the king of a chaotic, bloodthirsty country and so many of his knights to come into our capital city..." Virago shifts and looks as if she wants to rake her hand back through her hair in frustration, but she thinks better of it, instead clenching her hands into fists at her sides.

"I think that the attempt on Queen Calla's life was because of a Furo assassin," Virago tells me then, her blue eyes glittering with worry, her voice hushed in the stillness as King Charix's big boots tromp on the banquet hall floor. She growls softly in frustration. "But I have no *proof* of that, and Queen Calla would never disallow a country from participating in the Tournament—it is too unfair," she whispers, her face now showing anguish as she shakes her head with a sigh. "I am so worried for her, my love," says Virago, her eyes drifting up to her queen. "So very, very worried. I am worried that I cannot keep you safe. Or her safe. Or my beloved city safe—" Her voice breaks on those last few words.

I reach out across the space between us, and I take her hand in mine. "Hey, you know what? There's nothing to be worried about. You're *here* now," I whisper to her, and I finally make eye contact, holding her gaze, her worried blue eyes making my heart skip a beat. "Calla came to find you because you're the best knight for the job. I *know* that you can keep the queen safe. There's not going to be any assassin getting through *you.* I don't *care* what country they're from. You're the best, Virago," I whisper to her. "The very best."

Virago's mouth turns up at the corners finally, and though her brow is still furrowed, she offers me a small smile. "Thank you, my love," she tells me softly, squeezing my hand, too. "I will try my very best to keep you, and her, and *everyone* in my city safe during this tournament. It is my sworn duty. My honor to do so."

But Virago falls silent then, because the king is finally approaching the queen's table (did I mention that this is a *very* big room?), his boots sounding even louder on the floor now that he's closer to us. The echoing *thud, thud, thud* of the king and his men marching, and the advancement of so many people clad in black armor coming our way...it makes me shiver, just a little, and in a very not-good way.

And then King Charix arrives to stand before Queen Calla's dais.

I'm not exactly an expert in how members of royalty greet each other (is *anyone* an expert in that?), but if it were me, I'd probably do an awkward bow or nod my head or, you know, make *some* sort of gesture that I was in the presence of a person who was my equal, and someone I respected.

But that's not what King Charix does right now. Instead of deference or respect, or even a nod of simple greeting, he stands with his booted feet wide apart, folding his arms in front of him, his biceps flexing, his expression even angrier than before. And his imposing black-clad knights, fanned out behind him, don't make any sort of gesture, either, copying their king as they fold their arms and stare daggers at Queen Calla.

But Queen Calla, to her credit, doesn't seem to give a damn at all as she draws herself up to her most regal height and smiles beatifically at these silent, brooding (actually, they really look like they're sulking) men.

"Gentlemen," Calla says, her voice warm as she spreads her arms, a small smile flashing over her face. "Welcome to Arktos."

King Charix doesn't reply, only continues to stare at Calla, occasionally flicking his gaze to his sister Charaxus, his sister who is studiously staring off to the side, her face wooden, her jaw clenched tightly as she ignores her brother.

For a long, painful moment of silence that seems to stretch on and on (but what is, in reality, only a handful of seconds), nothing happens. There is a staring match between King Charix, who refuses to acknowledge the queen, and the queen herself, who stands on the dais, her chin tilted up, her eyes flashing. There is perfect silence in the entire room, and all you can hear is hundreds (maybe thousands) of women and men holding their breath, waiting, watching...

And then the spell is broken. It's obvious that King Charix was trying to make Calla look like a fool with his silent treatment. But she's too smooth for that.

She laughs a little, and the sound is low, musical, like bells pealing. She tilts her head to the side, her smile growing wider.

"It must have been a harsh journey, milord," she says, her eyes flashing merrily, and her mouth turning up mischievously at the corners, "for you are too tired to even speak! Do not worry; we will ply you with food and drink, help you get your strength back. Dancers!" she calls, clapping her hands, "help welcome the king!"

And then Calla sits down gracefully, leaning

back in her chair and threading her fingers together over her stomach as she watches the king imperiously. Her sitting down is obviously a dismissal.

Round one, Calla: 1, Charix: 0.

To my surprise, the king—who has a very pale face, as white as chalk—begins to flush. Through the back doors, dancers come rushing in, running in rhythm as they flood the room, a tidal wave of blue- and purple-bedecked women.

They're wearing wide-legged pants and a wide strip of shimmering cloth over their breasts, but other than that, these women are bare-skinned, with metal necklaces and bracelets and anklets shimmering as they begin to whirl around. And though these women are, technically, scantily clad, there is nothing overly sexualized about what they're doing. If anything, they look incredibly *wild*, tossing their heads and long hair, their muscled legs kicked high as they spin, their arms upheld to the sky. I'm mesmerized watching them move in rhythm, watching them spin and leap and run past us. Again, I can't see any band playing, but there's music in the room now, and it's louder, wilder, too.

The dancers spin around Charix, and he has no choice; he must retreat, back to the table on the far side of the room, because they'll make him part of their act if he doesn't. There was room for him to sit up on the dais with Queen Calla (I'm assuming that the other people sitting with her are other dignitaries and rulers from other countries), but there were too many women between him and the dais for him to wade through, so he's stuck on the outer edge of the room. It's a snub from Calla, who surely had this orchestrated if he decided to be a jerk about things; she strikes me as the planning sort. But then my stomach clenches, and I worry about what this will mean for relations between Arktos and Furo. A snub from Calla won't sit well with that angry king...

I can't worry about all of that for too long, though, because the women whirling by the table draw my attention. They're so damn *energetic* (seriously, if I attempted a single flying leap, I'd probably end up in the hospital with a broken foot or something), and they're such a pleasure to watch as the music spirals faster and faster, and the women move, adjusting to the music as they kick higher, leap off of each other's shoulders or over each other, the fabric on their costumes shimmering, their bodies, in every earth-tone color you can imagine, living personifications of the music that swells around us.

Finally, the crescendo of the music cuts out, and the women sink to the ground at the same moment, falling artfully where they stood. For a long, drawn-out moment, there is complete stillness, and around the edges of the room, a smattering of applause breaks out from people who aren't sure if this is the end of an act. But then the applause stops, because a different kind of music begins to fill the banquet hall, a single strain that sounds like a flute being played mournfully, the notes falling over each other to climb higher and higher, swirling in a minor key that tugs at my heartstrings so much that I reach out to Virago and take her hand, squeezing it, emotion filling me.

And, one by one, the dancers rise around us again, like seeds growing up within the earth, unfurling leaves, starting small, still curled up tightly on the ground, and then one arm reaching up elegantly, a questing vine, searching for light. And another arm reaches up, their balled hands opening slowly, fingers spread to the air and the light overhead as they rise, opening their hearts as they arch their backs, their eyes still closed until the very last moment. They begin to hold onto each other, and they hold each other close, drawing closer still, closer, as a drumbeat begins to fill the hall, a slow, sensual beat that stirs something inside of me.

I didn't sense anything sexual in the women's movements before, because there *wasn't* anything sexual about them. But now something is changed, because they are, in essence, moving *together.* It's heartbreakingly beautiful, how each woman looks at her partner, how tenderly she holds her as they spin slowly on the floor. Every action, every delicate change of hand or foot, is in rhythm with the music, and as the two women begin to merge, the drumbeat starts to throb faster, like your heart starts to beat quicker when you see someone you love, when you look at them across the room...when you look at a woman and just *know.*

The two dancers right in front of us are pretty equally matched. They're both tall; they both have long, wavy black hair. One is bronze-skinned, and one is black, their muscles in arms and thighs and calves and stomachs comparable. They're moving with their hands on each other's hips; they turn, gazes locked, their eyes glittering in the lit hall. Despite the crowd, they have eyes only for each other as the drumbeat thumps, as the music moves, as they move with it. They aren't doing anything particularly sexual, not like anything you'd see on the VMAs or in a pop star's music video. But it is very, very clear that they are moving like lovers would move, and we are privy to this dance of love. I feel honored to witness something so intimate and lovely.

Again, the music stops as before, but the

women, instead of falling where they stand, remain standing, remain holding tightly to one another, their faces an inch or less apart, as if they were about to go in for a kiss. And, again, the wild music starts up, and the women push back from one another, beginning to whirl and kick and leap. My heart was beating quickly before, but now it's beating even faster as I watch the women directly in front of our table. One is bending over backwards, her stomach in a perfect curve aimed at the sky, and the other woman is grasping her hips, propelling herself upward to hand-stand on that woman's hips, vaulting over her smoothly.

Just as quickly as they came, the women leap and run through those double doors, spilling out of the room like water running down an opened drain. They are there, and then, just as quickly, they are not there.

But now the party has *really* started, because everyone is laughing, talking loudly, eating and drinking, and Charix—who is still staring unhappily at the queen, who has still not said a word, but now drums his fingers with savage precision on the top of his table—is forgotten in the cheerful atmosphere of the hall.

And this is when the Magin starts to kick in.

I'd almost forgotten that I had a drink earlier, and that I had it on an empty stomach. In a matter of moments, I'm noticing that there are shimmering lights gilding everyone around me, lights that shimmer as brightly as glitter.

"Virago?" I murmur, dabbing a napkin at the corners of my mouth after I take a big bite of a vegetable pie. "Um...what happens with the Magin? After you've had it?"

"It makes everything..." She twirls the goblet in her hand around as she searches for the right word.

"More lovely," she finally settles on, and watches me with a pleased expression. "Is it kicking in yet?"

I stare at Virago's eyes, and I lean back a little more in my chair. Virago is always beautiful to me, but there's a soft haze around her now that makes her look like an exquisite painting. "Yeah," I murmur, and the music begins to change *again,* now a fast, thumping drumbeat of a tune...and the knights at the our table leap up excitedly.

They're getting ready to dance.

"Come on," says Virago, her smile as bright as the sun as she gets up, too, holding out her hand to me. "Dance with me," she breathes, and I'm laughing as she reels me into her arms, as she holds me close and pulls me out between the large tables, into the area that the dancers used earlier. And everyone begins to dance.

I know it's not *everyone* dancing, but the effects of the Magin makes it *feel* like everyone in the world is dancing with us as we move together to the music. I grip Virago's hips, the feeling of the armor—cold like metal, but it doesn't feel like metal against my hands—sends a thrill through me as my fingers hold tight to my knight, as my knight holds tightly to me, wrapping her arms over my shoulders, drawing me close for a kiss.

And is it me or are the lights dimming overhead? Because they seem to be lower in this moment, this moment where it's just me and Virago and the music and all the bodies swaying and moving with us to the beat. I can feel the heat of her, radiating out through the leather and the armor, and she tastes of citrus and chocolate, because Virago has been drinking Magin, too, and everything starts to merge, somehow. Because my fingers gripping her waist suddenly *feel* the strength in her, feel the muscles even beneath the leather, feel her hip bones there, and as her mouth is on mine, I can feel her tongue, feel the strength of that, too, and the strength of my own, and how hot we are when we move together, and suddenly...

Wow. We need to go back to our room. Right. This. Minute.

I break off the kiss; I stand up on my tiptoes, and I whisper into her ear, my head reeling from the effects of the drink, but feeling so very, very turned on that I can't help it. I tell her what I need, what I always need, but what I need so badly in this moment that I'm going to die if I can't get it.

"I need you," I whisper.

And Virago looks into my eyes, her own eyes darkening with desire, and in a single moment, she turns and, gripping my hand tightly, begins to move through the banquet hall, angling for the staircase.

As I look back towards Charix's table, I can't see him anymore. He may have stormed off; few of his knights remain in the banquet hall. I don't know what that means, but it can't mean anything good.

Still, I'm not concentrating on that as we stumble up the stairs, holding onto each other and feeling the heat thrum through our bodies.

I'm concentrating on Virago, holding tightly to her as we climb together.

The fire of my want is roaring through me. *Magic* roars in my veins as I kiss her again and again. And somehow (I mean, I trip on a *lot* of stairs; my shins are going to be black and blue tomorrow), we get to our room.

Chapter 8: I Need You

When I shut the door behind us, I can still feel the music down below moving through my blood, the drumbeat pounding like my pulse. Virago stands there in the half-light from the fireplace, crackling merrily in the room, and her eyes are hooded. When she stares at me with that potent desire, her mouth wet, her lungs breathing hard...I can't take it another second.

I step forward, and then I'm curling my hands into the sides of her breastplate, turning and pushing Virago up against the door behind us. Instantly, my mouth is on hers, and I can feel my veins thrumming with the drumbeat of my blood. I feel the heat, the need, rising in me, fierce and strong.

Shelley, blessedly, is curled up in front of the fire. She's taken care of, sleeping, dreaming—so all I need to think about is *this*. Now. This moment. I break off the kiss, I curl my fingers under Virago's metal, against the leather, and I press a kiss to the thrumming pulse point under her chin, on her neck, feeling the heat of her skin, the softness of it, searing me with desire.

And then Virago whispers those three words back to me, her voice low, growling, strained...desperate: "I need you," she tells me, the words soft and dark.

Virago has never once spoken that phrase to

me, though she has obviously made it clear that such was the case—many times. But those words, spoken between us, like an incantation...they're *magical.*

On another world than mine, with an enchanted beverage rushing through my veins, I grip Virago's hips tightly, digging my fingers into them, and I cover her mouth with my own, kissing hard. I drink her in, the soft strength of her mouth and tongue, the taste of her, the taste that I know, so deeply and intimately, as *Virago*, interlaced with that sweet chocolate from the drink. I gasp as she bites my bottom lip, as she sucks on it gently, and I move against her, fumble at the sides of her ribs for the ties that keep her breastplate in place.

But, no, she created this breastplate, this armor, and there are no ties for my fingers to find. I make my frustration known with a low groan, my fingertips curling over the leather, foiled in their quest to untie, unlace, unclip. I need to feel her skin under my fingers *right now.*

Virago senses this, because beneath my fingers now, I start to feel the metal heating up, and there's a small flash of light, and miraculously, the armor is gone. Virago is standing in her boots, her leather pants and her leather shirt...

And is there anything in the world hotter than a lady knight wearing leather? I really don't think there is.

My mind, my heart, but especially my body responds to the warm leather against me, because I'm working on the ties of her pants instantly, undoing them as I kiss her deeper, as I bite her bottom lip now, sucking, pulling. Virago's breath starts to come faster, more ragged against me. I pull her pants down, but just a little, just down her hips, and then I'm spreading her legs with my own, pushing them apart with precision as

I hold her against the door, as her knees buckle just a little to let me in.

And I come in, I enter, pressing my fingers down, into her pants, twisting my hand upward so that it has purchase against the leather, and my fingers find her center in that moment...and oh, my God, she's wet, so wet, dripping wet as I stroke a single finger across her opening, as she shudders against me, her strong fingers gripping my shoulders as she groans, bucking her hips, throwing her head back to rest against the door. She growls out something unintelligible but needing, wanting, asking...begging.

A thrill races through me as I shiver against her, as I realize how much she needs me in that moment, and I can't hold out, even though I want to, even though I want to tease her, want to make her beg for it again. Virago is good at teasing, at drawing out of me that exquisite desire that she waits to fulfill until I think I can't possibly take it anymore.

But there's no time for that teasing; there's no time for anything but what she wants, and what I want so desperately to give to her. So I curl my fingers upward, pushing up and into her as Virago hisses out against me, as her hips buck, and we settle into this fast, exquisite rhythm, just as quick as the drumbeat that I can still hear, even this far up in the tower.

My other hand pushes up her leather shirt until her breasts are exposed, until her hot skin is against the front of my dress, and I lower my head a little, press my hand over her left breast, squeezing the nipple, tugging it and pinching it as I take her right nipple into my mouth, running my tongue over it, pressing it against my teeth but not biting down, not yet, as I pump my hand in and out of her, as we find that perfect cadence together. She moans against me, exhaling her desire.

We move together faster now, my thumb stroking over her clit with each pressing in of my hand, with each curling of my fingers. She must have wanted me for so long, because she's so ready, so willing, and it takes just a single bite down on her right nipple, just a slight increase in my stroking, and then, suddenly, I feel her tense against me, feel her insides clench as my fingers stroke up higher, faster, drawing it out of her.

She gasps when she comes against me, pulsing her hips against my hand, riding my fingers as she groans, shuddering, leaning against the door with the entirety of her body because she can no longer hold herself up. The climax moves through her, potent, undoing her.

Finally, after a long, tremulous moment, Virago draws her head down, kisses me with her trembling mouth. A surge of heat moves through me right now, because I am so turned on by the sounds she made, by the feeling of her wetness against my hand, by the feeling of her climax against my fingers, of *her* moving against me. I breathe out hotly as she kisses me, as she wraps her arms around me tightly, tightly, squeezing me gently as she lets her forehead fall to my shoulder in surrender, as she breathes out, still shuddering. I draw my hand with its wet fingers out of her pants, and I curl those wet fingers around her hip. I press a hot kiss against her nipple now, just standing against her, helping hold her up.

Her strength returns quickly; Virago is able to stand under her own power in a matter of seconds. I take a step back from her, and I raise my brow, a mischievous smile stealing over my face. Because Virago is hooking her fingers into the edges of her curled down pants, and she takes the waistband in her hands, pulling them down in one smooth, effortless motion. The leather peels over her skin (the clothing must be tight because of the armor over it), and soon she's standing there with nothing on at all, her shirt drawn up and over her head and tossed to the floor in an instant.

When Virago is wearing her armor, she also wears this crescent moon necklace; all the knights wear it, a horizontal moon with different-colored stones dangling from it. Virago now stands before me naked except for the wolf tail draped over her shoulder, held tightly to her ponytail with a leather thong, and that crescent moon necklace, glittering at her throat in the firelight. Her nipples are peaked, the tops of her thighs are wet from my ministrations, and she stands there easily, her hands on her hips, staring at me with glittering, lust-filled eyes.

Getting me out of my complicated dress is not as easy as removing a leather shirt and pants. But this doesn't deter Virago. She prowls, naked, around me, like a wolf pacing a large circle around its prey, and a shiver moves over my spine as I glance sidelong at her, as I stand there, perfectly still as Virago comes up behind me.

She draws out the bow of the laces from the top of the corset. I can feel her hands against the fabric, and I shudder a little as Virago leans close to me, as she whispers, her hot mouth at my ear, "Put your hands on the door."

I gulp down air, desire pouring through me. My knees are weak as I step forward, as I spread my legs beneath the skirt, as I place my palms flat on the door in front of me, my arms straight.

And Virago begins to undo my corset.

I can feel the laces sliding through the grommets, the corset loosening from the top down. My breasts come free from their restraint, and my nipples are hard against the fabric. I shudder a little as the last lace falls way, my corset completely undone.

Virago pushes the shoulders of the dress down, and with the corset gaping open, my back is exposed to her. She scratches her fingernails down lightly, lightly over my back as I gasp; my head goes up and back as I moan, feeling the sensation of her moving against me in every part of my body, but—most significantly—in the pulsing center between my legs. I hiss out, trying to breathe as, again, Virago draws her nails over my back, coming up behind me to press her front to my back now. I can feel her breasts against my skin, and I shudder involuntarily as Virago reaches around, beneath the fabric of the dress, to find my breasts.

She leans against me, breathing hotly in my ear as she takes both nipples in her fingers and pinches them, her palms hot on my skin. The sensation of her skin against mine, the euphoria of the Magin rushing through me...it's all too much, too intense, too searing and strong, but I crave more, and Virago knows it. She pinches my nipples, twisting them gently, then harder, and her right hand leaves my breast. She leans against me a little more, and then she rakes her fingers over my stomach, over my hips, over my thigh, aiming for my center.

When she brushes her fingers over those Supergirl panties, a shudder moves through me so powerfully that I gasp out loud. Virago chuckles, low and growling, against my ear, and then she moves aside the fabric of my panties, tugging them a little so that they're tight against my center, before she moves them fully aside, questing beneath with her fingers.

I see stars when the pad of her thumb grazes my clit, stars because everything is even more intense now, my center throbbing with such a deep ache that I'm going to come, just from that simple touch (how powerful *is* this drink?), but no...Virago's not having any of it. She passes her thumb over my clit again, but so soft, just a mere brush of skin against skin, and it's not enough. It's too teasing. I need more.

That's when Virago moves, quick and smooth, and she begins to stroke me gently, too gently—she's teasing me—but increasing pressure, her touch coming faster now, harder, as she strokes my clit with her fingers, with her thumb.

My knees are weak as she finds almost instantly that perfect rhythm, that perfect rhythm that moves through me. I'm going to come, and it's going to be so fast. My knees are already weak, my eyelids already fluttering as I moan out, tipping my head back for her mouth to find my neck, for her to kiss me there, licking my hot skin...

It is quick and dirty and perfect, how fast I come, pulsing against her fingers as I breathe out, as my knees weaken so much that I can't hold myself up. But Virago supports me. She has her other arm around my middle, and she holds me against her tenderly as my orgasm moves through me, filling me with a bliss that undoes me in every way.

"I love you," Virago whispers into my ear, her words thick with emotion as she holds me tightly to her, as my breathing comes fast. I see stars when I close my eyes.

I reach around behind me, thread my fingers

through her ponytail, draw her mouth down to mine with a kiss.

We curl up together tightly on the bed, twining, my dress dangling off of me and me not really caring as I hold Virago close, breathing in all that she is. The moment I close my eyes, I'm asleep.

Well, in my defense, it's been a *very* long day.

Chapter 9: The Tea of Queens

We wake up to pounding on our door.

I blink, eyes blurry, and sit upright. I'm still partially (but not really) wearing that enormous gown from last night, and it's slipping off my shoulders. I try to pull the gauzy material back up and over my breasts, but I'm so sleepy that I can't really get a good grasp on the fabric.

"Oh, my God," I mutter, yawning and glancing out the window closest to the bed. It's still pitch black out. "What time *is* it?" I blink.

"It's time to get up!" someone yells from the other side of the door cheerfully, before pounding said door again, this time even harder. That voice sounds a *lot* like Alinor. It probably *is* Alinor. "Virago! Holly! Rise and *shiiiiiine*!"

"They have that saying on this world, too?" I mutter, yawning and rolling over on top of Virago, who chuckles a little and places her hands beneath her head, raising a single brow as she glances up at me.

"Good morning," I mutter to her, with a soft, secret smile, and then I kiss her.

"There's no time for that!" yells Alinor from the other side of the door.

Okay, *that* gets my attention.

"Um...how do you know what we're doing?" I ask, sitting bolt upright after rolling off of Virago and covering my bare breasts (ball gowns weren't really made for shenanigans in bed) with my arms.

"I can see you," Alinor mutters, as if it were obvious. The "duh" is implied in her tone.

"She has the power of far sight," says Virago, her mouth twitching up at the corners as I stare at her, horrified. "She can see through pretty much anything she wants to."

"That's...great." I bite my lip, my head tilted to the side as Virago gets up, chuckling a little as she rubs the back of her neck, then stretches.

"We'll meet you in the practice yard in a little while, Alinor. Go wake someone else up," Virago says, and I can hear Alinor sighing from the other side of the door.

But all this pounding has caused Shelley to stand up, and she bounds over to the door, whining and scratching at it.

"Actually, can you take the small beast with you? She'll love the practice yard," says Virago, turning to me. I nod, still a little bit mortified, and Alinor opens the door (didn't we *lock* the door last night?) and sticks her head through, positively beaming at us.

"Did you have a good night, you love birds?" she asks, batting her eyes, and Virago picks up one of her boots from beside the bed and throws it at the door. It does not hit Alinor, even though Virago has pretty spectacular aim. Instead, it bounces off the already closed door that Shelley was just whisked through.

Hmm. I hope my dog behaves for that knight.

"The day's assignments are given out to the Royal Knights at sunrise every morning in the practice yard," Virago explains, picking up her leather shirt from the ground and sliding it on over her head. She crosses the room, and I try very hard not to stare at her toned rear; then I don't care at all, and I stare away. Virago notices, glancing over her shoulder and chuckling at my expression.

"So we best get going," she tells me gently, opening the wardrobe and taking out a new pair of panties. These are obviously handmade, black, and of great quality (they look super comfy, actually). It's gratifying to know I've at least got underwear options here, in case I run out of my own.

"What about me?" I ask, as she starts to pull on her leather pants. I let the gown fall the rest of the way to the floor, and then I get up and glance around the room. There's a washbasin in the corner with fresh water. How the water is fresh and cold, I'll never know, but I'm assuming it has something to do with magic. "What am I going to do today?" I ask her, pouring a little water out from the big pitcher into the washbasin and splashing my face with it. I pick up the little cake of soap on the corner and start to wash up. The soap smells a little bit like lavender—but not quite.

"I figured you'd come with me," says Virago with a shrug. "I'll be given an assignment, but you can certainly come along, no matter where I go. There are a lot of things for you to see in Arktos City, and we could get a start on that." She has a soft smile as she turns to me, beginning to lace up her old silver armor, picking up the pieces from where they were neatly stacked on the trunk at the foot of the bed. "If that's what you want to do," she amends, as she places her chest and back pieces on over her head. She starts to tie up the thongs along her sides. "Of, if you'd rather, you could stay in the castle. I have many friends you might spend the day with..." She trails off.

"I want to stay with you," I tell her softly, as I dry my face on a very soft, woven towel. I'm standing there in just my Supergirl panties, but Virago crosses the room to gather me in her arms, my breasts pressing against the cold metal of her chest plate. I shiver against her, the sensation sending a little thrill through me as she holds me close, as she bends her beautiful face down to me and kisses me fiercely.

"Whatever you choose to wear today," she says, kissing my nose gently before breaking away, "make sure that it's comfortable for a lot of walking. And, perhaps, horseback riding."

I stare at the wardrobe in dismay. Pretty much everything in there is a dress. I usually only wear dresses, but I'm kind of doubting they ride sidesaddle here.

I dig through the wardrobe and find a forest green dress with a *very* full circle skirt, so even if I am riding on a horse, it's going to work out okay. I hope. It's a simple, medieval-style dress with embroidery along the hem, the sleeves, and the neckline. I pull out a new pair of panties from my own bag (today's geek underwear is brought to you by Wonder Woman!), and then I'm drawing on a chemise from the wardrobe, settling that forest green dress over it, and tying my hair in a quick ponytail with a matching ribbon.

"Good?" I ask Virago, whose eyes are hooded with pleasure as she glances at me, then draws me close.

"Perfect," she breathes. She's kissing me again...but then there's more pounding at the door.

"Virago? Holly?" It's Magel. "I'm here to wake you two."

Virago opens the door to Magel, who is raising

her hand to knock yet again. Magel smiles quickly at us and lowers her hand, glancing inside the room. "Wow, these are nice accommodations. The queen likes you, Holly," says Magel, her brow up as Virago and I move past her, shutting the door behind us.

"She does," Virago agrees, as Magel falls in line beside us. "Which is good. It distracts her from her heartbreak," says Virago, her mouth falling into a thin line.

Heartbreak?

"Um...what happened to her?" I ask now, clearing my throat, but Magel and Virago are both shaking their heads.

"If she wants to tell you, she'll tell you," Virago says firmly. And that, of course, makes me feel terrible for asking.

I grimace, shaking my head. "Sorry. It just looks like she was really hurt, is all," I mutter, shrugging a little uncomfortably. Virago glances sidelong at me and wraps an arm around my shoulders gently.

"Just be kind to her, like you're kind to everyone, my love. It will mean a great deal to her," says Virago, as Magel raises a brow, glancing at us but saying nothing.

We go down about a million staircases (give or take a few), through about a hundred halls (approximately), and then we're exiting a wide set of double doors, made out of thick, wooden beams. Finally, we're outside in a yard filled with women wearing armor.

Along the edges of the yard—though it's difficult to see since the sky is just starting to lighten—there are dummies that are vaguely human-shaped, made of burlap-type sack and stuffed with straw. There are large wooden contraptions with bulls-eyes painted on them, hay bales with bulls-eyes, more dummies with bulls-eyes... It looks like a lot of target practice happens in this yard. In the far left corner, there are several very large horses, already tacked up with big saddles and thick leather bridles with different-colored saddle pads that droop over their rears. Each horse has a different color combination, and every single one of the horses is *massive.* I would have guessed you'd need a big horse for such tall women, but, seriously, they must feed the horses whatever they feed the knights to get them that damn tall.

The knights are all milling about, but when Magel enters the yard, they stand to attention. I'm also realizing that most of the women are glancing my way, curiously.

"Is this the woman from the other world?" asks the closest knight, a tall redhead with a chainmaille circlet around her forehead, her armor just like that of the other knights. She's gazing at me so inquisitively that I smile a little, and then she's beaming back, her own smile huge.

Magel's voice raises as she chuckles. "Get a good look, ladies. This is Virago's lover, Holly, and, yes, she does hail from another world."

There's whispering and murmuring amongst the knights as Magel leaps up onto a table in the center of the yard. In a moment, though, the women shift their attention from me and back to her when she raises her arm.

"Your orders," says Magel, her mouth turning up at the corners as she crosses her arms, "if you're awake enough to receive them, are..."

She begins to instruct each knight who steps up

to her as to where she is stationed, and what her mission for the day is, overtaking the night shift of knights. (Which, even to Magel, was kind of fun to say). She talks about things like the west gate of the city and the field that they'll be using for the opening ceremonies of the Hero's Tournament (taking place tonight). And then she gets to Virago.

"The queen has expressed a wish to spend the hours leading up to this evening in the royal library, preparing herself for the opening ceremonies," she tells Virago. "You and Kell both are stationed there today, specifically near the entrance of the library, but keep the queen in sight at all times, understood?"

Virago stiffens a little, and Magel cocks her head. "Yes?" she asks in a lower voice, so only the knights closest to us can hear.

"Only two knights to watch the queen today, Magel?" asks Virago, crossing her arms in front of her, her face cloudy with worry.

"You and Kell are the best," says Magel with a soft smile. "You know you can call for aid should a situation arise. Do not worry."

Virago sighs for a long moment, then nods. "As you wish," she says, then turns to me. "Let us go," she says. "We'll pass through the kitchen to get breakfast on the way."

We cross the yard and head into the palace by a different door. This one leads immediately into the kitchen. The room is long and low, and there are many tables heaped with fresh vegetables and woven bags of grain. Several women are making tarts and pies, their fronts covered in flour. We're halted by a stout woman wielding—I kid you not—a rolling pin.

"Virago, you are a *knight*, and like the other

knights, you must abide by the rules," she intones, threatening the much, *much* taller Virago with the rolling pin as she brandishes it overhead. This woman is shorter than me, and she's wearing a plain black dress and a big white apron, her thick, curling black hair cut short around her face, a dab of flour highly visible on her copper cheek.

"Asha," says Virago, bowing low with a wide smile and a flourish, "I would like you to meet my lover, Holly. Holly, this is Asha—head cook to the queen, and one of the most lovely—"

"Save it," Asha mutters, but she looks mollified and even indulgent as she smiles a little at Virago. "There are seven sister pies on the back stove. Take what you want for breakfast."

"You're a wonder," says Virago, darting forward and placing a kiss on Asha's cheek. "Come, Holly. We don't want to keep the queen waiting!"

Virago approaches the back stove, scooping up several hand pies from one of the pans. She balances them in her palms, wincing a little, as they're evidently hot, but she tosses one to me, and I catch it, anyway, wincing as the pie burns my thumb.

"The dinner was marvelous last night!" Virago calls over her shoulder, and this causes Asha to roar.

"I had to use the Cauldron of Plenty! *Me*! Resorting to that sub-par piece of junk!" Asha moans, setting the rolling pin down on the counter and wiping her hands off on her apron with a sigh. "Please tell the queen that I was happy to do it, but that it—"

"That it wounded you to do so. Got it," says Virago, opening the kitchen door for me. I step through as Asha laughs.

"Have I said that before?" she asks

absentmindedly.

"Every time you use the Cauldron," says Virago, offering another bow as she takes a bite of the pie and then closes the kitchen door behind her.

"Asha," says Virago, one brow raised as she chuckles, "is Magel's sister. Head cook and head knight. It runs in the family, needing to be in charge, I think."

"Oh, my God, this is so good," I say around a mouthful of pie. It tastes like there's squash in the pie, and onions, but it doesn't *exactly* taste like those things. Regardless, it's one of the most delicious things I've ever had, and I burn my entire mouth while devouring the thing as I follow Virago down the hallway.

I'm licking my fingers when we turn a corner, and the serviceable, plain carpeting beneath our feet—a mouse gray—turns into the sumptuous cobalt blue rug that was in the main hallway at the entrance of the palace. Virago inclines her head to me as she points forward, toward the tall, white double doors with golden handles.

"This is the royal library," she says in a hushed voice. And then she smiles, and her smile is as warm and bright as the sun. "I think you're going to like it," she says mildly; then she take the final step forward, grasps the handles, and pulls the doors open.

I let out a low whistle, my heart literally skipping a beat.

"Wow," I whisper.

Imagine every book you can possibly think of, imagine every large bookstore you've ever been in, then multiply that by ten. We step into the room, and I look up, and up (and up) and realize that we must be in the center of the palace, and that this room must be the central tall tower I saw when I was down in the Meadow of Memory after we first arrived in Agrotera.

There are countless shelves of books before me, with wide, white staircases leading up to different open-air levels. The center of this wide, sprawling tower is hollow, so you can see up and up and up to the different floors with each one's uncountable number of books.

And, seated in front of us, in one of the many comfortable-looking, carved wooden chairs, is Calla. She's wearing a simple gray gown, shot through with strands of silver (the gown shimmers a little when she turns and smiles at us), and she's holding a thick book open on her lap.

"Virago," says Calla, setting the book on the small table next to her chair and rising. She's smiling when she says Virago's name, but Calla isn't looking at Virago; she's looking at me. "So good of you to come," she says, and then she gestures to two knights I hadn't even seen standing there. They were positioned on either side of the door when we entered. "Rami, Lilla, you can go. Thank you so much for your watch over me last night."

The two knights stand at attention, bow low and turn to leave, but Virago stops the closest one, reaching out and curling her fingers over the woman's black arm.

"Was there any sign of threat, Rami?" she asks, her voice dropping low as she gazes into the knight's eyes.

Rami shakes her head, her full mouth set in a grim line. "No, but tonight is the opening ceremony... Be careful," she murmurs.

Virago nods, then tightens her grip on the

knight's arm and draws her in for a small embrace, each knight tapping the other on the shoulder once with a fist before letting go.

Rami and Lilla are already out the door when I hear running steps in the hall outside. The rug goes down the center of the hallway, but there is bare wooden floor on either side of the rug, and this is what the person is sprinting over, sounding as if they have the hounds of hell behind them.

The woman skids to a halt outside the door, but she was going so fast that she skids right past the door and keeps going.

It's Kell.

"Sorry I'm late!" she chirps, ducking inside and shutting the door before Rami, who had an angry look on her face and was about to say something, can speak. "Your Majesty!" announces Kell, leaning forward in a sweeping bow. "Sorry, sorry," she tells the queen with a small wince. "I know I'm late."

Calla hides a smile behind her hand, and when she clears her throat, she looks all business. "And you are late *because*?" she asks, one brow up.

Kell grins widely. "I met a lady last night, Your Majesty."

"That was last night," says Calla coolly, though her mouth is trying to twitch upwards at the corners, despite her best efforts to look stern. "This is this morning."

"Well, I was still, um, *meeting* her this morning, too," says Kell, her grin almost splitting her face in two.

Calla chuckles at that, and Virago just sighs, shaking her head with a small smile as Kell leans against the door, adjusting the buckle of her scabbard over her chest and running a hand through her hair to "comb" it. All this achieves is to make it stick up in crazier angles, her curls spilling over her shoulders.

"And what about you two?" asks Kell, grinning at us now. She waggles her eyebrows. "How was last night?"

"Good," says Virago, glancing at me with a soft smile. "Holly tried Magin!"

"How much did you drink?" asks Kell, looking impressed in spite of herself.

"Just one glass," I tell her with a shrug.

Kell shakes her head and rolls her eyes. "Virago, she should have had more than one. None of the good stuff happens until you have more than—"

"The merits of drink aside," says Calla, clearing her throat, "I would love to speak with Lady Holly, if you would both not mind."

"I dunno," says Kell, sniffing. "She looks like an assassin to me." And then Kell starts to laugh. It's a jerky laugh, an I'm-kind-of-an-asshole laugh. The kind of laugh that says, "Yeah, right, she probably can't even wield a vegetable peeler."

I'm about to say something in my defense, but Calla shakes her head, inclining her chin toward me, and I cross the room, glowering a little, to stand before the queen.

"Come walk with me," says Calla softly, and we both cross the floor, getting farther and farther away from the knights until we're definitely out of hearing range.

"Now, Holly," says Calla, turning toward me, her face warm and open, "you were very kind to me yesterday. I thank you for that." She looks earnest, relaxed, and so much younger than when she puts on her game-face of queenliness. "And I feel like I can talk to you freely. That's...precious. Something that's in short supply around here," she tells me with a small, sad smile, but then she's shaking her head quickly. "Not that the knights aren't wonderful. I *could* tell them anything, really," she says, folding her hands in front of her, "but they are so protective. They don't want to hear about my heartaches. They just want to take action and *destroy* whatever or whoever made me sad. They're good people, all of them," she adds softly, "but I feel as if I can tell you what happened to me."

"Of course you can. But only...only if you want to, Calla," I stammer, shaking my head. "I just want you to know," I tell her quietly, my voice solemn, "that before Virago...I had my heart broken."

Calla raises a brow. "What happened?" She gestures to two chairs close by, big, plush seats with embroidered pillows. I sit down, holding her gaze.

"I loved this woman," I say tentatively. I haven't really told my story like this, not since it happened. "Her name was Nicole, and I thought I was going to marry her. But she started to lose interest in me, stopped caring about me...and then I found out she'd been cheating on me for over a year with her assistant." Even saying the words reminds me of how Nicole *used* to look at me, used to care about me. I'm head over heels in love with Virago; I think it's true love, and I never believed in the concept before. But Nicole's betrayal still hurts, as do all of the betrayals I've experienced in my lifetime. Even if the wounds heal, there is some small part of me, deep inside, that will always bear the scars.

Calla pales as she stares at me, her green eyes flashing. She clasps her hands in her lap again, but I can see that her knuckles are bright white, as if she's holding herself too tightly.

"I'm sorry you went through that, Holly," she tells me, her voice hoarse. "Like you, I also suffered a betrayal..." She trails off, her eyes glistening.

"Calla, you don't have to talk about this," I tell her, but she smiles sadly and shakes her head.

"If I don't talk about it," she whispers, "I'm going to die. I have to tell the story… I have to release it, or I will never start to heal. And I think," she says, flicking her gaze to me, "that I want to start healing."

"All right." I spread my hands in my lap. And then I smile at her, holding her gaze. "I'm listening."

Calla stares down at the floor for a while before clearing her throat. Her eyes are distant, unseeing, but then she begins to speak. "I loved a knight once. Her name was Bel. I...I met her when I was a very little girl, and we grew up together here, in the palace. She was..." Calla sighs, closing her eyes. "She was the most beautiful girl in the world. She had long brown hair that fell in waves, an upturned nose, eyes that sparkled like gems. She was perfect," says Calla, opening her eyes. There is such sadness in her gaze; the sight guts me to my core. "But she wasn't perfect. Not truly. I gave her my heart; I showered her with gifts, with palace privileges… She had anything, everything she wanted. I just wanted to make her happy. But I think I went too far. I loved her, but I don't think she ever really loved me. She saw my crown—and not my heart," Calla whispers. "We used to go to this place in the woods. It was a little castle my mother built for me. Just a playhouse, really, but we went there when we were small, so we would go there to tryst when we were older. And it was there that she told me that she was seeing several women, *had* been seeing several women since we had gotten together. And she told me that she did not love me."

Calla pronounces this in a soothing voice, but I can still hear the pain in every word. "I don't know how to articulate," she says, folding her hands into hard, small fists, her fingers curling against her palms so hard, her nails must be cutting into her skin, "how very, very much I loved her. And how very, very much she broke my heart," she whispers.

A single tear escapes her glittering right eye and traces its way down her pale cheek.

I reach across the space between us and take up her hand in my own. "I'm so sorry, Calla," I tell her, and mean it from the deepest place within myself. "She should never have been so dishonest with you. You didn't deserve that."

Calla glances up at me in surprise, her eyes wide, the tears shining in them.

"It's true," I tell her, shaking my head. "You didn't deserve that. Beyond the fact that you're queen, you're also a really awesome person. I mean, I haven't known you that long, it's true...but you're really nice. You're generous and kind and giving. And you deserve a woman who will adore you for all of those parts of you—not just the crown," I say, with a little smile. "Bel didn't deserve you. I'm so sorry that she hurt you."

Calla shakes her head a little, her eyes downcast. "She said that no one would ever love me, *because* I am the queen. That I would never really know if people loved me for *me*...or if they loved me for my title alone."

"And...that's a hard one," I say, frowning. "You'll have to kiss a lot of frogs to find your lady, I'm sure. But don't stop believing, okay? I'm so sorry your childhood sweetheart broke your heart—I can't even imagine that pain," I say, shaking my head. "It hurt enough when a woman I'd known for only a few years did it to me. I still bear that scar," I say, patting my heart, "and you'll always have yours. But you deserve love. And I think you'll find it. You just have to keep looking."

Calla stares off into the distance, her eyes still bright. "I don't know if I believe in love anymore," she says softly. "Oh, what you and Virago have...it's beautiful," she says, as she glances back at me with worried eyes. "I just don't think I'm ever going to experience something like that." And then tears begin to stream down her cheeks.

For a long moment, I don't say anything. We sit together, the pain between us pulsing, as alive as any living thing can be. I touch Calla's hand, and she holds my fingers tightly, as soft, quiet sobs wrack her shoulders.

She is in so much pain that I wonder if she really *can* love again. If she can trust someone enough again. God, I hope so. She deserves happiness. She deserves a woman who will see her, see every part of her. She deserves to be seen to the depths of her heart.

"Thank you, Holly," she whispers, then, her voice soft. "But...but if it's all right with you, it's very difficult for me to cry in front of people," she says, fishing an embroidered handkerchief out of her sleeve and covering her face with it in her hands. "Please go," she whispers to me.

"I would love to, uh, get some fresh air, anyway," I say, clearing my throat and standing quickly. "You take as much time as you need, Calla," I tell her, reaching out and touching her shoulder lightly. And then I turn and leave, rubbing my arms, feeling disquieted.

How many women have been so hurt? How many women are afraid to love again?

And, heart in my throat, I consider the possibility that, if Virago had never found me… What might have happened? I wonder if *I* would have been able to trust again. Or was it *because* she found me that I learned to trust?

Was it because she was exactly the right person for me?

And if so...I hope the right person is out there for Calla, too.

I reach Kell and Virago, and Kell glances over my shoulder at me, her brows up.

"What did you do to Calla?" Kell asks suspiciously, but I shake my head.

"She just...wanted to talk to me about something," I say, then glance at Virago. Virago gives me a small, sweet smile, and I hold her gaze for a long moment.

Because she always, *always* makes me feel seen.

"I'd like to get some air—and give Calla a little privacy," I say then, glancing from one knight to the other. "Go outside, maybe?"

Kell considers this. "Well, I was about to head out and fetch Calla some tea from from her favorite tea shop. But if you'd rather do it..." Kell shrugs and hands me a single gold coin, warm from her palm. "It's a nice walk there, and it's a nice day. And, honestly, I'm still very tired from last night," she says, waggling her eyebrows.

I laugh in spite of myself. "Okay. Yeah, that'd be fun. It'll give me a chance to see a little bit of the city, too," I tell her with a shrug, turning to Virago.

"Just be safe," says Virago worriedly, stepping forward and wrapping her arms around me, drawing me close to press a warm kiss to my forehead.

"Goddess, Virago, she'll be safe. It's Arktos City," snorts Kell. "All right, Holly. When you leave the palace, you'll be on the main road. Walk down until three streets pass by on your right. On the fourth street, turn right, and the shop will be there straightaway. It's called A Cup of Magic," she says, with a wide smile. "The sign has a little cup of tea on it, painted purple. Really, you can't miss it."

"Of course," I tell her with a small smile, and then I'm curling my fingers tightly around the gold coin, which feels surprisingly weighty in my hand. "That sounds easy enough. I...just don't know how to get to the front of the palace."

Virago inclines her head toward the library door. "Bear left out of this room, and then right. Keep going straight, and you cannot miss it. And if you see anyone, they will gladly direct you."

"I'll be right back, okay?" I tell Virago, lowering my voice.

She shakes her head, though I can see that she hesitated for a long moment. "Just...just be careful. I know my fellow knights have the city well protected," she says, though her jaw is clenching. "But still, be on your guard. There are knights everywhere, especially so close to the palace. If anything happens, just find the closest one, tell her that you are Virago's lover, and they will defend you to the death," says Virago seriously, curling her hands tightly over mine.

"She's getting *tea*," Kell says, rolling her eyes, "not challenging a pack of werewolves. She will be *fine,* Virago," Kell mutters then, one brow up.

"Of course, of course," says Virago, taking a step back and lifting her chin, though I know that she's more than a little conflicted about setting me loose in the city.

"Do I have enough here to buy tea for you guys, too?" I ask, holding up the gold coin.

Again, Kell snorts. "Calla always spends a gold coin for her teas, and a gold coin is worth about fifty teas," says Kell, with a small laugh. "But Calla is a good queen."

"I'll be back," I say, blowing a kiss to Virago, and then I'm out the door and into the hall beyond it.

I stare down the enormous hallway, biting my lip, as I try to remember the directions. For the record, I'm *terrible* at directions, whether I can remember them or not. "Um...right and then left?" I mutter to myself, setting off with a shrug to the right. At least, I think this was the way I was supposed to go...

All along the hallway, there are different suits of armor. I guess this is an "armor through the ages" sort of display, because some of the suits of armor look ancient, like they should be in a museum, not out in the open collecting dust (though, admittedly, there's not a speck of dust on them). And some of them look newer than Virago's armor, and much shinier. As I walk, I admire the different types of metal plating, of leather armor, of chainmaille armor. Some of the armor even comes with helmets, complete with vividly colored plumes, long, draping feathers that, on some of the helmets, nearly graze the ground.

I'm intrigued by the suits of armor until I reach a turn in the hallway and see a row of doors on either side of me, impressive-looking doors that are tall and pointed at the tops, like Gothic windows. I pause. I'm not exactly certain if I went the way I was supposed to when I left the the library, but *this* doesn't look right to me. Shouldn't I have found the door leading outside by now? Ah, well, I must just have to go down the corridor and make another turn...

But when I'm halfway down the hallway, I hear voices. Loud voices. They're coming from up ahead, from around another turn. These are voices that are familiar to me, but I can't quite place them yet...

Normally, meeting someone in a corridor wouldn't be a problem. I'm certain I'm already lost (how is this even possible?), and getting directions from a more knowledgeable resident would be great.

But as I stand, my heart thundering in my chest, I realize where I recognize the voices from. Because one of the voices belong to Charaxus—I would know her deep, dark, grating tone anywhere.

And talking with her is a man. A very angry man.

A lump rises in my throat as I realize he must be Charix, Charaxus' brother.

I have no idea why I do what I do next. No idea in the world, honestly. Maybe it's because of the assassination attempt; maybe it's because Virago doesn't trust Charaxus at all; maybe it's because I got a look at Charix last night, and I really, *really* didn't like what I saw. Either way, my next action is purely ridiculous.

Because I sprint around the edge of one of the suits of armor and duck down behind the suit, wedging myself in between the marble stand that the armor is on and the wall behind me.

The suits of armor are positioned in niches in the wall, but still—my hiding place is less than great. Scooby-Doo level, really. My heart is pounding inside of me, and I feel absolutely stupid, crouching here where they're probably going to spot me instantly, and then think I'm a complete idiot. And *why am I even doing this*? Because I don't like the look of Charix? This is crazy! They're going to see me right away...

But they don't. There's a long moment of boots clumping on the floor, and then Charaxus and Charix walk right by the armor, still engaged in a heated discussion.

And they pause quite near me.

My blood is pounding so loudly through my veins that I'm terrified they'll be able to hear it. But, instead, *I* hear this:

"You *swear* to me that this will be done, sister?" hisses Charix. I can see his boots around the corner of the pedestal, and the hem of his fur coat drifting down to the ground as he pauses, as he takes a violent step forward, gripping his sister's arm aggressively.

"Unhand me," she growls savagely, and she pulls her arm free from his grasp, but he grips her again, even tighter, his fingers curling in. I can actually *see* the metal plate on her arm bending away from his fingers.

"You *swear* to me," he murmurs, his voice a low snarl, "by the Goddess herself that you will do this thing you promise."

"I swear by Cower," whispers Charaxus, leaning closer, her face dark, "that the queen will be yours before the end of the Tournament."

His eyes dart around and almost bulge out of his head as he lets her arm go. "Speak not so loudly and where anyone can hear you," he growls, but his tone is softer now as he gazes at his sister. Softer by a hair. "You were born and bred by Furo," he says, lifting his hand and tapping the place over his heart, "and you are loyal to Furo," he tells her, reaching out and tapping her heart, too.

Charaxus' jaw tightens, but she says nothing else as she stares at her brother, as her eyes narrow.

"We have nothing further to discuss," says Charaxus, shaking her head, her long mane shifting over her shoulders. "We must not be seen together," she tells her brother in a warning tone.

Charix shrugs indolently, turning on his heel. "Goddess bless you," he tells her in a mocking tone, a sneer evident on his face as he shakes his head and chuckles, stalking back down the hallway in the direction that they came, the hem of his fur coat billowing out behind him.

For a long moment Charaxus stands very still, her hands curled tightly into fists, her breathing coming quick, her face cloudy. I hold my breath, my heart racing through me. She knows I'm here. She *knows* I'm here; that's the only reason she's staying behind.

But no. I glance around the pedestal, and I let out my breath in a soft gasp.

Because Charaxus stands there, and a single tear leaks from her right eye, tracing its way down her pale cheek to slide off her chin. For a long moment, she simply stands there, the glimmering trail of the tear still etched on her face. But then the moment is over. Charaxus turns on her heel, and she continues on down the corridor, the way that she and her brother had been headed before they stopped beside my suit of armor.

I get out from behind the pedestal after waiting for her to round the corner. I hear no other sounds, no voices or footsteps, for a good, long while. I stand up, and I'm shaking as I lean against the suit of armor. I wonder what the hell I just heard...and what the hell I should do about it.

I mean, it seemed obvious to me. Charix wants the queen, and Charaxus is going to give her to him.

For a long moment, I stand there, uncertain as to what I should do. It seems clear to me, but then...maybe I misheard them? I know that sounds ridiculous, but I have no idea what that conversation meant. I don't know. *I don't know.*

As I stand there, I realize that I'm trying to convince myself that Charaxus doesn't *truly* have any dark intentions. Because how could she be the vice queen if she has such poor character? I have no idea how a vice queen is chosen, but I'm assuming that the queen herself has a say in the matter. And why in the world would Calla choose a vice queen who couldn't be trusted?

I glance down at the palm of my hand and look at the golden coin that rests there. It's perfectly round, and on one side is a smattering of raised five-pointed stars. I rub my finger over the stars as I try to figure out what to do, and—in frustration—I set off down the hallway in the direction that Charix took.

I promised that I would get the queen tea. Charaxus said before the Tournament was over, Charix would have Calla...so I probably have *some* time to try and figure out what to do. I don't want to start a witch hunt if I'm wrong.

But I don't want Calla taken, either. Kidnapped.

God. I don't know what to do.

And, honestly? Picking up some tea sounds like the perfect antidote to all of this confusion. *Tea.* Yeah, I like the sound of that.

Chapter 10: Conspiracies

I don't think I've ever been so glad to enter a tea shop in my life.

There's a bright, silver-sounding bell that rings out merrily when I open the door to the shop (that was, admittedly, relatively easy to find, once I managed to get out of the palace itself), and then I'm shutting the big, wooden door behind me, my eyes scoping out the interior.

The shop is dimly lit, and the diamond-paned windows don't let in that much light, so it takes a long moment for my eyes to adjust to the darkness. I take a few steps in, and then I notice the lady behind the counter.

“Hello,” she tells me with a bright smile, leaning on the counter and putting her chin in her hands.

Like me, she has long red hair, but it's much curlier and poofier than mine. I love it. She has it drawn back from her face with two pins above her ears, and she's wearing a bright purple dress with a bright blue apron.

“Welcome to A Cup of Magic!” says the woman, giving me a sweeping bow as she spreads her arms.

There are warm, cozy benches around the shop, and little circular tables, and along one wall, there are actual wooden booths with small rectangular tables covered in lace doilies and comfortable-looking, worn patchwork cushions on the benches. But the most important part of the shop is the staggeringly tall set of shelves behind the woman. The shelves hold about a million (give or take) glass jars, all filled with different herbs and teas. The scent of the shop is positively amazing, and I inhale again, through my nose, smiling at the woman as I breathe in the heady aroma of all that tea.

"Um...I'm here for Queen Calla," I tell her, crossing the room and setting the gold coin down on the counter. "She would like her usual. And I'd like three other teas..." But I stare over her shoulder at the many, many jars. "I just don't know which ones," I admit.

"Ah, for Calla," says the woman, and stands up on her tiptoes to tip a glass jar down towards her from the shelf. The jar is falling one second, and then caught expertly in her hands the next as she turns around, plunking the jar on the counter with a bright smile.

"Now," says the woman, leaning on the counter again. "As the water heats for the tea, tell me—what do you need right now?"

I stare at her. "Um...I need some tea?" I guess.

She laughs at that, the sound as clear and bright as the bell on her door. "No, no—what do you *need*? In your life?" she asks me, her head tilted to the side, her eyes glittering perceptively. "How is your love life?" she asks, her voice dropping an octave and becoming jokingly sexy. "How is your gold? How is your happiness?" She puts her chin in her hands and leans forward on the counter. "What do you *want*?"

Normally, I'd be asking her what tea has to do with happiness or money or love, but I'm on another world, so I'm just going to go with this for right now.

"I want to know that my girlfriend and I are safe and happy. And the Queen, too. And just...everyone. I want everyone to be safe and happy," I say, taking a deep breath and letting it out. My shoulders come down from around my ears, and I relax a little as the woman's face softens with kindness.

"Good choice," she says, and then she sets four tall mugs made of pottery in front of her, and she puts in equal amounts of the tea from the jar she took down from the shelves for Queen Calla, scooping it out into the cups with a small silver spoon.

"Queen Calla wants that, too?" I ask her, mystified as she puts the jar of tea back up on the shelf and wanders away into a back room.

"It is always what the queen wants," she calls out. And then she reappears with a piping hot burnished metal kettle, held in her hand with a bright patchwork potholder.

"How did you know I was coming?" I ask her then, indicating the kettle that just started boiling when I arrived.

The woman smiles at me mysteriously as she pours equal amounts of water into the four mugs. "I always know," she says, with a small shrug, and sets the empty kettle down on a flat stone on her counter.

I nod (because what do you say to that?) and run my fingers over the counter as I turn and look at a table full of washed and clean teacups and saucers.

I'm still frazzled from all of the events of the day, and the woman behind the counter seems to sense that as she turns a small hourglass upside-down to time the tea. Then she comes around the edge of the counter to stand beside me, a comforting hand resting on my arm. "Are you all right?" she asks me then, concern etched on her face.

Her words are kind, and I nod uncertainly. Well, I can't exactly tell her that I just overheard a conspiracy against the queen... I run my hand through my hair and sigh for a long moment.

"Yeah," I tell her. "I think so."

"You know," says the woman thoughtfully, reaching into one of the teacups that's stacked neatly upon the others, "it's an odd time to be in Agrotera."

"Really?" I ask her, mystified, as she takes a crystal out of the teacup...

I'm staring at her hand, then, dumbfounded.

It's the rose quartz crystal that Aidan gave me. The crystal that I *know* is sitting on the little bedside table up in the room that Virago and I are sharing at the palace.

The woman smiles at me mysteriously and hands me the crystal, curling my fingers around it with her other hand. "There are strange things afoot," she tells me softly, gently. "And I know you're not from around here..."

I stare down at the little tumbled stone, confused. "You could say that again," I whisper.

"There is a lot of talk," says the woman, her head to the side as she stares at me with glittering eyes, "about how the Hero's Tournament will bring about the end of Calla's reign. They say it will be dangerous, and people should stay away from Arktos City, because bad things are destined to happen." She shakes her head a little. "But it will all turn out well in the end. You'll see," she says with a firm nod. She glances back at the counter as the last sands in the hourglass sift through. "And your tea is done, milady!" she says triumphantly, rounding the counter again to spoon the tea leaves out of the cup with that same silver spoon, tossing them into a little wastebasket expertly.

"Um...how did you get my rose quartz?" I ask her then, feeling a little silly as I palm my stone.

The woman glances up at me with a bright smile. She places pottery caps on top of the cups. "I'm a witch!" she says brightly, snatching up a little wooden box from under the counter. "I'm sorry. I should have introduced myself. I'm Isabella," she says, holding out her hand over the counter.

I take her hand, and I shake it gingerly. "My name's Holly. And my brother's a witch, too," I manage, and that earns an even brighter smile from her.

"He's probably a better witch than I am," she says with a chuckle, placing the pottery cups in the wooden box. "I'm not very good at magic, but I can see some things, do little parlor tricks, like conjuring your crystal...*and* I make a wicked cup of tea," she tells me, with a little wink. "I'm often up at the castle, bringing tea to the queen, so I suppose I'll see you around. But no matter what happens, Holly, stay true and strong to what you believe. Stay true and strong to those you care about. It'll all be right in the end. Promise."

"Okay. But that...that sounds a little ominous," I say, mouth dry.

The sparkle has gone out of Isabella's eyes as she nods a little. "It's going to be an interesting week," she says with a little shrug, pushing the box of pottery mugs over the counter to me. "And tell Calla that I want these mugs back," she says, with another wink.

"Um. Sure," I smile, lifting the box and pushing the golden coin over the counter toward her.

"Be careful, Holly," she says, picking up the coin and depositing it into one of her apron's large pockets. Her face is solemn as she gazes at me now.

"I'll...try..." I tell her. I want to ask her if she knows anything else, want to ask her more, but it seems like this is all she's ready to tell me. So I nod goodbye, and I turn to go, ready to push the door open with my rear while I carry the box of mugs in front of me...but the door opens by itself. As if by magic.

And it really *is* magic, I realize, as I step through and realize there was no one on the other side to open it.

"Good day," says Isabella, wiggling her fingers at me as she smiles.

"Good day," I repeat, smiling to her as the door shuts behind me.

"That took an *eternity*," Kell tells me when I'm finally back in the library of the palace, and she picks up one of the mugs from the wooden box without even looking at me, sipping at the hot tea and making a face.

"You're welcome," I mutter to Kell with a little laugh, and then I'm glancing at Calla—Calla who looks like she's never cried a day in her life, her face a mask of pleasantness.

"Thank you so much," says Calla then, rising from her chair and taking up one of the mugs, as well. "Did you like Isabella?" she asks me with a small smile.

"She's very nice," I tell her, handing a mug to Virago and then taking one myself. Virago looked so happy to see me, but then she noticed that I wasn't smiling, and now she's gazing at me with concern. I clear my throat. "I know that Virago has to keep watch over you, Calla," I tell the queen, setting the wooden box down on the little table beside the chairs, "but can I speak to her somewhat privately?"

My stomach churns inside of me, but I really, *really* feel like I have to talk to someone. And Virago, of course, makes the most sense... But she *hates* Charaxus. I swallow, offering a small smile up to my lover, who frowns with worry as she gazes at me.

"Surely," says Calla graciously, sinking back down onto her chair and sipping at her tea with a smile. Kell flops into the chair beside the queen, gulping down some of the tea and making another ow-that-hurts face. It's far too hot to drink so recklessly, but she's soldiering through, anyway.

"What is it?" asks Virago, when we've walked to the far corner of the library and, hopefully, out of hearing range.

I turn, and, immediately, I'm talking, my heart hammering in my chest. "Something happened today," I tell her, holding her in my gaze, my mouth set in a narrow frown. "Something between Charaxus and Charix. I don't know...*exactly* what I think I heard. But Charaxus said that Charix would 'have Calla' by the end of the tournament," I tell her quickly, feeling sick in my stomach.

I don't know much about Charaxus, granted. And, admittedly, the way she looks at Calla...there is genuine affection there.

But I had to tell someone what I heard. And Virago is my girlfriend, the love of my life...

Still, I don't expect *this* reaction. I don't expect Virago's face to become stony with anger, her mouth downturning into a sharp, hard frown.

"What happened *exactly*?" she asks me, her voice a low growl. So I carefully recount the events of the morning, trying to be as specific as possible, but I don't remember, word for word, what was said. I try to emphasize the fact that I'm not certain what was being discussed but that I thought Virago should know about it.

Virago glances back now, toward the queen. Kell is still lounging in the chair like she's, well, a professional lounger.

"Was anyone else there with you?" asks Virago then, searching my face.

I shake my head. "It was just me and the suit of armor," I offer wryly. "Why? What's going on?"

"This is not the first time I've heard something of this nature," says Virago in a hushed tone, curling her fingers around my arm. "Please… Say nothing of this to anyone, *especially* the queen. She couldn't endure another betrayal from one she trusts. Not right now," says Virago, shaking her head in disgust. "I'm going to tell Magel about this, and we'll discuss what action to take. It was right of you to tell me, love," she says then, drawing me into her embrace.

But if it *was* right, then why do I feel so wretched about it? I remember the tear tracing down Charaxus' cheek as she looked after her brother. I remember the look of pain that passed over her face.

I lean back from Virago and gaze up at her. "I just..." I swallow as she searches my eyes, her brow furrowed. "I don't know. I don't know if that's *exactly* what I heard..." But Virago is already shaking her head.

"Charaxus comes from Furo," she tells me gently, squeezing me tightly in her arms. "And those who come from Furo bring trouble, the whole lot of them. They are cruel, and they are bloodthirsty, and they worship the Goddess Cower. You remember the Goddess Cower," says Virago, with one brow raised. "You bested her yourself. You should feel no sadness for Charaxus. She will get what is coming to her," she says with a low growl.

But as I look up at Virago, I can feel something deep in my gut. Something—intuition, maybe—that warns me I've made a mistake.

"I love you," I whisper, holding her tightly, too.

But as Virago kisses me, I can still feel that tremor in my belly, can still feel that I've done something I shouldn't have...

Something bad is afoot in Arktos City.

But I'm just not sure what Charaxus' role is in it.

It's no secret that, aside from me, Aphelion is the most important person in Virago's life.

Aphelion, by the way, is a horse.

But, hey, I get that. Shelley is one of the most important people in my life, too, and she has four paws. But I'm nervous as hell as I stand in front of the doors to the stable. Virago stands there beside me, her chest all puffed up with pride as she opens the door for me. She's been waiting to introduce me to Aphelion since we got here, but we haven't had a free moment, and when Virago got off of her guarding shift, she said it was time.

I would have rather we could have put it off a little bit longer...

I'm honestly worried that Aphelion isn't going to like me.

If you've never been in a relationship with a woman who loved her pet more than life itself, let me explain something to you: meeting that animal for the first time is comparable to meeting the woman's parents and her child and her best friend, all rolled up into one furry (or feathered, or finned, or scaled) body. That's what it always felt like when I introduced Shelley to my girlfriends; and if Shelley didn't like the person I was dating, it set off alarm bells in my head…

I've never been with anyone who loved an animal as much as me—until Virago.

So when Virago steps into the stable alongside me and glances down the hallway, her face radiating joy, I feel that tremor of nervousness move through me, and I pat the pocket of my dress (yes, this dress has *pockets*!) to make absolutely certain that I have the bits of carrots that Asha, the head cook, gave me when we went through the kitchen.

"Be careful with that beast," she'd said, wrinkling her nose as she passed me a handful of the carrots, her brow raised. "She's a *terror*."

That didn't lessen my nervousness at *all*.

I love horses. Growing up, I took riding lessons, and I'd entertained the idea of continuing the lessons into adulthood, and maybe owning a horse and leasing a stall in a stable in Boston… But then the reality of a librarian's salary made me fall back to Earth; I realized that just wasn't ever happening. I've never been afraid of horses (not even when the calm, docile pinto bucked me off when I fourteen years old, my body thudding into the sawdust of the arena like it was a hundred-something pound sack of potatoes), but then again, I'm not going to meet a normal horse right now.

I'm about to meet a *battle mare*, a mare who has

been trained *specifically* to help Virago fight in combat situations, rendering herself as much of a dangerous weapon as Virago's sword.

I gulp some air and walk down the corridor with Virago, my knight gripping my hand tightly with excitement.

"It's been such a long time since I've seen her," says Virago, sighing with raptures as she glances at me. "I'm so happy to have you meet her," she repeats for the seventeenth time. "Don't worry. Aphelion is going to *love* you."

That's when I hear this very distinctive banging sound. It sounds, actually, a little bit like a sledgehammer hitting an anvil over and over again. I think nothing of it; after all, we are in the royal stables. I'm assuming a blacksmith is close by. But when we walk further down the corridor, I'm beginning to realize that the banging is not coming from outside the stable or from some distant blacksmith's forge...

It's coming from *inside* the stable. From inside a stall, actually.

The stall that Virago stops in front of.

At that moment, an enormous dapple gray mare sticks her head out over the stall door, angling her long nose to glance toward us. When she spots Virago, she snorts, tossing her head up and down, baring her teeth at me. Now, when I say *enormous*, I mean *eno-o-o-rmous*—she towers over Virago, and she has a gorgeous gray mane, and she's objectively beautiful with her horsey muscles and her pretty coloring...

But she's also snaking her head at me, teeth bared, her eyes blazing with a heated fire of hatred that on any animal is usually the prelude to a vicious attack.

"Aphelion," says Virago sternly, holding her

hand out to the horse from hell. "Be easy, old friend," she says in a soft, gentle voice.

And immediately, Aphelion—because this is obviously Virago's battle mare, much to my dismay—gentles and puts her nose inside of Virago's cupped palm, her nostrils flaring.

"Come, come," says Virago, looking up from petting her horse with shining eyes. "Put your hand on her; she will come to know you better that way."

I've been bitten by a horse before—a really nasty gelding named Puck who terrorized a lot of the other kids at summer camp. I was feeding him a carrot one day, but it was a pretty tiny carrot, and he was pretty pissed off, in general, so he kept on chewing once the carrot was done—specifically, on my pointer finger. He didn't inflict any lasting damage, but I still remember what it felt like to have those horsey teeth close around an appendage.

But I also remember that horses can sense fear, and I'm assuming that a battle mare would be *spectacularly* good at smelling fear. So I take a deep breath, I lift up my hand, wincing a little (darn it, but I'm human), and I lay my fingers on her neck.

Her skin is quivering beneath my palm, and she turns her head immediately, thrusting it against my chest as she begins to sniff me all over.

It's then that I realize that she must smell the carrots.

I'm laughing a little as I pull one out of my pocket. Okay, this is normal horsey behavior that I can handle. I place the carrot in the palm of my hand and hold the palm out to her very flat (something I learned after the mistake I made with Puck), and Aphelion snatches up the carrot and crunches on it delicately, nodding her head with happiness as Virago chuckles, patting her neck on the other side.

"She likes you," she tells me companionably then, her face beaming as she gazes at me (and, admittedly, her horse, too) in pride. "That's good. I need my ladies to cooperate together," she says with a little chuckle, smoothing the hair on Aphelion's jaw.

I pat Aphelion's nose, but since she already ate the carrot, she's glaring at me, waiting for me to produce another one from my pocket. I gingerly fish another out, holding it up to the giant beast, and again she lips it up, chewing on it thoughtfully as she stares at me, her ears back—not slicked back, like she's going to destroy me any second, but with a thoughtful air to them, as if she's saying, "I'm watching you."

It's really not comforting, but Virago doesn't seem to notice as she slaps Aphelion's neck a few times affectionately and then rubs her nose with a soft palm. "Aphelion and I have been through some pretty rough times, haven't we, girl?" she asks the horse with an affectionate voice. Aphelion takes her attention off of me and instantly has eyes only for Virago. Her eyes actually get a little droopy, and her bottom lip becomes loose and flapping as she relaxes, placing her head against Virago's chest in a soft, gentle bump.

It's wonderful to see this massive war horse relaxing and being loving with Virago. But then, Virago is very good with animals; it stands to reason that she would have a great connection with her horse. But as Virago takes a step back, staring at her mare with pride, Aphelion gives me a little sideways glance, and her ears go back again, just a little. It's a warning, I think with a sigh. A "really, don't mess with me; I'm just putting up with you for Virago's benefit" sort of look.

I smile and pat her gingerly before tossing the rest of the carrots I brought her as a peace offering into her manger.

Virago peeks into the grain bucket over the edge of the stall door and sighs. “Poor Angela. She’s the stablehand here. She hasn't gotten to grain the horses yet.” She glances about curiously. “Actually...she hasn't come by to sweep up yet, either, or muck out the stalls. That's odd.” She wrinkles her nose, then smiles sidelong at me. “I could do the mucking out quite quickly, if you'll hold Aphelion for me while I clean her stall.”

“You want me to hold Aphelion?” I blink at Virago, my voice about an octave too high, but she's smiling so encouragingly, how in the world can I possibly say no? So I nod miserably, and as Virago rounds the corner to go get a lead tie, I glance up at the mare.

“Be good, okay?” I ask her quietly. She slicks her ears back as flat as they can go and snakes her head at me.

Okay, so we aren’t getting along like two peas in a pod, and I'm not quite sure why Aphelion doesn't like me. When she snakes her head toward me again and sniffs me all over, ears still slicked back, eyes narrowed in suspicion, I begin to think about that… And when Virago comes around the corner, Aphelion perks up her ears and nickers at her, her eyes softening like they're melting butter. And that’s when I *know.*

Aphelion absolutely, one hundred percent, more than life itself, loves her knight.

And I'm...kind of getting in the way of that relationship.

I can see it right now, the slow-motion montage

(set, of course, to an overly sappy love song) of Aphelion and Virago riding into battle, Virago spending a lot of time on Aphelion, brushing and preening her mare, Virago and Aphelion going on adventures and quests together, Aphelion and Virago having a really awesome time together...

And then I come along, and Virago is whisked away to another world, and where does that leave Aphelion?

Without Virago.

I took Virago away form Aphelion. And she *knows* it.

My suspicions are somewhat confirmed when Virago steps forward, the pitchfork in one hand and the broom in the other, and she places her strong arms around her horse's neck. For a long moment, Aphelion bends her head around Virago's shoulder, giving the knight her version of a horsey hug. But when Aphelion's left eye rotates toward me, again she lays her ears slick back against her head (Virago can't see this, because her face is buried in Aphelion's mane), and Aphelion bares her teeth at me in a very clear "this woman is mine, not yours, you jerk" sentiment.

Virago takes a step back and threads the lead rope through the rope halter, handing me both ends of the rope as she puts the halter on over Aphelion's head, smoothing her ears beneath. Virago then opens the door, taking a step back, and gives me an even wider smile as she pats Aphelion's neck. "If you could just take her out into the stable yard, I'll only be a minute. Let her get some sunshine this afternoon," she says.

"Sure," I croak, narrowly avoiding Aphelion's very calculated bite at my arm (she gets a little fabric from the sleeve of my dress and nothing more). I turn around, leading this massive war horse down the corridor of the stable and out into the brightness of the stable yard, trying to keep an eye on her but failing. Aphelion gets in two more nips of fabric before we've cleared the stable.

"You're brave!" Kell remarks from across the stable yard, grooming her own mare who stands, one back leg cocked, her head down, absorbing the sun. Her mare is a gorgeous palomino color and is just as tall as Aphelion, but she somehow looks less vicious. Maybe because Kell's mare is not currently trying to bite my arm again, pawing at the ground like she wants to dig a grave and bury me in it.

"And why's that?" I ask Kell, sidestepping another vicious bite.

Kell snickers, smoothing the curry comb over her mare's withers. "Because Aphelion *hated* Virago's last lover, and it looks like she hates you even more!" She says this blithely as she grins at me. "So, yes," she tells me in a singsong voice, "you're *very* brave."

I sigh for a long moment as I avoid another bite, taking off in a brisk walk along the outer edge of the yard with Aphelion, trying to keep ahead of the mare. "Your horse is nice," I tell Kell as we circle around past her. Aphelion chooses this inopportune moment to try to kick with her right back leg at Kell's mare, but the mare snorts, lifting her head and sidestepping the kick with her own ears slicked back.

"Hey, Ayla, calm yourself," says Kell, rubbing her mare's neck. "And, yes, she is," she says affectionately, slapping the mare on the rump before casting me a sidelong glance. "I wouldn't be worried so much about her bites as I would about her kicks," she tells me helpfully. "Aphelion has a *mean* kick."

Aphelion is walking behind me innocently when I turn around, but in another moment, she's not quite so innocent, because she's risen up on her back legs just a little, doing a strange, horsey hop (I'm assuming this is some sort of war horse move, but she looks a little ridiculous, this enormous horse hopping on her back legs), and striking out at me with her front hooves.

My instincts take over, and I step back quickly, but it's not quick enough. Those enormous hooves are totally going to strike me...

And that's when Virago peers around the corner of the stable. And Aphelion drops to earth as quickly as if she were a thousand-pound stone. The horse literally bats her eyes, chewing contentedly on her bit as she gazes at Virago.

"How are my girls getting along?" Virago asks me brightly.

Aphelion and I share a secret glance of mutual dislike.

"Just peachy," I say, as Aphelion bats her eyes again at Virago.

And that is what we call an enormous white lie. For love.

Chapter 11: The Warning

It's about an hour (give or take) until the opening ceremonies of the Hero's Tournament, and the palace is in an uproar.

I never thought I'd be putting those words together in any sort of real-life scenario, but there it is. Palace. Uproar. My life has gotten infinitely stranger this past day and a half...and more magical than I ever could have thought possible.

But what's not magical is the reason for the uproar.

"I don't think it *wise*, milady," says Virago, her jaw tight as she stands at attention in front of Queen Calla, "for you to go through with this."

But Calla isn't even looking at Virago. She's being snugly tightened into a corset, and she's gripping one of her bed posts with white-knuckled hands, taking tiny, shallow breaths.

"My dear Virago," she says, gripping the post even tighter as Joy, resident head tailor to the queen, pulls on the laces for all she's worth, gritting her teeth, too, as she leans back, arm muscles flexing beneath the tight fabric of her sparkling black top. "I appreciate your concern," Calla gasps out, taking even shorter breaths as her waist becomes smaller, "but what sort of example would it set if the queen wasn't present in the city procession?"

"My queen—" begins Virago gruffly, as Joy glances sidelong at me, cutting Virago off with a raised hand.

"Can you hold these for me?" she asks, and I step forward with trepidation as she starts to make an elaborate knot in the corset ties. She hands me back some of the ribbons, and I hold onto the loose ends (thankfully, they're already tied off). "You were saying, Virago?" asks Joy wryly.

"My queen," says Virago, giving Joy a rather withering look, "you will remember that I advised you to cancel the procession entirely."

"Virago," says Calla gently, as Joy finishes lacing up the ribbons and tucking the ends away. Her waist is now *tiny* and looks wholly unnatural, but Calla straightens, settling her right palm against her squished stomach, and she smiles beatifically at Virago. "You are my best knight, and I am so grateful for your service, always," she says, stepping forward and laying a gentle hand on Virago's arm, "but you must know that if we did not have the procession, it would inform the whole world that we are afraid. That we are afraid that Charix has come to power, that we are afraid of our neighbors to the north. And nothing could be farther from the truth. Arktos is full of strong, capable women, and the men from Furo must see that, must see what we are capable of, and they must see that we *never* show fear. Surely you know this to be true."

"Milady, the *gesture* of being in the procession is worthless if it costs you your life," Virago beseeches, her voice coming out in a low growl.

Joy takes up the gown that Calla's going to be wearing in the Hero's Tournament procession: it's a big, burgundy number with a million tiers in its wide,

Scarlett-O'Hara-reminiscent skirt, and a very plunging neckline with off-the-shoulder puff . She lifts the concoction over Calla's head. "Arms up, milady," she says, a smile playing on her lips.

But Calla is turning to Virago. I don't know how she's managing to look incredibly serious in a corset and undergarments, but she's pulling it off as she draws herself up to her full height. "Virago," she says softly, quietly, "thank you for your concern. You are so good to me." Her face hardens. "But if I do not go out in this procession today, we have already lost. Don't you see?" she asks, placing a hand on Virago's arm again, her eyes narrowed as she holds Virago's gaze. "If we change how we do things because of a threat, then Furo has already won. They have already destroyed our livelihood. And that I cannot allow."

Virago's jaw tightens, and she nods only once. "I understand, milady."

"Well, I don't," scowls Kell, who—up until this moment—has remained perfectly quiet, sprawled in one of the queen's sumptuous, plush chairs. Aside from the overstuffed chairs, the queen's bedroom is actually pretty modest. It looks similar to the room that Virago and I are staying in. When I came in and remarked as such, Calla told me that she's no different from anyone else here in her kingdom, which was pretty damn awesome in my opinion, no matter how romanticized I'd built up the queen's bedchambers in my head (I'd imagined something on par with Marie Antoinette's rooms).

Virago and Calla turn to look at Kell. Joy simply puts down the gown and takes a pipe out of her pocket, lighting the thing up and puffing away at it as she sighs, leaning against the bedpost, waiting for us to be finished with our "debate."

"You're going to get yourself killed, my queen," says Kell then, rising. In this moment, there's nothing casual or sarcastic about her demeanor. She's impassioned as she takes a step forward.

Calla lifts her chin, staring at her knight. "Stand down, Kell," she says mildly, but there's a dynamic of power that's crackling between them.

Kell obeys. She takes a step backward, and then she places her fist over her heart as she sighs for a long moment. "I'm sorry, milady," she murmurs then. "But you know it to be true."

"I know," says Calla, her voice gentle again, "that I have a duty. As have you. We all do. We are all part of the web of life, and we must pull our own weight, all of us, and do what we were meant to. You know this, Kell."

Kell and Virago exchange a look, their brows up, but I can read Virago's face in that moment. She's glad that Calla is actively working for her country, but it's obvious to everyone here...there's a great risk to her being in that procession, being seen so openly in the streets of Arktos. Every single person in the city, those who live here and those who are visiting because of the tournament, knows the route that the procession will take. Which means there could be an assassin on every corner.

"We must be watchful," says Virago to Kell, and Kell snorts, her eyes flashing as she tosses her wild hair over her shoulder.

"*You* be watchful," says Kell, raising a brow. "*I'll* be ready."

Calla casts me a glance as Joy puts down her pipe and places the dress, at last, on the queen. The sumptuous folds of burgundy satin fall in waves over her cream-colored skin, and as Joy does up the tiny buttons on the back, Calla clasps her hands over her stomach. Kell and Virago have walked away: they're discussing, in soft, sibilant whispers, who else Magel has planned to be on the queen's closest guard for the procession.

"I hope you don't think me foolish, Holly," says Calla with a small, sad smile. "I have a duty I must perform, and I am determined to see it through."

"Not foolish," I tell her, shaking my head quickly, patting the pockets of my enormous dress (it's similar to a medieval gown in construction, but it still has pockets, because Joy is awesome). "They're just worried about you," I say, pointing my thumb toward the knights. "I mean, everyone's worried about you. It must be so hard," I hazard then. "Having people who want you dead." I swallow, shaking my head. "I can't imagine it."

Calla's eyes unfocus as she gazes out the window. Her hair, long and loose and curly, flows over her milky shoulders, and the silver circlet on her head glistens in the sunshine.

"I loved two things once, you know," she tells me softly, and my ears perk up as I stare at her, silent. "My country, and my love." Her gaze flicks to me. "It sounds noble and poetic," she says, giving a bitter laugh, "but it was true. If *my* knight were here now, she would persuade me not to go on the procession. I would still have to, but I would know she was there. Watching me. There, if I needed her." She gazes at me now, and the hurt is so evident in her expression that I actually take a step back. She looks so pained. "But she's gone. And I have to do this alone," she tells me with a small shrug, gazing down at her hands as she straightens them, then crossing them in front of her over her stomach. She sighs out for a long moment. "I'm sorry, Holly," she says, lifting her face and gazing at me with genuine remorse, her eyes glittering with unshed tears. "I didn't mean to become so maudlin."

"No, you have every right to be sad. What your ex did to you was unforgivable," I say, shaking my head. "But you don't have to go in this procession if you genuinely think that there's danger to yourself. And Virago really seems to think that there might be," I say, hooking my thumb over my shoulder to point to my knight. "Couldn't you… I don't know," I say, my mind grappling as I try to think of something. "Couldn't you just go to the opening ceremonies, not participate in the procession? Wouldn't that be almost the same thing?"

"The ruler of the country in which the Hero's Tournament takes place *always* participates in the procession," she tells me firmly. "To not do so would show weakness, and at this time, Arktos cannot afford to show any weakness at all."

I swallow. "Well, then the knights will just have to keep you safe," I tell her, giving her a watery smile. "But you're not alone."

"I'm sure they will," says Calla, with a bright smile that I know is fake. I swallow a little, turning to look back at Virago and Kell.

"I've got a bad feeling about this," mutters Kell loudly from the corner of the room, lifting a single brow and crossing her arms in front of her unhappily.

I didn't have a bad feeling, but when we get down to the gates at the entrance to Arktos City, I'm beginning to understand what Kell was talking about. I ride through the city behind Virago on Aphelion's back (getting onto the horse was a begrudging allowance on the war mare's behalf, and an oh-God-this-might-be-the-end-for-me experience on mine), and by the time we get to the front gates, the skin on the back of my neck is crawling. It seems like every hair on my body is standing on end. It's the way you feel when you can sense someone staring at you across a crowded room. I feel watched, and I feel scrutinized, and I don't even know where that sensation is coming from.

But it's very strong, and it's very apparent. And I'm pretty sure everyone else is feeling it, too. The knights, all on their separate mounts, all wearing their best armor, keep giving one another uneasy glances, and even though we didn't go down the main thoroughfare through the city ("We'd ruin the suspense if we rode down and came back the same way," Calla told me), I can hear the crowds gathered on the main street through Arktos City. Everyone is shouting, and the general murmur and merriment of the crowd can be heard clearly, even this many streets back. I'm assuming that pretty much everyone in the capital city has gathered on the streets, or is pouring out of the windows and on top of the roofs, to see the procession of champions about to enter the Hero's Tournament.

And that means that there really *could* be an assassin posted at every corner, in every nook.

The knights are out in full force. Even though we're on the side streets only, I can make out their familiar armor and their horses' uniforms (the big saddle, the bridle with the silver headstall, the colors of cobalt blue and gold across the horses' rumps in the form of the saddle blankets): knights that I've already met, and knights I've never met. There are a *lot* of royal knights in Arktos City, and they are all flanking the streets today, keeping everyone safe.

And keeping their eyes on the queen.

I'm holding tightly onto Virago (and it may be just me, but I'm pretty sure that Aphelion is prancing extra high, so that I'm having the bumpiest ride of my life back here. I would normally think that a horse wouldn't be so devious, but then, I'd never met Aphelion before today), and I lean forward now, putting my mouth as close to her ear as I can, her ponytail flowing over my shoulder, her wolf's tail with it, giving me a little bit of comfort. "Do you think everything's going to be okay? Do you really think something bad is going to happen today?" I ask her with a grimace. Virago frowns, turning a little so that only I can catch her words.

"I do," she says, gritting her teeth together. "But we are ready for it, whatever it may be. Come what may."

"Come what may," I repeat, swallowing a little and gripping her waist.

Life in Arktos certainly isn't dull.

We get down to the front gates, and we move through them, eliciting a bright cheer from the assembled people located near the wall. They're already pretty drunk (it's late in the afternoon at this point), hefting up goblets of a drink that I'm suspecting is Magin as they cheer loudly and raucously, raising their arms to the queen.

I have no idea how Calla is sitting astride her mount since she's wearing that big-skirted burgundy gown, but somehow she's managing it—and making it look very easy to boot. And she is *not* riding sidesaddle. Her mare is a tall, lean blue roan, the smoky color of her coat striking. And the horse is a heavy horse, like the others, so when her large hooves strike the ground, sparks are elicited from the horseshoes as they hit the cobblestones. The whole effect is particularly magical as Calla rides in the middle of all of the knights, her blonde hair blowing back in the wind, her gown spilling over the rump of her horse, the horse prancing through the streets like it's a show pony.

We pass through the front gates, and then we move around the left edge of the city, toward the encroaching forest. Here is where all the champions of the Hero's Tournament are gathered, different people from different countries, all present to vie for the title of "hero"—and, I've been told, a pretty cool-looking trophy, and a lot of gold. I'm thinking of this as Agrotera's version of the Olympics, but there are no silver or bronze medals awarded here. It's a winner-takes-all kind of game. The champions form a line, ready to march into the city.

As we canter smoothly (well, everyone *else* seems to be cantering smoothly; Aphelion suddenly seems to forget how to run, and I'm being tossed around like a sack of bruised potatoes) along the lineup of tournament contestants, I catch a glimpse of glimmering armor. There's the knight from Lumina, wearing her crystalline armor, astride her unicorn. My heart goes up into my throat to glimpse something so beautiful (and, you know, otherworldly), but then the rest of the contestants look pretty amazing, too. There's a guy astride a gigantic boar (with equally gigantic tusks), and a woman astride something that looks a little like a giraffe but that is pure white, and then there's a woman astride something that looks a little like a cross between a dragon and a dinosaur, standing up on its two hind legs, its two smaller front legs resembling those of a T-Rex, its scales an iridescent black. The rider is wearing armor made entirely of scales, her long black hair cascading down her back in a million intricate braids that are then knotted together to form shapes that remind me of Celtic knots.

Everywhere I look, there are interesting, fantastical-looking people, often laughing and talking together, but some are tensely sitting astride their mounts, waiting for the procession to begin. There are people other than knights and champions among us, too, because I see someone who I'm assuming is a queen or empress or something up on a dais, carried by four enormous cats. The animals look a little like a cross between tigers and lions, if tigers had lion manes.

And I also notice King Charix. He's in line in the procession with fewer men than he brought into the banquet hall last night, but there is still quite a crew of big, black-armored guys standing around, looking sullen and like they'd rather be anyplace else (since they are, apparently, too cool for school).

The champion of Furo is easy to spot. He looks like a guy on steroids who ate another guy on steroids for breakfast. He is almost *twice as tall* as Virago. I'm going to let that sink in for a minute. He doesn't look real; he looks, instead, like one of the parade floats that Macy's might blow up for the Thanksgiving Day Parade. He stands there like the Incredible Hulk, glowering and staring forward, and not taking part in any of the muted conversations that the other men from Furo are currently having. But as we canter past him, he watches us. The face-grate of his black helmet is lifted, and he watches us go by, and he actually smiles. But it's not a nice sort of smile.

This is the kind of smile that a wolf makes before falling in for the kill.

Giving me a little more to go on with this wolf metaphor, when the guy smiles? Yeah. His teeth are pointed. They are filed to tiny, sharp points. A chill lances through me as I catch his eyes.

I know, in that moment, that if you met this guy in a darkened alley, said darkened alley would be the last place you ever saw.

Virago holds the champion's gaze as we race past, and her jaw is set in that particularly hard line that I've come to know as determination and just the right amount of stubbornness.

"That's a big guy," I mutter to her, and she smiles tensely, glancing back at me.

"He's not so very big," she says, shaking her head. I shudder a little, and then we're finally past him, and we're all standing at the back of the line, ready for the procession to start.

I can hear hoof beats up ahead, and I glance up, surprised to see Charaxus cantering leisurely toward us, her head held high, regal, as her long black hair billows behind her. She is riding a tall black mare (I don't think they have any short horses or ponies in Arktos), and with her black armor, and the black saddle and bridle, the effect is pretty impressive. And slightly scary, especially paired with the scowl she's wearing.

"Are we ready?" she asks in a low growl as she comes alongside Calla. Calla nods, gripping the reins on her mare a little tighter. The mare tosses her head at Calla's tension, and the queen relaxes a little, giving a sidelong glance to Charaxus.

"Is it time?" she asks, her chin held high, bravely.

I realize at this moment that Calla really could die this afternoon, right in the middle of this procession.

I grip Virago tightly, taking a deep breath as all of the knights look up to the top right of the wall surrounding the city, above the front gates. One of the knights is standing on that wall, her armor glinting in the sunshine as she holds up a blue- and gold-colored flag. She holds it high, the stiff breeze taking it and fluttering it in the wind.

"We ride," says Charaxus then, gathering the reins of her mare tightly in her hands. The mare rears up, striking the air before her with dinner-plate-sized hooves, tossing her head and eliciting a bugling sound of challenge that seems to spread out through the other mounts lined up in the procession, no matter what animals they may be. The woman on top of the wall lets the flag fall down to her feet, and the people at the very beginning of the line begin to move forward.

I've been in a few Pride parades in my day, and the one thing about parades that's true, even across worlds, is that they're slow to start. And when they *do* eventually start, they're very stop-and-go. The people at the beginning of the procession may be moving now, but that means the knights and Queen of Arktos (and, you, know—me), being last in the lineup, will have to wait forever (give or take a couple of minutes) to move. But we don't have to wait as long as I thought we would.

And good thing, too, because all of the battle mares here, at the end of the line, are starting to act nervously, tossing their heads and stomping their hooves. But it's more than that. They keep lifting their noses to the wind, their nostrils flaring, as if they're sniffing out trouble, and they shift their weight back and forth. Some of them, like Aphelion, are even dancing in place, their necks arched unnaturally, chomping at their bits, their necks flecked with sweat.

"What has the horses so spooked?" I ask Virago, who leans forward and places a calming hand on Aphelion's broad neck.

"I don't know," she says, her voice tense with worry. She glances sidelong at Kell. "They only act like this before a battle."

"They can tell we're tense," says Kell, shrugging elegantly and tightening her grip on her reins, too.

But out of all the mares here, only Charaxus' remains calm, her four feet planted firmly on the ground. Actually, her back right hoof is cocked, and her head is lowered almost contentedly. Charaxus sits on her mare's back with perfect posture and poise, while the other mares dance around, tossing their heads, their knights sitting them expertly but taking a little bit of time to calm them down.

Charaxus chooses this moment to turn to look at Calla. Charaxus has positioned her mare right alongside Calla's, and they are side by side; their knees might almost be touching, actually, but since Calla's dress is so immense, it's difficult to tell.

"We are here for you, milady," says Charaxus solemnly now. Her voice is low, a growl, and pitched so that it doesn't carry, but Virago has positioned Aphelion close to Calla, too, so I can make out what she's saying. "We will keep you safe," Charaxus says in a gentle growl. And at the very end of her words, there's a catch to her voice.

Calla glances at her quickly, then away, but I can see that she swallowed. "Thank you, Charaxus," she says, and like Charaxus' words, Calla's are pitched to be heard only by Charaxus, but I'm close enough to hear her, too. And Virago also hears, because her jaw is tight as she tenses in front of me. I can actually feel the tension spreading out from her belly beneath my hands, can feel it even through the armor.

We start to move, the horses prancing in place, held close and tight by their knights, reins gathered into gloved hands, but the horses aren't having any of it. They dance sideways; they dance forward in slow motion (held in check by watchful knights), and every one of them—except for Charaxus' mare—is breaking out into flecks of sweat, the sweat gathering beneath the leather reins along their necks.

Ahead of us, along the curve of the outside edge of the forest, I can see the men of Furo. None of them are on mounts, which I find interesting. Every single other group of delegates is on mounts, or at least the champion is. They're the only people on foot.

Admittedly, I'm not quite certain what type of mount could *carry* their champion, since he seems to be a *giant.*

That giant chooses this moment to turn back and look at us. Virago stiffens against me and raises her chin. I can tell that they're gazing at one another.

And then, very slowly and methodically, the man lifts his massive hand, sticking his thumb up...and he traces his thumb across his neck.

My first reaction to this is a cold dread. The second (admittedly, much later) reaction: they have that gesture on this world, too?

The "you're dead" gesture.

Virago lifts her chin even higher and doesn't rise to the bait, much to my relief, but still...that was kind of chilling to witness. I can't even imagine that guy in hand-to-hand combat. He could beat an elephant, if he wanted to.

As I sit there on the back of the horse, as I hug Virago as tightly as I can, all of the horses moving forward in a stately procession, I feel a shiver come over me. I feel every hair rise on the back of my neck, and a tremor quakes through me. My brother, Aidan, always posits that everyone in the world is psychic, and he told me that, since he's so psychic (he's not a very humble guy), this means that I'm psychic, too. I don't know if I believe that, but what I'm feeling right now really can't be explained. I feel as if something's wrong, something's off, and that things are about to get worse.

There's music in the procession, moving along with us. Musicians are located between the groupings of champions and their delegates, playing mostly woodwind-type instruments, as well as people carrying drums and banging on them in perfect rhythm. The musicians directly ahead of us are playing something that sounds dignified and lively, but there's this minor-key type sound that's also working its way into their music, weaving through the melody...and that's not making me feel much more relaxed.

"My love," says Virago as we near the city walls and the front gate of Arktos City. The city itself was once so beautiful and atmospheric, but now the sight of the gates looming above us just fills me with anxiety: anything could be waiting for us in the city, anything ready and waiting to kill Queen Calla. As if she can hear my thoughts, Virago leans back and says quietly over her shoulder, "Be ready for anything. But know also," she says, lifting her chin, "that I will die before any harm comes to you."

"Don't go dying anytime soon," I tell her, trying to keep my voice light, but it betrays me, catching on the last word. I clear my throat. "Just watch Calla. I've got a bad feeling," I tell her, gripping her waist.

"Me, too," she says solemnly.

And then we pass through the open gates into the packed streets of Arktos City.

When I say "packed," I mean that the streets are literally teeming with people, wedged in tightly, waving little banners (most of them here, in the beginning of the city, are cobalt blue covered in gold-embroidered stars), tossing paper confetti. There are bits and bobs of magic spiraling around us and making stars appear in the air above people's heads, falling stars *whooshing* around the horses and exploding with loud pops of sound and color. Sparkles rain down on the people with miniature, magical explosions. The horses are actually pretty good about all of this noise and magic as they prance in place but still move forward, showing no signs of spooking.

"Long live the queen!" starts a chant close by. Virago smiles at the people in the crowd, though I can tell she's uneasy about this. We start to wend our way down the main thoroughfare, through the city, our horses steadily striding uphill, and a smattering of "long live the queen!" chants follows with us as we rise higher and higher toward the palace.

I'm beginning to notice that, when the champion and knights of Furo and King Charix move through the crowd, the voices on either side of the route grow hushed. Everyone's cheering like mad for the people before them, and then they're cheering like mad for the people after them...but, as one, the crowd falls to silence when the Furo delegates walk past. It's an odd, eerie sensation when a cheer suddenly stops; it reminds me a little of a wave performed badly in a sports stadium.

I'm not the only one noticing the lack of enthusiasm in the crowds here in Arktos for the Furo men. The black-armored guys are starting to grumble amongst themselves. They strike me as very poor losers (I'm not sure why; maybe it's because they were standing around like sullen toddlers earlier), so it's starting to bother me that they're grumbling. I know that relationships between Arktos and Furo aren't stellar at the moment. And I paid attention in Social Studies: when the relationships between countries are strained, it's a land of dry tinder, and it doesn't take much to set off the spark that ignites everything.

So I'm gradually starting to feel more uncomfortable and more worried, and it's when we round the final bend and are on the straightaway toward the palace that I realize my heart is in my throat.

It's the home stretch. We're *almost there*. Most of the other groups in the procession are already inside the palace, getting ready for the opening ceremonies that are going to take place in the banquet hall.

But *we're* not there yet.

I lift my eyes. There's a tiny glint up high. I don't know why I look up; there are glints and glimmers and shimmers everywhere, with all the magic in the air, making miniature pyrotechnics. But I look up, anyway. And though there are people spilling out of every window from the buildings surrounding us, though there are tons of people crowding the rooftops, too, there's one rooftop that's noticeably empty...

Save for one lone figure positioned in the corner closest to us.

Calla's mare is starting to ascend the wide marble steps in front of the palace, picking up her hooves daintily and placing them with care on each step. All of the horses and other mounts ascended the steps, too (which impressed me—it's not always a simple feat for animals to climb stairs), and Calla is giving the mare her head with the reins to make it even easier on her. It's because I noticed Calla right before I looked up that I realize something in this moment.

It's difficult to see the figure up on the roof, because this person is far back from the edge of the building; I can hardly make out their head. And their head is swathed in a hood...which is odd, given the day. It's warm out here, far too warm for a cloak and hood. I've already pitied the knights at least a dozen times, wrapped up in their leather clothes and armor; they must be positively roasting.

So when I look up and see this cloaked figure—this cloaked figure who appears to be hiding—I pause. But then I also see that the person is holding something, something that's being pointed toward Calla...

I just saw where Calla was, saw it very clearly, and there's no mistaking the direction of that object. It's so far up that the shape is hard to make out, but cold dread fills me as recognition dawns: an arrow. They're holding a crossbow, and the arrow is being aimed directly at Calla.

"Virago, look!" I whisper, pointing upward instantly, and then, heart hammering, I shout, "Calla, look out!"

Instantly, everything changes.

I've seen the knights move quickly; I saw Virago best the woman at the bar. But how fast the knights reacted, up until this moment, was slow in comparison to here, now. Because, in a single heartbeat, they have leapt into action, vaulting off their horses to surround Calla.

Kell, who was riding behind the queen on her own mare, is off of her mare's back in a second and then launching herself in a graceful leap to settle behind Calla on the horse. Instantly, Kell's eyes are closed, and there's a shimmer of strange, iridescence around both her and Calla, as well as Calla's mare. I think she's shielding Calla with magic.

Everything seems to shift into slow motion, because Virago has remained on her horse, and I remain on the horse, too, holding tightly to Virago as Aphelion rears up, striking the air with her hooves. I can feel myself slipping off Aphelion's shiny rump. She's a huge horse, so if I fall now, I'm going to drop a long way down to the ground. I try to hold on, but there are a ton of people shouting, and there's the sound of something *swooshing* through the air.

In a second, it's all over, because there's a loud *thwack* as an arrow hits the flag post closest to Calla, the post that's carrying the now-familiar blue and gold pennant of Arktos City. The attacker wasn't aiming at Calla, after all, but the message was communicated loud and clear: they *could* have killed Calla if they wanted to.

The arrow vibrates in place for a long moment, and there are already knights headed toward the building where the archer was positioned, but he or she is no longer visible when I shield my eyes against the glare of the sun and stare upwards at the rooftop.

Magel dismounts her horse and strides over to the arrow, drawing it out from the post with a vicious yank.

"There's a note attached, milady," she says with disgust. I've never seen Magel so upset, but it's a cold, calculated anger. If there is a person still standing on that roof when the knights get up to it, the archer stands no chance.

"I will examine the note later," Magel is saying, but Calla, very pale, is sitting with her back poker straight on her mare, Kell sliding over the horse's rear to stand again on the ground.

"Read it now, Magel," says Calla, her voice soft and quiet.

"Milady," Magel begins, but Calla simply looks at her, and Magel sighs for a long moment, then unrolls the thin bit of parchment that was attached to the arrow's shaft.

The crowd around us has hushed, but a murmur starts up now, a low one, thick with worry and fear.

Magel glances down at the note, and then her mouth falls open. She looks up at her queen with beseeching brown eyes, but Calla nods.

"The note, my knight," she says, and there is weariness in her voice.

Magel clears her throat. She holds up the piece of paper. She says, in a steady voice that shakes, only at the end, "Cower will rise. Calla shall fall."

Chapter 12: Fire and Ice

Virago's eyes are a steel blue, a dark blue, a rage-filled blue.

"I will kill him," she says simply. And, in that moment, I know she means it with every fiber of her being.

"We do not *know* that King Charix had anything to do with this. *Officially.* To go after him now would jeopardize our entire country," Kell snaps, unceasing in her frenetic pacing across the library floor. Back and forth, back and forth she paces, while the rest of the knights stand around tensely, all of them watching their queen, who sits in the center on one of her plush library chairs, holding the thin parchment threat in her pale hands.

"If the archer wanted her dead, she would have made certain it happened," says Magel tiredly, rubbing at her eyes with the back of her gloved hand. "She wanted to frighten the queen. But, most importantly, she wanted to do so in front of all of the people of Arktos, so that they would think the queen is weak. They wanted Calla to appear weak."

"But she is *not* weak," snarls Kell, turning to look at Calla now. "Milady," she says beseechingly, her rage evaporating (or, at least, she's hiding it) as she kneels down in front of Calla. "Are you all right?" she asks tentatively. "You have not said a word since the note was read."

Calla glances at Kell now, her blue eyes almost colorless. She was gazing at the note for the longest time, but she didn't look like she was even really seeing it. "Where is the archer now?" she asks, and her words sound so tired.

"In the dungeon," says Magel, her arms crossed in front of her. "I am going to interrogate her shortly."

Calla shakes her head, rolling her shoulders back. "Do not harm her."

The other knights stare at their queen. "Your Majesty?" asks Magel quietly.

Calla rises, lifting her chin. "I want to see her."

"My queen, no," says Kell, rising too quickly, a storm brewing over her features. "The opening ceremonies for the Hero's Tournament are at sundown," she says, pointing out one of the open windows in the library where the sun is descending low along the horizon. "We don't have much time to—"

"To break the archer?" asks Calla, lifting a single brow. "To inflict enough pain to retrieve the information you need to keep me safe?"

"Frankly, Your Majesty, yes," says Magel, her jaw tense. "You are our top priority," she says, spreading her hands, her words soft, soothing, "and that archer could have killed you. We *must* ascertain where she came from, who she is in league with, and who *precisely* wants you dead, or you will still be in jeopardy—"

"And I will die," says Calla solemnly, her eyes glittering. "Is that what you were going to say, Magel?" she asks, her voice soft, dignified.

Magel shifts uncomfortably. "Calla," she says then, her words soft. "It is our sworn duty to protect you, and to protect all of Arktos. You can't die."

Calla folds her hands in front of her, her chin lifted. "I have made peace with the Goddess," she says then, drawing herself up to her full height. "If I die, Charaxus takes over, and I know she can lead the country as well as I could."

"You can't be *reckless*," Kell begins, but Calla turns, and a single glance from the queen silences her.

"To protect me, you are *all* reckless," says Calla gently. "I will not have someone hurt because of me, even if she is an enemy. These are dangerous times to be queen, my friends," she says, looking around at all of the knights with genuine affection, her face softened now. "I accept that, and I have made peace with it. The opening ceremonies must go on, and I am the queen of Arktos," she says, spreading her hands and bowing her head, "and I have my duties to the Hero's Tournament. It has been an honor and a privilege to be your queen," she says, glancing at every knight in turn. "I hope you know how much I have loved all of you," she finishes, her voice quiet, small.

"You are saying goodbye," says Magel flatly.

"I am being realistic," says Calla firmly. "As I was realistic that something might happen during the procession this day. If anyone is going to make a move, it's going to be during the opening ceremonies, when every citizen of Arktos is there to see it, when so many people from neighboring countries will be there as witnesses."

"But we *will* keep you safe," Kell says, her voice adamant, her hands curled into fists.

"I have no doubts in any of you," says Calla, shaking her head. "You are my knights, and you are fearless. But there is darkness afoot," she says, her voice dropping low, “if Cower is involved. And I cannot predict what will happen now.”

I finger the edges of my sleeves, my stomach tying itself into knots. Virago stands beside me, her arms crossed in front of her, her jaw hard as she watches the queen, eyes glittering. Our arms touch, and the warmth of her, emanating through the leather and armor, is comforting to me.

“Now, please,” says Calla, sighing. “Show me the archer. And,” she says, a single brow raised, “I want to see Cower.”

The knights glance among themselves, but they can't argue with a queen who has already made up her mind.

I don't know how much time we have until the opening ceremonies, but it doesn't matter. We have enough time to get down to the dungeons, to see the woman who threatened the queen. And to see Cower.

But at the very thought of again seeing the goddess who turned into a beast, a beast who tried to destroy everything near and dear to me, my stomach twists into even tighter knots, knots that I can’t begin to undo. Virago glances sidelong at me as the knights assemble, falling into a line, and we all get ready to leave the library.

“Are you all right with going to see Cower?” she asks me, holding my gaze. “Because you do not have to go, my love,” she tells me, voice soft. “There is no reason that you should—”

“Yeah,” I tell her, shaking, “I can handle it. She's powerless now, right?” I ask, licking my lips and trying to calm my erratic heartbeat.

“Powerless,” Virago repeats, nodding. “She can do no harm, and she cannot touch any one of us. She is locked away forever."

I swallow, remembering Virago's stories about what Cower accomplished when she was loose and a powerful goddess. She destroyed so very many people, so many places...so much *life*. And now it's difficult to imagine that someone, once so powerful, could be felled by someone...well, like me. I never wielded a sword in my life, and I know that I had complete dumb luck, but I managed to vanquish a *goddess*. So I'm guessing that she...probably doesn't like me very much. And that's putting it mildly.

"Let's...go," I tell her, gesturing forward.

During all of these proceedings, Charaxus has stood silently by, watching the queen intently. Her eyes are narrowed, and her cheeks are pale, but then aren't her eyes *always* narrowed, and isn't she perpetually pale? Still, there's something about the way that Charaxus is looking at Calla now. She's gazing at the queen with such softness, such kindness…

Such *love*.

"Hey," I whisper, tugging on Virago's elbow and drawing my knight aside. "What happened with what I told you? About Charaxus and Charix?"

Virago shifts her gaze to Charaxus, standing quietly beside the other knights, but definitely separate from them. And Virago bends down to me, putting her mouth by my ear, her warm lips brushing against my skin.

"It is no small thing to accuse the vice queen of treason," she tells me softly, "but the knights and I are watching her relentlessly. Do not worry, my love. She will not pull anything on *my* watch," she says, her eyes flashing dangerously.

I take a deep breath, feeling sick to my stomach.

I glance sidelong at Charaxus now, taking in how she's gazing at the queen, her eyes fond. The only time she softens at all is when she looks at Calla. I glance back up at Virago. "I just don't think she's capable of—" I begin, but Calla is stepping forward, leading the procession now, and Kell look at us, her brows up.

"Come on, kids," she says. "Time to go visit a goddess."

The library is at the summit of the palace, so I'm assuming we would have a long way to walk to get down to the dungeons—but not so. Joy, head seamstress, tailor and all-around awesome lady, is waiting for us outside the library, leaning against the wall and looking cool. That's really the best way I could describe Joy on any given day.

"You summoned me, milady?" asks Joy, pushing off from the wall and smiling brightly at the queen.

"Yes, Joy, thank you for coming," says Calla, lifting her chin. "Can you please transport the lot of us down to the dungeons?"

Joy blanches a little at that. "But, milady," she says, shaking her head, "what about the protections in place on the dungeon? Only two knights are allowed down there without you. You alone are the key to the dungeons. I can't just transport us in—"

"If I am the key," says Calla, spreading her hands, "then you can transport us if you're with me, yes?"

Joy thinks about it for a moment, then nods.

"Are you sure that's where you want to go?" she whispers, and Calla nods, too. And then, tight-lipped, Joy glances at Magel to see what she has to say about the matter. Magel shrugs, just a little, and then

Joy is stepping forward, holding out her hand.

"Everyone, hold on tight," she mutters, and then we all link hands as reality blurs around us, and we're instantly plunged into darkness.

Well, no—that's not exactly true. It's much darker than the well-lit halls in the upper towers of the palace, but it's not pitch black. My eyes take a moment to adjust to the darkness, and I notice the orbs hanging suspended in the air along the walls, glass spheres full of dim light.

When I imagine a "dungeon," I'm not ashamed to admit that my mind goes to a Monty Python sketch or two, or a medieval torture chamber, so my assumptions are pretty skewed. Still, I don't think I could have ever imagined this very stone floor, clean stone walls and ceiling. There's no dripping water or dank smell; everything is very neat and dry. And there's not a bit of dust or dirt anywhere. It shouldn't surprise me—I've seen the rest of the palace, after all—but it's nice to know that even the dungeons are well maintained in Arktos.

When we near the cells, I'm trying to keep my breathing steady, but my erratic heartbeat is kind of out of control. My palms are clammy, my vision is starting to tunnel, that I almost fail to notice that there are only six dungeon cells here, each one of them meticulously kept. They are positioned off of the main dungeon chamber, where there's a desk and chair and a very bored-looking knight with her feet up on the table, a leather-bound book in her hand, and a steaming cup of tea on the table in front of her.

"Milady!" she yelps, jumping up to her feet immediately, her book falling to the floor, but Calla raises a hand.

"Don't worry yourself, Brunna," she says with a small smile, though she still looks very pale. "I am here to see the new arrival."

"The archer? She's here," says Brunna, stepping around the edge of her wooden desk to fish her keyring off of her belt. "She won't say anything, milady," says the knight, but Calla nods tightly, and Brunna steps forward, placing the key in the lock.

The door opens without a single creak (seriously, the knights keep the dungeon doors *oiled*? I thought it was a prerequisite for dungeons to at least have creaky hinges), and Calla, Magel and Kell step into the room. I can just see around Magel's curves that there is a woman sitting on a sturdy wooden chair in the corner, her back to the wall, her arms crossed in front of her. She's wearing a cloak, but the hood is pulled down from her face, and she's scowling. She has extremely pale skin and long black hair that falls in waves over her shoulders.

I glance sidelong at Charix. I know I haven't seen everyone who hails from Furo, but they seem to have several things in common. They're all the palest people I've ever seen, and every single one of them has black hair. Granted, I've only seen the knights that King Charix brought with him, Charix himself and Charaxus...but they all have a certain look to them.

And this woman, sitting in the cell, staring at the queen sullenly?

She's wearing black armor beneath her black cloak. And she has similar features to the others from Furo.

I swallow a little, glancing at Virago. Virago didn't get a chance to see this woman before, on the city streets, and she's paling now as she stares at the stranger sitting in the cell. Virago fists her hands, her shoulders rising with tension as she stares; her lips curl up over her teeth in a snarl.

My heart is hammering against my ribs as I reach out and place a calming hand on Virago's arm.

This isn't good.

"Do you know me?" Calla asks simply, clasping her hands over her belly. The woman looks up from her position on the chair, and she narrows her eyes even further. But she doesn't say a thing. Instead, she sneers and spits. The spittle flies through the air and lands on the stones at Calla's feet.

Magel takes a single step forward, her hand raised to hit the woman across the mouth, her face cold and callous, but Calla stays her, reaching out and placing her palm on Magel's arm.

"Then you know me," says Calla, her voice tight. "Who sent you, archer? Who do you owe allegiance to?"

The archer does nothing, only crosses her legs in front of her, tapping her toes in the air, her head tilted to the side, a sarcastic smile lighting up her features.

"I am prepared to die, of course," the woman says then, her voice lightly accented, though I have no accent to compare it to. Maybe something slightly British. "But me and mine have no fear. Your time is over, *Calla*," she says, enunciating the name with a smirk. "And I hope when you die that you—"

"*Enough*," growls Charaxus, and the floor beneath us, made of firm stone, begins to shake. I grip Virago's arm tightly, because if I didn't, I'd be falling to the ground. I don't know how the knights withstand it, but they do, bracing themselves upright, their legs wide apart, to ride the shock wave of reverberation that rolls through the dungeons.

The woman stares at Charaxus, her eyes wide...but she doesn't say another word.

Charaxus' hands are curled into tight fists, the leather of her gloves creaking as her fingers press against her palms, her shoulders leaning forward. Waves of energy seem to be shimmering over her entire body, radiating outward.

"Tell the queen who you owe your allegiance to," commands the rather terrifying Charaxus in a deathly whisper.

The woman lifts her chin, and her eyes flash defiantly, but Charaxus takes a single step forward.

"Cower," says the woman then, lifting her chin, her eyes shifting to the wall to her right. "The goddess you so piggishly cast down here in the bowels of the earth. But you forget, stupid queen," she says, her lips curling over her teeth, "that Cower rose from the ground before. And she will again."

"Enough," says Calla this time, shaking her head and turning to leave the room. "Keep her down here until I've decided what must be done with her," says Calla to the guard at the desk, Brunna. "And, if you'd be so kind," she says, her jaw tensing, "open the door to Cower's chamber."

Brunna pales at that, shaking her head slowly, then more adamantly. "Milady, you gave me strict orders to never let a living soul into that room, and that included you," she says miserably, as if she already knows how this argument is going to end.

Calla shakes her head. "Desperate times, my dear Brunna, call for desperate measures," she says softly. "Please open the door for me."

Her hands shaking so hard that she drops the keys twice, Brunna locks the cell door of the archer, once the other knights have left it, and then she unlocks the door to the right.

The door beside the archer's door looks nothing like the other doors in the dungeon. Not that the others look like cardboard constructs that are going to fall over at any moment; they're all built of thick, solid beams of wood, reinforced with metal bands along the tops and bottoms and middles of the doors, with sturdy, burnished metal locks. But this door?

This door is *solid metal.*

And it also looks like it has...well...*dents* in it. Dents along the bottom, like someone or something hurled itself into the door repeatedly, again and again, a solid metal door that—when it's opened—I realize is about five inches thick. *This* door creaks when it's opened, because it probably weighs a ton.

The entire room inside is not stone, but metal. There's pounded, poured metal that was probably once molten, then shaped along the wall, over and over again, poured into place and drawn along the wall to create a metal fortress within. Metal lines the ground, and in the corner is a metal bed with a thickly stuffed pad on it, and blankets.

But there is no one on the bed.

There's something in the corner.

I remember the last time that I saw the goddess Cower. She had just transformed from her enormous beast self into a small, thin woman. And that's what's sitting in the corner right now. A small, thin woman, wearing a crude dress stitched from the skins of animals, her hair jet black and matted and sticking up in all directions. Her back is to us, her legs are drawn up, and she has her arms wrapped tightly around her knees. She's rocking in the corner, and she looks small, yes, but I know what she's capable of, the destruction she loves to wreak, how she wants all worlds to end. She is chaos, in and of itself, and she wants death. Death to all living things, because she is the darkest darkness.

I shiver as I stare at her slight, convex back; she curls her body forward, but Calla doesn't falter. She steps into the metal room, even though the rest of her knights lift hands, trying to stay her.

She steps past all of them.

"Cower," says Calla, lifting her chin, her voice ringing out regally in the metal room.

Cower does not turn to look at her. But she does laugh. It's a low, mocking laugh, the kind of laugh that you hear and begin to wonder if someone is laughing at you. A soft, dark, whisper of a laugh.

"You are cursed, Calla," she says then, and the voice that she uses sends chills through me. I suddenly have blurred vision, and the room is very dark and cold, even though it wasn't a moment ago. The other knights shift uncomfortably, and I can tell that Cower is doing something to them, but I don't know what. I shiver again, wrapping one arm through Virago's and the other across myself, across my heart, resting the fingers of my right hand on my left shoulder.

"Cursed," Cower repeats, the word soft, sibilant, like an ill wind rushing through dead wheat in a frozen field. Everything about Cower reeks of death. "I will not rise today. Or tomorrow. Or the day after. But know this—I *will* rise again," she whispers, the words echoing in the room, bouncing off the walls and coming back to us to burrow into our ears, digging tiny, sharp claws in our brains. "And when I rise again, there is no knight of this world who will vanquish me. I will be...unstoppable."

Calla stands, poker straight, her hands clasped strongly in front of her as she stares down at the crumpled goddess. "No, Cower," she begins, her voice as unmoving as a world itself, but Cower glances over her shoulder just then—and she's laughing. A breathy laugh, the kind a dying person makes.

"Cower will rise," the goddess hisses. "And Calla will fall."

Calla stands there for a long moment as Cower, with her jet black eyes, stares at the queen. Then Calla simply turns and exits the room, motioning to Brunna to shut and lock the door behind her.

"She is weak," says Calla, her face white as she folds her arms in front of her. "Whatever will happen this day, or soon...at least it will not involve *her*. But the time is coming that she *will* rise again." She glances around at the knights, who stand silent, patient, surrounding their queen with their love and protection. "And I pity all of us when that day comes," she whispers.

"Milady, we will vanquish her again," says Virago, her low voice a rumble as she gazes at Calla, brows furrowed. "We did it once—Holly did it once," she says, proudly putting an arm around me. "Cower can be stopped, no matter what," she murmurs firmly.

Calla shivers a little, passing a hand over her face then. "I hope so," is all she says, glancing back at the metal door. "There is mischief afoot this night, my beloved knights," she says, raising her arms. "Let us rely on each other. We are strong together."

As one, the knights fold in, and they all huddle, embracing each other and the queen in one large, many-person hug. I'm part of it, too, because Virago draws me in, and on my right, I have my arm around Calla, and on my left, I'm holding tightly to Virago.

"The show," says Calla tiredly, glancing at all of us in turn, "must go on. The Hero's Tournament must begin tonight, with the opening ceremonies. There are knights stationed everywhere, yes?" she asks Magel, and Magel nods solemnly. "Well, then," says Calla simply, taking a step back, spreading her hands. "No matter what happens, we'll be ready, right?"

The knights roar in agreement, raising their right arms into the air, their fists pumping with energy...

But as I stand there, surrounded by the love of the knights, next to this incredible queen...I have a feeling that tonight will change everything.

Chapter 13: The Stolen Queen

Life has been a whirlwind since I arrived here on Agrotera; so much has happened in this short amount of time… I have seen unicorns, flying horses and knights; I have met and befriended a queen; and I have seen magic. I've fallen even more in love with Virago (which I didn't think was possible, but every day that I spend with her, I'm finding myself falling more deeply in love), and I feel like I've grown as a person. I've yet to lift a sword, but I've ridden on the back of a very cranky war horse, and I've made love in a completely different world...

But things are starting to unravel. Arktos is such a beautiful place. I'm beginning to think of it as a second home. But things are wrong right now, and I don't know how to fix them. The Hero's Tournament is about to start. I remember when the opening ceremonies aired for the Olympics. They were supposed to be a jubilant, exciting time, full of expectation and the magic of possibility...

But, right now, all I feel is sick with fear. Fear that something is going to happen to Calla, that something is going to happen to the knights… There's an ill wind blowing, and I can feel it deep in my bones.

And I don't know what to do about it.

Virago and I are up in our tower room, getting ready for the opening ceremonies. Shelley is asleep on the bed again (she's been sleeping a lot while here, which is typical Shelley; when faced with another world, she'd rather snore on a comfortable quilt), her tail wagging intermittently, and her paws moving in blurred motion since she's currently experiencing a dream where she's running around chasing something (I'm assuming bunnies, since she loves chasing the bunnies in the backyard at home). Virago is sitting on the edge of the bed, shining her sword, and I'm doing up the front of my bodice with cold fingers.

I bite my lip, tying the knot savagely over my chest, and that's when Virago looks up. She knows I'm unhappy.

"Something's going to happen tonight," I tell her simply. Virago's brows are up, but when she hears what I say, she sets the sword beside her on the bed, standing smoothly.

"Yes," she says, the word simple and full of regret. "But no matter what happens, I will keep you safe, Holly. And I will keep Calla safe."

"But...but..." I take a few steps forward, and I wrap my arms around her neck. Her skin is hot beneath my fingers, and it's so comforting, the softness and heat of her. "But what about *you*?" I finally manage, gazing up into those ice blue eyes I love with all my heart. "I love you," I tell her, pouring all the heat and desire and adoration I possess for her into those three perfect words. "I'm worried that something terrible is going to happen tonight," I tell her, wincing, "and I...I'm worried *you* aren't going to be safe."

"My beauty," Virago whispers then, her voice dropping as she bends slowly, carefully, falling to her knees in front of me. She wraps her arms around my hips and waist, and she draws me to her so tightly, resting her head against my stomach and breasts, breathing me in. I hold her, my heartbeat thunder through every inch of my body. I can feel every place where she touches me, feel her nearness radiating through me like sunshine: the physicality and weight of her hands at my waist, of her arms around my middle, of her face pressed against me, inhaling me deeply as she sighs, then leans away, gazing up at me now as she kneels at my feet. Her eyes, so blue, so bright, hold me to the spot with a warmth and love that fills me.

"My beauty," she repeats, her words a low, sweet growl, "do you remember when you saved me?"

I swallow, thinking of the weight of the sword in my hands, the feeling I had when the sword entered the Boston Beast...which became the goddess Cower. I thrust the sword into the creature, because if I didn't...Virago was going to die.

"Yes," I tell her, taking a deep breath.

Virago stands smoothly, rising and moving away from me. I bite my lip as Virago crosses the room, scooping up her sword from the bed and gripping the hilt in her leather-gloved hand.

"You know," says Virago lightly, turning back to me, "every sword is made specifically for one knight. Made for that one person alone." She lifts the sword. "And within this hilt here is a bit of my blood and a bit of my bone, hammered into the metal."

I stare at her as she moves easily over to me, letting the shining blade of her long sword fall to her arm and shoulder as she turns, curling her fingers around the pommel of the sword now, holding out the hilt to me.

"We do this," she says quietly, "so that the sword will only ever respond to one person. Wolfslayer will only ever respond to me. If anyone else tries to pick it up, it is too heavy for them. It is magicked, and it is alive, in every sense of that word. When you first tried to pick it up, it was too heavy, yes?"

"I could hardly lift it. I just thought you were crazy strong," I tell her with a soft smile.

Virago laughs, the sound of that laughter filling me. Shelley lifts up her head, and she blinks at us sleepily (probably a little miffed that we woke her from such an awesome dream about rabbits).

"Well," says Virago, raising a brow impishly, "I *am* strong," she tells me, wrapping an arm around my waist and lifting me easily. I sling my arms around her neck and kiss her deeply before she sets me back down with a small chuckle. "But it is magic that makes the sword so heavy. When you bested Cower with the blade...it began to know you. See? Try to lift it now."

Virago usually keeps her sword with her, and if it's not with her, it's on the couch or in the backseat of my car. That being said, I haven't wanted to touch it since that night with Cower, and I've had no occasion to lift it since. Here and now, I reach out, and I curl my fingers around the hilt of the blade.

And I lift it as easily from her shoulder as if I were picking up a pencil.

"Wow," I manage to say, and Virago smiles gently at me.

"You have all of me, Holly," she tells me then, her eyes glittering. "Even my bones and my blood respond to you, answer to you, bend to you and fall to you, because you have captured my heart."

I gaze at her, holding the sword alongside the both of us as Virago takes a step closer, erasing the space between us.

"You called to me, across worlds," she whispers to me. "You saved my life from a goddess. You and I are together, because we are as meant to be as stars and worlds." She wraps her fingers around my waist, and I feel the solidity of her, the strength of her, as she holds me gently. "Whatever happens this night, I know the Goddess watches over us—not a goddess like Cower," says Virago, shaking her head as my brow furrows, "but the Goddess who drew us together. She who made all."

I lick my lips. "Virago," I tell her, shaking my head then, "I'm not really religious. I don't know if I believe in any sort of greater power bringing us together..."

She smiles softly, cupping my chin with her hand. "Belief in something doesn't make it true or false. I believe in us, and I believe the Goddess brought us together," she murmurs, her eyes flashing with a bright fire. "You don't have to believe, my love," she tells me gently. "Because *how* it happened is not so important as the fact that it *did* happen. We are together. But I believe," she tells me, her voice strong, "that we will be all right. That I am not meant to leave you now. That we are meant to have a long, happy life together. Do you trust me?" she whispers.

I look up into her eyes, and I *know* that I trust her; I trust her with everything that I am or yet could be.

"Yes," I tell her, the power of the universe in that one syllable.

"I love you," Virago tells me, holding me close, her sword beside us, held up in my hand, the blade glittering in the half-light of the room as Virago bends low, giving me one last, sweet kiss.

There's a knock at the door, and when I cross the room to open it, Kell stands in the hallway, looking regal (she might have actually put a brush through her hair) and very serious.

"Okay, ladies," says Kell, lifting her chin. "It's showtime."

If I thought the banquet hall was crowded before, I had obviously never seen it stuffed to capacity.

Like it is now.

Everyone stands, packed shoulder to shoulder, talking and laughing. It's completely deafening down here, which is why I'm grateful that we move through the banquet hall pretty quickly. I see people from many different countries, like those from Lumina, in their crystal armor, and the knights from Furo in their black armor, standing around scowling. The knights usher Calla through the crowd toward the hallway on the far side of the massive room.

But as we're walking through the room, I bump into a lot of people, of course, because everyone is drinking Magin, and it makes you less aware of your surroundings. Nearly every person that I glance at is carrying a goblet with the precious liquid spilling down the sides of their cups, sloshing over the edges and sprinkling on pretty much everyone. The scent of citrus and chocolate is thick in the air, and everyone already looks like they're partying heartily.

We weave through the press of people, and then Calla stops just a little bit ahead to talk to someone.

I peek around Virago's shoulder and smile: it's

the woman from the tea shop, Isabella.

Calla embraces Isabella, because she's just that sort of person, but when Calla pulls back from the woman, Isabella stays her, whispering something into her ear. Calla's face clouds, and she nods once, glancing back to see that the rest of her knights are around her—and then she continues on.

When I move forward, I wave a small hello to Isabella, but she stops me, too.

"Just be careful today, all right?" she says, her eyes a little cloudy, as if she's looking at something that's almost too small to see. "I have a feeling..." she starts, but then she shakes her head. "Just be careful."

I swallow, then nod, following after the knights.

I want to ask Calla why we're even doing this, why she's present for the opening ceremonies when there is a threat to her life, but I already know why. I know that Arktos was chosen to be the host for the Hero's Tournament, and I know that there are so many people here who are from the neighboring countries of Arktos, dignitaries that will see, in a moment, whether Arktos is weak. Arktos is *not* weak, and Calla is *not* weak, and she's working very hard to show the entire world that Furo doesn't concern her, that King Charix does not frighten her, that these assassination attempts mean nothing, and that she is strong.

And we have to let her do that. Or, like she said, Furo will have already won.

Once we are past the crowd and through the wide, double doors leading into the hallway beyond, Kell shuts the doors behind us, and that closes out a lot of the noise.

Here in the hallway, it's almost quiet. The knights stand close to Calla. There isn't a big group here with us—just Alinor, Magel, Kell, Virago, Calla, and me—along with Charaxus, who stands off from the knights with her arms folded in front of her. But she doesn't have the typical scowl on her face. No, this time there's something different about her expression, something that worries me.

She looks worried. Charaxus.

I lick my lips nervously, stepping away from Virago.

And I approach Charaxus.

I know she's the vice queen, and, technically, she's almost as powerful as Calla. That means that she's different from the other knights, and that power dynamic is very real in a magical world where knights serve a queen. But, at the same time, I've watched how the knights interact with Charaxus. It's obvious that they adore Calla. They love her deeply and would die for her, pledging their lives to her out of genuine affection. But Charaxus?

I'm fairly certain the knights hate her.

It's not just Virago, though Virago and Charaxus apparently have had a rivalry going on since knight school. No, it's *everyone.* I have a theory that it's because the knights are loyal to each other, so if there's a person that one knight doesn't like or has a conflict with, then the other knights will back their sister up. Loyalty is important, and so is honor...

But I've seen how much of an outsider Charaxus is. And it hurts to witness it.

I don't think it bothers her that much; she's a very self-efficient kind of person. And, yes, I know, I overheard her talking to her brother Charix about possibly handing over the queen… There are a lot of reasons I shouldn't like Charaxus (she did, after all, hate me on sight for being the girlfriend of her arch rival), but I'm deeply hardwired to remember what it was like to be an outsider.

My high school years were a living hell. I came out in my teens, and that was just Not Done back then. I didn't have *any* friends at *all* until I met Carly.

No. Friends. At. All.

I was so isolated and alone, and I craved companionship, yes, above all, I wanted to be seen.

I doubt that Charaxus has ever wanted that. She doesn't strike me as the type of person who needs human companionship, either. She's standing now with her back poker straight, her arms folded in front of her, her jaw tight as she gazes down the hallway. Her eyes are unfocused, as if she's thinking deeply about something.

Am I really going to bother her now?

Um, yeah. I guess I am. Because I'm suddenly standing beside her, clearing my throat. As if shaken from a trance, Charaxus gazes down at me in surprise, but that surprise lasts for exactly a nanosecond before her all-too-familiar scowl appears.

"Yes," she says dryly, and it doesn't even sound like a question.

"Nothing," I tell her with a little shrug. "I was just wondering how you were doing. You looked...worried." Inwardly, I cringe. Am I really trying to be all touchy-feely with the woman who literally makes the ground beneath her quake when she's trying to make her point?

But Charaxus gazes at me then, and there's bewilderment in her eyes. "I am fine," she tells me gruffly, though her words are softer now. "Thank you for your concern," she adds, like she's trying to remember the social niceties for a situation like this, like she memorized them out of a book but isn't used to practicing them in real life.

"Are we ready?" asks Calla, and the knights turn, Kell poised at the door.

Outside, I can hear the banquet hall quieting.

And then...music.

The swell of stringed instruments begins softly but builds rather quickly, as my heart rises in my throat, as Kell's hands tighten on the doorknobs.

"Go out with the other knights; they're going to stand by and keep Calla in their sights. Stay with them, all right?" pleads Virago, hooking her fingers around my elbow and drawing me close—and away from Charaxus. Virago's jaw is tense, and it looks like she wants to say something more as she stares down at me, her bright blue eyes glittering with an expression I can't read, maybe because it's a bunch of things all at once. Trepidation, worry...love.

"I love you," I tell her quickly, putting my arms around her shoulders and kissing her on the cheek, on the nose, on the mouth, soft, quick kisses that are infused with the million things I'm trying to convey, too.

"My love," says Virago, leaning back, gazing at me with a small smile, "I'm not going to another world. I'll be right here. Right behind this door."

"I know. I just...I just love you," I tell her again, squeezing her hands as I take a step back, as Kell, Alinor and I step closer to the door. Magel, Virago, Charaxus and Calla remain behind as Kell opens the door an inch. Instantly, we're awash with sounds, so many people's voices raised in jubilation, so much music, so much laughter. Kell enters the banquet hall, and then Alinor, and then I turn to look back at Virago.

"I love you," she mouths to me. I nod, blow her a kiss, and step through the door, too, and Kell pulls it shut behind me.

The dancers from the banquet are here, now clad in more elaborate costumes, ribbons braided in their hair as they leap onto the empty tables in the hall, dancing to the beat of the drums, to the delicate cadence of the stringed instruments. I watch them with unseeing eyes, remaining as close to the door as possible.

There's the queen's table on a dais at the back wall, and the table is covered with a long cloth shot through with strands of silver and gold. Calla's throne has been moved to sit at the center of the table—to elevate her above the crowd, I'm assuming—and in the very middle of the room, the central table has been removed. It looks like a sort of stage has been constructed of several tables pushed together, covered with a cloth. Several of the dancers are leaping up onto that big, center stage now, propelling themselves across it like they have wings on their feet (to my knowledge, none of them actually *do*, but I'm on Agrotera: I wouldn't even be surprised if a woman leapt by with Hermes-esque sandals sporting little wings).

I'm tense. I can't actually enjoy this pre-show, because I'm concentrating too much on wishing that I had a sword. It's ridiculous. I'm no expert with the blade, regardless of the fact that I vanquished Cower. That was only luck. Still, I wish I had something that I could use to help the knights.

Because I believe, very much, that something is going to happen soon. I try to take deep, even breaths, as I watch the women dance...

And then, something *does* happen.

The music stops.

I remember a few days ago (has it really just been a few days? It feels like a lifetime ago), when the music stopped playing in the bar in Boston...a literal world away. Then, it was because Charaxus had stepped down into the bar, wielding a sword, wearing black armor… The scene looked sinister, but it wasn't, really. She just has that aura about her.

But, here and now, something *is* sinister. Because it's not Charaxus who is causing the music to stop, not Charaxus who is causing everyone to fall silent. Not Charaxus who has inspired a deep, disturbed hush to fall over the people assembled here, ready to celebrate, ready to open the Hero's Tournament with one big party.

A big party that isn't going to happen, I'm realizing.

Because it's not Charaxus who changed the atmosphere of the banquet hall.

It's Charaxus' brother.

Charix, king of Furo, ascends the stage of tables by striding up the small set of creaking, wooden stairs that had been discreetly tucked around the back of the stage. The dancers back away from him instantly. It's pretty obvious that this is not the moment for him to be on the stage, if he was even supposed to go up there at any point in the first place...but when he turns right now, the lone person standing in the middle of that stage, I shudder a little.

He's smiling.

He doesn't look particularly happy when he smiles.

He looks smug. Dangerous.

Evil.

He spreads his leather-gloved hands wide, and the hall is so still that I can hear the leather creaking when he uncurls his fists. Slowly, slowly, he raises his hands, gazing around the room with an expression of supreme disgust. He's not even trying to hide it now.

"People of Arktos," he says, his voice carrying to every corner of the room like he's shouting into a megaphone—but he's just whispering. "It is...unfortunate," he says, raising his lips up over his teeth, "that you would imprison our goddess Cower. It is...*unfortunate* that you dare to defile her by *keeping* her imprisoned. It is because of this that you will fall today."

He gazes around the room, his eyes glittering with malice...

And then he disappears.

King Charix *completely* disappears, disappears without a trace, like he was never standing there to begin with, and I somewhat wonder if he *was* really there at all. Regardless, the crowd is still silent, still tense, still...waiting.

I move quietly through the press of people, listening now as they begin to murmur, as the crowd starts to mill about, shifting uneasily. That's the best word to describe the situation in the room right now: uneasiness. Everyone's looking around, as if they're waiting for the other shoe to drop, and, honestly, I have no idea what's about to happen. Why did Charix disappear? Why did he make such a ridiculous speech? Was he trying to cause the people of Arktos City to panic? Doesn't he know that they're brave people who can't be scared off so easily?

I move through the crowd, and then I'm at the

door I came through, from the hallway where Charaxus, Calla, Virago and Magel were waiting. I open the door, pressing it open amid the murmuring crowd, and slip through it, shutting it just as quietly behind me.

The minute I close the door, I realize that something is wrong here.

At the far corner of the hallway, just around the bend, where I can hardly see them, is Charaxus. She has her arm around the queen's shoulders, and she's pushing her through...

I swallow, my mouth instantly dry.

Charaxus is pushing Calla through a portal.

And Virago… Virago is lying in a heap on the ground. Next to Magel, who is also sprawled unceremoniously on the ground, the both of them out cold, like they were clocked over the heads with something heavy.

"Charaxus!" I call out, taking a step forward. I don't know what's going on, but it can't possibly be good, not with Virago and Magel lying there, and with Charaxus shoving Calla through a portal. But Calla wouldn't go anywhere she didn't want to go. She's not a fainting flower; she's a strong woman, a queen. But somehow Charaxus is still managing to push her forward...

Charaxus glances over her shoulder at me at the exact same moment that Virago comes to, shaking her head, reaching up her hand. She grabs the hem of Charaxus' cloak as Charaxus steps through the portal...

And then Virago, Charaxus, and Calla disappear.

They're gone. The portal evaporates into nothingness.

They're *gone*.

"Oh, my God," I whisper, all the blood draining from my face. "Oh, my God," I repeat, racing to close distance between myself and Magel.

I throw myself onto the ground beside the unconscious knight, and I glance at her hurriedly, trying to see if I can spot any visible injuries. But, no, she appears to be all right: there are no stab wounds, no wounds of any sort. Magel chooses that moment to moan a little, moving her head back and forth, her eyelids fluttering.

"Magel? It's me, Holly," I tell her, leaning down and nervously tapping her on the shoulder as gently as I can. "Magel, what *happened*? Where did Charaxus go?"

"Cha—Charax..." Magel manages, her voice low and quavering as she takes a deep breath. Then she coughs a little, rolling onto her side, pushing herself up onto her elbow with great difficulty. I try to help her, but Magel is solid muscle and much taller than me; she's also covered in heavy armor. She sits up a little, her hand to her head, blinking.

"Where am I?" she asks then, looking around and blinking.

"You might have a concussion," I say, sitting back on my heels. "Do you remember what happened?"

Magel blinks hazily at me. "No..." she says, shaking her head again. "I was standing here one moment with Virago, Calla, Charaxus...and then...darkness." She glances around now, her eyes wide. "Did you say that Charaxus went somewhere? Where's Calla?"

"Charaxus took Calla through a portal," I tell her miserably, "'and I think Virago went with them.

She grabbed onto Charaxus, and then she just disappeared. I just don't know where they would have *gone*."

"Charaxus took Calla," Magel repeats flatly, and then she's staggering to her feet, even though it's obvious that she shouldn't be trying to stand. I hook her arm around my shoulder and try to help her right herself, but it's hard; she's still really out of it.

"I don't think you're all right, Magel," I try to tell her, but she shakes her head adamantly.

"Charaxus knocked me out," says Magel, gritting her teeth and wincing as she puts one leather-gloved hand to her head. "And she took Calla through the portal, Holly," she tells me, holding my gaze, "because Charaxus has kidnapped the queen."

Chapter 14: The Knight, the Witch and the Portal

"What?" I whisper, staring at Magel. And then, taking a deep breath, I blurt it out, not realizing what I've said until it's too late: "But she wouldn't do that. Charaxus is in love with the queen."

Magel stares at me, her eyes narrowing, her usually warm, brown gaze now flashing with an inner fire that stops me in my tracks. "What did you say?" she asks me quietly, raw power in her voice.

"I mean..." I blink, licking my lips. "Isn't it obvious? She's in love with Calla. Calla doesn't notice," I say, shaking my head, "but of course she wouldn't. She's been going through a rough time lately, and she got her heart broken. But I figured that pretty much everyone else noticed...right?" I whisper.

For a long moment, Magel says nothing. And then she shakes her head, her jaw tense. "Charaxus," she says, enunciating every word, "loves *no* one and *nothing*. Least of all our beloved queen. She's from *Furo*," she says, spitting the word out.

"Magel," I say, taking a deep breath, remembering what just transpired out in the banquet hall. "Something very weird just happened—"

And then there's the sound of screaming.

Magel reacts instantly: she's moving away from

me, even though she's incapable of walking in a straight line (I really do think she's concussed), and she has her hands on the doorknobs to the hallway, pulling them open.

"We're locked in!" a man is yelling over and over again in the chaos that has erupted in the banquet hall.

The party went from perfect happiness, Magin sloshing out of cups, laughter and merriment everywhere, dancing women moving to bright music—to silence...and then to *this*.

There is panic in the room, and I can see why now. At the far end of the room is the door leading out to the main hallway of the palace. And that door is locked tight. Kell is at the door currently, and she's tugging at it, putting her weight into it, pulling on the handles with her considerable strength, her arm muscles flexing impressively. The doors do not budge.

She bangs against the door with one massive pound of her fists before stepping back with a growl of frustration that I can hear even here.

"Kell!" shouts Magel, leaping up onto the stage. Kell turns, a deep frown etched across her features, until she spots Magel.

Alinor comes up beside me, shaking her head, running a hand back through her hair. "It's bad, Holly," she tells me, as Kell makes her way through the crowd, heading toward Magel.

"What's going on?" I ask Alinor, and she still shakes her head, her brow furrowed.

"We are locked in," she says, gesturing around the hall at all of the shut doors. "I have tried every door. They are sealed with metal, and metal," she says, her lips downturning, "is impervious to magic."

"But how...how is that possible? What about the hallway out there?" I ask her, pointing over my shoulder, back the way I came, where Calla, Charaxus, Virago and Magel had been waiting. I can see doors from here, in the hallway, doors that lead out to the rest of the palace. But Alinor's face remains stony.

"I doubt that the doors beyond that hallway will work, either," she says. "But I will try them." Then she straightens a little, glancing at me. "Charix has locked us in on purpose. He has staged a coup, and he wants to do this as quickly and painlessly as possible. He has one goal, and one goal only," she tells me softly, searching my face to see if I understand.

And I do.

"He wants to free Cower," I whisper, and Alinor nods, her face cloudy.

"Cower will rise," she says with a small shudder, "and Calla will fall."

I think about the conversation that Charaxus and Charix had in the hallway a few days ago, a conversation that I shouldn't have overhead but did. I think about how Charaxus reacted to her brother, how it was apparent that she dislikes him. How apparent it is that she loves Calla.

I know I'm not making it up. I'm perceptive; I've seen the signs. Charaxus loves Calla, and I really can't believe, in my heart of hearts, that she would do anything to harm Calla. She came for her, after all, across worlds...

Across worlds.

I turn to look at Alinor, my eyes wide as I reach across the space between us, gripping her arm.

Alinor looks at me in surprise, but I'm spluttering. I don't know how to articulate that

Charaxus came to find Calla *across worlds*. She opened a portal by herself to find Calla… This is not the type of person who then kidnaps the queen to hand her over to her brother.

But I don't know that for certain. I've been wrong before about a lot of things (I mean, look at my history of ex-girlfriends, for example), but I just don't think I'm wrong about this one.

I'm just not *sure*.

I only know that Charaxus took Calla through a portal before everything went down. And that she took Virago, my Virago, with her.

"Where..." My mind starts to churn at a million miles a minute. "Where's Joy? Can she transport a few of us out of the banquet hall?" I ask Alinor, who shakes her head.

"You can't transport past iron. A binding spell has been put around the entire banquet hall. They're staging a coup, and they want no one to interfere. It's better than bloodshed," says Alinor quietly, her eyes wide, "but we don't know what he's planning *after* Charix has released Cower. Bloodshed might be exactly what he has in mind. Keep us all penned in here, like animals awaiting slaughter." She stands up straight then, tilting her chin. "But if he thinks *that's* going to happen, he has another think coming—"

My mind is still going, still grasping at possibilities. And that's when I remember who else I saw here tonight.

"Alinor," I tell her breathlessly, then, my eyes wide. "Where's Isabella?"

"Isa-who?" she asks, blinking. "Wait, the witch from the tea shop that Calla likes?"

"Yes, *that* Isabella!" I tell her excitedly, gazing

out into the crowd. "She's a witch, right? If Charaxus opened a portal, a portal can be opened again, can't it?"

"Maybe. I don't know much about portals," says Alinor with a shrug, but she's beginning to look out through the crowd, too.

"Hey, Magel!" I call to Magel, who's deep in quiet conversation with Kell up on the stage. Magel glances through the crowd and spots me with surprise.

"Can you call out for Isabella?" I yell to her. Magel cocks her head to the side, but she does it, cupping her hands around her mouth.

"Isabella?" she says, her voice ringing through the press of people.

"Here!" says someone, shooting up her hand. I can see her hand in the air, and then I see her cascade of red hair. Yes, it's the right Isabella.

"Over here!" I shout, jumping up and down so she can find me in the crowd. Isabella moves toward me as quickly as she can, and in a few moments, she's standing beside us, breathless.

"What is it? What's happening?" she asks in a hushed voice, biting at her lower lip. "My wife is still down in Arktos City, and I'm so worried about her—"

"I'm sure that King Charix isn't going to harm any of the residents of Arktos City just yet," says Alinor, using a voice I've never heard her use before. Right now, she sounds like a policewoman, calming down a frightened civilian with a warm, no-nonsense tone. "Don't worry," she tells Isabella with a smile. And it's a genuine smile. Isabella nods a little, but it doesn't look like she's going to stop worrying anytime soon. And then she looks to me.

"Why did you have Captain Magel call for me?" she asks, her eyes wide.

"Isabella," I tell her, licking my lips that are suddenly dry because I'm so nervous. "Do you… I mean, I know it's a long shot, but you're a witch, so… I mean..." I swallow and shake my head. "Do you think you can open a portal?" I ask her all in a rush.

If I'd just asked Isabella if she had a pet purple rabbit, I don't think she would look any more surprised by my question.

"A *portal*?" Isabella repeats, her voice hushed. She looks pale. "I'm so sorry, but I don't think I should do that," she tells me then, saying it quickly, like the sentence is one long word.

"What?" I ask, spreading my hands. "Isabella, we need to follow Charaxus. She took Queen Calla and my girlfriend, the knight Virago, with her, and I don't know where she's taken them, or for what purpose..." I'm starting to talk too quickly, and I'm in very real danger of bursting into tears, so I reel it back. I take a deep breath. "We need the queen back. We need your help," I tell her then, quietly. "I know it's hard to open a portal," I say, "and I'm sorry that it would take so much out of you to open it, but—"

"Oh, Goddess, it's not that," says Isabella, shaking her head adamantly, her red curls flying. "Um...it was me," she says then, her voice so quiet, I can hardly hear it over the crowd.

"What?" I ask, paling. "*What* was you?"

"Um...when the goddess Cower went through the portal, taking Virago...when Virago came to your world for the first time," says Isabella, swallowing, "*I* was the witch in the village who opened the portal for her. Um. The thing is...that's why I run a tea shop now. Because I was never a very *good* witch. It was almost impossible for me to open the portal that night," she says, shaking her head, her eyes wide, "and when I did manage to open it, the portal went to the wrong place, anyway, and I jeopardized Virago's life, and..." Again, she's spoken all of this very quickly, and in one breath. She looks panicked. "I don't know if I could open the portal to wherever Charaxus went, and even if I *could*, there's no guarantee that you'd be safe going through it," she finishes miserably.

Alinor, standing next to me, her fingers hooked in the edges of her leather skirt, glances at me with brows raised. Magel has been wading through the crowd, and she finally reaches us at this moment.

Isabella shifts her gaze to look at Magel nervously before looking back at me. "I'm really sorry," she says then, straightening stiffly. "But I can't help you."

"Wait," I tell her, swallowing. "I mean, you're the one who brought Virago and me together, Isabella," I explain. "Without you, we never would have found each other. We were *worlds* apart, but you brought us together."

Isabella, about to walk away, her back stiff, her shoulders curled forward...stops. She turns back a little, her eyes wide. "But...I made a mistake," she says, shaking her head, her eyes swimming with tears. "I could have cost Virago her life."

"But you didn't," I tell her, fear making my words shake. Because of course I'm afraid.

But I have to find Virago. No matter what it takes. And Calla, too. Charaxus has taken Virago and Calla, and I have no idea where she took them, or for what reason. Right now, we're trapped in the banquet hall while King Charix is doing God knows what outside those doors, and he might do God knows what in here at any moment. Calla has to be found.

"Alinor," says Magel quietly, "organize the knights for whatever may happen. Holly, what do you have in mind with Isabella?"

"If we can figure out where the portal that Charaxus opened leads to, maybe Isabella can reopen that portal, and then..." I trail off. "Then I can get Virago back."

Magel's jaw tightens, and she's already shaking her head at me. "Out of the question," she tells me then. "*If* Isabella can open the portal—no offense," she says to Isabella, who's already blushing, "but I was there that night," she says. "You are very good at making tea, but you are *not* good at magic. You almost got Virago killed," she says firmly. "But *if* it's possible…" She trails off, taking a deep breath. "Then I and my fellow knights must go through it in order to bring the queen back."

"Just...just test it on me first," I tell her. "It's true that this is dangerous, yes?"

"Yes," say Isabella, Magel and Alinor together. They then gaze uneasily at each other.

"Then test it on me," I say, drawing myself up to my full height and lifting my chin. "I'll go through the portal first and make sure it's safe. And then, if it's safe, you can follow me through with a few knights."

"It's true. I must leave the bulk of them here to protect the citizens of Arktos," says Magel, raking her fingers back through her hair in frustration. "But it is too dangerous, Holly," says Magel then, in a soft voice. "If Virago knew that I was even *contemplating* letting you—"

"I am my own woman, Magel," I tell her kindly, calmly and evenly—but firmly. "I do what I will. And you know it's better to test the portal on me. Virago would be asking you to do the very same thing right now if it were me Charaxus had taken. You know that to be true."

Magel sighs for a long moment, her eyes downcast as she thinks about it, her arms crossed firmly in front of her. Then she nods, flicking her gaze to me. "If it is what you wish to do, Holly..."

"*Yes*," I tell her, breathless; then I turn to Isabella. "Will you do it?" I ask her, my hands clasped in front of me, pleading. "Will you reopen the portal?"

Isabella's eyes are still wide, and there's a great amount of fear in her expression right now, but she nods once, slowly. "Yes," she says, biting at her lower lip. "If you really want me to. But...Holly," she says, stepping forward and grasping my hands in hers so tightly, I can actually feel her fingernails poking into my palms as she squeezes. "This is dangerous, okay?"

I squeeze back, nodding, my heart in my throat. "I...I love her," I tell Isabella with a little shrug. "Anything could be happening to Virago right now. I don't know why Charaxus took her and Calla. But I have to find her. I have to save her. No matter what."

Isabella nods then, her cheeks bright red, her mouth in a thin line. "I know what you mean," she tells me earnestly. "All right. Show me where you saw Charaxus create the portal."

I glance at Magel, who nods, and then we all turn, moving through the unsettled crowd until we reach the door to the small hallway.

"Alinor," says Magel, turning back and placing a hand on Alinor's shoulder. "Use your calm, my friend," she says, offering up a small, tense smile. "Give the crowd some peace. Tell them nothing about Calla," she says, her voice dropping to a whisper, "but give them some kindness."

"Yes," says Alinor, bowing her head and turning quickly to make her way back through the crowd.

Once through the doors leading into the hallway, Magel turns to shut them behind us, but before they click, I can hear Alinor's big, cheerful voice filling the room with a mighty, "People, all is well!"

The doors close, and we're cast into shadow. There's not much light in this hallway, and all that's available comes from one small orb of light that hangs suspended in the air above us. It is a very low source of light, and I can hardly see as I make my way down the hallway to the far end, where I saw Charaxus last.

The door at the bend in the hallway is, of course, locked. I try it because I wanted to, but the knob doesn't even turn in my hands. I sigh in frustration and point to a spot in the thick, plush rug.

"This is where Charaxus formed the portal," I tell Isabella. "I...think."

"Just a general area is usually enough," she tells me nervously. She's tugging down on the front of her dress, which she has done about a thousand times since agreeing to do this—but that's just her tell. When I'm really nervous, I bite my lip or chew on a fingernail. We all have those tells, but it's making *me* increasingly nervous that she's so worried about doing this.

But I knew my plan wasn't going to be a walk in the park. I want to ask Isabella to tell me all the ways that this could go wrong, but my imagination is pretty active, and I've already come up with my own worst-case scenarios, including (but not limited to) being cast out into deep space. Actually, the first thing that my overactive imagination thought of was being erroneously dumped on a planet full of dinosaurs, which *could possibly happen,* for all I know. I am currently standing on a planet with magic and unicorns, after all.

Isabella is walking around the spot on the rug in a slow circle, staring down at it. She tries to roll up her sleeves, but they keep falling down.

In the tea shop, she was funny and confident; I suppose she was in her element. Now she looks uncertain as she walks that circle.

"I wish I had my cat with me. She's very helpful for spells," Isabella says, pausing on the rug and shaking out her hands. "But she's with my wife. Okay. I can do this." She looks up, raising her hands toward the ceiling. "Can you please stand together, Magel and Holly?" she asks, not looking back down at us. "Just hold hands and put your other hands out flat in the air, palms down."

Magel and I clasp hands quickly, and then we put out our free hands.

"Okay!" says Isabella, taking a deep breath. "Here goes nothing!"

She stands with her arms up, Magel and I hold hands...

And absolutely nothing happens.

"That's about right," Magel mutters, shaking her head, but I shake my head, too, as Isabella looks down in dejection, lowering her arms.

"No, no, Isabella, try again. Do you want us to imagine something, or try to draw up energy, or..." I trail off, because she looks despondent.

"It's not going to be any use. Don't you see? I can't *do* this," she tells us, shaking her head again, her voice plaintive. "Please—there are probably a few other witches out there in that crowd. We could try to find them, get together, create the portal that way—"

"We're running out of *time*," I tell her, breathless, my heart beating so quickly that I can feel all the blood rushing through my veins and racing under my skin. My hands are cold and shaking as I let go of Magel, take a step forward. "*Please*, Isabella, anything could be happening to them. They could be anywhere..." I try not to think about the distinct possibility that Charaxus could have done *exactly* what she told her brother she'd do. She could have already brought Calla and Virago to King Charix and given them up. And then what's going to happen to them? I shudder to think. I take a deep breath. "I'm sorry," I tell her slowly, trying to keep my voice steady, "but...but put yourself in my shoes." I gesture down at my feet. "If it were your wife through that portal...wouldn't you be doing anything in your power to get through it, too?"

For a long moment, Isabella just looks at me, her eyes wide, her breathing coming fast, her nostrils flaring. And then she closes her eyes, clenches her hands into fists and nods once, sharply. "You're right, Holly. I'm sorry. Okay. I'm going to try again," she says, and holds her hands out in front of her, arms straight, palms down. "Just...just imagine a portal of white light in front of us," she says, voice quavering and unsure. But at least she's trying. I close my eyes while Isabella says, "I'm trying to figure out where the portal opened up, but tracing it feels kind of...fuzzy..."

My eyes are closed, and I reach across the space toward Magel, to take her hand, and she does take my hand, but she leans forward. "Are you sure you want to do this?" Magel whispers into my ear. "I know Virago.

Wherever Charaxus took her, and for whatever reason, Virago is going to be all right. But if something happens to you under my watch, Virago will never forgive me," she tells me softly.

"I'll be okay. I've *got* to be okay. I've got to find her," I tell Magel firmly, eyes still shut as I try to imagine a portal of white light rotating in front of me.

For a long moment, all is silent. It's too silent, really. I can hear Alinor speaking to people out in the banquet hall, but here in the hallway, all is still.

I actually peek at that moment, opening up my right eye, my left eye still shut tight.

And there, in front of us, is the now-familiar tall, white portal. It's a little more see-through than usual, but as Isabella's hands shake, held out over the ground, the portal wavers, flickering...and then remains steady.

"Is this it?" I ask Isabella in a hushed voice. Her hands are shaking even harder now, and her brow is furrowed; a thin sheen of sweat is breaking out over her skin.

"Yes," she says. "Go through—hurry. I can't hold it for very long. It's too unstable."

I swallow, glancing at Magel, and Magel nods, unsheathing her sword over her shoulder.

"Ladies first," she tells me, indicating the portal.

"Okay," I whisper, and though my heart is in my throat, though I feel like I'm about to be sick (I could literally end up anywhere in existence, *anywhere in the universe...*), I take a deep breath. I gather my skirts in my hands.

And I step through the portal.

Chapter 15: Brave

I'm falling.

When I stepped through the portal before, it was like walking into a darkened room. You take those tentative steps, hoping a light will turn on, and then it does, and the world appears around you, safe and sound.

But that's not what happens this time.

I'm falling, and I can't see a damn thing. Everything is as pitch black as the darkest night, and my body is whistling down, down, down through the air, and I'm going to throw up, and I hold myself as tensely as I possibly can, because when I hit the ground, I'm going to die...

I gasp, the breath leaving me as my feet rest gently—as gently as a feather—against land.

I open my eyes, shut tightly against imminent destruction, and I gasp again, clutching my stomach, tears swimming in my line of sight...

Because I'm in my living room.

My living room.

I'm...back on Earth.

"No," I whisper, looking about frantically. "This isn't possible," I manage, and then I'm crouching down, touching my couch, picking up my remote, feeling my body, making absolutely certain that I'm really here, that this is all really physical and not a dream...

No. Not a dream. I drop the remote onto the coffee table, and I cross the room to look out the back door.

It's nighttime.

And it's storming outside.

I shiver, flicking on the overhead light in the living room. I turn to look back. Magel isn't here. That's weird...

And I notice something else I didn't see before.

There's a light on upstairs.

My senses seem to focus sharply in this moment. I can hear everything distinctly: the rain pelting the back door; I hear it dancing on top of the roof. I can smell the warm, comforting scent of my kitchen with its chamomile tea stored in different containers. I can see the brightness of the light on the hallway wall upstairs, can feel the floor beneath my feet...

And everything crystallizes as I stare at the hallway upstairs, and at the shadow I'm seeing there, reflected on the far wall...

"Virago?" I whisper, and then I'm shouting her name, rushing up the steps, tripping...

And there she is. Her ice blue eyes are wide as she stands at the end of the hallway, and when she sees me, she rushes forward, grabbing me around the waist, picking me up, lifting me into the air, kissing me fiercely.

"Holly, what are you *doing* here?" she asks, setting me back down gently to earth and trailing her hands quickly up my body to cup my face. She searches my gaze, her brow furrowed. "Are you all right?" There are actual tears in her eyes as she stares at me. "What happened? Has there been a coup, as Charaxus said there would be?"

"Charaxus? What happened with Calla?" I ask her, but then Calla is in the doorway behind Virago, the doorway to my bedroom. She looks completely fine, not a hair out of place on her head. She's actually holding one of my cups, and tea is steaming out of it. Either Virago or Charaxus had enough time to make her a cup of tea—so that's reassuring, at least.

"Oh, Holly," she says, rushing forward, setting the cup on a table and then embracing me tightly. "What has Charix done?" she asks, her brow furrowed deeply as she gazes at me.

And then Charaxus appears in my bedroom doorway.

She sighs heavily, leaning against the wooden frame. Charaxus looks shockingly tired and gaunt, her normally pale face even paler, her blue eyes bright, as if she's fevered. "There is no time," she says, stepping forward.

But she's not strong enough to take that step, and she stumbles a little, falling forward.

It's not elegant, the way she crumples—and it's not elegant, how Virago has to catch her, hooking her arm around Charaxus' ribs, all the while trying to keep her face from flickering with distaste.

"Charaxus used up all of her power and energy to bring us here, the only place she could think of that would be safe for us—on another world entirely," says Calla, her mouth downturned. "She was trying to keep me safe. Virago," she says, gesturing behind her, "grabbed hold of the edge of Charaxus' cloak when Charaxus stepped through the portal, so Virago was brought along by mistake. Charaxus was just trying to keep me safe," she repeats, her face worried, "because her brother is after me."

"We could have fought him," says Virago, her voice a low growl.

"Virago," says Calla, one brow up, "Charaxus did what she could, with Charix changing his plans at the last moment—"

"Yeah, did those plans include throwing a coup? Because that's what happened the moment you guys disappeared," I say with a small frown. "It's bad. He has everyone locked in the banquet hall. I don't know where he is, or what he's thinking of doing—"

"Wherever my brother is," Charaxus manages, as Virago sets her down onto the floor, leaning her against my hallway wall, "you can be assured that he is, right now, trying to retrace my steps. You did badly in following us, Holly," says Charaxus now, and even though she's as white as a ghost, even though she doesn't even have the energy to stand of her own volition, she's still reprimanding me.

I try to take the high road and shake my head. "You looked like you were kidnapping the queen—and you really did take my girlfriend. I wasn't about to sit by," I tell her, lifting my chin up, but Charaxus' eyes—so sad—give me pause.

"Be that as it may," says Charaxus, her voice low, grating, subdued, "it's probably too late, now. I have tried so hard to keep you safe, milady," she says, and her voice sounds broken as she looks up at Calla. "But I have failed you."

"No, you haven't," says Calla, sinking down in her gown beside Charaxus, her skirts billowing up around her so that she's in a nest of fabric. She reaches out and touches her hand to Charaxus' cheek, cupping her face gently with her hand. Charaxus closes her eyes, breathes out and leans into Calla's palm, and it's absolutely impossible for me to think, right now, that Calla doesn't know how very much Charaxus cares for her.

Or how very much Charaxus is in love with her.

"Charix wants you," says Charaxus, her voice so soft now, it's faltering, as she stares up at her queen, "to open the dungeon, and to open the door to the goddess Cower."

"Well, then he just won't have me," says Calla calmly, kindly, as she gazes down at her vice queen, her green eyes brimming with tears. "You must rest, Charaxus, my faithful friend," she says, rubbing her thumb against Charaxus' pale cheek. "Your energy is almost spent. You did well saving me. Rest now."

"You are not safe," Charaxus whispers.

The skin on the back of my neck is prickling as I hear something above the raging storm overhead. Thunder and lightning crackle across the sky; the rain pours down onto my roof... But above all of those sounds, I hear something out of the ordinary.

I hear my sliding glass door opening.

It makes a very distinctive *whoosh* when it opens from the outside, a small creak from the handle, a little groan from the lower part of the glass as it's pulled wide.

I hear that now, hear those small sounds merging together, even over the roaring rain, even over the bolts of lightning summoning thunder right outside the window. I turn, and I grip Virago's arm, my eyes wide as I lock gazes with her.

"There's someone here," I whisper to her, and one brow goes up as she turns, glancing down the stairs, reaching up and over her shoulder for her sword.

Charaxus glances up, too, as does Calla, all of us turning to look down the hallway, toward the steps that lead downstairs.

The only light on in the entire house is the light above our heads, here in the hallway. It's not a very bright bulb, but it gets the job done. But now, as the lightning flashes overhead, the thunder booming on its heels, the overhead light flickers...and goes out.

We are plunged into absolute darkness, punctuated by the flickers of lightning dancing through the sky.

Every time a portal has been created, every time someone comes through, something goes wrong with the lights. This isn't wholly unexpected, but it's the exactly wrong moment for it to be happening.

Because I can hear a footfall on the first stair, down below.

Someone is ascending the stairs, coming for us.

I look around, looking for something I can use as a weapon, and I've got nothing, not a single useful object in the hallway, unless you count the vacuum cleaner I have sitting in the corner because I figured that, if I tripped over it every night on my nightly pee, I would actually vacuum up Shelley's fur fluffs that collect in the corners of my hallway. But since moving the vacuum up the stairs last week, I've not used it once.

Well, I'm about to use it now. I grab the vacuum cleaner, and I'm getting ready to heft it up when my knees grow a little weak, and I swallow.

Because I can see what's coming up the stairs now.

Knights in black armor. The men of Furo,

marching quietly, stealthily, including the giant champion, who towers over the rest of them. And right there, right in their midst on *my* staircase...

Is King Charix.

His big fur coat makes him look larger and more imposing than he already is—which is pretty damn imposing. He has a sneer on his face, and his lips are up and over his teeth. His eyes glitter in the dark, reflecting the lightning through the window behind us.

When he reaches the landing, he pauses.

"You have your orders," he tells his knights dismissively, as if he's waiting in line at Wendy's for an order of fries. "Kill my sister," he points with a wide, terrible smile, "and kill the knight and the woman. Subdue Calla and put her in irons, and then we leave this world," he says, spitting out the last word as he glances around at his surroundings with disgust.

"Do you think you can best me so easily, Charix?" asks Virago, holding up her sword easily. "How many men did you bring?" she scoffs, tossing her ponytail and wolf's tail over her shoulder and sinking into an elegant crouch. "Twenty? I have bested fifty before, and not even on a good day," she says with a bright, wicked smile. And then she cocks her head. "I see we're protecting ourselves with a human shield. A nice touch."

Charix, who is surrounded on all sides now by very burly, black-armored men, sniffs, shrugging. "Why get my hands dirty with this butcher mission?" he asks with a cruel smile. "Admit it, Virago—I have seen you in battle. I know how you move, and I know what you will do in this enclosed space," he says, reaching out with a leather-gloved hand to pat my wall (painted this really awesome shade of lavender) condescendingly.

Everything he is in this moment reeks of condescension, actually, as he stares at my girlfriend with a smarmy smile.

"How did you even find us, Charix?" asks Virago casually, her head tilted to the side as she casts the king a withering glance. I glance sidelong at her. Is she stalling?

"I followed the trail, obviously," he says, shaking his head, pointing at me. "She tumbled through after that terrible witch opened the portal, and it was quite easy to follow. Come, now, Virago—surrender, and I will kill you quickly."

"Surrender, sir," she murmurs, her eyes glittering dangerously, "is not in my vocabulary."

"*Wait*," Charaxus growls then. Calla and I glance down to her, but Virago does not, only stiffens a little, raising her sword a bit higher.

But Charaxus is standing, having struggled to her feet, and now she's leaning against my hallway wall heavily on one shoulder, her breathing labored as she stares at her brother.

"Charix, you have Furo," says Charaxus then, her eyes glittering with pain. "You do not need Arktos, too. I ask you for the final time, brother, to leave off these grotesque plans of domination. You will look foolish when you fail, and our beloved country will suffer because of your greed."

"Sister," says Charix, snarling as he shakes his head slowly, "you *left* Furo. Do you not remember? You were a child, and you left, and you went to Arktos, and that day, you sowed the seeds of your own destruction. You are not loyal to us. You are a deserter. And that is why you must die. I tolerated you being Vice Queen of Arktos because I thought you would possibly prove to still be loyal, and therefore," he spits, "of use to me—but I was wrong. You are not loyal to us. You are loyal to *them*. And that is high treason. Kill her first," he tells the knights on his right side, and they begin to walk forward, down the hallway, their swords drawn in the small space.

I take a step back, holding tightly to my vacuum cleaner (that I'm beginning to realize isn't much of a weapon), but Charaxus and Virago and Calla don't budge, so I stand my ground, too, lifting the vacuum off the floor. It isn't just a bad weapon, but it's also really damn heavy.

Charaxus is stepping forward now, and she's unsheathing her sword from her back. She's weak—it's obvious how weak she is—and she could possibly be wounded, too, judging by the way she's favoring her right leg. But Charaxus stands up to her full height (which is impressive), and she lifts her sword up to the level of her heart. She points the blade unwaveringly, straight and true, at her brother.

"Leave off this," Charaxus hisses. "I challenge you, Charix. Will you face me one last time, brother?" she asks him, her voice soft but fierce, as she holds his gaze. "Or do you worry that your sister will best you yet again?"

"You are weak," he snarls, laughing, tilting his head back and roaring with laughter. Outside, a bolt of lightning touches down far too close by, and the thunder that follows it, booming through the house, is practically deafening. The hallway is dark, but it's still easy to make out the knights, to make our Charix, perched at the very top of the stairs. It's easy to make out Calla, too, standing next to me, holding her breath, and Virago, standing in front of me, gripping her sword, and Charaxus, all of us poised, ready to do battle in these close quarters, battle where life and death and the fate of entire country hangs in the balance.

Everything is so much bigger than us right now, and I can feel that, can feel the weight that every single second carries, every single heartbeat. I'm close enough to catch the scent of my beloved knight, the sweet scent of leather and metal, and something that smells a little of sandalwood. I can make out tiny details, like the creak in the leather of her gloves as Virago crouches there, hardly wavering at all; how Charaxus is standing, but her legs are quivering. I can see her from behind, can see how her whole body shakes, and how much she's trying to hide that fact.

Everything hangs in the balance in this one tiny moment that I'm going to remember for the rest of my life—for however long my life is slated to be.

It *might* not be for much longer.

"*Done*," Charix snarls then. He turns to his knights. "My sister and I are going to settle something, once and for all," he tells them in a low growl. "You know what to do."

The way that the knights look at us then is pretty disconcerting.

I have a feeling that, whether Charaxus wins or loses, it's going to end the same way—with all of us dead.

Charaxus turns to look at us, and for a moment, she wavers. She's not looking at *us*, per se: she only has eyes for Calla. Wide eyes, eyes full of pain, of sorrow...of words left unspoken.

Charaxus steps forward, cupping her fingers around Calla's elbow. For a long moment, she says nothing, but then she murmurs, "Charix must battle with me, because of past scars we both carry, of siblings who were always locked in battle with each other. This is the battle to end it," she says then, soft enough that only Calla should be able to hear it, but I'm standing right next to Calla. I glance away, but not before I see the tears glittering in Charaxus' eyes. "Get away, milady," she tells the queen softly. "Do whatever it takes to get away. I will face the music when all is said and done. This, and more, I would gladly do for you. I am ever at your service," she whispers, her voice breaking.

"Charaxus," says Calla sadly, "I never wanted you to be at my service. You are a good and loyal friend, and you are good to Arktos. Thank you for...for everything," she says, her voice catching. "You are a good friend," she repeats. And Charaxus nods, turning away. To see her face in profile, so etched with pain, within and without—it's heartbreaking.

Charaxus is Calla's friend--and that is all she will ever be.

"Come on, come on," bellows Charix from down the hall, gesturing with short, jerky movements. "I do this only to see the look on my sister's face when I run her through, by the way," he says with a wide grin, laughing with his knights, as if he shares a joke with them. "The battle is already won, sister. You do know that, don't you?"

Charaxus laughs then, too. It's a surprising laugh, a laugh of power as she glares, her eyes flashing. "Nothing is ever won...not until the very last moment. Do not be so pompous as to think you are the victor, my brother. This is why I bested you once...and I can certainly do so again," says Charaxus, turning her sword in the air, the blade aimed at his heart. She sheathes the sword in an elegant, smooth motion.

Now she's standing perfectly well on the balls of her feet, not a single sign of strain in her body. For a long moment, I wonder if she was playing her brother for a fool; I wonder if she's bluffing now. But, no, she said it herself; she showed us how weak she was.

Isn't she?

God, I hope she's not. I hope she's perfectly well, and that she's going to fight her brother and win against him, and then we'll all fight the knights, and it'll be okay. We'll be triumphant.

Somewhere in the back of my head, "Eye of the Tiger" begins to play as we're all ushered downstairs—in Calla's case, pretty roughly, one of the knights shoving her down the steps, but she manages to catch herself before she falls—and then pushed out into the pouring rain.

Overhead, the storm roars, and beneath it we stand, drenched in an instant.

We form a loose circle around Charix and Charaxus—the knights from Furo, and Calla, Virago, and myself. Lightning arcs across the sky at that moment, a vault of light opening up overhead, and down here, in the muck and mud of my backyard, two black-armored figures draw their swords again.

The rain is coming down too hard for me to hear Charix's blade leave his sheath, but Charaxus' makes this bright *shing* in the air as she artfully lifts it up and over her shoulder, laying it across her chest as she lifts her chin.

"How *is* your wife, dear brother?" she asks, and she sounds almost jolly as she takes a quick step to the right, starting to flourish the blade in front of her, drawing a complicated figure-eight pattern in the air with a couple more spirals to it. She's smiling wickedly as she begins to circle her brother. "Does she still ask about me, perchance?" she growls.

Charix has his lip drawn up over his teeth, his long hair starting to stream down into his face, the rainwater pouring down around all of us. "Keep my wife out of this," he says, sketching a quick, flashing circle in the air with the tip of his sword as he shifts the hilt in the palm of his hand, beginning to circle his sister now, too.

The two of them move in one large circle, taking dancer steps, foot over foot, as they crouch, as they study one another with almost unblinking eyes, prowling around like great cats.

Virago's fingers close over my elbow just then, curling gently but firmly. I shift my weight a little and glance sidelong at her out of the corner of my eye.

"Be ready," she breathes in a low, almost-silent growl, and I stiffen, my entire body zinging with electricity.

Ready for...what?

There is a roll of thunder just then so loud, so jagged-sounding and deafening, that the ground beneath us quakes.

And that is when their swords finally meet.

It's Charaxus who takes the first step forward. It's one long, graceful bolt, and then she's slashing down with her sword toward her brother, and her sword meets Charix's with a clash of metal and sparks, flying into the night.

Charix holds his ground, and Charaxus steps away lightly, spinning her sword in front of her like a metal firework.

"That's the problem with you, dear brother—

you fail to see things that are happening right under your nose." She shrugs elegantly and turns, feinting with her blade at Charix's right side. He sidesteps it, but almost too slowly, and a bit of his fur coat gets caught on the end of Charaxus' blade. She tears the coat with a ripping sound, and the fur flutters a little in the wind with its new hole as Charix glowers at his sister.

"That's the problem with *you*, sister—you talk your way through a battle." He steps forward, and with enormous strength, he brings the sword to the left, aiming for Charaxus' weak side. She parries the blade, thrusting forward, but his feint was enough to knock her a little off balance. Charix immediately brings the sword down from overhead, banging it toward Charaxus, who has to lift her blade high to parry it.

Was she acting when she appeared strong? Or was the weakness an act? Is she hurt, and is she bravely trying to fight him, anyway?

If she's hurt, how long can she possibly fight without finally showing a tell to her brother? And if her brother knows how very weak she is...isn't he going to destroy her?

My heart in my throat; I can only watch as the flurry of blades comes faster now. There is no time for talking anymore. Grunts and growls fill the air as Charaxus and Charix exist in the very center of this maelstrom of sharpness, the blades flashing as they move over and over, trying to find a weak spot, seeking flesh. I realize I'm holding my breath when there are small black dots appearing at the corners of my vision, and I take a deep breath as Charaxus feints to the right, then does a magnificent spin and turns, coming in for Charix's back now.

She moves so fast, her entire body is a blur, but Charix moves quickly, too. And though the rain is pouring down all around us, though the heavens are emptying everything they've got, though my eyes are full of water, and it's so very, very difficult to see...

I still see a small flash in Charix's other hand as he steps neatly backward.

And I see it again when his hand comes through the air, moving much too quickly, to connect with Charaxus' stomach.

She curves forward, and at first, I think the motion is elegant...but I realize in a moment, as she crumples forward, collapsing onto her brother, that it's not...

It's because he stabbed her.

Charix stabbed his sister with a dagger. That's what I saw glinting in his hand; that's what I saw slicing through the air toward her. He grabbed a dagger from a pocket within the lining of his coat, and he stabbed her.

It's over. The fight is over.

Charaxus is crumpled onto her brother, her sword sagging in her right hand, sagging down to the ground, the blade brushing against the grass and the mud there. Charix puts his other arm around his sister, the one not twisting the dagger in her guts, and he squeezes cruelly, laughing as she gasps.

"Don't you see?" he asks, hissing the words into her ear. "I will *always* win. I am better, faster, stronger, smarter than you will ever be. That is why I inherited Furo, and that's why you had to crawl away to Arktos, to try and make something of yourself. You crawled away to *Arktos!* The land of women." He spits onto the ground beside Charaxus' sword that has fallen completely to the earth, splashing into a puddle at her feet. "That is why *I* am the chosen one of the goddess, and that is why *I* will bring about the change this pathetic world so sorely needs."

Charaxus is gasping for air, and I'm gasping with her, my hands to my face, trying not to watch the dagger twisting up so deeply into her belly, into her lungs, probably. Tears are streaming down my cheeks, and Virago's hand at my elbow is even stronger, her fingers curling tighter. Calla stands there, her jaw clenched, her hands fisted at her sides, and all the black-armored knights are looking to us now.

"Kill the knight and the woman," says Charix, disgustedly pushing his sister to the ground where she gasps, curling herself inward, blood leaking out into the mud. She turns a little, her face to the sky, her eyes open, tears leaking from the corners of them. "And do it quickly," Charix mutters, cleaning his dagger on the torn edge of his fur coat. "We must go back through the portal with the queen."

Virago unsheathes her sword, bringing it over her shoulder at lightning speed, but there are about thirty knights here (and that massive champion), all with swords, all advancing toward us, and one is reaching for me. It's too many, too much.

This is how we're going to die—in my backyard, on my planet, but at the hands of someone who's from another world. As a child, I had so many hopes and dreams about magic. I never thought it would be the death of me.

But no. I'm not ready to go, and I'm *especially* not ready to go at the hands of such a *complete asshole*.

I dash forward, and because all of the knights have their attention trained on Calla and Virago, they don't even catch me bolting until the last minute, and then it's too late. Because I'm beside Charaxus, and I'm picking up her sword from the mud.

Virago said that when a sword is sworn to a knight, anyone else who tries to wield it will be out of luck. And...that is totally true. When I pick up Charaxus blade, it's like I'm trying to pick up an entire fallen tree trunk in my hands. I wheeze, holding it as "upright" as possible, but its blade is still stuck in the mud. I can't lift it any higher.

And Charix, of course, *laughs,* the bass sound of his laughter booming around me like the thunder.

"Holly!" Virago shouts, but since she's looking at me, her eyes wide, her face full of fear that I'm now in the middle of things, a few knights take this moment of her distraction to surround her, pummeling the sword out of her hand. It falls to the mud as they grab her arms, as she growls, struggling. They hold her arms tightly, and she stares at me with wide eyes, panting.

Charix takes a step forward, his eyes flashing and his smile poisonous.

"How funny," he says then, lifting his hands, gazing around at the rest of his knights. "Isn't this amusing? How many of you would like to try your sword practice on this new sword dummy? It'll be just like the practice yards back at home." Charix shrugs, taking another step closer. "Or do I, perhaps, want to run her through right now? I do so love to watch the life of a person leave their eyes. It gives me something to fall asleep to at night," he whispers to me, his gaze blazing with a fury and hatred that makes me take a step backward in revulsion.

But that's the only step I take. Because he is super tall, and he's got a million muscles, and he's wearing black armor and a black cape, and he's pure evil—anyone would take a step back from that. But no more. I am standing my ground today. I have a sword I can't even lift, I'm in my own backyard, and we're probably about to die.

But Virago would die with honor.

And, dammit, that's how I'm going to die, too.

"I love you, Virago," I shout to her, and my voice shakes when I say it, but I mean it with every fiber of my being. Virago shakes her head, already about to tell me to watch out, and the whole world seems to slow on its axis in this moment, this one moment...as she stares at me with wide, pained eyes, trying to reach across the space between us.

If the last words I ever say are "I love you," that's got to be okay.

I stand firm, I take a deep breath...and then I try to lift Charaxus' sword again.

If it were a just world, I would be able to lift up this sword right now, and it would come out of the mud with such force and power that it would arc through the air and aim itself toward Charix. But life isn't necessarily fair, and the world is certainly not just, so the sword? It doesn't budge. Instead, the blade sinks even deeper into the mud, squelching further into the earth.

It feels a little like trying to pull the Excalibur from its stone, and I'm not King Arthur material by any stretch of the imagination. The sword doesn't give; it doesn't even budge.

Charix laughs again, and it's the cruelest, worst laugh, the laugh of someone who is laughing so hard at you that he can hardly remember to breathe, his sides heaving, his head thrown back in slow motion as he lifts his sword, as he raises it to the heavens. The lightning dancing across the sky is reflected in the sword blade. I stare up at the blade, at the wicked gash of lightning tracing itself across the sky, the metal reflecting the light, and I realize this is it. It's over. That blade is about to come crashing down on me.

It's over.

I tear my eyes away from the terrible, glittering blade, and I rest my gaze on Virago, instead. Virago, who is standing there, held back by six knights now, seven knights, all of them pouring around her, because she's struggling so strongly against them. She's still struggling, still trying to reach me, but it doesn't matter. That sword is going to come crashing down, and everything will end for me.

But, at that moment, Virago's eyes widen, and she glances from me, down to my feet.

Charaxus is still curled up in the mud. I can see the gash in the chink of leather armor just beneath the edge of her metal chest plate, the blood gushing out of her belly, can see the blood pouring down her side, merging with the rain and the mud and spilling out onto the earth. But at that moment, she lifts up her hand, pain tracing itself across her face, contorting it, but she reaches out to me—and she touches my foot.

I'm wearing these little green slippers that go with my dress. They're very thin, and now they're completely mud-soaked, so when Charaxus touches my foot, she's touching my skin and curling her fingers around my heel.

"Now," she growls.

And suddenly, there's power. Raw, pulsing, electric power pouring through me. I realize in that moment that Charaxus is lending me her energy, her power, so that her sword will respond to me, and in that exact same instant, it *does* respond. I'm lifting it, lifting it like it weighs absolutely nothing, and Charix takes a few quick steps toward me, raising his sword above his head, his face contorting into a leer of sadistic pleasure, because he's about to murder someone.

But *not today.*

I lift the sword, and because Charix expected it to be leaden, expected me to be completely unable to lift it, he is not prepared, not prepared at *all*, and because he's moving so quickly, he can't stop his trajectory.

And as lightning and thunder arc across the sky, roaring, the storm above us powerful and potent and completely magical (I'm convinced), King Charix of Furo falls onto the blade of the sword.

And it cuts right through him.

His face contorts, but now it's not contorting with pleasure but with *rage*, blind, animalistic rage as he staggers back, as the blade slides out of him, and I'm left holding Charaxus' wickedly glittering sword as Charix—with blood dripping down his side—hefts his sword and takes another swing at me, this time aiming for my neck and head.

I ran him *through*—why the hell is he still coming for me?

I lift up the blade, and I parry his sword, but just in time. I can feel the power thrumming through my hands, can feel the sword *helping* me (it's a really odd sensation, like I have complete control over my arms and hands, but someone else is helping me make those decisions in my own head—like the sword itself is sentient in some way. Weird, right?). His sword *shings* through the air, coming at me from the other angle, and

I lift up Charaxus' blade, and I block it.

I can't move, really. If I step backward, there's Charaxus, and if I step anywhere, she won't be touching my foot, and I am *highly* aware of the fact that this is the only thing keeping us alive right now, her hand on my foot, filling me with her power. But out of the corner of my eye, I see Virago break away from the men holding her tightly, and then she's grabbing for her sword in the mud at her feet.

She lifts it up, and the blade is shining in the lightning as she turns, swinging it wide. The black-armored knights take a quick step back, but then Charix is roaring at them.

"Stand your ground, men!" he bellows. "It is but one knight!"

"Two!" shouts Calla, tripping one of the knights neatly with her foot and taking his sword from his sheath in one lovely, elegant move. And though the sword is very, very difficult for her to lift (her brow furrows with strain, and her arms shake, because that sword is not bonded to her), she manages to use it against the next knight who comes for her, hitting him in the back of the head with the pommel as she neatly sidesteps his rushing bulk, moving aside in one graceful motion as he falls, unconscious, at her feet.

"Three," I manage, lifting up Charaxus' sword again as Charix begins to take out all the rage over his day *really* not going as he'd planned...on me. He begins to bang his sword down over and over again as I hold up my own sword, trying to keep his strength from pushing me backward. Over and over again, he beats it down, treating the sword like a club he's trying to use against me, but I hold up Charaxus' blade, and somehow the energy keeps thrumming through me, even when my arms start to shake.

Charix still bleeds, his blood rushing out of his open wound and leaking down his side, the mud devouring it eagerly at his feet. But still, even with the wound, even with the bleeding, he *still* comes for me.

And there's murder in his eyes.

The lightning at this point is almost constant, the storm roaring around us so much that I'm wondering if we're nearing the eye of it, and I'm wondering exactly how much magic played a part in creating this storm. Because this is no normal summer storm. This is a storm full of power, a storm of roaring winds and rains and thunder and lightning at such deafening and blinding levels that it's all I can do to concentrate on holding the sword and keeping Charix from killing me… Because the storm raging around us is something out of legend.

I hold up the sword, my strength failing me, and I can feel the source of the energy pouring through me beginning to lessen, too. Charix takes another step forward, and I have to take a step back—I have nowhere else to go. But I step back, and the back of my sodden dress, the backs of my legs, are against Charaxus now. She's holding my foot with fingers that are growing looser with each passing heartbeat. I chance a glance down at her, and I see that her eyes are closing.

She's dying.

The sword is starting to feel heavier in my hands. Virago is trying to get to me, and so is Calla, but we're all surrounded by so many different knights, and their one goal is to kill us. They're trying their absolute best to do this as Charix rages, beating his sword down on mine. Virago and Calla are not going to reach me in time.

I have to do this myself.

And, in a moment, I'm not going to be able to.

I've never held a sword in my life, other than that one time with the Boston Beast—or, should I say, the Goddess Cower. I don't know how to use swords, and I've watched a million movies involving them, and about a million more sword fights at Renaissance festivals, but *watching* and *doing* are two completely different things...

But somehow, at this moment, everything standing against me doesn't matter.

Virago is there, and she needs my help. The love of my life is trying to get to me, is battling so many more men than is fair, struggling, thrusting her sword and parrying and smashing it down right and left, and still managing to look elegant and graceful as her feet complete a sword dance that is breathless to watch, in the tiny glimpses I've caught of it. She is not wounding anyone but making them all fall unconscious, just like Calla is. They're not killing the knights, though the knights are trying to kill them.

I need to help Virago.

I need to help the love of my life.

And that means I need to get to her.

And Charix is in my way.

Charix wants me dead. There is an evil spark in his eyes, in the way he's smiling as he uses his sword like a club, not displaying a hint of the artistry that Virago and Calla are using to fight against the knights. Instead, he is brutish, trying to thrust his strength against me because I'm smaller than him.

I flick my gaze to Virago. And somehow, through the whirlwind of blades, through the swords and armor and life and death...she sees me. Her ice blue gaze, in that instant, cuts through everything else, and it finds me. And I find her.

We lock eyes, and as I feel the power weakening, as I feel Charaxus' hand begin to slide down my foot, her eyes closing, the power ebbing and leaving me...

I lift my sword.

Charix was bringing his sword around again to my right. By lifting my sword now, my right side is completely exposed If this doesn't work, his momentum will follow through, and his sword will slice through me. But I put everything I have into this one movement. I lift my sword, and I step forward, feeling Charaxus' hand completely leave my skin. It's gone; her power is gone, her energy leaving me in a single instant. In that second, it's just me lifting this sword that is much too heavy for me. But I'm already in motion, already stepping forward, already thrusting forward, up...and in.

The sword goes straight through Charix and out the other side. He crumples into me, and then we're both falling into the mud together. I lay there, stunned, as he vaults over me from his momentum, and he falls into the mud beyond me.

Charaxus, Charix and I are in the mud, and around us, a battle rages on. But as I scrabble up, trying to find Charaxus' sword, a hand reaches out, and fingers curl around my ankle.

I turn back, my heart in my throat, half-expecting it to be Charix, but it's not: it's Charaxus.

And she's holding something out to me in her black-gloved hand.

"It's the shard," she whispers, blinking back the

rain, her lips pale as she uncurls her fist and drops the shard into my hands. "It's ready," she says, and then she slumps a little, back into the mud.

It's ready? I stare down at the shard in my palm.

This is the shard that can create portals. As I stare down at the little sliver of glass, I see lightning reflected in its surface.

I give a quick intake of breath and stare up at the sky. Charaxus reflected light onto the shard to get it to work.

The only light source I have...is lightning.

I glance around. I'm not exactly sure what Charaxus had planned. A retreat? Yeah, a retreat sounds pretty damn good right now. Because while Charix fell, that doesn't mean he's not going to get right back up again, like he's trying to now, pushing himself to his hands and knees in the mud with a snarl. Calla and Virago, as elegant and amazing as they are at fighting (Calla, by the way, is *completely badass*), are vastly outnumbered. And the knights are starting to push them back to back. They're doing well, their swords are flashing blurs, even with the magic making it difficult for Calla to lift hers, but it's only a matter of time. They are outnumbered. They will fall.

The lightning flashes again overhead, and I turn the shard in my hand, wiping the rain out of my eyes, concentrating the reflection of the lightning on the shard, and the reflection onto the ground in front of me.

The lightning flashes, is reflected...and, in a heartbeat, a portal is opening. But this is not like any of the normal portals I've seen open before. No, this one is very, very different.

Because there is a hole in the ground, a wide hole of white, pulsing light.

And it's spinning like a very fast whirlpool.

And it's beginning to tug at me.

Virago and Calla leap back from the knights at the same moment that I realize that Charaxus did something to the shard. It opened a portal that would take anyone nearby with it, a portal with its own power source and gravity.

This means that I need to get away from the portal if I want to get away from Charix and his goonies.

And I need to do it *right now.*

But saying and doing are two completely different things, and as I try to take a step backwards, I can feel the suction of the whirlpool portal pulling me in. It's tugging at me, pulling at my arms like a dangerous undertow.

"Holly!" Virago yells over the roar of the storm, over the roar of the portal tugging at me. She's holding tightly to Calla, and together the two of them are trying to reach me, but Virago is gripping the banister of my porch, and she's holding out a hand to me. "Let go of the shard!" she shouts.

I uncurl my fingers, and in that moment the shard goes zipping out of my hand, arching through the air toward the portal.

Charix moves past me, grappling toward me, but, like the shard, is pulled inexorably toward the portal, too. His face is equal parts rage and equal parts fear as he tries to clamor toward me, but he can't quite manage it—and then he's pulled down through the portal.

Almost all of the black-armored knights—

including the giant champion—are through it then, and the portal is pulsing with a strange blue-white color now, pulsing every heartbeat or so. It's going to close. I feel it in my gut. It's going to close. It's almost over.

I'm backpedaling as fast as I can, but the portal is tugging at me so strongly, I'm beginning to feel like it's impossible to fight it. I fall to the ground, start to crawl backward, back toward the house, back toward Virago and Calla, each holding out their hands to me, their faces stricken.

But, beside me, Charaxus lolls her head on the ground, and she begins to move toward the portal, her body dragged by the suction, by the gravity.

"No!" I cry out, trying to grab her. I manage to snatch up her hand as she swings past me, but she locks her ice blue eyes on mine.

"No," she tells me softly, quietly, almost impossible to hear over the sound of the portal and the storm, but I know her intent. I know what she's about to do, and I scream out, cry out, but I can't save her. She lets go of my hand, and then she's spinning into the portal, her body swallowed in a heartbeat by the light.

And, in that heartbeat, the pulsing blue-and-white circle on the ground disappears.

Calla and Virago collapse, and I lay down, too, for a long moment. But then, somehow, I find myself on my feet, shaking and racing across the relatively small expanse into Virago's arms.

"She's gone," I tell her, gripping her shoulders and locking eyes with my lover. "Charaxus saved us, and she's gone."

Virago's jaw is hard as she glances to her queen and then back to me. "I'm sorry, beloved," she says. And then she wraps her arms around my waist and draws me closer to her. We embrace for a long moment as Calla gets to her feet, stumbling toward the spot in the earth where the portal appeared. She kneels down next to it, putting out her hand over the place on the earth.

"Where did they go?" asks Virago, getting to her feet and helping me to mine. I'm still shaking, and she knows that, has her arm around me as I hold her tightly.

Calla sits there thoughtfully. Then her hand curls into a fist on her lap, and she glances at us over her shoulder.

"Somewhere," she murmurs. Overhead, the storm abates, the lightning now only intermittent, and the rain coming down in an almost soft mist.

Not everything is right in the world. Charaxus is gone. I don't know if she's alive—she was so badly wounded—and Charix and his men have gone, too, and I don't know if *they're* alive, but somehow...I doubt that they'd die. They went through this portal, yes, and it saved our lives, but they could be anywhere in the entire universe. And that's kind of a terrifying thought, because when I close my eyes, I still see Charix's blood-mad face as he tried to kill me.

But right now, my lover is beside me. I wrap my arms tightly around her waist, and I press my full weight against her, and she holds me.

Calla sits back on her hands on the mud on my lawn, staring up at the sky. Her eyes are wide, but she closes them, then, lifting her head back, letting the soft rain wash over her. She's alive.

And we're alive, too. I reach up on my tiptoes, wrap my arms around Virago's neck, and I kiss her fiercely. I drink her in, I drink in all of her; I drink in the rain and the storm and the fact that we are all okay.

And Virago kisses me back, her arms wrapped so tightly around me it feels like she'll never let me go, her mouth on mine, the heat of her skin sending a warm tingle through every part of me.

We're *alive.* And we're together.

Overhead, lightning dances.

And beneath the storm, the rain falls down, covering Virago and me as we stand, kissing away the darkness.

Chapter 16: Other Worlds

"Oh, my God," I mutter happily, rolling my eyes back as I lick the whipped cream off of my straw and then shove that straw back into my ridiculously sugary drink. "This is one thing Agrotera *doesn't* have," I moan. "I missed this."

Carly raises a brow and then chuckles, sitting back in her chair as she waves to the three drinks in front of me. "You were gone for a couple of days, I'd like to remind you."

"And I'd like to remind you that *they don't have frappuccinos* on Agrotera, Carly," I tell her, horrified, and then I pick up the frap on the right, this one a double caramel with an extra shot of espresso. I take a big sip and smile beatifically. "Ah, that's the stuff."

"Do you miss Virago as much as you missed Starbucks?" asks Carly with a little laugh.

"Well, she's only been gone an hour," I tell her, as I set the cup down, but then I blush a little. "But, yeah, I do. She promised she'd be back tonight, though, with my poor baby Shelley. I can't believe she's on Agrotera without me right now! She's probably still sleeping," I say with a little laugh, "but it's the principle of the thing. So, yeah, Virago will be back soon."

Carly's smile grows a little more genuine. "You really love her, don't you, Holly? Like..." She leans forward, presses her hands to the table, spreading her fingers, "Like the kind of love that lasts forever, complete with tacky greeting cards?"

"Well, I don't know about the greeting cards...but, yes," I tell Carly, and I say that single word with all the fervor I have in me (and, considering that I'm completely hyped up on sugar *and* caffeine right now...that's a *lot* of fervor). "*Yes*," I repeat, leaning forward. "*That* kind of love. I'm...I'm going to spend the rest of my life with that woman," I tell her then, and—at first—I'm surprised I said that, but the more I think about it, the more I realize how completely and utterly true the statement is.

I want to spend the rest of my life with that woman.

"Okay," says Carly decisively.

And then she glances at her watch.

"Um...I'm sorry if I'm keeping you from work," I tell her quickly. "Do you have to be back yet?"

She flicks her gaze up to me and shakes her head with a soft smile. "Not just yet. I was just...checking on something. So," she says, drawing out the word as she picks up her coffee. "Do you know if the Hero's Tournament will continue?"

"I doubt it," I tell her, shaking my head. "With everything that happened, Calla told me she was going to postpone it. And since it's definite that Furo wanted to overtake Arktos, that's enough of a reason for a postponing. They need to make sure that King Charix is definitely somewhere that he can't hurt anybody."

"Yeah, how are they going to do that? Didn't you say that since the magical crystal bit—"

"The shard," I tell her, trying to keep a straight face. I grin, anyway.

"The shard," she says, chuckling. "Since *that*

made the portal, it was impossible to trace?"

"Yeah," I tell her, poking at my straw and thinking about how Charaxus let go of my hand. It was so stupidly noble, but she didn't have to do it. She didn't have to, but she did, anyway.

And now she could be anywhere. In all honesty, she might be dead. But, whatever happened to her, in the darkest moment, she had kindness and strength that most people only dream of.

"Well," says Carly, reaching across the table and patting my arm, "I'm sure it'll be all right. I'm sure they'll find her."

But I'm not so sure.

The front door of the Starbucks opens, and I don't usually look up at the people coming in, but for some reason, right now, I do.

And my jaw falls open.

"Aidan, what are you doing here?" I ask him excitedly, standing and hugging my brother tightly. He grins at me, shaking his head as he hands me a Tupperware of cupcakes. Orange-vanilla—God, I'm probably going to eat all of these in one sitting..

"Because Carly told me to come here. Didn't you tell her, Carly?" he asks, looking down at my best friend, his brow furrowed.

"Tell her what?" asks Carly with a wide smile.

"Uh-oh," I mutter, sitting down. Aidan goes up to order his usual extra-vanilla, extra-whipped cream, extra-sprinkles frap from the barista, and I stare at Carly, my eyes narrowed. "What's going on, Carly?" I ask her.

"My beloved Holly," she says, spreading her hands and leaning back in her chair so far, I'm fairly certain the front two legs are up off the ground. "This is an intervention."

"Oh, no," I groan, and my brother heads for the table with his frap, already drinking it down.

"What'd I miss?" he asks, and Carly grins at him as he takes a seat.

"I just told her this was an intervention," she says, nodding, and my brother groans a little, too.

"No, no," he says, waving his hands and smiling at me, "it's a *good* intervention."

"Are there really *good* interventions?" I ask them, and Carly folds her arms in front of her and just smiles at me, quite a bit like the Cheshire Cat grinned at Alice.

"Look," says Carly, "we love you—"

"Here it comes," I moan, shaking my head. "But I talk too much about Virago? We're too lovey-dovey? I'm sorry, guys," I tell them with a sigh, "but I *really* love her, and I can't dial it back, and—"

"Well, no, we don't want you to," says Aidan, and he looks a little sad as he reaches across the table and takes my hand in his own. "But that's why we're here."

"You guys are scaring me," I tell them as I look from Carly to Aidan, and I note that both of them are no longer smiling.

"Holly, we love you," says Carly resolutely, "and we want you to be happy."

"And you're *really* happy with Virago," my brother continues.

"So," says Carly, drawing out the word, her head to the side, "we think you should go live on Agrotera."

I stare from Carly to Aidan, and back again to Carly. "You can't be serious," I manage.

"Why not?" asks Carly, shaking her head. "It's a magical world. Even though you almost *died* on it, you haven't been able to stop talking about it since you got back. You obviously love it there."

"And what's more important," says Aidan, raising a finger, "you're *happy* there. Because you're with Virago. And she makes you happy."

I stare at my brother and best friend, and then I glance around me. I glance at the tables and chairs in Starbucks (really, one of my favorite places on this, or any other planet). I think about how very, very much I love Aidan and Carly, and how very, very much I'd miss them. It's hard to go through portals, if shards aren't involved (and, anyway, we still don't know what the shard was costing to create those portals, and maybe we never will), and I don't know how often I'd get to see them.

But, really, besides books and my job...there's a lot I don't love about this world. The hate and the greed and the global warming… I mean, I'm assuming Agrotera has two out of those three, but somehow, Arktos and Arktos City makes all of it better. I didn't get to explore the country of Arktos like I wanted, but I *love* Arktos City. I love it. I love everything about it. I love that it's populated with women like me, I love the magic, I love the magical animals, I love...

Everything about it.

Just like I love everything about Virago.

"But...but what about you guys?" I manage, tears springing to my eyes as I think about how little I'll be able to see them. "I love you both so much," I say, shaking my head.

"And we love you, too, Holly," says Aidan with a long sigh. "Which is why we want you to be happy."

"And, when we *do* get to see you," says Carly, tears standing in her eyes as she gives me her biggest and bravest smile, "you'll have even *more* ridiculously romantic stories to tell us, so, hey—you can save them up," she says with a watery laugh. "And then you can get all of your love-colored confetti out at once."

"We *will* see you again, Holly," says Aidan, holding my gaze. "And, in the meantime, I can try to figure out inter-world communication. Hey, I'm a witch," he says, puffing out his chest. "It should be a snap for me."

"Guys, I can't leave you," I start, but Carly shakes her head.

"Are we really the only reason you'd be staying on Earth?" she asks quietly, her head to the side.

I laugh a little, a single tear streaking down my cheek as I squeeze my brother's hand. "Well, that and Starbucks."

"One of those two things is a good reason," says Carly sternly, but then she's smiling at me. "You've loved magic your entire life, Holly—and you finally have a chance to live a magical life with the *love* of your life. Do you know how many people get that chance?"

"Very few," my brother agrees. "Hell, I'm still waiting for my lady knight in shining armor. But you found yours."

"Just love her, Holly," says Carly, holding my gaze. "Love her and live, and be happy. And that's enough."

Every time I close my eyes, I see Virago. I see her smile and her ice blue eyes. I see her long waterfall of black hair. I see the way her mouth turns up at the corners as her eyes travel the length of my body. I see the way she grins with delight when she's around her knights or when she looks at her horse. I see the way she crouches down to get on Shelley's level, and how she speaks so seriously (and with a great deal of love) to my dog. I see the way she fills out those gorgeous leather pants, and the way she crosses her legs, her brow furrowed, as she reads poetry, often speaking lines out loud in a quiet, hushed whisper, like she's saying a prayer. I see the way she moves, the way she simply is.

Love her and live, and be happy. And that's enough.

"I will," I tell them, the promise in those words as powerful as any sword.

And that's exactly what I do.

The End

The next book in the Knight Legends series is out now!

Search for "**Forever and a Knight**, Bridget Essex" wherever you buy your books!

Made in the USA
San Bernardino, CA
29 November 2016